REINCARNATION BLUES

REINCARNATION BLUES

BY MICHAEL POORE

Up Jumps the Devil
Reincarnation Blues

CONTENTS

For Dad and Barbara

Copyright © 2017 by Michael Poore

Published in the United States by Del Rey,
an imprint of Random House, a division of
Penguin Random House LLC, New York.

Del Rey and the House colophon are
registered trademarks of Penguin Random House LLC.

Hardback ISBN 978-0-399-17848-1
Ebook ISBN 978-0-399-17849-8

Printed in the United States of America on acid-free paper

randomhousebooks.com

2 4 6 8 9 7 5 3 1

First Edition

Book design by Elizabeth A. D. Eno

REINCARNATION BLUES

A Novel

MICHAEL POORE

DEL REY • NEW YORK

CHAPTER 1

The Wise Man of Orange Blossom Key

This is a story about a wise man named Milo.

It begins on the day he was eaten by a shark.

The day didn't begin badly. Milo woke up before sunrise, tucked his fifty-year-old self into a pair of shorts, and walked out to meditate on the beach. His dog, Burt—a big black mutt—followed.

Milo sat down in the sugar-white sand, closed his eyes, and felt the warm salt breeze in his beard. He took note of his ponytail feathering against his back and seagulls crying. That's what you were supposed to do when you meditated: *notice* things, without really thinking about them.

Milo was not a particularly good meditator. He cracked open a beer and watched the sun come up. Meanwhile, as always, the more he tried to think of nothing, the more he thought of ridiculous, noisy shit like his big toe or France. Maybe he would get a new tattoo.

He drank his breakfast, noticing the ocean, welcoming its ancient indifference. He tried to match its breath—the breath of time itself—

and fell asleep, as usual, on the beach with his beer and his dog, until the tide rolled in far enough to wet the sand under his ankles.

He was, perhaps, the crappiest meditator in the world. But he noticed this, accepted it, and let it humble him. Humility was one of the things that made him a wise man.

He walked back to the house to open a new bag of dog food.

The shark that would eat Milo in a few hours was miles away at that particular moment. It patrolled the surf off St. Jeffrey's Key, looking for manatees.

The shark knew it was hungry. This required no thought. The shark lived in the moment, every moment, in a perfect equanimity of sense and peace, meditating its way through the sea without even trying.

Milo worked in his garden for a while.

He played with his dog and read a book about fossils.

He went online and spent twenty minutes watching dumb videos.

Then he drove his old pickup truck to St. Vincent's Hospital, because visiting the sick is an important part of a wise man's job. He took Burt with him.

Petting dogs was good for people; it was a scientific fact. Burt was a wise man, too, in his way. All animals are.

On this particular day, Milo and Burt visited Ms. Arlene Epstein, who was dying of being a hundred years old.

She was asleep when Milo arrived, and he stood there looking at her for a minute.

Hospitals had an unfortunate way of reducing people, he thought. Looking at Arlene Epstein in her bed, tissue-delicate, you'd never know that she had once been a legendary bartender, keeping rowdy tourists in line with a sawed-off hockey stick.

Burt hopped up and rested his forepaws on the mattress.

"Milo," yawned Arlene. "Is it Thursday already?"

"Saturday," he answered, kneeling.

"I always liked Saturdays," mused Arlene. "I think I'll die on a Saturday, if I can help it."

"Not today, though," said Milo. "You look good."

"Fantastic," she replied, sitting up and giving his beard a tug. "You can take me for a walk."

Arlene was not supposed to go for walks. There was a sticker on her door that said she was a fall risk. Milo ignored the sticker and stole a walker from a closet down the hall.

Arlene took one step about every three seconds. Milo stuck casually by her side, ready like a hair trigger to catch her. Burt walked along the wall, sniffing like crazy. (Dogs love hospitals. Think of all the different smells you can never quite get rid of.)

When they had traveled ten feet, Arlene asked, "Milo, do you know what happens when we die?"

He was honest with her. He said, "Yes."

One step. Two steps.

"Well?" she asked.

"You come back as something else."

Arlene thought about that.

"Like another person?" she said.

"Or a dog. Or an ant. Maybe even a tree. Burt was a bus driver in his last life."

The old woman stopped.

"Don't fuck with me," she said. "I'm going to die soon, on a Saturday, and I want to know."

Milo looked down at her with deep, honest eyes.

"I've lived almost ten thousand lives," he told her. "I am the oldest soul on the planet."

Arlene looked into one of his eyes, then the other. Seemed to like what she saw. She set the walker aside, took Milo's hand with both of hers, and leaned on him some.

They resumed walking.

"Will I still be *me?*" she asked.

"Sure," said Milo. "More or less. Of course, you're supposed to make improvements."

"Well, I don't think I want to come back as a tree."

"Then don't."

Arlene patted his hand and told him he was a good boy.

Burt sniffed out something nasty on the floor and gave it a big, fat lick.

If Milo had gone out swimming then and been eaten by the shark, it would have been a wonderful, generous note for his life to end on. But he didn't.

The shark, always hungry, had eaten a mess of ocean perch and some floating garbage and now cruised the deeps between islands, coming up slowly across the outer reefs of Orange Blossom Key.

The shark had *been* an ocean perch in a former life. It had been food of all kinds. It had been the Strawberry Queen for the 1985 Strawberry Festival in Troy, Ohio. Sometimes, in dreams, it remembered these other lives.

For now, though, it swam and was hungry, and swam and was hungry.

Milo still had his workday to look forward to. Part of being a wise man was knowing the importance of work.

Milo did two things for a living.

Thing One: He was a fisherman and a sport fishing guide.

He owned a boat called the *Jenny Ann Loudermilk* and charged people a fortune to catch fish. You could charge tourists in the Keys practically anything.

Today, Milo's workday involved housecleaning aboard the *Loudermilk*. Maybe a customer would appear, but he kind of hoped not. He was hoping to go surfing, if the waves built up.

He stood on the deck of his boat, wielding a garden hose, spraying away seagull shit and old fish guts. Burt curled up on the floor in the pilothouse and lay there watching the flies on the windshield.

Milo thought about Arlene Epstein and wondered if she was scared.

He hoped not. Death was a door. You went through it over and over, but it still terrified people. That's what he was thinking about when something bright and colorful caught his eye, down on the dock.

A tourist, in an ORANGE BLOSSOM KEY T-shirt. A chunky man of middle years, wearing a mustache, sunglasses, brand-new boat shoes, and a straw hat.

Suddenly Milo didn't feel like working that afternoon. Suddenly he just wanted to head for BoBo's Pub and sit at the bar and drink beer.

"Are you going out again today?" asked the tourist.

Aw, great balls of shit.

"The customer's always right," said Milo. "You want to go out, we'll go out."

"How much?"

Milo quoted his fee, which staggered the man. (O, shining hope . . .)

"Listen," said Milo, "you get three or four other fellas, it's easier on your wallet, and we could go out and hit it tomorrow morning—"

But the tourist seemed to be in the grip of some urgency.

"No," he said. "Let's go ahead and go."

"Hop aboard," said Milo, offering a strong, tanned, tattooed hand.

The tourist introduced himself as Floyd Gamertsfelder.

"I sell carpet," he said.

"That's awesome," said Milo, casting off.

Burt jumped ship and trotted away down the dock, heading home. He didn't belong out on the water, and he knew it.

Floyd Gamertsfelder didn't give a shit about catching fish. This was something Milo knew the instant he saw him, the moment he heard that strange urgency in the carpet salesman's voice. About half of Milo's customers were like that; they paid heavy money for his time, fuel,

and tackle, but they were there for something deeper and more difficult than amberjack or marlin.

This was Thing Two, the second part of Milo's job: professional
wise man and counselor.

People came to him because they had problems they couldn't sort
out on their own and they had heard of him. Just as people in cartoons
climbed mountains to find wise men, real people traveled serious dis-
tances to consult Milo aboard his boat, upon the sea, for the price of a
half-day charter.

They were smart to do so. When you live almost ten thousand lives,
after all, you can learn a great deal. Milo had squeezed so much learning and experience into his one, single soul that the knowledge had
grown pressurized and hot and transformed into wisdom the way coal
changes into diamonds. His wisdom was like a superpower.

It showed in his eyes—like green fire in outer space—and in his tattooed skin, which was creased and furrowed as if his suntan had put
down roots.

"I really just want to talk to you about some stuff," Floyd admitted
as they motored out of the marina.

"I know," said Milo.

Past the breakwater, a decent-sized swell lifted the *Loudermilk*. The
kind that promised good surfing later. He hoped Floyd was a fast talker.

Patience, his *boa* reminded him. Compassion.

Milo nodded, formed the *mudra* with his thumbs and forefingers,
goosed the throttle, and steered out to sea.

Floyd Gamertsfelder was not a fast talker.

Milo was kind of hoping he'd open up and spit out whatever his
mystery problem was before they got too far out, but no. Floyd made
his remark about wanting to talk, and then he just clammed up, watching the horizon, looking glum.

Milo wasn't surprised. It took time, usually. The puzzles people
brought were hardcore and personal. They had to ride the waves

awhile before they opened up. They had to glimpse his outer-space eyes and hear the ocean roll in his seaworthy, biker-dude voice.

Milo nearly always took his customers to the same place, the same coordinates. Out of sight of land, an hour over open water, to a place only he knew about. In ninety feet of water, he dropped anchor directly over a forgotten submarine wreck, an artificial reef that hosted almost every species in the Gulf.

"A dead man could catch his limit here," Milo told his customers.

He and Floyd drifted around for two hours over the sub, catching bonito and sunfish.

Floyd opened up a little cooler he'd brought, and they each had a beer.

"Have you ever been married, Milo?" Floyd asked.

Ah, a marriage problem. Marriage counted for 80 percent of the wise-man business.

Milo said, "Yep." (Nine thousand six hundred forty-nine times.)

"Well," said Floyd, "basically I don't think my wife is very nice to me."

Milo made a sympathetic noise.

"Not like cheating on me. I don't mean that. Maybe this'll sound dumb, but she doesn't ever do nice shit like bring me a glass of lemonade when I'm mowing the lawn. Am I being old-fashioned? They say it's the little things, right? Well, she doesn't *do* any of the little things."

Milo reached behind him to damp the throttle, cutting the engine noise.

"Do I do little things for *her?*" Floyd continued. "Hell yes. Last week I made spaghetti, and—whoa, something's happening!"

A nice amberjack had hit Floyd's line, and they spent fifteen minutes reeling it in.

The wind picked up a little. Down below, in the ribs of the old submarine, thousands of fish watched the shadow of the *Jenny Ann Loudermilk* as it lurked across the sea bottom. A mile away still, the shark that would eat Milo chased a school of mackerel and glided north along the drop-off.

"Is your wife nice to other people?" asked Milo.

"Not particularly," said Floyd.

"What do you think the problem is?"

Floyd took a deep breath and said, "I pretty much think my wife is an unpleasant person. I think she doesn't like me very much, or anyone else, either."

"Why don't you leave her?" asked Milo.

Floyd digested this question for five full minutes.

"I'm trying to be mature about things," he said at last. "I thought maybe we just needed time. Marriage is work. So what"—here, he finally turned to look straight at Milo—"so what I think I need to do is, I need to grow up and *want* things to get better. My parents didn't raise quitters."

Milo didn't meet Floyd's eyes. He watched the sea, looking for something in particular.

"'Scuse me a minute," he said, and cast a tube lure waaaaaaay out, watched it splash down. Silently counted: Four, three, two, one—and then yanked back hard, cranked like mad, and dropped a giant angry barracuda onto the deck, right in front of Floyd.

"Christ!" screamed Floyd. *"What's wrong with you?"*

The barracuda thrashed, all huge jaws and razor teeth, instantly making hash of the deck hose.

Floyd exploded in panic, dancing and spinning.

"Be mature about it," suggested Milo.

The barracuda flipped into the air, snapping at Floyd's hands.

"Give it time," added Milo. "Fishing is work."

The barracuda mowed through an empty beer can and went for Floyd's ankles.

The carpet dealer, like most people, was brave when he needed to be. He swallowed his panic, bent down and grasped the fish around the middle, and flung it out of the boat with something between a sob and a grunt.

Then he stood there shaking, pumped full of adrenaline, trying to decide if he had enough courage left over to shout at Milo again.

"The problem with a barracuda," said Milo, "isn't that you aren't being mature. The problem is that it's a barracuda. If you don't like being in the boat with it, one of you has to go."

Floyd sat down in the fighting chair. After a minute, he said, "Yes."

He said it in the saddest way, but he looked happy.

Milo mashed the throttle and sped for home, hoping to save the tail end of the afternoon.

If he had died just then, it would have been a poetic and satisfactory end. But he didn't.

He chose to get drunk at Bobo's Pub.

BoBo's was famous across the Keys for BoBo himself: a stuffed baboon with exposed fangs and a life preserver, eternally crouched on his haunches, one paw wrapped around a healthy erection. The bartender had to take BoBo home at the end of each night; otherwise, kids would break in and steal him.

For about a year, Milo had been shacking up with the weekday bartender, a forty-five-year-old former soccer pro named Tanya. After closing, he helped her stack chairs, and then they went back to her bungalow (BoBo rode in the back of the pickup), where they killed half a bottle of wine and made love.

Outside the open bungalow window, waves hissed and crashed. Then, suddenly, one wave made a different kind of sound, a *boom* like a bass drum in a hollow log.

It was a surfing sound.

"Come surfing with me," said Milo.

"Not tonight," she said. "I'm going to get a little drunker and go to sleep."

"I'll wake you when I get back," he said, leaning down and kissing her.

"No," she protested. "Are you kidding? Let me sleep. I gotta work early tomorrow."

"Okay."

Isn't that dumb? That was the last human conversation Milo had, in that life.

He paddled out past the shallows, muscled his way through breaking waves, and slid downhill into the deeper country, where the waves were still swells, right before they began toppling.

It was his favorite thing. Sitting on his board out there, waiting. Glimpsing the candlelight in the bungalow window. Wondering what Tanya was thinking about. Wondering how Burt was doing at home, a few miles up the beach. Sleeping? Hunting along the shore?

That was Milo's status in the minutes before the shark. Not bad, as such minutes go.

He even managed to meditate a little, folding himself up inside the moment. He noticed the moon, like an anklebone, like a story, up in space. The night and the breeze and—

The shark hit him.

It drove upward like a rocket and smashed into the air with the surfboard in its jaws. Milo experienced it the way you might experience getting hit by a bus. Sudden and hard, and knowing something bad was happening without knowing what yet.

And then knowing and being afraid.

Getting eaten by a shark wasn't any different for a wise man than it was for a shoe salesman or an aardvark. He felt what was happening with terrible clarity—the awful tearing, crushing—and he screamed and yelled just like anyone else.

Too bad. He had always kind of thought he would go into death like an explorer, in a golden flash of peace and wholeness, and here he was being chewed up like a ham.

His last words were "No! Fuck! No!"

The voice in his head began to go quiet; the light inside him started to go out.

Burt, Milo thought, before he went totally dark, would be smart enough to go find a new friend, someone who would appreciate what a fine dog he was. It was a good and kind thought, a wise thought, and then something like a fast-moving interstellar night flooded through him and snuffed him out like a—

With a flick of its tail, the shark dove for the middle depths, leaving behind a cloud of gore and pieces of surfboard.

It didn't stop to savor or to be appreciative. It was still hungry, so it looked for more food.

One half of the shark's brain noticed the ocean, noticed the sounds and heartbeats of the sea.

The other half noticed the warmth of good food digesting in its belly and remembered being a perch, and a mackerel, and a clam, and a whale, and a dog, and a cat, and the Strawberry Queen.

CHAPTER 2

The Unlikely Joy of Being
Catapulted into Vienna

Dying was nothing new, of course.

Milo had died nearly ten thousand times, in almost every way possible.

Some deaths were horrid; some were not so bad.

The best way to die, of course, was instantly, but this was rare. Milo had died instantly just one time. A tower crane dropped an iron girder on him. It was the only time he got to the afterlife and had to ask, "What happened?"

Of course, even if you knew she was coming, Death was never routine.

Four times, Milo had been executed and therefore had known in advance the exact hour he would die. He had been burned at the stake in Spain, beheaded in China, hanged in the Sudan, and gassed in California. Knowing death was coming, you could usually manage to act brave. But it was just an act. Inside, it felt like someone was working on you with a plunger.

Milo hated the ones that hurt. Fourteen times he had died in combat: speared, knocked off a parapet, wounded and bled out, speared, run over by a chariot, paralyzed with a mace and run over by a horse, kicked in the face by a horse, speared, bayoneted, exploded, shot and bled out, shot and dragged by a horse, fallen on by a horse (Milo hated horses), and choked to death by a giant German infantryman. Once, he had been captured by the Turks and flung by catapult back over the walls at Vienna. This was his favorite. Crushing speed, and then flying through the night in a universe of battle smoke, the fires of the starving city beneath him. Horrifying but wonderful, wonderful!

There were deaths of haunting beauty. As an Arctic explorer, freezing to death, he felt nothing but the illusion of warmth, and his brain released little chemicals of peace and satisfaction. He slipped away as the sun rose, flashing on the ice like a knife catching fire.

He didn't always get to grow up before dying. He knew what it was like to spend all summer at Children's Hospital, with his hair falling out, and to die holding Charles, his toy alligator.

Milo had died during orgasm, died after rich dinners in fine company, died in moments of perfect love. Died, in one future life, in a starship crash at the speed of light, in a moment that resonated forever inside the envelope of time, so that it was always happening, like a guitar string that would never stop humming. He had fallen from trees and choked on waffles. He had been eaten by sharks and cancers. He died of bad habits and angry husbands and killer bees, once, and dumb accidents like sticking a high-pressure air hose up his nose when he was working in a tool shop, trying to be funny.

Between lives, when he could remember it all, he sometimes wanted to relive being catapulted into starving, besieged Vienna. How strange to want to relive a death. Forty times he had asked Death to make this happen.

"Why?" Death had asked him.

He thought it over. "I flew!" he answered. "I was weightless."

She said, "Nothing's weightless; that's why we die."

He settled for the memory: weightless and perfect and closing his eyes, remembering the fire and the speed and the rushing wind and some rising kitchen smoke he had flown through, smelling of onions and roast dog.

CHAPTER 3

Suzie

You don't come from dust, no matter what they say. You come from water, and you go back to the water when you die, like a river rolling downhill.

Milo woke up by the water, as he'd done almost ten thousand times. Woke up on a railroad bridge over a dark, sleepy old stream full of stumps and catfish.

Death was there with him, sitting cross-legged, leaning against an old steel truss. She was always there when he awakened, watching him with those watery, sensitive eyes, wearing her long black hair like a cape.

She didn't *have* to be there. She could snuff out his life and leave him to wake up on his own. But she never did. Not once. It was okay; the universe would get along without her for an hour. There were other Deaths on the job, dark and pale and sensitive just like her.

"Suzie," he whispered. (She didn't like to be called "Death." Who would?)

"Shut up," she said. "You know better than to talk right away. Give it a few minutes. Be still." She chewed on her hair, hiding a smile.

It took a few minutes for your soul to get its shit together, moving from one world to the next. You had to let yourself come into focus, let the memories of all your lives gather. Even if you'd done it a bunch of times.

Milo was not surprised by the railroad bridge or the catfish stream. Things were the same everywhere; what they had on Earth, they had up here. You needed food and language and shelter and air and coffee "down there," and you needed them "up here," too.

Milo's body was very much like his Earthly body, except young again. He wore a pair of jean shorts and nothing else. All as it should be, the way it always was.

After a minute, he cleared his throat and said, "Thanks for the shark."

"You know I don't decide how you're going to get it," she said. "The universe has its own *boa*."

"You could have yanked me out of there, you know, before—I mean, it really fucking hurt."

She looked angry for a second. Her eyes blazed (literally). Then they cleared.

"You're messing with me," she observed.

"I'm messing with you."

Miles away, a train gave a honk and a wail.

The railroad bridge, Milo observed, was a rusty, forgotten thing, with weeds and wildflowers shooting up out of the cross ties. Abandoned obviously, but in the afterlife, that didn't mean a train wouldn't come cannonballing along, despite the rust and weeds. Things in the afterlife had a way of changing when you weren't looking. Or when you were.

Milo climbed down into the tall grass by the river, looking out for snakes. He reached up to help Suzie down, and she *let* him help, which was nice.

He wished they could have more time together, getting him focused and settled. But he knew that wouldn't happen. The others would be here soon.

He examined the woods and the water. He'd been awake for five or ten minutes now, which meant—

"Five," he whispered. "Four, three, two—"

"Milo!" sang a voice behind him.

He turned to see two women picking their way along the river-bank, sidestepping rotten branches, surprising a—*croak!*—huge frog and—*splash!*—a snapping turtle.

Suzie heaved a theatrical sigh.

"I'm going to bug out for now," she said.

"Suzie—"

"It's been a long day. I mean, a whole ferryboat overturned in the Sea of Cortez this morning. A hundred and fifty lives all at once. Yeah, yeah, it's my job, but . . ."

Milo started to say something, but she was gone in a burst of wind and dry leaves.

"Okay," he said, and turned to face—

"*Milo!*" The first of the two women, a big old Earth mother with a giant Oklahoma smile, bustled up and threw her arms around him.

"Milo," she warbled, squeezing. "Milo, Milo."

"Mama," said Milo, speaking into her armpit (she was not his mother).

The second woman, smoking a cigarette, looked like a cranky of-fice manager who had retired to Florida. She was followed by a cat.

"Nan," said Milo, shaking her hand.

"You're late," she said, as always.

They were not angels, and they were not gods. Milo knew a hun-dred things they were not but could not have said, for sure, what they were.

"You look fit," said Nan. "Do anything useful this time around?" A second cat appeared from beneath her skirt and shot off through the grass, chasing something.

Mama said, "Shhhhh!" and waved her big hands in the air. "Talk is for later. Hush now, and let's just get him home."

She took his arm, and the three of them set off down the riverbank.

Through the woods, until the river emerged by a motorway, and they followed the road into a small town. Rode a bus for a while, still following the river. Crossed over a shining lake, with houses afloat on the water.

You were expected to be quiet and meditative in the hours after you died. You were supposed to think about what a good job you had done (or had not done). Your new home, when you got there, was a reflection of this. If you had been Gandhi, or someone similar, you'd probably get to live in a big house with a garden and a pond. If you cooked and ate cheerleaders, on the other hand, you might have to rent a shack beside the landfill.

They got off the bus and walked through a neighborhood of bridges and canals. The farther they walked, the less clean the sidewalks became. Milo, who hated litter, picked up a French fry box. No trash can in sight, he just carried it.

They stopped eventually at a warren of apartment buildings. French fry boxes and other trash populated the dead grass out front.

"Aw, man," said Milo. "Really?"

Mama avoided his eye.

"Disappointed?" asked Nan, giving him a crooked look. Five or six more cats had accrued around her.

"I was a wise man!" Milo protested. "A spiritual master! I helped people. I was in tune with the planet—"

"You went fishing," said Nan, "and gave advice. Everybody does that."

Fuck it. Milo tossed his French fry box onto the grass, beside a discarded sock.

"You didn't actually achieve much," said Mama, laying her big hands on his shoulders. "You had nine thousand nine hundred ninety-four lives of experience behind you. Don't tell me that was the best you could manage. Not my amazing, electric-souled Milo!"

"Don't coddle him," snapped Nan. "You always coddle him. God forbid he should actually *do* something."

Milo itched to give them both the finger. Instead, he let them lead him into his building (Propane Estates 2271) and up three flights of stairs to his own door (Number 12). Painters had painted it shut, but Mama body-slammed it open.

It was like every other apartment in the universe. Furniture that didn't match. Light fixtures from the 1970s.

"Get settled," said Mama. "Take a nap. See what's in the fridge. We'll be back for you sometime soon."

She looked at Nan then, as if some communication, something subtle, had passed between them.

"What am I missing?" Milo asked.

Neither of them would meet his eyes.

"We'll talk later," said Mama. "Rest."

"'Kay," said Milo.

Mama and Nan and a hundred cats walked out the door.

"Cat piss," he said. This time he'd really gotten screwed. It could be hard to tell, down on Earth, if you were living a truly soulful life. Up here, the hindsight was clear. Too much beach, too much beer, not enough changing the world, blah-blah-blah.

Fine. Screw it. There was always next time.

He tried a light switch over by the door. No lights. He tried a switch in the kitchen. Nothing. The power wasn't even turned on yet. Man . . .

He made his way down the hall, letting his eyes adjust in the half-light. The hall opened into a single bedroom. Over here, the shadow of a bed, an end table, a clock radio—

The air stirred.

Dust and dry leaves whirled up in a funny little tempest. The leaves formed a shape and slowed down, until only the shape remained.

Suzie coalesced beside the nightstand. Nearly cocooned in black hair, eyes softly (but literally) burning.

She wrapped long arms around him and gave his lips the lightest flicker of a kiss, the way a snake might kiss.

He drew her closer. The flickering kiss deepened.

"You should at least let them get out of the neighborhood," Milo said. "They're not blind, you know."

"I think maybe they suspect," said Suzie.

"Well, if they do find out—and they will—they won't approve. You know they won't."

"Shhhhh," Suzie hissed.

Then she coiled around him, forcing him to the floor.

Cheap carpet, he noted. There were going to be burn marks.

Eventually, the half-light from the windows became a deep purple dusk.

Morning, noon, twilight, and night didn't always happen in order in the afterlife, the way they did for the living. Order was often an illusion. There were fewer illusions here.

They had worked their way up onto the bed. Both were nearly exhausted and damaged here and there.

Milo buried his face in her hair, breathing deep. She smelled like midnight.

"I missed you," he said.

She propped herself up and looked down at him.

"Please," she said. "You don't even *remember* me when you're down there screwing around with your Tanyas and Amys and Batangas and Li Wus and Marias—"

"I can't help that. It's what happens when you live a life. I still sort of miss you, somehow, in a something's-missing kind of way."

"Liar. But you're sweet." She bit him a little, on his neck, drawing blood.

"I brought something for you," she said.

"Yeah?"

"Do you remember this?" she asked, and from the depths of her hair she produced a copper circlet. Banged up, half-green with verdigris, it was a rough sculpture of a snake swallowing its own tail.

"An armband," Milo said, taking it from her hand. Holding it, feeling its weight, he realized the armband was familiar.

"From my first life," he said.

"And your first death," she added. "Remember?"

He remembered.

He turned the armband over and over in his hands and let the memory rise up like a dream.

CHAPTER 4

The Barbarian Problem

INDUS RIVER VALLEY, 2600 B.C.

Milovasu Pradesh opened his eyes, when he was able, and the world flooded into him, a river of color and sound. The parents who had brought him into the world lived among green trees and mountains. Between the mountains, green fields. A river flooded by, tumbling into a deep, misty gorge.

The world was full of voices: The roar of monsoon rains, the sounds of insects and night. His father telling stories, his mother singing songs.

No one in his village knew that he was a brand-new soul. How would they? You don't come into the world with numbers on your forehead, telling how many lives you've lived. The only way anyone might be able to tell, at a glance, is by watching your eyes. New souls have the hungriest eyes, drinking in the world for the first time.

"He's like a stone," said Milovasu's father. "When he is watching something or listening, he is completely still. He barely breathes."

"He's like the sun," argued his mother. "You watch. One of these days all this watching and listening will catch fire inside him, and he'll be like a god; you watch."

"He will be a leader," said the village leader, and everyone agreed.

The village leader had once been a warrior of some distinction. He wore a soldier's copper armband, a ring in the shape of a snake swallowing its own tail. He slipped this ornament from his arm and allowed Milo to wear it around like a hat one afternoon.

Milo learned quickly. He walked when he was three months old. Walked, in fact, all the way to the gorge and had to be chased and snatched up at the last second. Potty training was a breeze. His first words came out in a sentence, proper and whole: "Father, do you hear the wind blowing in the trees?" To which his father replied, "What? Yes, I hear it. Holy shit!"

Always, he was the leader in the games the boys played. Until the year he turned six and stopped growing. One day, it seemed, the other boys shot up another foot, and Milovasu stayed the same. No one knew why.

"Maybe he's just gathering his strength," mused his father, "and in a month or two he'll put on a great burst and pass them all."

But he didn't. He stayed small. Sometimes, too, he had trouble breathing. His chest would tie itself in knots, and he would have to sit down, wheezing and croaking until his chest loosened again.

The other boys no longer let Milovasu play games with them. When he insisted on running among them, anyhow, they snatched him up off the ground and began passing him back and forth like a ball.

"I won't allow this!" howled Milovasu. As he was passed through the air, he made a hammer with his fist, and the boy who reached up to catch him received such a blow on the nose that he staggered around like a drunk and was laughed at. Milovasu strode off in triumph, trying to hide the fact that he couldn't get his breath. He was hoping to get out of sight around a tree before he passed out.

Before he got far, four boys overtook him and knocked him to the ground, and the boy he had hit filled his mouth with dirt.

The next day, however, he was back. Again, he ran among the boys.

This time, when they grabbed him, he took hold of the largest boy, Sanjeev, by the wrist and gave his arm an expert twist. This was something he had learned from watching his father and the other men wrestle. Sanjeev cried out in pain at first, but then stifled himself. Pain, the elders taught, was transitory. Like most things outside a person's *boa*, it came and went.

"Let me go," he said to Milovasu, "and no one will lay hands on you again."

Milo let him go.

Standing, Sanjeev said, "It was childish of us to treat you that way."

Milovasu shrugged and answered, "Well, we are children."

"Nevertheless. But let me say this: It is a fact that you are smaller than all the rest, and you do make an excellent ball. An ordinary ball doesn't turn and thrash in the air and make itself difficult to handle. May we use you as a ball, Milovasu?"

Milovasu appreciated the respect shown by Sanjeev. And his father had taught him not to be overly proud. He agreed.

His father, when he first witnessed this new game the boys played, was puzzled and angry. But when he watched awhile and saw how it was, he was even more proud of his son.

"Milovasu will be the smallest leader this village, and maybe the world beyond, has ever known," he said.

But that wasn't to be. This is what happened instead:

One day, as the children were playing and their parents worked in the fields, a general commotion arose in the center of the village. Voices called out, sounding surprised and upset. Neighbors hurried between houses, trading cloudy looks.

Milovasu left the children's games and met his father and mother at their front door.

"Let's go see," said his father, and the three of them joined the rest of the village at the well, where the elders were just arriving.

The focus of the uproar was a man who looked as if he should be dead; his whole left side was covered in blood. He spoke briefly to the elders, then fell over and died.

The leader of the village raised his hands and made everyone be quiet and told them some terrible news.

The dead man, he said, had been a farmer down in the valley, on the lower part of the river. Three days ago, their village had been threatened by barbarian raiders, so he and his fellow farmers had armed themselves the best they could. They fought bravely and were slaughtered. The village had been burned and the survivors dragged away to be slaves. Only this one man had escaped to warn them.

The raiders were coming their way now.

In the wake of this news, silence.

Barbarian raiders were not a new thing. You heard about them, from time to time, in the stories of traders. They were the stuff of nightmares and worry, certainly, but they had not actually shown up within the lifetime of any of these particular villagers.

Except one.

Old Vashti, the most aged among them by thirty years. She might have been a hundred. Even Old Vashti didn't know. She looked like an old stick that had begun to melt.

But she appeared strangely bright-eyed and clearheaded now, as she stepped up to speak. She also looked troubled.

"These raiders came when I was a child," she croaked. "They're bad people. They peel children like grapes and let the ants have them. They like to rape people for days on end, before and after they're dead. The only reason I survived was because I reminded the chief of his mother, except that she wore a mustache. You can't fight them, and there's nowhere to run. My advice is to get a knife and stab yourselves to death."

And Old Vashti took out a knife and did just that, right there in front of everyone.

A cry went up. It went on for some time and got louder and was about to become panic when a ringing sound, not unlike a bell, cut through the noise, subdued the cries, and got their puzzled attention. Looking around, frightened and annoyed, the villagers discovered that the source of the ringing was not a bell but little Milovasu at the nearby blacksmith's forge, banging a hammer as hard as he could on the great anvil.

Several adults, including the village leader and his own parents, moved to snatch him up and put an end to this childishness. Really, at a time like this!

"Please," Milo said. "I offer a suggestion. Something other than stabbing ourselves."

Silence. They were ready, all of them, to hear options.

"Since I was even smaller than I am now," said Milo, "the goat herders have talked about building a rope bridge across the gorge, so that the goats can easily graze the pastureland on the far side. It has never been done; I don't know why—"

"Because we're lazy," offered Drupada, one of the herders.

"—but I don't see why we couldn't do this now and escape across the gorge, gathering the bridge up behind us."

"That," said Drupada, "is what inspires the laziness. In order to build a rope bridge, someone—not me—has to climb down into the gorge, down a half mile of slippery rocks, and risk his neck, taking with him one end of a very long rope, and then climb a half mile of slippery rocks up the other side."

"There's no time," added one of the elders. "That would take a couple of days. The gorge is difficult."

"What," said Milovasu, a curious look in his eye, "if you didn't have to climb?"

The whole village stared at him.

"Go on," said the village.

"What," said Milovasu, "if there were someone small enough, yet strong enough, that he could be *thrown* across the gorge, holding one end of a rope? Once he was on the other side, other ropes could be tossed back and forth and quickly worked into a bridge."

The village stared at him.

"We'd need an awful, awful, awful lot of rope," said Drupada.

The village burst into action.

By early morning, they had strung together enough rope to make a sort of tightrope across the gorge. They had also contrived enough rope for a handrope, as it were, on either side, all strung together with twine. All that was needed was for someone to carry, one way or another, a single length of rope over to the far side and pull the rest up behind him.

It would take the raiders days to follow, if they *chose* to follow, and by then the villagers would be well hidden in the mountains.

They took everything they could easily carry, which amounted to very little, and made their way through the morning mist, toward the gorge. Up at the very front walked Milovasu, his bare head and shoulders draped in orange blossoms. Beside him walked his friend Sanjeev. Behind them walked the coppersmiths and their assistants from the forge, bearing great coils of rope around their shoulders.

As they neared the gorge, the village leader slipped his copper armband into place around Milo's biceps.

"Just for today," he said, "you are our leader."

Milovasu tried not to be overly proud, just as he was trying not to be overly terrified.

"A practical consideration," he said. "The armband is much wider than my arm. It will fall off and be lost."

Sanjeev removed the armband, wrapped part of it in twine to make it thicker, and secured it once more on Milovasu's arm.

Moments later, they stood at the lip of the gorge.

There was no ceremony. There wasn't time. Already, if you listened hard against the booming of the water, you could hear rough voices far away.

Umang, the strongest of the coppersmiths, built as if a bull had mated with a stump, stepped forward and checked to make sure that Milovasu's end of the rope was secured about his waist.

"Are you ready?" he asked the boy.

"I'm ready," answered Milovasu, frightened out of his mind, breathless, using all his mental strength to keep from pissing himself. The far side of the gorge was fifty yards away. It seemed to grow farther as he looked at it, so he didn't look at it.

Then Umang took him by the wrists, swung him around in a fast, tight circle, and hurled him with a mighty grunt across the abyss.

It didn't work.

Milo rose into the air, spinning just a little, arms and legs spread like a flying squirrel. But a boy is not a flying squirrel, and before he could cross over the deep and the dark and the roaring water, he flew down and down, the rope following him like a graceful knotted tail.

He pissed himself, but he did not cry out.

The bad things he felt were too many and too much to be called one thing, like sadness or fear. There was the immediate knowledge and horror of his own life ending. There was also the horror of what, in all likelihood, would happen to his home and his family. The whole terrible thing gave one huge stomp inside his head, like an angry elephant, and then left him in silence as he passed out of the morning sunlight and fell and fell and fell through the dark.

The fall didn't kill him.

He struck branches and the steep flank of a mossy cliff and plunged backward into churning water. The water flung him up on a rock, choking and paralyzed. In a little while, the voice and the light in his head would fall silent and go out. But for now his wide eyes and listening ears still looked and heard. Just for a moment. He fell asleep for a while.

When he awoke, a little girl sat on a nearby stone, staring at him with eyes nearly as big as his own. She stared as if she'd never seen a boy before, let alone a boy broken and dying at the bottom of a gorge. She was wrapped in something long and black—maybe a robe, or wings. Her long black hair lay drenched across her shoulders.

He knew who the girl was. What else could she be?

"I didn't know Death was a girl," he said, his voice no more than the sigh of a moth. "I didn't know Death was so young."

"I'm not young," she answered. "I'm old enough to get tired just thinking about it. And I'm a girl because I want you to like me. You're very brave and wise for your age."

Milo felt himself getting dark and quiet inside.

"I don't want to take you," the girl whispered. "You were living your life so wonderfully. I've never seen anything like it. They must have accidentally packed an extra soul inside you."

Milo wanted to say something, but his breath wouldn't cooperate. His body jerked. He began to choke.

The girl leaned over him and kissed his forehead, and he felt himself go out like a—

He lay on a wooden bridge, over a slow blue river. The river flowed through a green meadow bright with wildflowers.

He was whole again. He was even a little taller.

His armband, he noticed, was gone. Too bad. He'd earned it, he felt.

The girl was gone, too. In her place was a woman.

A woman with pale skin and black, deep eyes. She wore something like a cape, or maybe it was wings.

She reached out and cupped his head in a long, willowy hand.

"Try and survive 'til you're a grown-up next time," she whispered.

"'Kay," he said.

The woman and the little girl were the same. Milovasu understood this, without understanding quite how. But before he could ask, she straightened up and stepped back and was flanked by two other grownups. An enormous, planetary woman, and an old lady holding a cat.

"Come," said the big woman. And they took him across the bridge to a town on the river's far side, into a neighborhood of nice houses. They ushered him into a mansion with a fountain in the courtyard, and peacocks.

"Holy shit," said Milo, after his father's example. "Why? How can I possibly have earned this?"

"Beginner's luck," said the old woman with the cat. "Enjoy it while it lasts."

"More than luck," said the big woman, giving the cat lady a sour look. "You have had an exceptional first life. Who knows—you might reach Perfection very quickly."

They turned to go.

"Wait!" Milo cried. Who were these people? What was happening?

"Are you goddesses?" he asked. "Or perhaps the souls of my ancestors?"

The big woman laid a warm, heavy hand atop his head.

"We're a little bit of everything," she said. "Think of us as slices of the universe."

Which meant squat to young Milo.

"Do you have names?" he asked.

"Everything has a name," answered the old woman, a little crossly. "My name is—"

The air exploded with a sound that was beyond words or music. As if the stars themselves were humming or the whole entire Earth were getting ready to sneeze. His ears would burst! His mind would tear—

It stopped.

"But you may call me Nan," said the old woman.

"I am Mother," said the big one. "Or Mama, or Ma, or—"

"Who are you?" Milo asked Death.

"She's called Death—" Nan answered.

"I'm Suzie," Death interrupted.

Milo liked this name. It sounded futuristic.

"Since when?" asked Mother, rolling her eyes.

"Since right now. Calling me 'Death' is like calling him 'Boy-soul' or a dog 'Dog.' Besides, how'd you like to be called 'Death'?"

" 'Suzie' is pretty," offered Milo.

"We should go," said Mother gently. "He'll be needing his rest."

"Rest from what?" Milo asked. "With respect, all I did was fall down and die. I just got out of bed, like, an *hour* ago."

But Mother and Nan turned their backs and left the courtyard, arm in arm. Suzie vanished in a sudden gust of wind and blue clover. Milovasu let his head spin and his thoughts whirl while he had a long pee in the fountain, then he went into his house and found some fruit waiting for him and managed several hours of troubled sleep.

Later, the universe women came back and they had a sit-down.

The purpose of the sit-down was simple: They explained how the universe worked.

In Milo's new kitchen, Mama waved her big arms, and a roaring fire appeared on the stone hearth.

"That fire," she explained, "is the Great Reality. It represents the universe the way it really is: Raw and wordless. Alive and pure. You can't really understand it, and if you got too close to it, you'd burn up. It has a lot of names. Sometimes we call it the Oversoul, because it's like one giant perfect soul. Okay?"

Mama had made one hell of a fire. Milo shielded his eyes and backed up.

"Okay," he said.

Mama turned away from the fire and pointed all around at the rest of the kitchen. "Notice how the farther you get from the fire, the cooler and darker everything gets? That's because the Oversoul casts its heat and light—its *reality*—out into everywhere. But as the heat and light radiate out, they get thinner. They diffuse. I mean, look at the fire, there—"

Milo looked.

"—and you see bright, perfect light. Look out here, and it's bright in some places and dark in others, and the light flickers and changes. And this is like where we are now."

"The afterlife," said Milo, always an eager student.

"It's not called 'the afterlife,'" rasped Nan. "Because it's the 'before-life,' too, isn't it? It's called *Ortamidivalavalarezarationaptulsphere.* Means 'middle.'"

"'Afterlife' will do," said Mama. "Don't be difficult. Anyhow, things here are warmer and brighter, more real, than out there in the rest of the universe."

"All right," said Milo, "so if I see a bridge here, in the afterlife, it's more *real* than if I see a bridge down on Earth."

"Not bad," said Nan.

"Exactly," said Mama. "Here, it's the *idea* of a bridge. Or a spoon. Or a fencepost. It's a pure form."

Nan and Mama, Milo now noticed, seemed to shimmer in a way that other things and people did not. As if they were wrapped in a wonderful second skin. Now that he glimpsed and considered this phenomenon, it did seem as if they were more *there* somehow. More *real*. Suzie—Death—had shimmered in this way, also. How curious.

"And *those* forms," said Nan, waving her hand at the back of the kitchen, which was comparatively dark, "go out and diffuse even more, until they're mostly shadows, with a few flickers and flares now and then. Harder to see the forms for what they are. Harder to tell what's real."

"And that's Earth," said Milo. "Where we go to live our lives."

"Where *you* go," said Nan, "to live *your* lives. *We* don't have to go anywhere."

Milo still didn't understand what Mama and Nan *were*, exactly.

"We're like tiny slivers of the fire," said Mama, "come out into the dark to help you."

"Help me what?" asked Milo.

At that moment, Mama waved her arms again, and the next thing Milo knew, they were outside, walking down the street. The street led straight downhill to a quiet little park.

"We're here to help you become part of the fire," said Mama, putting on a pair of sunglasses. Milo had never seen sunglasses before. Interesting! And cool. "We're here to help you get through the illusions and into the real universe."

"The Oversoul," said Milo.

"Yep," said Nan. "Every life has something to teach you. Chances for you to learn and grow and eventually become perfect. It may take thousands of lives."

"It's our job," said Mama, "to help you decide what kind of life to attempt next."

"I need to give that some thought," said Milo. "Obviously."

They reached the park, where Milo turned and looked back the way they had come and noticed that the street now led downhill, back to his house.

"It was downhill coming here," he remarked. "How . . . ?"

"Flickers and changes," said Mama. "Changing forms. Reality is elusive. Down on Earth, it's even more elusive."

"Which would seem," said Milo, "to make it even more difficult to decide what kind of life would lead toward truth and growth."

"Smart kid," said Nan. "Let me tell you, it's not always the obvious choice."

"How long do I have to choose? How long before I have to go back?"

Mama and Milo sat down in the grass, while Nan lit a cigarette (interesting, thought Milo, observing) and stood watching a new house materialize across the street.

"You go back when you feel like it," said Mama.

"And what if I—"

Mama shushed him.

"Lay back and watch the clouds," she said. "Let your mind be quiet. Just be."

Milo tried to just be, but his mind kept filling up with thoughts of Suzie. Was that okay? He fell asleep thinking about that, feeling uneasy.

It was decided, after a week, that Milo would be reborn as a radio personality named Milo "Pork Chop" Zilinski, in Cincinnati, Ohio.

And he went and lived that life and died when he was forty-nine. When he woke up in the afterlife on a rusty old railroad bridge, he found his head cradled in Suzie's lap. She stroked his hair but didn't kiss him or anything. It wasn't like that between them yet and wouldn't be for a long time. They had a minute or two to themselves, to enjoy being grown-ups together, before Ma and the cat lady showed up.

"What was your favorite thing?" Suzie asked. "What will you miss the most?"

"From life?" Milo gave his answer some thought. Life as Pork Chop Zilinski had been kind of sleazy. He doubted they were going to give him a nice house this time.

"Christmas," he said. "That was my favorite."

Liar. His favorite thing had been a girl named Peanut, backstage at Ozzfest.

She let him get away with it. That's how people make friends.

CHAPTER 5

Your Soul Can Be Canceled
Like a Dumb TV Show

Milo drifted up through oceans of memory and opened his eyes.

The afterlife, after the shark got him. In bed with Suzie.

He slid the armband over his wrist. A perfect fit.

Suzie lay against his side like a jigsaw piece. They fit together the way people do when they've held each other a hundred thousand times.

She gave his arm a squeeze and said, "Look sharp. You've got company."

A knock at the apartment door. A loud, fat knock. A Mama knock.

Shit. That's right. They wanted to talk to him about something.

"Do you know what they want?" he asked Suzie.

Suzie bit her lip.

"No," she lied.

He let her get away with it.

"Just go," she said.

He left the bed with a sour feeling in his stomach.

"Milo?" she called after him.

"Mmm?"

"Pants, baby."

He followed Ma and Nan and forty-some cats out of his dingy little neighborhood, walking quietly once again. Meditating as they went, supposedly. Milo kept thinking about the weather and his third-grade teacher and a troublesome refrigerator he'd once owned.

He also thought about the two women he found himself with. He had known them for thousands of years by now, but did he know them any better? Was he supposed to love them? He did, a little, he supposed. But they scared him, too.

They passed into a comfortable, cozy little neighborhood. There were hummingbird feeders and fences. You could hear somebody playing music, just barely.

Then, quite suddenly, everything fell away.

The sidewalk simply extended like a pirate-ship plank out into empty space.

It was like a magic trick. There was the sidewalk, and the end of the sidewalk, dripping clods of dirt and little scraggly roots . . . and then nothing. A touch of vertigo played cement mixer with Milo's senses.

A soft breeze blew. It should have smelled like spring or like a neighborhood, but it smelled like nothing.

"What is this place?" Milo asked.

"It's Nowhere," said Nan.

Milo waited. There had to be more.

"When you go back this next time," said Nan, "it will be your nine thousand nine hundred ninety-sixth life."

One of the cats twined between Milo's ankles, as if trying to nudge him off-balance. His stomach lurched.

"So much suffering," said Ma, "being alive. Being born, living, dying, being reborn. I'd think you would want to break out of the cycle, Milo."

They'd had this talk before.

"I *like* the cycle," he said. "I *like* living lives."

"That's fine," said Ma, "but you're not supposed to keep going back forever. You're supp—"

"I know what I'm supposed to do."

"You," snapped Nan, "are like the kid who's been held back in fifth grade for the eighth time. Achieve Perfection already!"

"I think this 'Perfection' thing might be overrated," Milo mumbled.

Mama stepped up beside him. Bowing her head for a long moment, she said, "Think of yourself as a rocket ship."

"Not the rocket metaphor," sighed Milo.

"Every life you live should take you higher, learning more, becoming wiser, growing in every way. Eventually you reach orbit, living higher and higher lives, circling the planet, until one day, at last, with one final push, you reach escape velocity and fly away into the stars. Remember the fire? That flying away is your destiny, Milo. It's every soul's destiny. Weightless and free."

"Right, right," said Milo. "Escape velocity. Perfection. Do you know how not-easy that is?"

"Yes," said Nan. "That's why you get thousands of lives to do it."

"I've heard this a million times," Milo fumed.

"Then maybe you need to hear it a million and one!" bellowed Mama, patience gone, swelling like a mighty, psychotic cow. "If you'd try and *understand* it, maybe we wouldn't still *be* here, having the same stupid argument we've had *over* and *over,* and maybe you wouldn't be on the verge—"

She stopped.

"On the verge of what?" asked Milo.

"Tell 'im," rasped Nan. "Hurry up. I'm missing my shows."

"The thing is," said Mama, drawing up closer, facing him, "you don't get to keep trying forever."

Here it comes, thought Milo.

"A soul gets ten thousand lives," said Nan. "Ten thousand tries. After that, it becomes Nothingness."

Milo froze.

Huh?

"That leaves you," said Mama, "with five more lives to get it right. If you do, you will go through the Sun Door in a flash of golden light and become part of the Great Reality."

"The Oversoul," added Nan. "Everything."

"The universal *boa*," barked Milo. "I get it."

"I hope so," said Nan. "Because if you don't, we'll bring you here and push you off the end of the sidewalk, and you'll vanish forever from time and space. Your soul will be canceled like a dumb TV show."

Milo almost threw up. He dropped to his knees to keep from reeling into space.

"I *have* grown!" he yelled. "Every time I've lived a life! When I'm down there, I'm the wisest guy on the planet. I could be president, except I know power is a crutch! I could be rich, but I know money is a siren song. I live by the governing dynamics behind all the traps and illusions—"

"Wisdom," said Nan, "is not the same as Perfection."

Frustration.

"Do they give extensions?" Milo asked. "Maybe I can convince them to let—"

"Them?" said Mama. "There's no 'them.' The universe doesn't have a judge or a landlord. It's like a river. It flows and changes and does what it has to do to stay in balance."

"Two plus two equals four," said Nan. "It's not personal. And it doesn't matter how you feel about it."

Over thousands of years, Milo had gotten used to the glow that Mama and Nan—and Suzie, and all universals—wore. The skin of superreality that enfolded them. Now he noticed it anew and, for the first time, found it frightening rather than motherly or protective.

"Enough," said Ma, sounding tired. "Listen. We have sort of a plan, if you're interested. What you should do, for your next life, to set yourself up."

"Okay," said Milo.

"Your next life should be all about self-denial," said Nan. "Like the great hermits, back in the old days."

"You live in a cave and starve yourself," added Mama, "and speak to no one, and ignore everything but all that wisdom packed up in your soul. No distractions. No family, no great food or great journeys or girlfriends or achievements. You sit, and you understand."

Milo considered this.

There were, he knew, many ways a soul could reach Perfection. After eight thousand years, he had tried them all. You could love, you could become some kind of savior, you could achieve a great peace or teach something new and powerful. But one of the most successful, if your soul was old and wise enough, was the hermit thing. You tortured your inner self with isolation until—*pow!*—one day it turned into some kind of sun or soul diamond, and—*poof!*—off into Perfection you dissolved. Trouble was, it was enormously unpleasant and hardly anyone could pull it off. Sooner or later, most souls crawled to the nearest village and started wolfing down baloney and pinching college girls, and that was the end of that.

"No," said one of Nan's cats. A black cat with a fluffy tail, staring up at them with huge, familiar eyes.

"Eavesdropper!" hissed Nan.

The cat stretched and changed and became Suzie, who stood on the sidewalk with her arms crossed.

"You're setting him up for failure," she said. *"People* are Milo's talent and skill. It's how his soul is shaped. Two plus two."

Mama reached out and pulled Suzie away from the edge. "You're giving me fits, honey," she whispered. "That's better."

"Well," rasped Nan, "he had better do *something* extraordinary. The usual horse poop isn't going to get it."

Milo rose to his feet. They all spent a minute examining the sidewalk.

The temperature dropped again. The sky advanced into twilight.

"It doesn't make it any easier," said Nan, "the two of you boinking around behind our backs like a couple of teenage jackrabbits."

Suzie's head whipped around.

"That was tactful," remarked Mama.

"I'm sorry," said Nan. "You didn't imagine it was a secret, after eight thousand years? Well, how cute."

"Jackrabbits?" repeated Suzie.

"Sorry for the reality, sweetheart, but it's just one more way our boy here is out of balance. People-souls don't do the Hokey Pokey with universal-souls. He's a person. She's Death, for crying out loud. You think that's been a big fat help, all this time?"

"Um," said Milo, "I rather thought it might be an advantage. I thought it meant I was really, really advanced."

"It *should* be an advantage!" spat Suzie. "You *are* advanced!"

"Balance!" growled Mama, eyes closed, trying not to lose her temper. "Listen: This isn't the first time that someone like her has been in love with someone like him. Ages ago, Spring—the season of spring, you understand—fell in love with a woman. At first, this was wonderful. The woman reveled in this giant spirit that loved her, this Perfection of warmth and rebirth and new growth, plus I suppose he made himself just awfully handsome, bursting out all over with health and goodness and freshness. And he got to be alive and living in an everyday way he'd never known. He learned to pick out new carpet, and sleep, and eat breakfast, and make love. She called him 'George.' And when he held her, he showered her with young leaves and dandelions and dogwood petals. Sometimes, when they held each other, he was a man. Other times, maybe he was rain or a fabulous tree. And, naturally, she became pregnant.

"At first, that was fine news. The woman's belly became great and firm, like the ripe Earth itself. Then it became *too* great and firm, until it seemed she must burst. And then she *did* burst. She exploded with meadows and cowslips and warm breezes. Miraculous, except, of course, she was dead."

Twilight deepened around the sidewalk and the neighborhood.

"It's worked okay so far," said Suzie. "The two of us."

"And I'm glad for you," said Mama, "both of you." She patted Suzie's cheeks as if making a pie. "But I think it's part of what's keeping our Milo here from moving on. It may even move him straight into Nothingness. And I think I'm done talking about it for now."

"Me, too," said Nan.

"Fine," said Suzie.

"Fine," said Mama.

Mama and Nan vanished in a golden flash.

"Fine," repeated Suzie, disappearing in a dash of wind and leaves.

Milo blinked his eyes. Clicked his heels. Tried to beam himself back to his crappy apartment.

No dice.

He shoved his hands deep in his pockets and walked, and pouted, and walked.

CHAPTER 6

The Eleanor Roosevelt of the Sea

Death doesn't pout.

It doesn't chew its nails or get frustrated and throw fits.

Suzie reminded herself of these things, storming away from the sidewalk, glaring and grinding her teeth, hurling her cosmic self through space and time.

"Assholes," she muttered.

It wasn't the first time she'd been party to an argument over the Way Things Are Meant to Be.

She hadn't been Death very long, the first time they butted heads.

It was yesterday, or it was a thousand years ago. There wasn't really a difference. Time was a swamp inside a giant washing machine.

She came upon a blue whale lying on a beach, moaning softly to herself. The whale was a sister and a mother and a grandmother. A great-grandmother, actually. Whole worlds of life had passed through her, and now here she was, the victim of a trick in the tide, washed up on land, being crushed by her own weight.

Suzie let the whale see her. Tried to look friendly ("friendly," she had learned, was important to humans and other mammals). She made herself look like a whale, somewhat, and stood looking into one vast dying eye.

Hi, said the whale (whales are telepathic).

Hi, said Suzie. And she left it at that. Being Death was kind of like being a therapist; it worked better if you let *them* do the talking, if there was going to be talking.

She told Suzie her name, which was AiiOOOOOnuuUU. The spirit inside the old grandmother was exactly what you'd expect of such a creature: huge and dreamy, crackling with plans and memories. She did *not* want to die yet, and certainly not like this.

Being trapped on land, for a whale, was the marine equivalent of accidentally locking yourself outside with no clothes on.

AiiOOOOOnuuUU lay there missing the sea. The picture in her head (and Suzie's head) was like an endless blue heart. Living in the ocean was half-dreamlike, an act of worship without the complication of gods.

Suzie let AiiOOOOOnuuUU's mind fill her senses. She leaned forward and rested against the whale, against a hundred seasons of memories and voyages and names she had known.

Suzie let the whale feel her own memories. Let her feel what it was like to fly, what it was like to be timeless.

Death took a million forms. Suzie shared some of her favorites.

Fire. Chocolate. Silence. Sleep.

Bicycles. Being melancholy.

One time, she had brought a dying girl a present—an Eiffel Tower snow globe. The girl had wanted to see Paris but never got to go. The girl held the snow globe and was transfixed and happy when Suzie touched her head and snuffed her out, and that was one of the few times Suzie was mortal enough to cry on the job. She gave this memory to the whale, who was puzzled by it, but grateful.

The whole idea of this communion was to get AiiOOOOOnuuUU to relax and become sort of peaceful and accepting and hypnotized before Suzie brought things to an end.

But it backfired.

The whale made a mournful, rattling sound and tried to heave herself backward, fighting to get to the water.

But Suzie already had her whale hands on AiiOOOOOnuuUU's head. The great eye went dim and went dark and went out, and just at that moment Suzie changed her mind.

"No!" she bugled, in whale language. Her voice emerged fierce and wet.

And before she knew she was going to do it, she pulled AiiOO-OOOnuuUU back from Between and breathed her into the dead, mountainous body.

The great lungs filled! The great eye moved in its orbit!

Frantic, Suzie looked around for a way to get AiiOOOOOnuuUU into the sea. Impossible! Aw, shit—the tide had gone out, leaving nothing but sand and rocks and clams for a hundred yards.

I'll talk to the ocean himself, she thought (she knew this ocean: a tall, deep-looking fellow with pearls for eyes and a taste for Greek wedding music). She called his name, which took ten minutes and made it rain but failed to get his attention. In the meantime, she became aware of voices on the wind, calling to her through the rain, and turned to discover several dark forms standing in the sawgrass, just uphill.

Death had more than one shape and name, after all.

"You can't do that," they said (Death is telepathic, too, but likes the sound of its own voice).

Suzie, defiant, said, "I just did! I'm not taking her yet." The whale was a great spirit. Couldn't they see?

"She's like the Eleanor Roosevelt of the ocean," she added.

"Not anymore," they all said. "Look."

They pointed. And Suzie looked, and saw, and it was awful.

The whale, half alive and half dead, lay shaking and gagging on the beach. Her mighty eye now had a bad, zombie-like glow.

Shit, thought Suzie. They were right; she knew better. She hated that they were right. Even more, though, she hated what she had done to the whale.

"No matter how good your intentions are," she muttered to herself, "you can't put the lightning back in the bottle."

"Huh?" said the other Deaths.

"Never mind," said Suzie, and waved her hand and let the whale die again.

And she turned to face them, ready to give a little lecture about how maybe death wouldn't be so awful so much of the time if only they'd take time to learn a thing or two about being alive, and they could roll their eyes all they wanted to, and—

But they were gone.

She made her way up on top of the whale and sat there awhile in the wind and the rain, being melancholy and enjoying it, and wishing she had some chocolate.

That was a long time ago now. Felt like it, anyway.

Suzie flurried to a stop in Milo's new apartment. The leaves and shadows slowed and vanished, leaving her feeling tired, groping for the light switch. Wondering if Milo was going to be mad when he got back, since she had basically left him out there on the sidewalk (that ridiculous, dumbass sidewalk!).

Well, the walk home would be good for him, mad or not. Milo needed to get his act together.

She decided to dye her hair.

A silly thing to do, if you're a universal idea, like Death or Spring or Music or Peace. But Suzie had learned something interesting about people: They knew the wisdom of simply being busy sometimes.

Chop wood; carry water. Do the dishes. Sweep the garage. Milk the cows.

Dye your hair.

She was about halfway done when Milo arrived. Hands shoved way down in his pockets, frowning.

"Thanks for the ride," he said.

"Sorry," Suzie answered, head down in the sink, kneading her hair through rubber gloves. "I wouldn't have been good company."

He just stood there, looking moody. As soon as he had a beer and changed his underwear, Suzie knew, he'd snap out of it (she knew Milo better than he would have liked).

"Do you have any questions?" she asked.

"No," he growled. "No questions."

"Good, 'cuz when I talk, I get chemical yick in my mouth."

They watched TV in silence. Deflated, Milo drifted off while watching a cat-food commercial.

"You can't let it happen, love," said Suzie, dragging him awake again.

He tried to roll over on his side, facing the wall, but she reached out, grasped his chin, and turned his head to face her.

"If I do what I'm supposed to do," he said, "if I leave the cycle, I leave *you*. If I don't, I get deleted."

He sat up.

"Who says Perfection is even desirable?" he asked.

"What do you mean?"

"What if I *like* my imperfections?" Milo asked. "I mean, when they say 'imperfect,' they're talking about human desires, right? Like wanting someone to love you, and having a cool job and a car, and your kids go to college, and people admire you. And painful things, like if your mom dies, or you live in poverty and danger, or you have diabetes, or raccoons get in your garbage. That's called 'being alive.'"

"It is painful," answered Suzie. "That's what I see when I take someone's soul out of the world. So many of them are glad to be free of the pain."

"So what? You guys taught me that pain is an illusion."

"And Perfection frees us from . . . ?"

"Illusion. I know. But you're talking in circles!"

"You only say that because you don't know Perfection. When you're perfect, you become part of Everything, like Kool-Aid dissolving in water."

Milo's hands were busy with nervous energy. He made a little bunny sculpture with part of the sheets.

"I don't *want* to join with Everything," said Milo, "or dissolve. I'm happy being me."

Suzie bit her lip and hugged her knees. "Now who's talking in circles?"

Milo grunted in frustration, trying unsuccessfully to rip the bunny's ears off.

"Peace," said Suzie. She took his hand, and some actual peace traveled up his arm and calmed him.

"Maybe there are possibilities," she said.

"Like what?"

"What if you try really hard, and do the Perfection thing. Hear me out! Just get it done. And *then* tell them you don't want to go."

"Go?"

"Into the cosmic whatever."

"They'll just tell me a math problem and explain that the answer doesn't care what I want."

"You'll have leverage, though. Credibility. If you've done the Perfection thing."

"Two plus two still equals four."

"So does five minus one."

Milo pulled her to him, kissing her.

But she pulled away. She looked sad.

"You don't think I can do it," he said.

"I do!" she shouted. "It's just that you tend to do, you know, too much. You try too hard. You've screwed things up before, taking things to extremes."

"I know. I have to be especially careful now."

"Remember the time you fucked it up so bad you had to come back as a bug?"

"I said *I know!*"

She played it over for him in her eyes, like a movie, an old life flashing before him.

"I hate when you do that," he complained.

"Hush," she said, baring her teeth in a certain way. So he hushed, and remembered.

CHAPTER 7

The Time Milo Had to Come Back as a Bug

WATER CARTEL SKYHOOK, EARTH ORBIT, A.D. 2115

He had been born fantastically rich, which was a chance to score big soul points. If you could survive early exposure to money and privilege and avoid turning into an asshole, the universe tended to be impressed. A hundred lives ago, Milo thought this kind of challenge was just what he needed.

He had been born aboard a gleaming space yacht (past and future were much the same, as far as the universe was concerned), heir to the chair of the Interplanetary Water Resource Cartel, the company in control of all the water in the solar system. From Mercury all the way out to the Neptune ammonia mines, if you wanted water, you paid the cartel. You paid whatever the cartel told you to pay.

He grew up aboard a private space station—Mother called it a "villa"—in orbit around the comet-smashed Earth. The villa supported a population of butlers, valets, cartel lackeys, and technical crew. From time to time, new structures were added. As a toddler, Milo requested a TerraBubble big enough to sustain his own private forest. As a young teen, he demanded harem chambers.

Normal people, living in poorer quarters elsewhere in the solar system, were fascinated with Milo the way people in previous centuries were fascinated with movie stars. They ate it up when he behaved badly (on his fourteenth birthday, Milo shot his valet with an antique pistol, then had him resurrected by medical robots) and took a weirdly personal pride when he behaved nobly (like the time he donated the Black Sea to a little refugee girl who was thirsty).

Like many children of privilege, Milo found that his primary difficulty lay in fighting boredom.

He traveled around and fed his libido. By the time he was twenty, he had been to every brothel and nightspot from low Venus orbit to the nautilus caves of Titan. He tasted everything there was to taste, felt every sensation, and satisfied every urge on the human menu.

He fed his mind, attending fancy schools, earning degrees in Game Theory, Leisure Theory, and Theory Theory.

Like a lot of rich people, Milo collected things. He had a collection of antique automobiles, a collection of deadly snakes, a gallery of paintings executed by cats, and a ball of string bigger than the Great Pyramid, parked in orbit around Mars.

His collections bored him. His travels bored him.

He was sitting around one day, thinking about shooting his leg off with a particle blaster just to see if the robots could put it back on, when an item on the news feed caught his attention.

It was a short film about Kennedy Pritzker Helleconia Gates, a daughter of the Helleconia Oxygen Cartel. Like Milo, she was rich and attractive. Unlike Milo, she was not young. At two hundred and ten, thanks to cosmetic nanobots, Kennedy looked a reasonably attractive thirty.

"Bully for her," muttered Milo.

Now, reported the article, in her most recent surgical eccentricity, Ms. Gates had ordered her virginity restored.

Milo sat up straight. He played this part of the article several times.

"You can't really do that," he said, consulting cartel scientists. *"Can you?"*

They explained to him that, yes, it could be done, in a physiological sense. The bored look in Milo's eyes gave way to a lively fire.

A fire of purpose, even zeal.

He would seduce Kennedy Pritzker Helleconia Gates and collect her famous virginity.

He arranged for them both to be ribbon-cutters for the new Martian supercolosseum.

"I liked what you did with the Black Sea," Kennedy said, shaking his hand in the green room before the event. "You're never boring when you make the news."

"Nor you," replied Milo. Plunging straight ahead, he said, "After the ribbon-cutting, will you join me for dinner in my shuttle? I'll cook for you. I make, as it happens, a terrific zero-g étouffée."

She turned him down with the faintest shadow of a laugh.

Later, alone in his shuttle with a bag of potato chips, Milo reflected. He saw Kennedy for what she was: a life that had aged like whiskey, growing mellow and deep. He saw himself as she must see him: a haughty child, a vacuum of character.

He couldn't win her.

Not the usual way, anyhow.

It came to him in a dream.

Past midnight, disheveled in his silk dragon robe, Milo summoned the cartel engineers and announced his plan to overwhelm the pants off Kennedy Gates.

"I will host the mightiest charitable ball in the history of human-kind," he told them. "There will be music by famous musicians, food by famous chefs, dances, narcotics, and erotics, hosted in a palace of my own design."

"Fine," they all said. "Where?"

"On the sun," said Milo. "You will build me a palace on the sun."

When a cartel chairman—or her son—tells you to build something, you build it.

So they built Milo his palace. Put it together in Earth orbit, explaining that when the time came, it could rocket to the sun and be lowered to the surface. A thing called the "Yesterday Field" made it possible. The palace would be protected by an invisible lattice of exotic particles. The lattice would send the sun's heat back through time—to yesterday, as it were—leaving the palace unburned.

"The only problem . . ." said the scientists.

But Milo was too excited to listen further. He jumped up and down, dancing, ignoring them.

"It's important," they said, but he had his headphones on.

The construction of the Water Cartel Sun Palace took three years. It became the most popular media item on the SolWide stream, with millions checking their newsgroups hourly to watch the fantastic turrets and spires take shape above the ruined Earth.

Milo concerned himself with one thing only during those three years, and he *got* that one thing. Kennedy Gates RSVP'd in the positive, on singing stationery, just twenty-four hours before launch. "I'll be there," she wrote, "one way or another."

The guests shuttled up to the completed palace the next day and entered a grand hall vast enough to have its own weather. Milo appeared on a balcony of polished obsidian, wearing a Nehru jacket and sunglasses. At his signal, engines blazed, the Yesterday Field shimmered, and they shot toward the sun in perfect style.

Milo surveyed the throng from his balcony.

Kennedy? He didn't see her. Fuck.

He had to leave the great hall to find her, but find her he did, drinking alone in the grand alabaster stables among the mighty Lipizzaner horsebots, feeding them apples from a leather shoulder bag. She wore a yellow sundress.

"The closest thing I'll ever have to children," said Milo, nodding at the horsebots. "May I?"

She handed him an apple. He fed it to his favorite, a mare named Elsie, who was programmed to tap-dance.

"I should think," said Kennedy, "you could have all the children you liked, without having to go to a lot of trouble."

"I think I like trouble," he answered. "Besides, I'm picky. I can't have them mothered by just anyone. They have to make up for my own poor genes."

Kennedy gave him a playful look.

"False modesty doesn't suit you," she said. "But I like that you try." She tossed her head to indicate the palace, all around. "I like the *way* you try."

She stepped up close to him then and touched his lips with an apple. He took it with his teeth and stood there holding it as if he were a boar's head at a feast.

"Sometimes," she said, "a woman just appreciates a little effort."

With that, she brushed aside her shoulder strings so that her sundress began to fall open. It seemed almost to bloom around her shoulders. Then she stood on tiptoe and bit down on the opposite side of the apple.

It was a perfect moment. The palace fired its retros just then and nestled into the surface of the sun.

Immediately, it began to melt.

A distant roar at first, and a trembling throughout.

Uh-oh. It occurred to Milo, for the first time, to wonder why all of the engineers had declined to attend the ball.

Solar fire came pouring back through time, through the Yesterday Field. All the heat and plasma and raw radiation from tomorrow—from five seconds from now—erupted like a fiery octopus around the towers.

Milo had worked too hard and waited too long to be here with Kennedy Gates and her falling sundress and her apple and her famous virginity. His eyes held her eyes.

She *would have,* he thought. She was *going* to. Did that count?

"I'm sorry," he said.

She caressed his cheek with a gentle, exquisitely painted left hand.

"It's okay," she said. "I'm not really her. She always sends droids to these things. Parties wear her out these days. She's not aging as well as they'd hoped."

Below their feet, a rise in temperature.

Well, shit, thought Milo.

The Kennedy bot retrieved a compact mahogany plaque from her shoulder bag and handed it to him.

I, read the plaque, MILO GALAPAGOS ROCKEFELLER BUFFETT GALIFIANAKIS CLXIII, TOOK, BY ROBOTIC PROXY, THE SURGICALLY RESTORED VIRGINITY OF KENNEDY PRITZKER HELLECONIA GATES.

Dated June 28, A.D. 2140.

"It'll have to do," said Milo.

"Well, good," said the droid.

He just barely had time to prop the plaque on one of the stall doors and stand for a moment, admiring it and stroking Elsie's neck, before everything came apart and the sun swallowed them down.

Milo's Sun Palace life was the cosmic version of flunking second grade.

He had set himself a challenge, and he had failed. Privilege had turned him into a ridiculous, self-important goat.

The universe sent him back to Earth as a bug. Usually you get to choose what kind of life you're going to live, but not if you really screw the pooch. He became a cricket. In China. In 1903.

This time around, he was a raging success.

A little girl captured him and kept him in a wooden cage, hung from the ceiling. He learned to chirp when she pressed her nose against the cage and giggled at him. It wasn't much, but it made her love him. Not many crickets get to be loved. Even fewer crickets receive elegant funerals, but when he died, the girl made him a tiny coffin and set him adrift amid lily pads on a pond in the city park.

He went straight to the afterlife, redeemed somewhat, after that. Lesson learned, one would hope.

CHAPTER 8

Holy Cow

The memory fell away, and Milo found himself back in his dumb apartment in the afterlife, looking into Suzie's eyes.

He blinked.

"I got the cricket part right," he noted. "I was an *awesome* cricket."

Thirsty. Was there beer in the fridge? He got out of bed to go see.

Padded down the dark hall, felt his way around the corner into the kitchen, and opened the fridge to—surprise! Light! The power was on!—discover a twelve-pack of cold, cheap beer.

He cracked one for himself and—hearing her sneak up behind him—one for Suzie.

"Yuck," she said.

"Cheap beer is an acquired taste," he told her. "Like expensive cheese."

"I had an idea," she said, hopping up to sit on the counter.

He waited. He sipped his beer.

"You think you're ready to really try and do something perfect?"

"Actually, *you're* the one who said—"

"Do you even know what it looks like? Perfection?"

Milo thought about it.

He said, "No."

"Would you like to see?"

He sipped his beer. He scratched himself.

"Yes," he said.

"Good. Come to work with me."

"By work, you mean . . . ?"

"Being Death. Picking up souls. Ending lives. Yes. One of the souls I'm picking up tomorrow is reaching Perfection. You want to see what that looks like? Come with."

"Are you supposed to do that? Take people with you?"

She kissed him.

He started kissing her back, but she pulled away and headed down the hall.

"Six o'clock comes early," she said. "Set your alarm."

"Six?"

"Workdays are the same everywhere, Milo. As below, so above."

He fell asleep watching a documentary about sweaters.

In the morning, she wrapped them both in her long hair, which became wings, which became a wind and dry leaves, flying. It was wild and fun and also scary. Flying with Death was like being in a sleeping bag with a sensuous woman and a tarantula.

The wind slowed and stopped, and his feet were back on the ground.

He was in someone's living room, where the only light was a flickering TV.

The room was trashed. Pizza boxes. Dirty plates. Some magazines. Clothes that had been tossed aside. On the couch, like one more piece of trash, slouched a young man with dirty hair in a Hank 3 T-shirt.

His eyes were dull. His skin matched his eyes, except where angry sores broke the skin. His mouth hung half open, like a wound that wouldn't heal. At first, Milo thought the mouth was full of popcorn:

some white kernels, some black kernels. Then he realized these were the man's teeth.

He heard Suzie next to him. She had a grip on his elbow.

"Um," said Milo, "this is the super-enlightened perfect life? *This* guy is about to go through the Sun Door and join the Oversoul?"

"Don't be dumb," she said. "I've got some stops to make first."

A slab of broken tile lay on a coffee table in front of the man, half-covered in something that might have been powder or crushed glass.

Suzie knelt in front of the man. He stirred.

"Chris," she whispered.

The man coughed. His eyes began to close.

"Christopher." A little louder.

"You let them see you?" asked Milo.

"Sometimes. If they're having a hard time letting go. Now shhhhh."

She reached up and laid a gentle hand on Christopher's cheek, and his eyes opened wide. He glanced around, and when he first saw Suzie, he jerked. He acted as if he wanted very much to get off the couch and run away but couldn't get his legs to work.

He said, "Sucks," foaming at the mouth a little, and was dead.

"That's it?" asked Milo.

"Yeah. He'll be waking up by the river any second now. We're outta here. Hang on."

Dark and wind again.

They stood beside a young woman in rags who sat on a wooden stool, nursing an infant. All around them, torrents of quick, barefoot children poured, chasing and playing.

Suzie reached down over the woman's shoulder and touched the baby on the forehead.

"Oh, shit," said Milo. "Are you kidding?"

Suzie kissed the woman on top of her head and rested her own head there a second, eyes closed.

Wind and dark.

They stopped to take a fat man working at a computer.

They took a big black dog.

They took a lonely old woman in a bed in a half-dark room. The second she died, a cuckoo clock in the hall went bananas.

Wind rushing, leaves flying. They landed in Mumbai, in India, at the edge of a buzzing neighborhood, on a street clip-clopping with donkeys and carts.

A cow walked by. One of the city's many sacred cows. It crossed the street, and traffic stopped. The cow might be someone's grandmother.

"Come on," said Suzie, tugging at Milo's hand.

"We're following the cow?"

"You want to see Perfection or not?"

He nodded.

The cow walked through a marketplace, where a Brahmin hung a garland of magnolias around her neck. Milo could have sworn the cow bowed to the priest a little.

They watched the cow do something very intelligent and surprising. She plodded around behind the bazaar tables, and when a shopkeeper was distracted by a possible deal, she stretched her neck, opened her mouth, and trotted away holding a butcher knife in her meaty, drooling lips.

They followed the cow out of the market district, through a district where houses gave way to shacks and pavement gave way to dirt, to a place where people were living in trash. It was one of Mumbai's many dumps. The ground itself was made of compressed refuse. People lived in huts made from trash, between towering hills of garbage. It smelled like putrid milk and sewage, beset by roaring clouds of flies. Children followed the cow, dancing.

The cow stopped, poking its head through the door of a house made entirely of wholesale-cheese boxes. Milo and Suzie peered over the cow's back. When his eyes adjusted, Milo gasped and withdrew.

"What's wrong with them?" he asked.

"They're starving," said Suzie.

"Lots of people are starving. They don't look like that."

"They've been too sick to look for work or even to beg. If they don't eat very soon, they'll die."

Suzie followed the cow into the hovel. Milo followed Suzie.

Inside, a man, a woman, an old woman, and four tiny children all expressed surprise that a cow had invited itself inside. But they didn't have the strength for a greeting or a protest. Their flesh stretched like drum skins over sharp bones. Their heads resembled skulls. The old woman hinted that maybe the cow was an incarnation of death, come to bear them out of this miserable life.

"I doubt it," said the man. "We're not that lucky."

The cow lowered her head, placed the knife on the floor, and said, "Please eat me."

"Whoa!" Milo whispered.

Other exclamations followed. Expressions of surprise. Expressions of gratitude.

The cow was kind enough to accept the father's thanks and to exchange bows.

Suzie reached out and stroked the cow's forehead. It knelt down and quietly died.

The family prayed before they began cutting.

"Suzie," said Milo, feeling shaky.

"Mmm?"

"What just happened?"

"You have just seen a soul achieve Perfection."

"Because it sacrificed itself?"

"Not just that."

On the floor before them, the cutting had begun. Slowly at first. Respectfully.

"That cow wasn't just a cow. She was formerly lots of other things, including a famous bodhisattva named Aishwarya. She gave herself to this family out of a perfect understanding that they could use her flesh to live and get better. And she was neither proud nor afraid. That's important."

Between them, a young woman with wonderful eyes had appeared, happily watching the family butcher the cow. She and Suzie bowed to each other. Then the woman vanished.

Milo stroked his chin. "I could do the sacrifice part," he said. "I think."

Suzie looked thoughtful. "You and this cow-person-soul have a lot in common," she said. "You're about people, one way or another. That's why I brought you."

It was getting pretty bloody down there on the floor. The old woman was especially fierce, ripping gristle with her bare hands.

"We need to go," said Suzie.

Wind and dark.

They stood by a river, in the afterlife, in the middle of a tremendous crowd. The crowd wore bright colors and waved banners of yellow silk.

Airships and balloons crowded the sky.

The bodhisattva and former cow, Aishwarya, strode to the river, wearing a beatific smile. The crowd parted for her, and she waded into the river.

The air itself turned golden around her. The gold flared and boiled, and then *flashed* out in a ring of cosmic light, casting a moment of unmistakable Perfection over everything, over thousands of souls and stones, the airships and the wind itself.

And then it faded.

And everyone turned and went off to do their own thing, as if someone had gotten on a loudspeaker and said, "The magic, perfect cow-woman has left the building. There's nothing more to see here."

Back at Milo's apartment, Suzie collapsed across the living-room sofa, and Milo occupied a beanbag chair. Some Styrofoam pellets popped out through a wound in one side.

"If a cow can do it," he said, "I can do it. If I can perform some kind of great sacrifice, then I will have achieved something perfect, and maybe I can have bargaining power to not go into the Everything?"

"It's not just sacrifice, Milo. If a wolf chews its leg off to get out of a trap, that's sacrifice, too, but it's also desperation. It's not Perfection. There has to be love."

"I have love!" protested Milo. "I'm in love with *you*."

"'Love'" said Suzie, "and 'in love' aren't always the same thing. 'In love' is a human thing. Chemicals. 'Love' is cosmic. I love you, too."

She took his hand, and some love traveled up his arm and burst inside him like a galaxy. For a moment, he contained wonders and stars and time, and could speak Spanish, and existed in twenty dimensions. He also began to explode a little.

"Babe," he wheezed.

"Oh. Sorry, sorry."

Kiss on the cheek. He fizzled back down to his usual self.

They sat in silence for a while. The light in the window began to change.

"Hungry," said Suzie.

They found a smokehouse down on the river. A woodsy joint called the Bucket. The piano player was drunk and loud, the air thick, the meat hot, and the beer, a local favorite called "Skeeter," was black. It was the kind of joint not frequented by Mama-types or Nan-types or other representatives of the universal mind.

"No Nan or Mama tonight," said Suzie, over her first beer and her first basket of wings. "All they do is watch. Watch people live their lives, watch people do everything that matters, while they sit off to the side and make their judgments."

She had insisted on wearing a disguise if they were going to go out. Baseball cap and a fake mustache. Otherwise, people pointed at her and whispered. Death was the original celebrity.

"You're one of them, you know," Milo pointed out.

"I know," she answered. "Shut up."

Like most conversations between people who have been together for eight thousand years, it was a conversation they'd had before.

"Goddammit!" Suzie tore off her fake mustache. She kept getting garlic sauce in it.

Milo struggled to get a rebellious chicken leg down before it fell apart in his hands.

You couldn't really eat and talk a lot at that particular joint.

Later, they walked along the riverbank.

"I may be one of them," said Suzie, "but I'm not *like* them. They've got a lot of nerve, getting all critical of us for, you know, being together."

"It's not like it doesn't make sense," Milo said. "You're like a god, and I'm just—"

"I am *not* a god. I've explained this a million times."

Milo decided not to say anything else for a while. They walked in silence. A dragonfly buzzed them and flew out over the river.

"I'm going to quit," said Suzie.

Huh? Milo thought. Was she serious? And was she crying? She hardly ever cried.

"What do you mean, 'quit'?"

"You know," she said, waving her arms. "Quit. Stop doing my job. I'm sick of this shit, always having to worry about whether I'm rocking the cosmic canoe."

"Can you *do* that?" Milo asked. "Quit being Death the way you quit waiting tables or teaching biology?"

"I don't know."

Out over the river, a dragonfly flew complicated loop-de-loops.

A fish jumped up and ate the dragonfly.

Milo put his arm around Suzie.

"A question," he said. "When a fish in the afterlife eats a dragonfly, does the dragonfly go to the afterlife?"

"It was already in the afterlife, Milo."

"Well, exactly, see? So?"

"It's complicated."

"You say that about *everything*."

"Everything's fucking complicated."

Another dragonfly zoomed between them. It looked a lot like the same dragonfly.

"I want to open a candle shop," she said.

He looked at her with one eye closed. A shop?

What would it mean, operating a business in the afterlife? People did, of course. But Milo had never quite understood how money worked up here. You could earn money if you wanted, but at the same time, if you needed something from a store, you could go get it, whether you paid for it or not. By the same token, if you went to a bank and asked for some money, they'd give it to you. Like everything else in the afterlife, it was change-y and shifty and unclear. ("I don't get it," he had once said to Mama, trying to understand. "Money in the afterlife might as well be air!" Mama had replied, "It's an Ideal Form, remember? It's the idea of money.")

Dealing with money sounded like an enormous pain in the ass. He raised an eyebrow at Suzie.

"A shop? You want to be a shopkeeper?"

"It's more about being an artist," she said. "I'd *make* the candles. In different shapes."

"Are you just saying that, off the top of your head, or—"

"Nope. I have wanted to make candles since they were invented. I mean, it's the greatest kind of sculpture. Say you made a candle of Michael Jackson, and it would be all cool and look just like him, and you'd show it to people, and they'd say, 'Oh, that's the cutest thing I ever saw,' and then you could light it and watch his head melt. Candles are awesome."

Twilight deepened into night. Something in the river jumped and splashed.

Milo said, "And that's what you'd rather do instead of being Death."

"Wouldn't you?"

Hell yeah! Milo thought. "Hell yeah!" he said.

———

In the middle of the night, Milo woke up and decided to go get reborn.

Suzie woke up, too. And knew.

"You just got here!" she protested.

"I know," he said, brushing her hair out of her eyes. "But I can't help thinking I ought to get it done with. I'll perform my great act of Love and Sacrifice, and when I get back we can be together."

"Don't fuck it up."

"Love and Sacrifice are pretty straightforward."

"There are subtleties, babe."

"I know," he answered. (What subtleties?)

She kissed him. Then she turned away and pulled the covers over her head.

She never accompanied him to the river. It didn't seem right to have Death on your arm when you were going off to get born.

At the river, he didn't undress. You didn't have to. He just waded through the mucky shallows and cattails into knee-deep water and the cooler, faster current.

Images flashed in the water. Possible scenes and faces, snapshots of lives he might live.

This one? No. That one? Interesting. Chances for Love and Sacrifice. Big chances.

When he finally chose, the choice frightened him. But he steeled himself and dove.

There was a brief shock, a pause, a Nothingness, and then he was being squeezed like toothpaste into the world again.

CHAPTER 9

The Secret Lover of Sophia Maria Mozart

If anyone was going to perform an act of perfect cosmic love, it was probably Milo.

He had been in love sixty-eight thousand five hundred and four times.

The first time he fell in love—really, *really* in love—he was an Iron Age farmer in middle Europe. He and his wife, Hyldregar, were married by a druidic shaman. By the time they were in their twenties, both were stooped from heavy work. They had ten children, two of whom lived to be grown-ups.

The tenth childbirth killed Hyldregar. After that, Milo aged even faster and died when he was thirty-two. His neighbors during the last seven years of his life called him *gragn luc moesse,* which meant "the sad old stargazer."

"Love means being torn in two," he was known to tell young people on their wedding day. You shouldn't say things like that to young people. He had to live a penalty life as a catfish, after that.

In future times, Milo and his lover Brii were born aboard a vast, world-sized generation ship on its way to Aurelae Epsilon, during the earliest colonization of the stars. Most of the passengers had forgotten that they were even on a ship. "This is the shape of the universe," they declared, "these halls and tunnels and great machines."

Milo and Brii attempted to reach the outer shell of the ship, passing through engine rooms the size of continents. They saw graveyards, artificial forests, and the great gravity gyros themselves. They passed through war zones. They saw a wasteland, where everyone had been dead for two thousand years. On the far side of this apocalypse, they found the hull of the ship, at last, and witnessed space passing by at one-tenth the speed of light. Then they went back down, back home, with their stories. Milo got a job in radio, and Brii published a magazine. They told the story of their journey to the edge of the ship and became famous.

The ship traveled for a thousand more years before reaching Aurelae Epsilon. Milo and Brii were the ship's great love story and became the first great love story of the new world.

In some lives, love is like a movie.

In Renaissance Vienna, Milo was a young musketeer who fell in love with Sophia Maria Mozart, a great beauty (and the composer's great-great-great-great-great-great-great-great-great-aunt).

Sophia Maria was the wife of Maximilian VanFurzelhaas, a minister to King Ferdinand and a notoriously angry man who was always off traveling. Every time Maximilian would go away, Milo would slip into the garden beneath Sophia Maria's window and sing funny songs to her. Eventually, he got her to come down into the garden and play Adam and Eve with him. He brought Venetian masks.

VanFurzelhaas was gone so often that his household staff became quite familiar with Milo and catered to him on his visits as if he, not VanFurzelhaas, were lord of the house. Even outside the household, the affair became well known. Milo's fellow scholars made up a tavern song—titled, with a refreshing absence of subtlety, "Milo Heidelburg Is Fucking Maximilian VanFurzelhaas's Wife, Tra-La"—which became popular enough that VanFurzelhaas himself finally heard it and came roaring home to bury his sword in Milo's throat. Milo, the superior swordsman, contrived to wound the aristocrat and escape to Salzburg. From then on, however, Sophia Maria was required to accompany her husband on his travels. This only broadened her pantheon of amours, which included some of the foremost heroes of the age, including the sculptor Leonard Duesel, the architect Zeinsfisthoffen, and the pope, once, quite by accident, in the dark.

Milo, in the end, fared less well, having the poor judgment to return too soon. He joined the ranks of Vienna's defenders during the Ottoman siege in time to learn that VanFurzelhaas had been placed in partial command of the defenses. His arm proved long enough to have Milo assigned to a particularly hot spot upon the ramparts, wherefrom he was famously captured and launched by catapult back into the city.

Sometimes, between his first hundred or so lives, Milo tried to spend his time with Suzie, though they weren't yet lovers in those days. They both enjoyed swimming and food. They enjoyed asking each other questions like "Would you rather lose an arm or an eyeball?" And sometimes Milo thought he caught her looking at him a certain way.

He wondered what would happen if Death went to bed with a plain old mortal man.

"I don't know," she said. "It might destroy our friendship. It might even burn you up. Like, literally consume you with fire. I seriously don't know."

Milo was flustered. "Can you read my mind?" he asked.

"I thought you knew."

"Well, don't. Jesus!"

After his hundredth life, he helped her open an exotic-food store called the Chocolate Squid. The store was fully stocked with squid and chocolate-covered butterflies and flowers you were supposed to dip in cheese, and more. When the gods tried to do human-style things, Milo observed, they often missed the mark.

The whole year the store was open, only fifteen customers came.

After Suzie closed the door for the last time, Milo tried to kiss her, but she turned away.

"I'm serious about the burning-up," she said.

On Earth, life after life, Milo fell in and out of love all the time.

He knew thousands of ordinary loves, the sort that grind out years like sausage.

He knew the love of family and good friends. He loved things like beaches and rain and well-made clocks. He knew what it was like to watch love flake away and die and leave you feeling as if you'd been eaten by wild pigs.

Once, in eighteenth-century Zambia, love saved Milo's life. The love of an entire village. The love of hundreds of people.

What happened was that Milo had a string of bad luck. Poor farming, drought, a snakebite, his mother died, a toothache, his house burned down with all his tools and possessions. Broke, tool-less, and too proud to ask for help, he became angrier and angrier, until one day he followed a wealthy man into the forest and beat him and took his money.

It was a small village, so of course he was identified. Some constables came and got him and brought him to the schoolhouse to face trial.

In many villages, Milo might have been beheaded or had his hands chopped off. But villages are all different, in one way or another, and Milo's village had an advanced idea of what a trial was supposed to be like.

An odd kind of trial (it was an odd kind of village).

What they did was love him.

How they loved him was that a couple of hundred people spent hours reminding him what a good person he was. They reminded him of how, when he was a teenager, he had saved a small child from a hyena, taking the brunt of the hyena's attack upon himself. The child was in her twenties now. She touched the deep scars on Milo's arm and spoke softly to him.

They reminded him that he had once walked to the Congo and back, just to visit his grandfather. He had worked on a highway crew for four years so that his younger brother could go to university and become an engineer. He refused to kill animals, even rats and snakes and spiders. He had also married the ugliest woman in the village, because he saw past the outside and romanced her heart, but no one said this aloud. The wife herself was there and reminded him how he sometimes got up early and did her chores for her, so that she might have time to herself.

When the villagers were finished, their love had untwisted the angry knot that had formed in Milo's head and soul, and they made him remember that he was good. And he went on his way and lived his life and was grateful. In time, with hard work, his luck changed, and he lived until he died.

He was a man named Owen who loved a man named Brad, in the Gayborhood section of Houston. They lived together in a small apartment and had a dog named Maggie. They lived together for fifteen years, until Maggie died and Brad was offered a dream job that took him to Switzerland. The choice was agonizing. It aged them.

He was a woman named Oko whose husband drowned in a sea battle. She became a famous widow, setting a place for her husband at the table every night. She waited for him on the rocks by the sea. At first she looked for his ship on the horizon. Then, as time passed, in the water itself, as if he had passed from one world, the world of having a body with arms and legs and hair and teeth, into another, the world of having the Earth itself for a body. Streams and currents were his arms. Storms were his voice. The moon and constellations were his changing thoughts and moods.

He had not been a handsome man. Sometimes she saw a fish that wore his face.

CHAPTER 10

The *Looking Glass* People

High summer.

Blue sky above and green corn below.

In the middle of the green, four silver ARK ships, each the size of an ocean tanker, lay waiting on the grass, their noses lifted into the soft wind. Depending on where you stood, the ships reflected either the sun or the grass and corn.

It was, thought Milo, standing miles away, near the fence at the ARK perimeter, as if each ship were a world trapped in a mirror.

He eyed the chain-link fence behind him, ten feet high and topped with razor wire. He traced its gray length across the hills, a rough circle maybe sixty miles in circumference. How useful would the fence be, really, if they came? There would be thousands of them, and they'd be angry.

How else could you expect them to feel, when they knew they were all about to die?

It had begun, five years earlier, with the Disappearances.

Scientists and engineers.

Just a few at first. They were not famous people, and their disappearances rarely made the news. There was enough going on in the news already, in the third decade of the twenty-first century. Everything the scientists had warned people about was happening all at once.

The seas were rising. The oceans had died, from plankton right up the food chain. The water tables had gone toxic. Computer viruses formed networks that shut down the Internet at least once a week.

A few vanishing eggheads didn't seem like a big deal.

The Disappearances caught Milo's attention when they started happening at Stanford, where he worked. Melinda Warnstein-Keppler, the electronics guru, vanished from her apartment, leaving dinner in the microwave. Zhou Chen-Barnhart, the builder of the orbital neutrino collector, was next, then Claudine Fraas, the Nobel laureate author of *Problems in Holographic Relativity*.

Milo didn't worry about disappearing, himself. He was a research assistant. An information-science gunslinger, but he would never be a giant. He worked for the giants and was honored to do so. They were all, in their way, trying to save the world, back when they still thought it could be saved.

Milo had come to science in a way that was both usual and unusual. Like most science-worshippers, he was curious. There was nothing he didn't want to know, and this made him absorb books and computer links the way other kids absorbed loud music. That was the ordinary part. The extraordinary part was *why* he wanted so badly to understand how the world worked (and how time worked, and space, and life and death).

He heard voices in his head.

Not the voices of schizophrenia but voices that seemed to be from the past. Other lives he had lived. Memories spanning thousands of years. Information that came to him out of nowhere, because he had once lived in Japan or had once been an Egyptian mathematician.

Hell, maybe he *was* schizophrenic. Maybe he had a brain tumor.

(You don't have a brain tumor, a voice told him. A former doctor.)

He wound up working for Wayne Aldrin, the rock star of Systems Integration Science. At twenty-five, Aldrin had published *It's Only an Island if You Look at It from the Water,* a treatise that revolutionized problem solving. At thirty, he had developed a food plant that would thrive in toxic earth; it broke down poisons, cleaned the soil, and dropped fruit that was basically a big yellow multivitamin. It could have fed half the world, Milo had heard, except that it would have cost the wrong people a lot of money.

"The trouble with problem solving," Aldrin often complained, "is that too many people are making money off the problems."

Aldrin was forty now. He wore his gray mane like an ocean wave, curling backward and breaking around his neck. His surgeon's hands were machines the way a flute is a machine. He was the sort of man da Vinci might have imagined.

Milo considered Aldrin the greatest human alive.

They were working, in those days, on the Nowhere Computer. It was a computer that existed only in cyberspace and worked like a vacuum: pulling in functions and data that were already "out there." It was immeasurably powerful, according to Aldrin, for something that didn't actually exist. When the Disappearances began, they hadn't gotten it to work yet.

Milo didn't let this bother him. To be honest, his attention was elsewhere. Not on the voices but on his fellow info-cruncher, Kim. The torch he carried for her was the lab's worst-kept secret. Someday he was going to ask her out. When he wasn't so busy.

One quiet Friday, Kim leaned over his desk and said, "I wonder if you could do me a favor."

"Sure," he said.

"I have a date," she said, "but no babysitter. I don't think anyone even *does* babysitting anymore. I wonder if you could come over and watch Libby for me."

She should have just shot him. All around the office, eavesdroppers winced. Ouch, ouch, ouch . . .

(No way! said some of his voices.)

Shit. Really? Fuck!

"Yes," he said. "Of course." Fuck.

"Seven?" she said.

"Okay."

He rang the doorbell at Kim's ground-level apartment, and she an-swered wearing a long, sheer dress that left one shoulder exposed. One tanned, smooth shoulder.

"Hey," he said, stepping in. "You look great."

"Why, thanks."

"Hey," he said to Libby (Kim's six-year-old), who was parked in front of the TV. It was a good TV night, meaning the TV stations were broadcasting.

Libby didn't answer.

"What time are you expecting the lucky fellow?" Milo asked. Maybe he could manage to be in the bathroom when the doorbell rang.

"He's here," said Kim, opening a bottle of white wine.

Here? Already? Shit. Where?

"Didn't I tell you, Milo? It's *you*. I'm going on a date with *you* to-night. If that's okay. It'll just have to be here, because, like I said, the babysitter thing."

She blinked at him with wide, sunny eyes.

Oh, wow!

"I . . . well, of course," he said.

"I was getting old," said Kim, "waiting for you to ask."

He felt silly for waiting and decided to balance it with an act of spontaneous courage. He slipped an arm around her waist, drew her to him, and kissed her on the lips. She returned the kiss, and they re-leased each other.

Libby watched them over the back of the couch.

"Are you guys getting married?" she asked.

(Are you guys getting married? asked some of the voices.)

———

They had dinner, the three of them, by candlelight. Milo found himself having a kind of double date.

"I have one of the lab computers here at home," Kim told him, over roast beef. "I've been working on the satellite problem."

"I hate spiders," Libby told him.

That's how it went. Two conversations, two dates, at once.

"It's been three years," answered Milo, "since anyone launched a new satellite. It's going to be like a new Dark Ages if we don't find a new way to transmit. I don't care for spiders, either. Aren't you glad they don't fly?"

"What if we teach data packets to ignore the existing systems? What if we could get info to just, I don't know, bounce off the magnetosphere?"

"Did you know some cockroaches can fly?"

Milo was stunned. That was frigging brilliant. It was the kind of thing Aldrin would get excited about.

"We should call the Doc," he said. "I *heard* about flying cockroaches!" he added. "Gross!"

"They're called palmetto bugs. I have to go number one."

There was lemon meringue pie for dessert, in front of the TV. They watched an old Batman movie and fell asleep on the couch together, all three of them.

The next morning, an hour before daycare opened, they took Libby along when they sped over to the university, hoping to catch Aldrin at his customary cafeteria table, with his tablet and his orange and his orange juice.

But he wasn't there.

He wasn't in his office, either, although his door was open. And he wasn't in the lab. Neither was any of his stuff.

Milo and Kim shared the same unbelieving look.

"Disappeared," they whispered together.

"What's that mean?" asked Libby.

Before they could answer, two scary guys in black suits marched into the lab.

"Milo Osgood?" they asked. "Kimberly Dodd and"—one of them checked a handheld tablet—"Libby?"

Ah, shit, thought Milo.

"Yeah," all three of them said, and, just like that, they were disappeared, too.

First they were driven to the airport. Then they were rushed aboard a small jet and flown east. On landing, they were driven down a bunch of farm roads, through golden morning light and corn, to a white building with no windows, surrounded by military tents and military people. They were escorted inside, down a long, spotless white hallway, and left before a spotless, featureless door.

The door opened before Milo could knock, and there stood Wayne Aldrin. He looked ruffled, if unharmed, and had a haunted look in his eye that hadn't been there before.

"First of all," he said, "I'm sorry. Second of all, come in and sit down."

Libby was about to say something, but at that precise moment a bright-looking teenager in a jumpsuit and ponytail came hurrying up, saying, "Are you Libby?"

Fifteen seconds later she and Libby were off, down the hall, hand in hand. "I'll get her breakfast!" promised the teen, "and have her back to you in an hour!"

Milo gave Kim's waist a squeeze as Aldrin ushered them into his new office. A cheap desk, a table, coffee machine, filing cabinets, computers, and some folding chairs. Aldrin, plainly, hadn't disappeared; he'd been transplanted.

"It'll be best," said Aldrin, "if I just explain, without interruption. Then you can ask questions or yell and scream, if you want.

"A year ago, some amateur astronomers sighted an anomaly in the night sky. The professionals took a look at it, and it's bad news. In October of 2025, a comet the size of Ireland is going to hit the planet Earth like a big, fat musket ball and probably kill every living thing. So they—let me finish, Milo—so they had a big conference to decide what we should do, and what they decided was this: to collect the right scientists and nuts-and-bolts people and have them build spaceships to carry humanity away from Earth. One ship for Venus, one for Earth orbit, one for Mars, and one for Jupiter's moons. The ships will serve as habitats and carry materials to build more habitats."

Milo had to lace his fingers together to keep his hands from shaking. Beside him, Kim softly gasped.

"So," Aldrin continued, "to do all this, we need to do a hundred years of science and engineering in just five years. Now, before you go asking a bazillion questions, let me see if I can anticipate you. One: How many people can go on these big ships? The answer is: Not many. Maybe six thousand on each of the arks. Two: What are they telling the rest of the planet? The answer is: Nothing for as long as possible, or they'll come here and rip us all to shreds. Third: Why are *you* here? You're here because I'm here, and I'm allowed a staff of two. Why am I here? Because in order to make this all work without breaking down, it has to be as simple as possible. I'm here to try and make it all . . ."

"Elegant," suggested Milo. Then he threw up on the floor.

"Exactly," said Aldrin. "Oh, damn. I'll call a custodian. Don't worry. I threw up, too."

They repaired to the hallway and kept talking while waiting for the custodian. Holding hands, Kim and Milo asked some questions that Aldrin must have anticipated but hadn't gotten to yet.

He listened patiently, gravely.

"No," he answered. "You are not guaranteed a place aboard one of the arks. Only the team leaders are guaranteed, at first. Yes, I'm one of them. No, Kim, I'm sorry, there's no special exception for children. As we get closer to our launch date, skilled workers will be selected, as we learn more about our needs. Later, there will be a series of lotteries."

Kim glared a hole in the floor.

"If you won't guarantee Libby a seat," she said quietly, "I will do nothing whatsoever to help you."

"Nor will I," said Milo, surprising himself.

Aldrin shook his head.

"They're not my rules, you guys," he said. "That's something you have to understand. Just because I'm a key designer doesn't mean I have any say where policy's concerned."

"Who *does?*" asked Milo.

"Money," spat Kim. "Who else? When it comes right down to it, there's about five or six world banks that hold the loan on everything."

"That's a myth," said Milo.

"No, she's right," said Aldrin. "Money's no different from anything else. It forms systems along paths of least resistance and collects in places. Those places, the banks, are the only ones with the muscle to pull off what we're trying to do here."

"What, then," said Milo, "we don't cooperate, they come and put a bullet in us?"

"I don't know," said Aldrin, eyes darkening. "Just don't make trouble. Play the game, and try to improve your hand. In the meantime, let's do our best."

The custodian arrived with his rolling tool closet and vanished with a nod into the office.

"We're in a whole new reality," Aldrin said, placing a firm hand on each of their shoulders. "Take some time to get your brain around it. I got you guys an apartment together. Go sit. Get something to eat. They'll bring you clothes."

"Together?" asked Milo. "How did you know? I mean, we just . . . last night was—"

"Jesus, you guys," Aldrin laughed. "Everybody knew, except you. Now get outta here."

Aldrin's door shut behind them. Way down the hall, Libby and her babysitter came galloping their way, laughing.

"*I* knew," said Kim, burying her head in Milo's shoulder.

The world outside of central Iowa continued to fall apart.

A dirty bomb turned Seattle into a ghost town. The pharmaceutical industry finally hit a tipping point and overcharged itself out of existence. All over the world, people who needed medicine to stay alive began to sicken and die.

Milo stopped getting his asthma meds. Now, when he had an attack, he toughed it out.

The ARK compound developed into a small city. A city no one knew about and no one was allowed to fly over.

In the largest buildings, they designed the gigantic arkships themselves. This was partly Aldrin's domain. Within a week, they had begun brainstorming spaceships based on living creatures. Their systems would breathe like lungs, flow like blood, see and hear and think like brains.

In other buildings, they studied ways for people—whole communities!—to live and work in space. One of the first things they decided was that people would be happier with fewer social restrictions. The need to restart the human race would make conventional marriage impractical. Human culture aboard the ships, it appeared, was going to be very "free."

These experiments and conclusions had a heavy influence on the current ARK culture. ARK became like a party school that was really, really, really hard to get into.

In their dormitory, Milo and Kim lived in much the same way other families lived. They made friends. They celebrated holidays. During the day, Libby went to daycare, and Milo and Kim worked in the spacecraft-assembly building.

They were invited to parties. They usually went.

They were invited to join Free Love cohorts and politely declined. Milo and Kim had decided to be monogamous.

It was not a bad life, if you were able to ignore the fact that the world outside was doomed and you were probably doomed right along with it.

———

Milo found himself fighting depression. Not the full-on, soul-crushing kind that could paralyze you, but an abiding and sublime sadness that seemed to well up from across the ages.

It was the voices again. They had all lived lives on Earth, supposedly, in every age of human history. And now that part of history was going to end. Violently and badly.

There was a Fauvist painter who feared the death of Earth far more than he had his own death, of pneumonia. There was a deeply religious farm girl from a thousand years ago who didn't mind her own death, because the world and God's works would endure. But now even that was in danger.

Most of the voices were silent. That's what depressed Milo—the silence. Eight thousand years of silent voices in his head, looking out through his eyes.

"What's the matter?" Kim asked him one night, catching him woolgathering by the apartment's one window.

"I hear voices," he told her bluntly, at last. "Usually, anyway."

"No shit," she said, taking his arm. "You talk about them in your sleep."

A year passed.

Within the perimeter, the spaceships themselves began to take shape. Mighty frames, at first, like cages the size of city blocks, swarming with workers, prodded by cranes. There were four. The *Looking Glass,* an experimental ship, would be finished first and would tour the solar system in the greatest sea trial of all time before the others— the *Avalon,* the *Atlantis,* and the *Summerland*—left Earth just ahead of the comet.

Outside, the economy evaporated.

"It's dying fast out there," Aldrin remarked. "And I don't get it. Everything that's happening was preventable. The whole last sixty years has been like watching our business leaders drive us all toward a brick wall without ever trying to turn or swerve."

They were in the computer lab. They were almost always in the lab these days. The ships' giant chemical lungs weren't cycling properly yet. Milo and Kim were pouring all their work hours into a computer model that Aldrin swore would root out the cause.

If it worked, they'd celebrate.

There was a lot of celebrating at ARK, because there were breakthroughs every day. It could rain Nobel Prizes at the ARK compound, and there still wouldn't be enough recognition to go around. There wasn't time.

The computer model worked beautifully. Food plants growing in the ventilator bronchia were reproducing too fast. They'd have to be spread out. Maybe some of them could be grown in the coolant chambers, where there'd be condensation.

They celebrated. Their achievement shared the news that night with a team that had discovered how to make radiation shielding out of cardboard and peanut oil.

After a while, tiring of the crowds and the bars, Milo, Kim, and Aldrin found their way to a wide-open space far from the compound, in the middle of open grass, under stars like an ocean of ice and fire.

They signed out a portable fire pit, and brought marshmallows, and sat in the middle of the Iowa night, drinking wine.

Then Aldrin said, "I miss my wife."

What?

"Did you know I was married?" he asked. "It was a long time ago. She died quite suddenly."

"I knew," said Kim. She gave his arm a squeeze.

"It's not that I would wish her back now, with things the way they are. It's only my way of observing that this project takes being alone and kind of shoves it right in your face. I mean, being a social species is what this is all about, right? Keeping the chain going. We're not like hamsters. Hamsters live alone. Know that? They don't even like other hamsters. We're more like wolves. When wolves are apart, and then they come back together, they jump around and lick each other and go all crazy. They call it 'the Jubilation of Wolves.'"

Something in the fire popped, sending sparks into the night.

"It's not an easy time," said Aldrin, "to be a lone wolf."

He put a hand on Kim's knee and gave it a squeeze.

Oh, man! thought Milo. What was happening here?

Kim's mouth wobbled open. She said, "I think I've had enough wine," and stood.

The hand dropped away. Aldrin focused on the fire.

"I think we all have," said Milo. He gathered up his jacket. He draped Kim's shawl over her shoulders.

"I'm going to stay out awhile longer," said Aldrin, so they said their good-nights and left him there.

When they'd gone about three hundred yards, they heard a long, broken howl.

"Drunk, horny bastard," muttered Milo.

Kim took his arm and said, "Be nice." Nice? Milo thought about the word.

His depression had turned to raw frustration now. All their work on integration, on building a ship that worked like an organism, had become so promising. And now the great man himself was proving too human. Not only that, but his sense of appropriateness seemed to have slipped.

Fuck.

Might have known it would get complicated, Milo thought.

Problems are complicated, said the Egyptian mathematician in his head. That's what makes them problems.

The night of the first lottery, they prepared Libby's favorite supper— mac and cheese, extra cheesy, with sliced-up hot dogs in it—and watched Libby's favorite movie, *Beverly Hills Chihuahua 47*. After the child fell asleep, they practically devoured each other in their tiny sleep pod.

Their message to each other was simple and unmistakable: They were a family and they loved one another.

They were not chosen.

"Libby, Libby, Libby," Milo heard Kim whispering over her home laptop, after midnight, as the last numbers flashed. "At least Libby, Libby, Libby, Libby, Libby," like a magic spell that wasn't magic enough.

The *Looking Glass* took its final shape, and you'd think they had built some kind of cathedral out there on the Iowa plain. She lay across the hills like a trick of the eye, out of scale and shining.

Watching her leave the Earth was like watching a whale made of fire.

Earth and air both shook, and the whale rose—slowly, at first, still reflecting the green hills and green corn, and as it lifted away, it was like watching the Earth lift away from itself. Then the great engine bells ignited, and she crossed the sky like a second sun.

The weather changed on the hills and blew their hair and their lab jackets and clippings from the freshly mown grass, and they all squinted, the three hundred thousand ninety-two of them that remained, as the ship shot across the sky, and up, and out.

And they all went back to work, and the countdown resumed, a little faster.

Finally, some amateur astronomers in Mexico noticed the comet. They were calling it Comet Marie. Other people outside the fence, in different parts of the world, started putting two and two together.

"Maybe this is why all those scientists disappeared," they said.

So a few of the ARK staff were assigned to get on the Internet and spread disinformation. There was, they said, a place in the Andes Mountains of Peru where you weren't allowed to go and weren't allowed to fly over. But here were some fuzzy satellite pictures of what looked like a tent city for thousands of people and several giant rockets under construction.

People swarmed into South America, storming the Andes in search of survival. They were hindered by the fact that it was getting damn hard to get around out there. Luxuries like passenger flight had crashed with the world economy. Ocean travel was expensive and dangerous and mostly under pirate control. Everywhere, law was breaking down.

Up in Iowa, they worked in peace for a while longer.

Months passed.

The ships took their final shapes. Their anatomical systems were tested, and the ships breathed and their hearts pumped and their brains crackled and their engines flexed.

Everywhere around ARK, work quickened and peaked. People worked harder, hit the bars harder, loved harder. They watched the clock and the skies, anticipating the reappearance of the *Looking Glass* and the exodus that would follow.

For the first time, many of the ARK staffers seemed to understand that their lives weren't going to go on for much longer. They hit the bars, but they were quiet about it. Some of them began disappearing over the fence at night. Some of them wanted to see friends or family before the world died. Some of them meant to survive and wanted time to prepare.

Milo and Kim didn't talk about it. Kim refused. On the outside, she clung to a prim belief that chance or justice would intercede and at least deliver her kid. On the inside, Milo could tell, she was coming apart. Instead of talking about it, they drank. They didn't hit the bars; they just drank. For a while they supplanted talk with lovemaking. And then the lovemaking grew sad, and slowed, and stopped, almost with a shrug. Then Libby began spending nights in their bed, between them.

The world had already ended, thought Milo. You could see it on people's faces; they had a stretched-out, jittery look to them now, as if something had bitten them and they didn't know what. You started coming around corners and finding people crying, and they'd look ashamed and hurry away.

Milo didn't cry. But he started having asthma attacks that were so bad they knocked him out. He told no one.

In his head—or in his soul, wherever that was—certain voices chimed in, trying to be helpful. A fisherman on Krakatoa who had seen the end of the world already, in a volcanic blast heard round the world. An eight-year-old who had seen the plague approach her village, take her family, and then crawl down her own throat. A banker who took too many risks, leaping from the roof of the Grain Exchange.

It's ended before, they said. Who would suppose it shouldn't end again?

This cheered Milo up a little, believe it or not.

Most nations dissolved into chaos and rioting. The Internet gasped, flashed, and went silent.

Milo walked into the lab one morning to find Kim and Aldrin in the midst of a heated argument. Both were red-faced and turned away from each other the moment they glimpsed him.

"What did I miss?" Milo asked.

"Nothing import—" Aldrin began.

"*What did I miss?*" Milo roared, kicking over the nearest chair. "I'd appreciate it if *one* of the two of you would have the courtesy to not treat me like an idiot."

"He," said Kim, her voice shaking, pointing a finger at Aldrin, "says he'll make a place on the *Summerland* for us, if we'll make him . . ."

She couldn't continue.

"Make him what?" asked Milo.

"Part of your family," said Aldrin. He was trying to be dignified, with his hands folded behind his back.

" 'Part of your family'?" said Milo, advancing. "Sounds like pig Latin for 'I want to fuck your wife.' "

(This, piped up the Egyptian mathematician, is yet another way the world ends.)

"It's not that simple," said Aldrin, "or that coarse."

They were nose-to-nose.

Kim stepped up beside them, looking worried. She'd never seen Milo hit anyone, but he sure looked ready to now, and that wouldn't help anything. They didn't tolerate violent people at ARK.

Something quite complicated was happening in Milo's mental wilderness just then. A strange inner voice was shouting at him, almost as if thousands of previous lives were trying to give him advice. Behind his anger, his soul was trying to be wise.

The thousand voices convinced Milo to be silent and thoughtful for a minute.

When he spoke, this is what Milo said:

"Wayne, we love you. And with the crazy future coming down on us, your suggestion even makes some sense. But I have a problem with something. Why didn't you come to *both* of us with this . . . proposal, if you will? But more so, how can we possibly get around the fact that it sounds like you're trying to use Libby, and your influence, to get Kim into your bed? That doesn't sound like you. It's not the Wayne Aldrin I know. Why don't you answer those questions, and then I'll decide whether to break your teeth with a wrench."

Aldrin nodded.

"Thank you for asking," he said. "In your way, you've been patient. The answer to the really important question is: I haven't changed in that way. I am not trying to get you to prostitute yourselves or to hold Libby hostage."

"Then what could you possibly mean?" asked Kim.

"They have announced a change," said Aldrin. "Only to the preselected team leaders. For whatever reason, the policy wonks have decided to give extra chances to our immediate families. I think things are getting a bit shaky. They need to make sure the teams stay cohesive and keep working, so they're throwing the team leaders a bone."

Milo's asthma launched an attack.

"Go on," he wheezed.

"Well, that's it. I'm not trying to get in bed with your wife. I'm try-ing to get your family aboard an ark."

Milo could swear he read Kim's mind at that moment. One thought, one priority: Libby, Libby, Libby, Libby, Libby . . .

God, he didn't want to do this.

They were *his* family, goddammit.

"We'll do it?" he said, looking at Kim.

Kim practically burst with relief. Rivers of tears.

"Yes," she said.

Then they all just backed away, awkward, awkward, awkward, and did computer stuff and didn't look at one another until lunchtime, when the three of them went to a notary office over in admin and got married by what was essentially a vending machine.

The comet appeared in the night sky.

"So beautiful," you could hear people say. They crowded the hills around the arks at night. Every night, on blankets, as if waiting for fireworks. Couples, here and there. Larger groups, whole teams of spouses.

Milo, Kim, and Libby moved into Aldrin's pod. It was more spa-cious, better appointed. "He has a dishwasher!" cried Libby, who obvi-ously felt that this, above all, signaled some kind of evolution for their family.

Milo and Kim spent nights in Aldrin's sleep chamber. Aldrin himself had the grace to sleep on the couch. They progressed through an un-comfortable cycle: At first, they didn't make love in Aldrin's bed, any more than they made love in their own. Then something desperate and wordless got ahold of them, and they made love three nights in a row. Then they didn't again. Kim actually shivered when Milo touched her.

"What's the matter?" Milo whispered. "Afraid your husband will hear?"

"What's the matter?" whispered Kim the first time Milo wouldn't put out. "Afraid *your* husband will hear?"

Libby spent days playing with the dishwasher, rolling the little cart in and out. She looked at Aldrin like some kind of tall, friendly dog they had come to live with.

They explained nothing to her, out of sheer cowardice.

The second lottery began at nine in the morning, the same day that administration reported contact with the returning *Looking Glass*.

All was well. The ship had flown like a silver swallow.

The separate lottery for the leaders' families offered an 80 percent chance. By nightfall, they knew Libby had drawn a seat. Kim went into the bathroom and cried. Not softly, but braying like a donkey.

"Why'd she even bother to go in the bathroom?" asked Aldrin, and the two husbands laughed together for the first time.

By nine P.M., they knew Kim's seat was assured.

They all had a glass of wine in the kitchen. Even Libby.

By midnight, the passenger lists were complete. Milo was not on any of them.

No one knew what to say, so they said nothing.

In the middle of the night, Milo left.

It was something he had decided, weeks ago, to do if the lottery turned out as it had.

He bought a sleeping bag, pup tent, and a mess kit from the commissary automat, left the dormitory, and made himself a little camp in the hills.

He wasn't alone. They dotted the hillside: Dark patches, sleeping bags, on dark grass. Campfires here and there, like red stars. These were the ranks of those who were staying behind. Putting some distance between themselves and the silver future-ships.

It was not comforting, Milo found, joining these ranks, this great pre-dying. It was empty and terrible and made him feel as if someone had performed a stomach operation on him. It brought his asthma on so strong that he went to sleep that way and dreamed he was strangling.

They called themselves the Earth People.

In the morning, some of them got up and went to work. Others slipped off through the corn. Milo did not go back to the lab. They were finished there. The Earth People who slipped away left holes in thousands of jobs, and those jobs still needed doing.

Those who remained became job-doers. This was all that remained of what had once been full, above-average lives. Now anything that required time and years and a future was set aside. Dreams and plans. Fears about growing old. Wishes. All that remained was the doing of jobs, and maybe memories and some indiscriminate sex. Milo's voices grew quiet, almost silent.

He took a job with the fueling teams, making sure the awesome chemistries stayed cold or hot. He worked in an astronaut suit, amid clouds of cryogenic steam.

He tried not to think about anything.

He was helping to fuel the *Avalon* when Kim found him. She rode up on the tiny crew elevator, at lunchtime. With an actual old-fashioned lunch pail and a baloney sandwich.

He was sitting on the fueling tower with his legs dangling into space. He saw Kim's lab shoes out of the corner of his eye. Felt her there, looking down at him.

"What are you doing?" she asked. "Why would you leave like that?"

He stood.

"You know why," he said.

"We still have three days!" she cried, hitting him in the chest. "At least it's *something!*"

Milo shook his head. "You have to try and be a family, the three of you, for real, before they strap you in and take you away, wherever. You need this time, and I'm giving it to you."

She gripped herself with both arms. Eyes squinched closed, but no tears.

He drew her to him and pulled their bodies tight together.

She tried to slip her hand inside his enviro-suit.

"No," whispered Milo. "Go be his. Make him yours."

Softly, she hit him in the chest again. They stood rocking, their foreheads touching.

"Libby?" he asked.

"We tried to tell her. We had to try and tell her everything, really—I mean, we're loading in two days practically. Plus, we had to try and explain about you, and . . . well, what do you expect? We had to sedate her. That's all there is to tell. She loves you. I love you."

Milo nodded. He kissed her forehead.

After a minute, she did what she had to do. She rode the elevator out of sight.

After work that day, Milo stopped in the lower hills and looked back down at the compound. The arks lay waiting, ready, their noses lifted into the soft wind, reflecting green grass and blue sky.

He eyed the chain-link fence behind him, traced its gray length for miles across the hills. How useful would the fence be if they came? Surely they would come, once they saw the arks go up. There would be no disguising it. They would see, and they'd come, finally.

The Earth People did their jobs.

On the third morning, they helped to load the arks.

They sealed the mighty hatches and primed the awesome engines.

They fled to the farthest hills.

And it happened.

The ships *boomed,* and the ground shook, and the air went blurry like water, and the shock waves arrived.

The *Avalon* flared, lifted, then burned away into the sky, white-hot, mirror-bright.

Then the *Atlantis.*

Then the real heartbreaker, the *Summerland*. And that tugged at them and hurt them in a way they hadn't anticipated, because when she was gone—which she was, too soon—it was really over. The great accomplishment had been accomplished, and now here they all were, a bunch of dead people standing around looking at one another, without even a job to do.

They built bonfires. Halloween bonfires. Beach-sized bonfires, college pep rally–sized bonfires. Some commandeered the surviving shipbuilding cranes and built pyramids and Jenga towers. There were architects and engineers among them, so there were marvels and wonders by the end of the week, spread over miles, drenched in everything from kerosene to leftover rocket fuel.

At night, exhausted, they slept.

Who knows what they did everywhere else on the Earth?

Milo worked on the construction of a giant wooden man. He had a giant wooden mouth and a pecker and everything.

On the last morning, people finally came to the fence.

They stood outside at first, fingers hanging on the mesh, looking in like jailbirds in reverse. Then they climbed over or cut their way through. Some of them were angry, but they didn't do anything to hurt anyone once they got a look at the bonfires, at the pyramids and towers and the huge wooden man. Whatever had happened here was over. All that was left was this tribe of doomed people, just like them.

At nightfall, they lit the fires.

The whole landscape went up in a garish false day, roaring, an elemental mockery of the launching of the arks. Where were they now, the ships? Hanging in orbit? Were they watching?

The night writhed in pagan howls. Everywhere, shadows leaped or clustered in groups. They sang in some cases. Some were silent.

Milo's voices were silent, too, finally and completely. They had all experienced their own deaths. No need to share this one.

Not long after full dark, the comet rose in the sky. Different from before. Dreadful.

A woman staggered past Milo, calling, "Terry? Terry!" (And Milo thought, That's how the world ends? People stumbling around, yelling, *"Terry"*?)

The comet brightened and moved with sudden speed.

An immense *riiiiiiiiiiiiiiiiiiiiiiiiiiiiiipping* tore the sky.

A knot of men and women came dancing along, drunk, naked, and crazy-eyed.

"Dance with us!" they howled, clutching at him. Milo tore himself away, baring his teeth like a dog.

Thunder like a million rockets.

The ground tore open and the air caught fire.

"Terry!" someone screamed.

And then dark. And then nothing.

CHAPTER 11

The Flood

Milo shot into the afterlife as if sprayed from a fire hose.

Everywhere, water crashed and surged. The river convulsed as if a universal storm sewer had backed up. That's what happens when tons of people die all at once. The afterlife can burst like a dam.

Milo found himself in a tumbling river full of struggling bodies and crying voices. Voices disappointed that they had just endured the end of the world and got to the afterlife, and now that appeared to be ending, too.

Suzie must be awfully busy, he thought.

A day passed. Now and then a house floated by, and people climbed on it. Occasionally, there would be an island of some kind, and the newly dead would crowd over it and overwhelm it.

Milo floated and relaxed.

The river passing between worlds wasn't like other waters. You couldn't drown in it. It would, if you let it, carry you along like a leaf or a water bug. It would hold you like a reflection.

Milo let it.

He even, after a time, allowed himself to sink and take root in the bottom muck, where he swayed like seaweed, sleeping.

———————

She swam down and pulled him like a cattail, raising mud in a boiling cloud.

Half awake, he protested like a sleepy child.

They sat on the shore together, dripping and holding hands. As his brain de-fuzzed, Milo noted that the river had gotten more or less back to normal. The shrieking crowds were gone. Flotsam and dreck littered the trees and a nearby park, but on the whole the crisis seemed to have passed.

Milo wondered how long the adjustment had taken.

"It's been a week," Suzie whispered.

"I was in the river for a week?"

She pressed a finger against his lips.

"I don't want to hear it," she said. "I assume you don't think I was sitting around all that time with my thumb up my ass. Listen: *Almost everyone in the world died.*"

"Peace," said Milo. "I get it. I was there."

She was so, so tired. Now that his eyes cleared, he could see it in the color of her skin, which had gone colorless and translucent.

She crawled like a cat onto his lap, and now it was her turn to sleep.

They both woke up sort of sprawled in the mud. Some kind of large shadow hovered over them and was tickling Milo's lip with a long, dry weed.

He batted at the weed, sitting up, blinking.

"Mama," he said. "Hey."

"You guys are cute," said Mama.

"Bite me," mumbled Suzie, who hadn't opened her eyes yet.

Mama clapped her meaty hands.

"Chop-chop!" she said. "Now that things are back shipshape, Nan wants everyone to come over."

"To her house?" asked Milo.

"Why?" asked Suzie, sounding combative.

Mama rolled her eyes. "I'm too tired for this shit," she said. "Can we just go, please, and make the best of it?"

They went. Muddy and bleary and talking to themselves, they went.

Many lives ago, as a little kid walking to school in Ohio, Milo (and all the other neighborhood kids) lived in fear of a scary widow named Mrs. Armentrout. They were super-careful not to set foot on Mrs. Armentrout's lawn, because she'd come to the door and curse at them or knock on her window like gunshots going off (one time she made a kid named Leonard shit his pants). Then one day a stray dog bit Milo as he was passing by, and she came out and drove the dog off with a leather belt. She brought Milo, crying and shaking, into her kitchen and gave him a Coke with a tiny bit of vodka in it while she smoked a Pall Mall and phoned his mom.

Nan reminded him of Mrs. Armentrout, and her house reminded him of Mrs. Armentrout's house.

The outside of the house would never catch your eye. It sat surrounded by a dead lawn and a dead garden. Once you passed inside, though, it came to life.

It was like stepping into a crowd, because Nan had about eighty-five television sets, all turned on all the time and set loudly to separate channels. They were not the slim, streamlined modern television sets, either, but the kind from the 1960s: wooden battleships with big dials. Nan's TVs all had huge doilies on top and supported hundreds of framed pictures. Nan rarely appeared to actually watch any of these sets, but if you turned one down or changed the channel, she'd yell at you, even if she was occupied at the far end of the house.

The house itself was a minefield of . . . things. Every end table (topped with doilies) was crammed with Hummels or bowls of plastic fruit. No surface of any kind was without its own ashtray, piled with old butts and lipstick stains. No wall space (with awful 1970s wallpaper) that wasn't hung with a tiny painting of Venice or a dog or a vase. And there were vases, too, and crafted mugs waiting to be knocked over. You walked through Nan's house with your elbows at your sides. You stepped carefully and sat carefully, because, of course, there were the cats.

Everywhere. Countless.

If the televisions were the eyes and heart and electric blood of the house, the cats were its breath. They moved from place to place in tides, as if the rooms breathed them out and then in. There were pauses and stillness now and then, as if the house rested, and then sometimes sudden flurries, as if the house had gasped aloud, some alarm sensed only by the cats, by a common neurology, secret and occult.

They left their muddy shoes outside and located Nan in her kitchen, smoking and watching *Family Feud* on a countertop TV.

"Nice to see you," Milo told her.

"Sit down," she said, neither kindly nor unkindly. "I'd offer you something to snack on, but I gave everything to the relief people when they came by."

"That was nice of you," said Suzie.

"Don't patronize me."

They all took seats around the table and then sat there saying nothing.

Eventually Suzie said, "Can we please get this silliness out of the way?"

"The silliness," said Mama, "as you call it, isn't the least bit silly."

Milo raised his hand like a schoolkid.

"Whatever the silliness is," he said, "it appears to involve *me*, and I haven't got the first idea—"

"I think what you did for your family in this last life counts as an act of Perfection," said Suzie. "I think it's obvious. These two bullies disagree. I vote 'yes.'"

"There's no vote," said Mama. "A lifetime either balances perfectly or it doesn't. Nan and I happen to understand why your recent life didn't balance, and Suzie does not."

Milo got up and started making himself a cup of coffee.

He hadn't thought about his evaluation yet. Things had been rather busy since the comet. Now that he gave it a moment's thought, however, he became angry.

"I would like to know," he said, "what was the slightest bit imperfect about the life I just led."

His eyes burned. He swallowed hard. A cat yowled, at the back of the house.

"You weren't even close," said Nan.

"Think it through," said Mama. "You went down there with a plan, right?"

"I went down there to promote Love, with a capital 'L,' through selflessness and sacrifice. And what did I do? I gave my family to another man so they could have a chance of survival. Do you understand what that means? The emotional cost? Of course not. That's why you"—he pointed at Mama and Nan—"always try so hard to fit into human forms and always get it wrong." He indicated the house, the TVs, and the cats.

Nan narrowed her eyes and pulled on her cigarette but said nothing.

Milo filled the coffeemaker and sat back down to wait.

Mama put a big, soft arm around him.

"Tell me about the fence," she said.

The fence?

"The huge fence you and your ARK people put up around the ships to keep everybody else out."

Ah, shit.

"It's like we were building a lifeboat," he said. "There's no way there was going to be room for everybody. Let me guess: The perfect thing to do was to somehow help the whole planet. Everyone on Earth."

Mama nodded. So did Nan. Suzie glared at the floor.

"What other kind of help did you have in mind?" Milo asked. "There was pretty much 'getting killed by the comet' and 'not getting killed by the comet.'"

"There *were* survivors," said Mama. "They will start rebuilding, bit by bit. You might have helped those people get ahead of things a little bit."

"Hindsight," said Milo. "How was I supposed to know there'd be survivors?"

Beneath the television chatter, an uncomfortable silence.

"If it was easy," whispered Mama, "they wouldn't call it 'Perfection.'"

"Helping those who were involved in the project," argued Milo, "was the best use of our time and resources. Even the gods can't suggest an alternative."

"We're not gods," said Suzie.

"Oh, hush," whispered Nan. "They can't tell the difference."

"In any case," said Mama, "it doesn't matter what any of us thinks. The ocean is wet. Two and two is four."

The coffee machine said *ding*. Milo ignored it.

"How am I ever supposed to make a perfect choice?" he asked. "It's always a trick question in the end."

"I don't know," snapped Nan. "Be trickier? Get smarter? That's *your* job. We'll know your perfect moment when we see you do it. It's supposed to be amazing and surprising and impossible, and yet almost everyone manages to do it within nine thousand lives. Everyone but you. That's all I know."

The light shifted in the windows. Cats began, a couple at a time, to fill the kitchen.

Feeding time.

Time for goodbyes.

To Mama and Suzie, Nan said, "His house ought to be ready by now. Go sit and drink his coffee and argue all night, if you want. *Master Chef* is on in three minutes."

Suzie rose from the table. "I'll take him," she said.

"Well, there's a big fat surprise," said Nan, lighting another cigarette.

———

Leaving the house, crossing the dead lawn, Milo took Suzie's hand.

"Is it far?" he asked. He hoped his new house was nearby; he liked Nan's neighborhood.

"We're not going there yet. I have something to show you."

Her voice had a rubber-band bounce to it. Excitement.

It wasn't far.

They walked uphill, along a brick street lined with shops and Victorian streetlamps. The shops had enormous windows with heavy wooden molding and plastered doors. Gilded signs on hanging shingles.

Suzie stopped before a nameless storefront. The windows were soaped. No sign hung above the door.

"They're closed," Milo was saying, but when Suzie produced a skeleton key and unlocked the door, he remembered.

"Your store!" he gasped. "Your candle store!"

"My space," she said, "where the candle store will be."

Inside, she clapped her hands, and a hundred candles leaped into full flame. "I took the first step and signed a lease. The next step is . . . what? I guess fill it up with candles. A coat of paint. A sign with a cute name."

Milo picked up one of the candles: a tall amber-colored sculpture of a rabbit.

Other candles wore other shapes. A knight. Snoopy. Buddha. Earthmother figures with round, pregnant bellies. Fruit candles. Candles shaped like cars and houses and horses and skulls. Cobras. Dancers. Angels. Ghosts.

They were beautiful and lifelike. Many of them looked as if they were about to say something.

"You've been busy," Milo remarked. "Which begs a question."

"Yeah?"

"Does this mean you quit? Your other, you know, job?"

She didn't say anything.

"Okay," he said, "obviously not, because you just wore yourself out for a solid week, bringing almost the entire world over from the other side. But you couldn't keep doing all three—making the candles, making people die, and tending the store when you open. Am I wrong?"

"You're not wrong. That's the next thing to check off the list, I think. But it scares me."

She took a deep breath and scrunched her hair up in her fingers.

Milo's eyebrows rose.

"Death," he mused, "is afraid of something?"

"Can you blame me? I mean, I'm not supposed to quit. Can Summer quit and join the circus? Can Beauty give notice and go work at the animal shelter? It will affect the balance—"

"Oh, God!" said Milo, shaking his fists. "If I hear one more time about how everything has to be in balance, balance, balance, I'm going to literally catch fire. I mean it."

"That's like getting mad at hydrogen or apple trees."

Milo stood silently fuming.

"I'm tired," he said.

"Well," Suzie answered, "I'm going to bed, myself. I put a cot in the back. I can sketch you a quick map to your house—which is very, very nice—or, if you come with me, we can do the Happy Pony."

"The . . . ?"

"I read about it in a magazine. Looks like a woman riding a pony. Makes you happy."

He followed her to the cot.

For the next two weeks, they played house just like a billion other couples. They slept together. They got up to go to the bathroom in the middle of the night. They had moods. They watched TV and left notes for each other.

They did laundry. They both sucked at it and were always shrinking things and turning white things pink. Suzie had some weird garments, like dark robes and velvet tunics and cloaks with a hundred pockets. Work clothes. One time Milo put on her voluminous, hooded nightwatch cloak and came up behind her, saying, "Your tiiiiime haaaas coooome!"

Suzie was painting the antique tin ceiling with a long, telescoping brush. She froze, favored him with an expression like ice on stone, and said, "Put. That. Back."

He put it back.

A lot of their time together was passionate. They had to go out and buy a bed, because they broke the cot.

Some of their time together was unusual. Like the time she went off to work and came home all upset because a lot of kids died in a school fire. It bothered her when death was hard for people, even though they went on and lived other lives. It was the kind of thing that made the living hate and fear her. That particular night, Milo held her for an hour while she shivered and stared at the floor and didn't want to talk. She didn't cry, as Milo would have.

Outside, the afterlife remained the same as always. Earthlike, and also dreamlike. Days came and went. Streets changed direction. The balance of Heaven and Earth followed its own inscrutable schedule. Clouds flew. Rain fell. The moon changed.

"I want it to be like this all the time," Milo told Suzie one Sunday morning (it was Sunday there, anyway. One street over, it might be Thursday, or Shoe Day. You never knew).

They were reading newspapers on the couch together, legs intertwined.

She gave him kind of a hug with her legs.

This, he thought. *This* is Perfection.

Very few people know how to leave a moment like that alone and not fuck it up.

Milo didn't know.

"That's why," he said, "when I go back this next time, I'm going to make sure I have what I need to get it right."

Suzie's face clouded.

"What does that mean, exactly?" she asked.

How to explain the idea that had crept up on him during their morning coffee?

"I'm not taking any chances next time," he said. "I'm going to have special powers."

Her eyes held a cautious interest.

He counted off on his fingers.

"One: I can choose to be smart if I want, right? Fine. I'm going to be really fucking smart."

"That's no guarantee."

"Of course not, but"—Finger Two—"I can also choose to have unusual strengths and challenges. Like, you know, being clairvoyant, or reading auras, or irresistible personal charisma."

"Which?"

"I haven't made up my mind." Finger Three. "I'm going to be born to smart parents, in a smart community. And I will use my abilities to do good.

"That's as far as I've got," he said. "But my last few lives, after consideration, I have been taking a knife to a gunfight. This time I will hit humanity like a bomb of goodness."

Suzie put down her portion of the newspaper.

"I like it," she said. "If you make it, maybe we really *can* be like this"—she indicated the couch, their coffee, a nearby brandy bottle, the sunlight, the shop—"all the time."

The sunlight shifted just so, the way it only does in candle shops.

"So you're going soon?" she said.

He nodded. "You know how it is. Once you get the itch, it just gets worse. It's like the Universal Cosmic Eye telling you it's time."

Suzie got a peculiar look on her face.

"I do know," she said. "I know exactly, in fact."

She got up.

Milo squinted at her.

"Suzie? You're puzzling me."

But she wasn't looking at him. She was looking up at the antique tin ceiling.

Not at it so much as through it. The way, Milo thought, you might look at the ceiling if you were getting ready to say something to the whole universe.

"I'm sorry, Milo," she said. "I'm afraid this might be uncomfortable for you."

Before Milo could phrase a question, she opened her mouth, and the room and the neighborhood and the universe itself turned inside out. The language of Everything That Was crammed itself into the candle shop's back room full of photons and hurricanes and sweater vests and dung beetles and Thursday afternoons. Pyramids and bathtubs and award-winning barbecue sauces—

Milo felt himself stretching like a rubber band.

It stopped.

The room quieted, leaving them both as they had been, standing in the back of the shop. Milo patted himself down, half-expecting a galaxy or Queen Victoria to fall out of his pants.

"You just quit," he said, "didn't you?"

Suzie nodded. She looked a little ashen.

"Are you okay?"

He crossed the floor and put his arms around her. Felt her forehead.

"I'm okay. I just surprised myself, is all."

"All right."

They stood that way for a while. Long enough for the shadows to lengthen.

He let her go. Turned to head for the bathroom.

"I need to give some more thought to my own Big Idea," he said. "A life with advantages isn't the same as a life with privileges, but there are still pitfalls. Similar pitfalls, really—"

"Milo?"

Suzie's voice was suddenly small and frightened.

Turning, he found that the room behind him no longer existed.

It was as if the walls and floor and the space between them had stretched. As if a lens had interposed, with Suzie on the opposite side. She stood just as he had left her but at the same time not quite there, as if she stood around a corner.

She cried out, called his name.

He reached for her, but she was light-years away.

"What's happening?" he cried, still reaching. But he knew.

Things were balancing, exactly as she had feared.

"*I love you,*" he said mournfully.

Tears left Suzie's eyes and shot across the room like sideways rain.

She streamed away like water, flashing in the half-light. Gone.

Milo called after her. His voice stretched like the howl of a train, then snapped back to normal, along with everything else. He paused a second, looking around, sizing up what had happened. Then reason left him, drained out of him like a flood in reverse, and left him on all fours, screaming like a child.

"She's not *gone*," Nan told him for the third time, handing him his third Coke and vodka. "She's somewhere, in some form. Somewhere."

Milo sat at her kitchen table, shaking. He had come to the door a stuttering, crying, runny-nosed mess. He wanted his moms. All ninety-nine hundred of them.

"I saw her go," he explained again.

"Nothing 'goes,'" said Nan. "Don't you listen?"

"Bullshit. That whole thing with the sidewalk."

"That's different."

"How?"

"Dammit, Milo, drink your whatever-it-is and be quiet awhile. *Wheel of Fortune*'s on. And *American Idol* and *Welcome Back, Kotter.*"

They sat there in silence through *Welcome Back, Kotter* and a fresh bottle of vodka and six more shows in a row.

When Milo finally walked down to the river, a week later, it wasn't because he'd worked it all out in his head and was healed and ready to begin a new life. His head and heart still felt like bomb craters.

That's why he was at the river.

He didn't want to think of it as a kind of suicide, but, hey, when you have loved a woman for eight thousand years and then the cosmic *boa* itself decides you can't be together, it's hard.

"Stupidest goddamn thing," he muttered. Then he shut up. Everything he said, everything he thought, just dug the crater a little deeper.

He concentrated on the new life he had chosen. Looked for it in the water.

Advantages. Special abilities. Superpowers, even. He looked for them in the water as he waded through the mud and the reeds, looked among the reflections as the river flowed around his knees.

The images were not always what you expected, but you knew them when you saw them.

A goose. A tall man in professorial robes. University buildings, ivy and stone.

The river filled with pictures and reflections and pulled him down.

A river. Mist. An old stone bridge.

Nothing.

CHAPTER 12

The Day Iago Fortuno Died of Old Age

A roulette wheel doesn't make choices.

There's a cause: The wheel is spun.

There's an effect: A ball pops around like an electrocuted cat and eventually comes to rest somewhere.

In much the same way, the cosmic *boa* doesn't make choices. Causes go in one end, a passive balancing takes place, and effects come out the other end.

So you can't blame the universe for the fact that Suzie, having spun her relationship with the universe as one might spin a roulette wheel, suddenly found herself wormholed out of her candle shop and materialized far, far away in the corner booth at Santana's Taco Palace.

It happened so fast, and was so terrible and awful, that she sat there for three whole minutes with a numb expression on her face.

She said, "Milo," one time, in a shaky voice.

But she didn't cry. In fact, when the server—a serious-looking woman in a cowboy hat—appeared at her table, she ordered a mess of tamales and a margarita.

"Rocks," she specified. "Not frozen."

"*Bueno,*" said the server, and started to walk away.

"In a bucket," Suzie further specified.

The server said, "Good for you," and walked away for real.

Crying wouldn't change the *boa* one bit.

Neither would getting drunk, of course, but she was going to do that anyway.

"*Tu mama estan gorda,*" she said to the universe. "Your mama is so fat . . ."

She was going to sit and drink and hate the universe in Spanish.

And it wouldn't be the first time.

It was a long time ago (or not).

She woke up one day feeling good and tired of it all.

Good and tired of what, exactly? One day she tried to make it rain on a drought-plagued Guatemalan valley, because three hundred million earthworms were drying out, slowly, in the soil. The universe twisted around and flipped her out of there, reminding her, in its way, that she was Death, not Rain or Mercy.

The next morning, giving the afterlife the finger, she emigrated downstream to a little fishing village on the Caribbean Sea and lived in a house there for a time.

She didn't quit. She still rode her winds and shadows and performed her work. But she also started wearing her hair in braids, eating mangoes, and having conversations with mortal people.

Odd conversations, because, naturally, most people mistook her for a witch.

"*Mi esposo tiene la respiración más horrible,*" someone might say. "My husband has the most horrid breath! What can I do?"

And, because of course she was old and knew things, she would maybe say, "*Probar algunas de las hojas de menta por la laguna.* Try some of the mint leaves over by the lagoon."

They called her *bruja,* behind her back, but they meant it in a good way and a bad way, both.

The grandmothers, though, knew exactly what she was. They looked at her the same way they looked at fire.

The children and the men simply accepted that she was mysterious in some way. Not unlike Don Chico, the mayor, who had been struck by lightning six times.

The village was called San Viejo. People fished and lived and played guitars in the evening before she started living there, and they did the same after. They played baseball before. They still played baseball.

When she first moved to San Viejo—the *edge* of San Viejo, on a hill above the beach—she made a good friend almost right away.

Maria Ximena had the same job as a lot of the women in San Viejo, which was to wait for the fishermen to come sailing home in the evening and then take a sharp knife and cut up the fish. One day she was standing at a little wooden table, doing that very thing and cut off the end of her finger. It lay like a tiny cookie amid the fish guts.

Suzie happened to be standing there. Some of the fish were still vaguely alive, and she quietly brought their little fish deaths to them. When she saw Maria Ximena's fingertip lying on the table, she stepped up close, took Maria's hand in her own, and made the finger whole again.

Maria said one thing about God and one thing about the devil, and after that they were friends. Maria started watching the sunset with her, every night down among the boats, and taught her how to play the tambourine.

At the same time, in those early days, the young men began falling in love with her. They couldn't help it. They were afraid to bring her flowers, though, because when they dreamed about her, she had sharp teeth. The only one who was not afraid was a man called Rodrigo Luis Estrada Alday. He was, as the old women said, one of those men God sometimes makes by mistake, the body of a man with three or four men inside it. He had wild eyes and a vast mustache.

"If I swim out to sea and kill a shark with a knife and bring it to you," he whispered to her one morning, after church, "you'll kiss me. Won't you?"

And she said, "No," and gave him a sad look, which he misinterpreted. And he swam out to sea with a knife, and the currents took him.

In time, another of the young men, Iago Fortuno, tried to court her. He started by tying bundles of flowers all around the door of her house.

"*Gracias,*" she said. "But flowers are sad, don't you think? You snip them and give them to someone, and then they die."

Instead of being hurt, Iago Fortuno looked thoughtful. Inside his head, he thought, Maybe there's a way to make flowers last longer or even, like birds, live free of the soil. And he quit being a fisherman and became a florist. He became one of those mysterious things that people didn't quite understand—like Suzie, or like Don Chico (who had been struck by a seventh bolt of lightning and was dead. No one could agree on a new mayor, so there wasn't one for years).

If the people of San Viejo noticed that they tended to die more often or more easily since Suzie had appeared among them, they shrugged and talked about other things.

Meantime, Suzie did her grim work. Like everyone who works, she continued to learn. She learned that every death was different. Sometimes it was good to go slowly. Animals, especially wolves and tropical birds, liked to be sung to as they died. Other times it was best to be quick. Presbyterians and hamsters, for example, both preferred a nice, quick, no-nonsense death.

The longer she lived in San Viejo, the more she appreciated the kind of things that went with living. Like having a window open when you slept, and grass, and tortillas. Being happy when people came to visit, and being happy when they left. The way certain things felt wonderful when you held them in your hands: a book, an ax, a baby, a beer, a big-ass pile of M&M's.

She loved living among these things, these sensibilities, in San Viejo, although she was content, as it were, to sit beside the water rather than to plunge in. She took no lovers (although she was tempted, out of kindness, once or twice, to kiss poor Iago Fortuno, who continued to bring her flowers, and damned if the flowers he grew didn't start to stay fresh and alive longer . . .). She almost took a job helping at the schoolhouse, but one thing the old women seemed to insist on, quietly, was that she not spend overmuch time around the children. She didn't start a store or organize dances or say political things.

She watched, though, and sometimes helped, while others did these things.

Maria Ximena married Jesus Franco, and they had three daughters. The fishermen started putting little five-horsepower engines on the back of their boats and catching more fish. One year there was a hurricane. For several years, there was a war. One year everything was wonderful! Sometimes that happens. The fish were bigger, everyone was healthy, and they had a festival with a bonfire twenty feet high. Iago Fortuno married a woman who, although not a nun, had nonetheless taken a holy vow of silence, and the other men were in awe of this and thereafter considered Iago one of the wisest and most clever of men, and they convinced him to fill the mayor's office.

A young man named Carlos des Casas Montoya tried to impress Suzie by swallowing a sword. Two swords at once! Three! And then died, coughing blood.

Maria Ximena Franco died of a fever. Jesus, her husband, went blind in one eye the day she was buried. Two of their daughters grew up and moved away to the city. The third daughter became a communist and carried a rifle everywhere.

A young man who called himself El Gato courted Suzie with poetry. He played his guitar for her and sang a song he had written, comparing her to the wind.

"El viento es una mujer y un canción y un sueño," he sang, and died in his sleep.

If the villagers noticed that Suzie had remained beautiful and unchanged for a great many years, they didn't mention it. The old women still looked at her with the same knowing eyes, although the original old women had given way to new old women.

A day came when she felt moved to sweep out the house one final time and go back where she belonged (technically). She knew it the way you know it's time to go to bed at the end of a day.

She knew it, not surprisingly, the day Iago Fortuno died of old age.

She walked through his garden and his greenhouse and found him in his bed, sitting up, waiting. Before she could lean down and kiss him on the forehead, he stirred, saying, "I have something for you."

And he retrieved something from the wooden table at his bedside and handed it to her.

A flower. A small yellow flower.

"Una flor inmortal," he said. "An immortal flower. You can just enjoy it and not be sad."

The flower was made of silk and wire.

Suzie said, *"Bueno,* Iago," and leaned down and kissed him on the mouth, and off he went to the afterlife.

Suzie went back up the hill and swept her house and closed the door behind her and became a wind along the beach.

The old women made respectful signs but whispered, *"La rana está fuera del pozo.* The frog is out of the well," and broke out a bottle of wine their grandmothers had put aside years before.

The waitstaff at Santana's didn't approach Suzie while she was drinking her margarita.

They weren't afraid. They just wanted to see if she could drain the whole bucket.

She could, as it turned out. Afterward, though, she fell asleep right there at the table, so someone had to wake her to tell her it was time to go. They fetched Santana himself.

"Señora?" he said, poking her in the shoulder a little bit.

"Milo?" she slurred, raising her head. Then: "Oh. Hi. Sorry."

She stood to go, staggering. As she staggered, she noticed something that disturbed her. She felt . . . less . . . than before. Like chunky soup that had been thinned with water. If she raised her hand to the decorative ceiling lamps, she knew, she would find herself becoming transparent.

"Shit," she said to Santana. "I'm starting to fade."

"*Sí,*" answered Santana. "*Lo siento.* The frog is in the well."

"It sure is," she agreed, and stumbled out and became an evening breeze. A thin, unsteady breeze that made snoring noises and wobbled around in the park all night as if lost.

CHAPTER 13

The Swami Who Could Not Be Poisoned

Milo had lived many lives in which he was talented in some way.

Sometimes the talent was developed through practice and hard work; other times it was more like a birthday present. Either way, special abilities always made things easier. It was like going into battle with a magical sword.

He was a racehorse named Across the Sea, with lungs like locomotives and hooves like war hammers, who couldn't bear to see another horse pass him by.

He (*she,* actually: Milona Oxygen Templeton) managed cargo for interstellar freighters—one of the hardest jobs ever. You had to be able to keep schedules in your head and coordinate quantum collapse points. She could imagine hyperspace the way other people might imagine a stick of chewing gum.

In India, long ago, he was a snake charmer. Just an ordinary snake charmer at first, until one day he wasn't careful and was bitten. He went home and lay down and waited to die but didn't. It turned out that he was immune to all sorts of poison. He became a swami, a holy man, and people would come to see him drink terrible things and be bitten and survive. He said prayers for pilgrims, and they paid him.

One day a lot of black fluid came gushing out of his mouth and eyes and pores, and he fell over dead. Things add up. You can't help it.

One time he had what people like to call "a way with animals." He became a famous cowboy, in an age of genetically engineered beef. He rode horses with legs like whips, careening among beef cattle like corn-fed tankers, under an artificial deep-blue sky.

"Gee!" he would yell, and "Haw!" and the horses flowed the way he wanted, because they loved him. The cows mooed at him like foghorns. They loved him, too, in their sad, doomed way.

He was Mona Rivette, the precocious daughter of a waveform physicist, a beautiful child with the misfortune to be one of the last victims of a terrible wasting disease. By the age of nine, she was almost completely paralyzed. Her condition, and her terror of being shut up within her own body, drove her to an act of singular genius.

She asked her father to let her use some of his cloud time on the solar supercomputer, and he did. She asked him now and then to bring her such-and-such a material or to have such-and-such a thing machined or molded, and he always did.

On her eleventh birthday, she presented her family and the District 45 Galactic Patent Board with an invention she called a "fish," a communications device that hovered over a person's shoulder and served to call people, or compute things, or record sights and sounds, or broadcast, or measure things with lasers, and so on. It was the ultimate personal assistant.

People loved the fish because it did a lot of the tedious technical work they often didn't feel like doing. The pricier models would even fetch things. They also loved it because it was cute, hovering beside them, or flying with them, or even swimming with them, if swimming was something they did.

"Holy shit," said the physicist, when his daughter showed him her invention. And he oversaw the patents and saw that they made his daughter wealthy.

For two years, Mona lived in a wheelchair, waited on hand and foot by her own invention. It enabled her to speak and write down thoughts and invent two or three other things before the day it helped her say, "Goodbye," and hovered nearby, purring sadly, while she died.

In some lives, Milo developed talents that were pretty much superpowers. In medieval China, he was the kung-fu master Mo Pi, who walked alone up to a Mongol encampment one day and quietly demanded that they turn around and go home. When the invaders laughed, Mo Pi stamped his foot one time on the ground, bowed, and went home. Three days later, an earthquake rolled through the countryside and the mountains. When the last aftershock had faded, the Mongols had gone home.

Often enough, great talents must also be great secrets.

Behind the Iron Curtain, Milosevic Kocevar became a respected shoemaker. He made sturdy shoes for reasonable prices, married a drab woman and raised drab children and ate a great deal of cabbage, and never bothered anyone. Or so it seemed.

Unknown to all but a few, Milosevic sometimes made bombs. He planted the bombs under the cars of the *snerkezeii*, the secret police, and in the dustbin of the little government building at the edge of town. Sometimes he planted bombs on the highway, where the Red

Army caravans passed. The bombs looked like discarded shoes. They were never detected in time to stop them from exploding.

Later on, when he was very old and the Iron Curtain came down and he told everyone what he had done, even his own family didn't believe him.

Sometimes you become good at something by accident. Centuries ago, Milo owned a brewery and brewed an excellent beer. His only competition was old Geoffrey Morgan, who had won the top prize at the Bristol fair every year since before Milo was born.

Geoff Morgan had a beautiful daughter named Igraine, and when she turned sixteen, Milo asked to marry her.

"Nay!" barked Geoff Morgan. "The day you get Igraine's hand is the day that swill of yours wins top prize at the fair!"

So Milo went home and brewed his finest beer and was almost finished when a battle broke out nearby between the king's men and the retainers of the Duke of Salisbury. The fighting spilled into town. The dead and their blood got into the open vats, and while a dead man can be fished out, you simply cannot remove blood from beer.

Milo arrived at the fair that year with a dark, bitter beer, instantly popular for its peculiar and aggressive taste. He won top prize, and won Igraine, and returned to a long, fat life making beer and children. And every year he grew more famous for the drawing of his mysterious dark beer. He and his lady always arrived at the fair just a shade too pale and with bandages about their forearms (though these were scarcely noticed and never remarked upon by polite folk). What *was* remarked upon was the way Milo and his bride were so devoted that there was nothing he couldn't ask of her, nothing she wouldn't do for him.

Milo enjoyed his brewing talent so much, he tried to take it with him when he died.

He spent hours and hours in the basement of his modest afterlife home (his reward for a modest life making beer), making more beer and still trying to find a way to make the perfect dark beer without having to open a vein.

"You're supposed to move on," griped Suzie, sitting on the basement steps. Her eyes watered and her voice sounded scratchy. She was experimenting with smoking cigarettes, her latest human curiosity. It wasn't working well. She stubbed out her smoke on the steps.

"I am moving on," said Milo, opening a tap and tasting his latest batch. He grimaced. "The last keg was too sweet. This one's bitter. A step in the right dir—"

"That's not what I mean," she coughed. "You're supposed to take what you learned and start getting ready for a new life. Not dwelling on the old."

A smirk twisted Milo's lips.

"I know what this is about," he said. "This is about *her.*"

Suzie scrunched her eyes up. "Her *who?*"

"Her. Igraine. The love of my life. The most recent one."

"You're off your pickle. Jealous of an Earth chick?"

"Be respectful," he said.

Suzie's eyes flared. "Listen to you!" she shouted. *"You're* the one who's got her on the brain. Not me."

"Okay," said Milo, closing the tap, rolling the barrel away. "Fine. She's on my mind. We were married fifty years, after all. And that makes you jealous."

She gave him a complicated look.

"You know we're just friends," she said. "Right?"

How could she be so dumb?

"I'm not dumb," she said, her tone pure ice. "I'm *Death.* Don't you get it? I bring things to an end. I don't do the Love thing. It's not my area."

Milo shrugged. Fine. He wasn't going to beg.

"Next time I'm alive," he said, "I'm going to be the first man to sleep with a million women. How do you like them apples?"

"Good. I hope your soul pecker falls off."

Milo went silent, inside and out.

Soul pecker?

After a life in banking, Milo had to serve a penalty life as an alligator snapping turtle, waiting in the murk at the bottom of slimy ponds. Claws dug in, holding his breath.

These were talents, too. Waiting. Striking fast, when the time came.

Sitting in the murk, raw talent fifty million years old, coiled like a spring in the swamp.

He was a jazz musician, saxophone, smoky and slow. Mookie Underwood, in pinstripes and suspenders and a tie with a perfect four-in-hand. Saddle shoes, shined like planets that clicked and tapped their way through orbit.

If you watched people listening, whether it was in a club or a hall or down at Smokestack Records, they all had a certain look, which they couldn't help, as if they were trying to get a peek down the bell of that big brass sax, because it sounded like something lived down there. Something wise and wet and not particularly happy. There was an old soul behind that sound, but whether the soul was in the saxophone or in the man himself was never plain.

CHAPTER 14

The Hasty Pudding Affair

KING'S COLLEGE, CHRISTMINSTER, BRIDGER'S PLANET,
A.D. 3417

An old stone bridge.

A primordial morning, full of mists and loomings. A river of mist
flowed under the bridge, and a shore of mist came to meet it.

The mist retreated before morning sunlight, and a stone church
emerged, as if rising out of time. It was followed, at a distance, by a
stone clock tower.

Three wooden sculls, flying like spears across mist and water, shot
out from under the bridge. Strong, hearty voices called out:

"Stroke, slow the slide!"

"Power three on five, boys! One, two . . ."

"Three, hands down and away!"

On the shore, shouts and cheers from people half visible:

"Huzzah!"

"Steady on, Harrow, that's the way!"

Somewhere in the fog, a finish line crossed. A climax of cheers, jeer-
ing.

The fog lightened then, revealing a hundred or more boys in jackets and school ties. Among them, the robes and gray hair of professors.

The assembly grew quiet at the crack of a distant pistol and craned their whole selves to see upriver, beyond the bridge, eyes on the next race.

All eyes, as it happened, except for the eyes of Mr. Daniel Titpickle, vice dean of boys, who excused himself through the crowd until he reached the towering robes and frowning soul of William Hay, professor of theology, and tapped him on the arm.

"What is it, Titpickle?" rumbled Hay.

"It's the Froosian Goose," whispered Titpickle. "It's gone missing from the Damocles Club again. There's reason to suspect the Barleycorn Society."

Hay, the Barleycorns' faculty adviser, raised a dread eyebrow. Something made him skeptical, although it was, in fact, traditional for the Barleycorns to make off with the Damocles Society's sacred Froosian Goose, just as it was the Damocles Society's duty, whenever possible, to kidnap the fabled Barleycorn Bones.

The Froosian Goose was an ancient stuffed goose (shot by King Edward II of Earth, founder of the original King's College), "a simbol of Fellowshippe" carried with solemnity and placed before the brothers at assembly. The Barleycorn Bones were, according to certain dark and secret lore, the skeleton of one Jonathan Poore, a famous priest and cannibal.

The Froosian Goose had been captured once or twice a year since the society's founding some hundred years ago. The bones had been stolen only once, and the brother with the misfortune to be asleep on guard that night, according to legend, lay buried under the dining commons in Oxbridge Hall.

"If you'd come with me back to my office," suggested Titpickle, "we can dial up Broode at security, and he can tell you—"

"No need for that," said Hay, raising a ministerial hand. "Not this time."

"But—" sputtered Titpickle.

Hay silenced him with a dead eye.

"It's not my lads," he said, "sinners though they are. Not this time. I'll involve the police, if they need involving."

He dismissed Titpickle without word or gesture. A slight flexing of the atmosphere about his person was all it needed, and the dean slunk back the way he had come, missing the unexpected triumph in the second race—and by four seats!—of the brothers of the Round Church Circle.

Hay taught his classes like a dark lord. His more-serious students worshipped him. The dilettantes scowled behind his back, until they learned that what the older lads said was true: Hay had eyes in the back of his head, and ears everywhere.

"Hay is diabolical," his acolytes declared, "like all great religious minds."

Hay usually took his lunch in Washing Commons, but not today. Today, to his wife's surprise, he went home and asked her to make him one of whatever she was making for Milo. Milo was their eight-year-old boy, a challenging young man who attended Sparrow, a primary prep school attached to the university. Most of the faculty brats went there. It was like a daycare facility where they read Chaucer.

So Victoria—Hay's wife—kissed him on the cheek and made him a meatloaf sandwich and fetched him a glass of milk. Then she went off about her housework, leaving Hay at the table alone, where he was sitting and waiting with his hands folded in his lap when Milo came banging through the door and dashing into the kitchen, all flying hair and shorts and class four tie.

Hay would have preferred for his son to stop and address him with quiet awe, but he settled for a quick "Hey, Dad!" and a wave of one not-too-clean hand as his offspring shot past, out of the kitchen quite as suddenly as he'd come in.

Hay terrified everyone on Bridger's except for his own child, which confounded him. He didn't know, of course, that his child was an an-

cient soul who had lived almost ten thousand lives, who had been everything from a king to a pollywog.

Hay waited. He took a bite of his sandwich.

He was rewarded with the boy's reappearance. Tie loosened, shirt
untucked, shoes jettisoned, but with his hands and face clean. He
mounted to the table and, with something like good manners, ad-
dressed himself to his lunch.

"How come you're home?" asked the boy, with his mouth full.

"I'll let you think that over," Hay replied.

The boy ate, and studied his father.

You could see the wheels turning, the way boywheels had turned
for a million years, like the minds of little poker players, judging
whether to bluff or fold.

"I've hidden the Froosian Goose in my closet," said Milo, pausing to
gulp his milk. "I was going to paint it blue or else with dots."

He licked away his milk mustache.

The Barleycorns, a club of some twenty-five promising nineteen-
year-olds, barely managed to get away with the goose each year without setting off alarms. Despite himself, Hay was impressed.

"Tell me how you did it," he said.

"Am I in trouble?" asked the boy.

"Naturally you're in trouble. Don't be foolish. How'd you manage
it?"

Hay kept watching for signs of the boy's infant-onset asthma to
show themselves. As a toddler, the boy would sometimes get red in the
face and short of breath when he was placed under stress or if he was
caught getting up to no good. The condition had been genetically
muted since, but sometimes the boy still seemed to labor for breath, if
called on his behavior.

Not lately, though.

"How did you know?"

"Young man—"

"I'll tell you how I did it if you'll tell me how you knew."

"Last night at dinner," said Hay, "you asked why a goose was symbolic of fellowship, and I explained that geese never leave one of their own behind if he is injured. One of them will drop out of the flock and stay with him until he recovers or dies. You seemed to find it all funny, in your way. When I learned that the Damocles Society's goose was missing, I put it together. It's the sort of thing you'd do. Now. How?"

"Sometimes they take it places. I was on my way home from school when one of the brothers brought it out and put it down beside his car. Then he went back in to look for his keys."

"You made it from the society clubhouse to our own door, carrying the Froosian Goose, without being stopped?"

"I wasn't carrying the goose. I was driving the car."

Hay dropped his sandwich.

"I beg your pardon?"

"It wasn't hard."

"How did you manage to start the car, with the keys missing?"

The boy suddenly seemed less plucky and cast his eyes down to the floor.

"Did you start the car . . . yourself?"

The boy nodded.

Hay had forbidden Milo to use *that* particular talent. Not until he was older, until his brain was more completely formed. It was for his own good. There were studies—right there at King's College—indicating that a kinetic could experience a decline in ability if that part of the brain was exercised too early.

"Where is the car now?" Hay asked.

"I left it on Braintree Street, by the war memorial."

Hay stood.

"Tuck in your shirt," he commanded, "and find your shoes."

When his son was presentable, Professor Hay drove him to the police station and saw that he confessed to his crimes.

Grand theft, for an eight-year-old, carried a penalty of one year's probation. At Hay's urging, the court also stipulated that Milo wear a

Dawson mole, a tiny electronic bug that nulled his telekinetic abilities. Milo made sure to wear it right between his eyes whenever his father was around. If this made Hay feel guilty, it didn't show.

For the next several years, Milo focused on school, setting a high bar for his own achievement. He read and learned, took tests and won prizes, and grew older. A lot of the energy he would have used moving things with his mind, he focused through the more-traditional lens of his intellect.

This focus paid off. At the tender age of fifteen, he enrolled at King's College on a faculty scholarship and blew the placement exams out of the water. He was permitted to major in subspace physics.

His father raised his eyebrows and said, "Hmmph!" as if Milo had impressed him. Not made him proud necessarily but impressed him.

He was *not* permitted to major in neuroapplications. Wearing a Dawson mole had rewritten his synapses, and those talents were gone. It was like losing a limb or a form of sight, but Milo swept the loss under his considerable mental rug and pressed on.

A faint, ancient voice way down in Milo's soul whispered, Oh, wow, we might actually make it this time.

College was a turbulent time for Milo. It's a turbulent time for most people, but Milo had to contend with being far younger than his fellow freshmen, as well as with being a faculty brat. Most of the King's College student body were smart kids from wealthy families, whereas Milo was merely smart. Fortunately for him, his intellect won him respect, and he was still somewhat legendary for stealing the Froosian Goose.

He faced the same challenges that bedevil every adolescent schoolboy. He struggled to be cool and handsome and to not go touching his penis every five minutes. There were girls at King's College, but not the girly kind he knew from middle school. College girls terrified him.

College girls terrify me! he appealed to his older, wiser self, a self he was getting to know and depend on.

His wiser self was no help with the college girls. The voices were afraid of them, too.

His fortunes became more interesting the day he tried to show off by challenging Professor Basmodo Ngatu in Literature 232, the Poetry of Colonial Resistance.

Professor Ngatu, a thin black man with a ponderous, imperial head, was not a lecturer. He was a discusser and a question-asker.

"Why," Ngatu asked one day, pacing before the chalkboard, "do you suppose Zachary Heridia wrote his attack on the oxygen cartel in verse rather than in an epistolary form? Was he trying to fly under the radar by having his attack appear where allies of the cartel were unlikely to stumble on it?"

Most students peered into their books, while their fish levitated slightly above their left shoulders, recording notes.

It was dangerous to make eye contact with Ngatu. But Milo did.

"Mr. Hay?"

"Sir, I wonder if Heridia's choice of form was more of an artistic decision. What if he wrote in verse and published in a literary forum *not* as a rhetorical tactic but simply because it was more beautiful?"

Ngatu strode up into the gallery, his own gold-plated fish swooping behind him, and peered down at Milo over antique glasses.

"'The Suffocation of Emeline K,'" said Ngatu, "was written three days after the oxygen embargo against the Ganymede terraformers and published a week after that. Four thousand people died in that embargo. Six hundred were shipped downplanet to the Europa prison islands. But you suggest that Heridia, whose own sister died in the Jovian monoxide 'accident,' was more concerned with art than with raising consciousness?"

The other students had their heads out of their books now.

Milo shook his head. "That's a false choice," he answered. "Art can encompass both social responsibility and questions of beauty. 'Themself are one,' to quote Emily Dickinson. And I think that's where Heridia was, at this decision point. He realized he could make the most of his message by making it beautiful and by presenting it to an audience who would appreciate that irony and be grieved by it."

"Grieved?" asked Ngatu, eyes narrowing. "You believe this writer chose to elicit an emotional response rather—"

"People are complicated," someone interjected.

All heads turned. The speaker was a female student, Ally Shepard.

"Miss Shepard?" asked Ngatu.

Ally Shepard shrugged. "Heridia might have written in verse for more than one reason. I think that's where . . . he . . . was going."

She waved her hand in Milo's direction. A wonderful hand! Ally Shepard was like an island girl, imported from the tropics. She fit into her King's College uniform like so many sleeping kittens. There was no place on her body that Milo didn't imagine his hands, petting. Indeed, the wide majority of King's College males and a number of females shared these imaginings. Ally Shepard was both president and premier talent of the Hasty Pudding Club, the vaunted campus theater organization. She was perhaps the closest thing King's College had to a celebrity.

A brainy celebrity at that.

"It's dangerous," Ally was saying, "applying hindsight to something as complex as why someone wrote a poem, because the temptation is to try and make it make sense. We *can* apply reason, but what we *can't* do is apply the storms and variations that govern a human mind moment to moment."

She looked Milo's way and winked.

"I would say," said Ngatu, descending again to his chalkboard, "that your point bears consideration. So let's hear about that. How did the artist affect the political chess player within the same mind, and vice versa?"

Milo barely listened. His entire universe was nailed to Ally Shepard—he didn't dare look. Hard as he tried to be cool, to be more than the sum of fifteen years, he could only sit there blushing, with a vacant look in his eyes and growing discomfort in his pants.

———

In the week that followed, Milo suffered a sort of identity crisis.

Was he a cute little phenomenon, like an ornament the freshman class wore with quiet amusement? Or had he made his age immaterial? Was he, in fact, a brooding future Lord Byron? He imagined himself being photographed in black and white or filmed without his knowledge.

Soon enough, he would know which of these was his true self. Any day, the intramural clubs would issue their fall invitations, and that would tell all. At King's College, future greatness was invited into clubs; mediocrity and cuteness were not.

The invitations—actual ancient-style paper messages—arrived under doors one wet, leafy October morning.

Milo did *not* receive an invitation from the Damocles Club. He *did* receive warm greetings from the Barleycorns, the Tycho Fellowship (a science organization), the Harrisons (a literary circle, publishers of the *Ilion*), the Harrow Intramural Team, and—what, ho!—the Hasty Pudding Club.

Just as he was thinking that he needed parental permission to join anything, his fish buzzed.

"Milo?" growled his father's voice. "Listen: If you haven't got plans already—oh. How have you been?"

Milo could vaguely hear Mom in the background, reminding him to "show an interest."

"Fine, Dad. You and Mom?"

"Good, fine. Your mother wanted to know if you'd care to stop by for dinner, Friday? She hasn't seen you for a while."

Dammit. Lord Byron didn't want to have dinner with his mom and dad.

"I'd be happy to," he said.

"Well, good. Come by around five, dinner at six. Have a good day."

The fish went dark.

"By the way," said Milo, "I need your permission to join the Tychos and the Harrisons and the Harrow Intramurals and the Barleycorns and the Hasty Pudding Club, you fucker."

Milo didn't rush right over to his parents' house on Friday.

When his classes let out at noon, he wandered the campus. The future scientist and author, hands in his pockets, windswept and poetic. Across the quad, through its forest of giant chestnuts. Down the cobblestone road between Stowe Hall and the pitch. Down along the canal, and there he stopped.

He watched the usual scattering of college men trying to impress college women by navigating the canal, standing in the stern of narrow wooden barges, steering with long wooden poles. Most of them were city boys who had never done anything of the kind before, and the rest were country boys whose whole boating experience involved no more skill than it took to yank a motor to life. Most of them went careening around the water at the very precipice of capsizing, their dates trying to keep a brave face.

Milo, on the other hand, had been paddling around on that canal since he was a baby—usually with his mother, on Wednesday evenings. He was in just the mood to get out there and show the older boys a thing or two.

"'Lo, young Hay," said the supervisor at the launch, Mr. LeJeune. "How's your mom?"

"She's fine, sir. I'd like to take a boat out. Is it still three?"

"It is, Mr. Hay. But you still got to have your majority. Are you eighteen, then?"

"Mr. LeJeune, you know I can paddle one of these—"

"Like the devil himself, sir. But I'd lose my situation here if something was to—"

"I'll sign," said a familiar and awful voice. "Pay him, Milo."

Ally Shepard.

He wished he were dead.

"I don't think—" he began, but then she touched his arm, and it was all warm kittens. Oh, did she smell nice.

She sat down in the bow of the nearest gondola, looking up at him through designer shades. And Mr. LeJeune handed him a receipt and an oar, and just like that he was master of King's College again.

Expertly, he stepped onto the stern and drove her into the channel. They might have been riding on glass, so smoothly did he steer. And it was just as he would have daydreamed. He cut through the rest of them like a shark through a lot of clownfish, pivoted to starboard, and made speed for the castle bridge. And, oh, did the young blades glare! And, oh, did their dates raise their eyebrows, impressed!

"You're good at this," she told him.

He shrugged, giving his hair a rakish flip.

They passed between stone walls, under two stone bridges, where Milo had to duck. The vast green plain of St. Martin's yard opened up on the port side of the canal. Beyond, the cliffs and spires of St. Martin's itself.

Ally slipped out of her loafers. And her stockings, too. Then she spun around on the bench, hiked her skirt halfway up her thighs, threw one leg over each side of the bow, and let her exquisite feet trail in the water.

Milo yanked his shirttail out of his khakis, anticipating an erection.

She tucked her head around one shoulder, looking at him upside down. How could he meet her eyes, when the rest of her was hiked up and spread out like that?

Be bold, advised Milo's ancient selves in the depths of his head.

Milo did what Lord Byron would do. He looked at her legs, gave the rest of her a burning stare, then turned the burning stare on her eyes.

In my biography, he thought, when they write about my women, they will say I was mad, bad, and dangerous to know.

She laughed, righted herself, and turned again to face the canal.

Milo bumped into another gondola. Oh, way to go.

"Jackass!" said the older boy.

"It's okay," said Ally. "Practice makes perfect."

What a bitch. He was her slave.

"Go to the castle," she said.

The canal proper ran to the end of East Green, where it opened up into a wide pool, a convenient turnaround. But you could, if you liked, continue upstream all the way to the Brandy River itself. Just short of the river, the canal wound like a moat around the walls of a castle. This was the automated gatehouse between the river and the canal, really, but it was part of King's College, so they built it like a castle and called it a castle.

"You don't seem like fifteen," said Ally. She leaned forward now, feet *and* hands trailing in the water, embracing the prow like a lover. It looked like something she was doing by accident, just relaxing. Was it an accident? *(Hell no, it's not an accident!* roared the old voices down inside him.) Did she know what it was doing to him? He could stare all he liked, after all, with her head turned away. Did she know that?

"How old did you think I was?" he asked, ducking beneath the castle bridge, steering them into the wilderness portion of the canal.

Plop plop!—turtles, startled, slid off logs and vanished in the water.

Ally sat upright, scanning the shore.

"I want a turtle," she said. And she slid sideways into the canal, almost without a splash.

Underwater, gone.

Splash!—bursting from the water hard by the shore and snatching blindly at a sycamore log there.

Damned if she didn't catch a turtle. A small painted turtle. She held it aloft in triumph, tossing her head to clear the hair from her eyes.

She half-stood, half-floated, half out of the water, drenched and running like a waterfall. And quite translucent, Milo noted with wonder. Her King's College uniform had all but become one with her pink skin.

"Shit," she said. "I lost my sunglasses."

But she didn't much care, it seemed. She swam out to the gondola, which Milo steadied while she climbed back in.

"See?" she said, holding up the turtle for his inspection.

"Painted turtle," he declared. "Watch it. They bite."

Ally snapped her teeth at him and let the turtle go in the waist of the boat, where it scratched desperately at the wood, crawling under the middle bench.

"He wasn't much fun," she said, pouting. Then she lost the pout and squinched her eyes at him, saying, "How about you, Milo Hay? Can you be fun?"

"I invented fun," he said, wondering what he meant. Wondering what *she* meant.

The woods opened up to port, revealing the castle. Tall stone walls, dripping with moss. Moat still and black, with leaves floating. Between tree branches, great spiderwebs caught the sun.

He let the gondola glide in, stopped her gently with a touch of the oar on the bottom, then shipped the oar and sat down on the stern bench. Let her float. He leaned back like Lord Byron, wicked and casual.

They didn't say anything for a few minutes. She seemed absorbed by the image of the castle and by the way the sun danced through the leaves. Milo, too, let the quiet fall over him.

"How do you know you're not a ghost?" asked Ally, still watching the castle. "They say ghosts don't know. So how would you know?"

"Maybe you don't," said Milo. "Maybe we are."

"I think ghosts go around thinking of all the things they didn't do," she said. "You know. Regrets. Like if you died right now, your ghost might go around regretting never being kissed."

Now she looked at him.

"I've been kissed," he almost said. Boys and girls in middle school did their share of kissing. But he absorbed the insult. The moment was like a boat you didn't dare rock.

She lowered herself into the bottom and came to him and lowered herself over him, smelling like the river. And she pressed her lips against his, and he pressed back. At first he thought that was all she meant to do, and he was happy with it. Then something new happened. A new lip introduced itself, and he realized this was her tongue.

While they kissed, he was generally aware that her hand was busy between them, below their collarbones. But he was lost and mindless and didn't think about it until she pulled away and sat up, straddling him, and he saw she had unbuttoned her shirt and unsnapped her bra.

Lord Byron would touch her.

He reached up with both hands, letting his knuckles stroke her belly. (Don't go grabbing for them all at once, voices advised.)

He felt her own hands at his belt buckle then, and his heart raced. She would feel, see how hard he was. Was that good? Would she be offended?

Standing suddenly, nearly upsetting the boat, Ally reached up under her skirt and pulled her panties down. Stepped out of them and straddled Milo. She worked her way down around him and he was inside her.

My God! His entire mind and body whizzed and sparked.

Immediately, orgasm approached like a surging, drooling beast. In that time, he was both frightened and astonished by Ally Shepard, who bucked with her hips and had a look in her eyes that, honestly, he didn't like very much. As if she were striking out at someone.

And then everything was topsy-turvy, with a scream and a laugh, and he was underwater, in all that murk, with water up his nose and his pants around his knees. Ally had jerked them over sideways, capsizing them.

The moat was shallow. He found the bottom and stood, sputtering. Fumbling with his belt.

"Dammit, Ally!" he croaked.

She was sputtering, too, and still laughing. She had recovered quickly and was onshore, shoes in one hand, turtle in the other. Shirt and bra still open.

"At least you've got that much," she said, "if you die in your sleep tonight." And she walked off into the woods, toward campus.

He loved her and hated her.

The gondola floated, half sunk, on the dark water. He dragged it ashore, dumped it out, and rowed home.

He felt kind of like Lord Byron and kind of like Little Boy Blue.

He was, for the moment, a happily confused young man.

Dinner at his parents' house was a stilted affair.

"You seem preoccupied," said his father, glowering over the roast beef.

"Oh?" said Milo. "No. Not really."

"Well, where are you?" asked his mother, laughing. "You're not here. I think it's a girl."

Milo's stomach lurched.

"There is something," he said, "but it's not a girl. It's about the clubs."

His father chewed ponderously, frowning.

"You've already taken on more than you should, for your age," he said. "Extras can wait until next year, I should think."

Dammit, thought Milo, Dad knew you got invited only once. You either got on board freshman year or you didn't get on at all. Before he could phrase this in a way calculated not to piss his father off, though, the doorbell rang.

Maybe it was Ally Shepard. It would be just like her, he thought, to surprise him and make him uncomfortable.

It wasn't Ally. It was two Christminster policemen.

"Milo Hay? Are you Milo Hay?"

"Yes."

"You're under arrest," they said, and grabbed him and spun him around and put handcuffs on him.

"Milo?" called his mother from the other room. "Who is it?"

"Jesus Christ!" cried Milo. "For *what?*"

"Rape, Mr. Hay. This way, please."

While he was sitting downtown in a jail cell, Milo's ancient-soul voices tried to comfort him. The forms your life takes are illusions, said the voices. Happiness or jail—it's transitory, like a dream.

"The truth will out," said his father, when they let him see visitors and an attorney.

Milo died over and over again, describing what had happened in the boat, in the moat. His father listened like a great stone owl, arms folded across his chest. But when Milo finished, his father did something unexpected.

He reached out with one great hand and cupped the side of Milo's head with something like affection.

"You didn't do anything wrong," he said. "Stupid, but not wrong. Don't let them convince you otherwise."

Milo nodded.

The attorney, a young man with a ridiculous pouf of bleach-blond hair at the very top of his head, shuffled some papers and said, "Fortunately, stupid isn't a crime. If you're innocent, you're innocent. Open and shut."

It didn't matter that he was innocent.

He thought about that on his way to the prison colony at Unferth, chained to a bunk in the belly of a warp transport. Three days with nothing to do but feel how unfair it all was and to be terrified.

What mattered, it turned out, was that Ally Shepard's dad was a rich Spartan banker and could hire a whole team of Ivy League lawyers. Professor Hay's powers, on the other hand, were confined to his classroom. His worldly salary covered only the expense of the single pouf-haired lawyer, who took one look at the opposing team and was almost sick on the courtroom floor.

Ally Shepard, said the opposition, had been seen by a hundred people, walking across the King's College campus soaking wet, in what might have been a ripped-open shirt.

"Mr. Hay's student record," argued the Ivy Leaguers, "is that of a precocious and impressively developed mind, accompanied by an equally developed ego. He believes himself to be a superior sort of fellow in every respect, Your Honor, and he treats his peers as mere prey. Given his sophistication, he is no more a child, sir, than you are. He is an adult and should be sentenced as such."

The pouf-haired attorney, to his credit, tried to say something about Ally Shepard and a long string of therapists, but the Ivy Leaguers had complicated reasons why this evidence should be disallowed.

Professor and Mrs. Hay sat in the front row, looking ashen and small.

"Unferth Prison," pronounced the judge.

Falling through hyperspace, Milo reviewed his transformation.

My exquisite life as the Lord Byron of Bridger's Planet, he thought, is over. Which bites, because it was going to be a pretty fine life.

His stomach gave a violent wrench, and he fought back tears.

Now I need to figure out how to stay alive in prison. That is my grim new truth.

Nonsense, insisted his deep soul. This is the truth: stars, time, Being, Nothingness. Your *boa*.

Okay, thought Milo, desperate for anything other than despair. He would let the truth flow around him like an ocean, where the waves moved through the water but the water itself was still. He would be like the water, like the still, black moat where that lying, pathological bitch had dumped him—

Milo, said his deep soul.

I will be like the water, he thought, starting over.

The Unferth prison colony, he had learned online, was one of the most fearsome examples of spacefaring justice. Almost fourteen hundred years ago, when humans first left Earth and began living aboard ships and stations and other artificial environments, the problem of life support had become the guiding light for everything, including law. Down on Earth, they could afford to be warm and fuzzy and lenient. Violent criminals were freed to hurt people time after time. Greedy corporate moguls hoarded wealth and squandered resources under the protection of puppet governments. Everyone knew where that had gotten Earth, didn't they? The moguls herded whole populations into debt slavery. Violent criminals made whole communities unfit to live in. Information and education were channeled so poorly that the planet lost its ability to look ahead, to think ahead, to plan. And so they drowned in their own polluted, shortsighted muck until Comet Marie put them out of their misery. All but a very few, spared and cultivated by the worst of the moguls.

Living in space had changed everything. On Earth, environments and communities had been vast, incomprehensible things. In space, the environment became something you could measure by looking at a gauge. The health of a community was something you could measure by glancing around a cafeteria. Air and water didn't just come from the sky and the wind; they had to be processed, recycled, and monitored. Machines couldn't just be ignored or argued about until they fell apart; you had to maintain them with knowledge and skill, or the monster hostilities of outer space would tear them apart and kill you. Quickly. Vacuum and gravity and radiation didn't care about your beliefs or superstitions; the *boa* of outer space was strict and unforgiving. What mattered was what you did and how well and fast you could do it.

The elements of life support became, in a sense, as valuable as life itself. There was no room for bullshit and waste. If you were going to use oxygen and water, you had to be useful. There was no more room for people who killed, raped, hit, cheated, stole, bullied, or otherwise did harm. The wealthy criminals—those who manipulated the resources for profit—lasted longer than their poorer brethren, but the *boa* caught up with them, too, before long.

In the earliest days, right after the comet, harmful people were "spaced." Authorities dragged them into an air lock and opened the outside door.

The result? Things got shipshape in a hurry.

When the OZ drive came along and opened up star travel, artificial environments gave way to planetary communities again. The reins of justice eased somewhat. Criminals weren't necessarily executed. Room was found for them in out-of-the-way places, and they stayed there. Felons rarely came home.

Unferth was one of those out-of-the-way places. It was an asteroid, hauled into deep space, light-years from anything. The surface was a barren, cratered dead zone. The outer hatches led down into a warren of tunnels, and that was where the prisoners lived their lives. They could open air locks to eject waste, including their dead. But they rarely did. Nothing was provided from outside, so the population was under pressure to follow extreme recycling protocols. The inmates found a use for *everything*.

So it was thought, anyway. News didn't really go in and out much.

"It's an *oubliette*," his father had said, by way of description, when they said their goodbyes. "A place of forgetting."

It was his way of acknowledging that they'd never see each other again.

The professor wasn't a dark lord anymore. He was a sack of clothes, tailored on a budget. A man who'd had all his illusions kicked out of him.

No one can live like that, thought Milo, crying, watching his parents shuffle away. Life in prison could take many forms.

Three days away from Bridger's Planet, the cruiser dropped out of hyperspace at Unferth. A guard escorted Milo to an air lock.

Click! Clack! Boom!

A hissing of pressure and air.

The opposite hatch opened, and Milo found himself peering through into a kind of bare, rusty cube. A stale smell filled the shuttle.

Milo stepped through.

"Bye, kiddo," called the guard. "Mind your cornhole."

The hatch spun shut.

Click! Clack! Boom!

The cruiser warped away, leaving Milo in the rusty prison air lock, waiting.

He waited for five hours.

Finally there was a lot of clanking and the inner hatch scraped open.

A skinny old man greeted him, wearing burlap trousers, sandals, and a set of enormous homemade eyeglasses.

"Heh!" barked the old man. "Got one in the hole. You coming?"

Milo ducked through the hatch and entered the prison.

"Shut it behind you," said the old man, coughing, and shuffled away into . . . dark.

"Hey!" yelled Milo. "Hey, um—" But the old man moved on, out of sight.

The court had warned him not to expect a welcome or any form of processing. His fish and its biocompatible wet-wiring had been stripped from him. He had not been assigned a number, and no record-keeping would follow him into the prison.

So where did he go? What did he do? He would need food and a place to sleep at some point. How did a prisoner procure these things? The courts had made it clear that this would be his problem.

The corridor was not, Milo found as his eyes adjusted, entirely dark. A set of softly glowing squares high on the wall provided enough illumination for him to discern roughly carved rock walls.

Down the corridor he went, feeling his way. About twenty feet along, the lights behind him dimmed into black, and another set came on just ahead.

It made sense, Milo thought. Conservation. There would be no combustible light sources, because they burned oxygen. Probably the lights operated on primitive motion sensors and a phosphorescent glow mix. It made him feel better, for a minute, knowing that the prison population was capable of such sense and subtlety. Maybe he wouldn't encounter raw brutality here, after all.

A hundred yards down, shadows jumped out of the black, knocked him unconscious, stripped him naked, and left him bleeding on the floor.

When he woke up, he reviewed what had happened.

The prison was a resource-poor environment. It made sense that inmates would haunt the corridors near hatches, in case of a drop-off. He'd have to anticipate traps like that.

Atta boy! said his voices. Keep using your head. . . .

Milo got to his feet and soldiered on. At least he didn't have anything else they could take.

The voices didn't comment on that.

An hour later, he encountered people. Real, discernible people, not just shadows and shapes. The hall opened up into a space about as big as an average living room, where several men and a couple of women sat playing a game with handmade cards. In the far corner, one man held a homemade-looking ladder for another man, who appeared to be doing something mechanical to a nest of pipes.

They all wore some form of burlap trousers, at least. Milo felt awfully, awfully naked.

He was hoping that this would be the point where someone would take him under a wing and talk to him and tell him things until he could learn—

A wise man, advised his ancient soul, isn't afraid to ask questions.

"Can someone please help me?" Milo asked, and that's as far as he got before three of the card players—two men and one of the women—jumped up, slammed him to the ground ("Look how *pretty!*"), and took turns with him until he lost consciousness.

Milo woke up with foggy senses and a body that felt bruised and crusty. He was crumpled up on cold, damp stone. He tried to make himself go back to sleep, but someone kicked him and said, "Get up. Clean yourself."

Milo didn't want to be awake. He wanted to retreat inside himself. At the edge of his mind, he felt something like a pit, something dark and gibbering. The pit was something like madness, something he could disappear into.

No, insisted the voices. You're going to remain human. Sit up, open your eyes, and survive the day.

So Milo sat up, feeling like a car wreck. He blinked his eyes clear and found he was sitting in a kind of hollowed-out hole, as if someone had dug a grave in the stone. There was a carpet of sorts, made of burlap and covering half of the tiny floor, and some bowls scattered about. A deck of cards. Some dark sticks that may have been charcoal or crude pencils. Something shiny and knifelike. The hole smelled like sewage.

Directly in front of him, so close that their knees touched, sat a heavy, round man with thick, long hair and a matching beard. His eyes, in the middle of all that hair, were like icy little points. Like Milo, he was naked.

"Clean yourself," the man repeated, thrusting a moldy burlap rag at Milo and pointing to a bowl of murky water.

Milo wiped himself all over. Some of the grit and blood came loose; the rest he smeared around.

Some basic communication was in order, Milo reasoned.

"I'm Milo," he said.

The man pointed to himself, saying, "Thomas." Then he said, "Eat this," and handed Milo a bowl full of something like camel sperm.

He couldn't do it.

"Not now," he said.

"You eat whenever you get a chance," said Thomas.

Milo ate. He tried not to think about what he might be putting in his mouth.

Go along, for now, he thought. Then, later, revenge.

No, said his old soul. Be the ocean, be the pond—

Revenge, Milo repeated, swallowing hard.

Sooner or later, the nightmare sense of it had to go away, right? Sooner or later, Unferth would begin to seem real, and he would become less sensitive to its horror. Right?

No. But Milo learned important things. He sensed that paying attention and learning were the keys.

Milo learned that he had asthma. Between the dark and moldy

damp and the unrelenting fear, he began to feel, at times, as if his own body were suffocating itself. Lovely, he thought, wheezing.

He learned that he "belonged" to Thomas. Thomas branded Milo's shoulder: Thomas 817-GG. This was the number, in the prison's home-made system, that described the location of Thomas's cell. He didn't keep Milo by his side all the time or on a leash, but if Milo wandered too far away, it was pretty likely that someone would return him and collect a reward.

Thomas was a plumber. Sometimes he left for hours or days, taking a bag of homemade tools with him. Everything in Unferth was home-made. There were people whose job it was to make things. There were people whose job it was to grow food, make clothes, make paper, glass, brew alcohol, take messages to people. There was even a sort of school system, where people shared their skills and their stories.

There were no janitors. You had to clean up after yourself or force others to do it. This kept people from being too messy.

When Milo had been Thomas's "girl" for a week or so, he found to his horror that Thomas could loan him out.

Thomas needed a new tool. So he took Milo to spend the night at the home of Gob the Blacksmith.

"You will not like Gob," Thomas told Milo, on the way to Gob's shop.

They had to go through a heavily populated zone of the prison, a place that had been developed for shops and industry, where larger, better-maintained plumbing was available and power was more reli-able. It was essentially a cave the size of a village. Phosphorescent lan-terns hung from mossy cables. Stacked along the walls like Anasazi cliff dwellings were commercial spaces and residential cells. There were rude streets and passageways, packed with shoving, smelly, bad-tempered foot traffic.

Gob was a giant, Milo discovered when they got to the blacksmith shop. Milo couldn't stop looking at him.

He had been born a giant, but then things had been done to him. One whole side of his cranium had been sculpted from an aluminum plate. His arms and shoulders looked as if a muscle bomb had gone off. Then levers and springs and other machinery had been worked into his flesh and bones. When they first arrived in his shop, he was tearing a piece of sheet metal with his bare semi-robotic hands.

"Are you shitting me?" Milo exclaimed.

"He has to be strong," Thomas explained. "He can't use heat, because fire uses air. So he can only pound and tear and cut and squeeze."

Gob began rolling the sheet metal into a tube. As he worked, he cast a red eye on Milo.

"He's pretty," said Gob.

"It's a loan," Thomas said. "You understand? Two nights. One thread cutter."

Gob understood.

To Milo, Thomas said, "You stay here for now," and was gone.

Gob reached across the shop, plucked Milo off his feet, and slapped manacles around his ankles.

"You don't need those," Milo whined. He had no plans to run. Where would he go?

"Be quiet," grumbled Gob. Casually, he reached down with a pair of crude, twisted scissors and snipped off a bit of Milo's left ear. It bounced off his knee and lay on the floor amid iron shavings. Milo's stunned brain could only think how dirty it looked and wonder if the rest of him was that dirty.

His asthma rose up and overwhelmed him.

In his two days at Gob's forge, Milo watched the giant whittle metal as if it were wood. Watched him bleed, sometimes, when his muscles and machinery tore through overtaxed skin.

Sometimes Gob asked him to fetch things, and Milo fetched. Sometimes Gob had other uses for him. Milo tried to force himself to sleep when that happened. Breathe in, breathe out, be someplace else. In this way, he found, he could keep his asthma at bay.

The second morning, a round, heavily scarred man came in and cut thin strips of skin from his legs, for which Gob paid him. Gob ate one of these and offered Milo another. Milo refused.

"Obey," rumbled Gob. "You eat when you can."

Gob threatened him with the scissors. Milo refused.

Roaring, Gob made a noose and hung him from an iron peg high on the wall.

"No!" Milo cried, before his airway collapsed. He kicked and swung, feeling his vertebrae stretch, feeling nothing, and then dark.

Gob laid him down on the floor. Milo's neck and lungs burned. He wanted to vomit, but his throat wouldn't work right.

Gob straightened and glared down at him like an evil god.

When Thomas came back, he wasn't happy with his new tool.

"It won't cut straight," he muttered, turning it over in his hands. "The threads will stick."

Gob made a dark, inquisitive noise. The noise seemed to make Thomas nervous.

"No," he said. "I can make it work."

Turning to Milo, Thomas said, "Let's go. I've got something to show you. Something you'll like." He actually seemed excited and almost happy. Weird. What could he have to show that he would think Milo might like?

But Gob reached out with those great, half-robotic arms and grabbed them each by one shoulder.

"The boy," said Gob. "Let's talk about the boy."

"You can't have him," answered Thomas, though he didn't seem too sure of himself.

Gob shook his head. "Not that," he said. "I tried to hang him."

Thomas's eyes flared, but he also inched toward the door. "Goddammit, Gob! You promised me—"

"It didn't work," said Gob.

"Well, good," said Thomas, through his teeth.

"Think about that," said Gob. "Stop trying to walk out the door. Think about it until you see what that means."

"What it means," Thomas told Milo, when they finally left the blacksmith's shop, "is that we can get rich. As rich as you can get in here, anyway."

Milo had listened to the two big prisoners talk, and all he had gotten out of it was that he, Milo, was going to be "trained."

They shoved their way through the crowded streets. Thomas was in a hurry, still excited about something. He wouldn't say what.

"Trained to do what?" Milo wanted to know.

"Tested first," said Thomas. "*Then* trained, if you pass. You'll see tomorrow. Right now, look! We're here."

Thomas had led them up into the cliff dwellings and stopped before an open doorway on the second level.

"Where's here?" asked Milo.

"Home. A new home."

"How?" Milo asked. "Is it expensive? I don't get it."

Thomas shrugged. "I wanted it," he said.

They stepped inside, and there was the explanation. A naked man lay crumpled against the far wall, neck twisted, head smashed open. The floor was a dead sea of drying blood. Milo could taste the tang of iron on the air. He shook and then threw up.

"I took it," said Thomas.

The room was bigger than their grave hole, Milo noted. Maybe four times as big.

"You decide about dinner," Thomas said, laying a heavy arm around Milo's shoulders. "I can go out and get . . . you know, food . . . or we can . . . you know."

He indicated the dead man.

Milo threw up again.

"We call it 'long pig.' "

And again.

"It's called 'diving,'" Thomas explained.

They were on their way up-tunnel, toward the surface. Toward the test Thomas had hinted at.

"Diving?"

"Do yourself a favor," said Thomas. "Breathe in and out as deep and fast as you can."

"Why?"

"*Do it!*" Thomas shouted.

So Milo began hyperventilating. They turned a corner and started up a steep ramp.

"Stop when you feel faint," advised Thomas.

Milo started feeling faint just as the tunnel opened up into a chamber roughly the size of their new dwelling back in the village.

One whole wall was a window, overlooking a rugged crater. Beside the window, a door, and near the door, an old woman who looked like a wizard. Long white hair and blue eyes. Not just blue irises—both eyes were completely blue. Was she blind?

He stumbled and would have passed out on the floor if the woman hadn't caught him.

"Been hyperventilating, have you?" she asked.

"He told me to," gasped Milo, jerking his head at Thomas.

"Good. I'm Arabeth. As soon as your head clears, we'll go."

Milo's head cleared rapidly. His thoughts and vision came back into focus.

"Does he know . . . ?" Arabeth asked Thomas.

"Not a thing."

"Good. Less likely to panic if he doesn't have time to think about it. Now, boy, listen to me. Look and listen."

"All right," said Milo.

She slapped a big metal knob in the middle of the door. The door, which looked as if it had been hammered together out of old steel buckets, hissed and popped open. Beyond, a rusted air lock.

"We're going to space you, boy," she said. "What you need to do—"

Milo howled, backing away, but Thomas caught him and held him.

"When that outer hatch opens, you'll have about ten seconds to get to the next hatch, about twenty feet that way"—she pointed—"before you go dark."

Thomas hurled him into the air lock. Milo tried to claw his way back, but they were shutting the hatch.

"*Hey!*" he screamed.

Pppppppppssssssssst! Thump! He heard the hatch seal.

He sprayed urine, flinging himself against the hammered metal.

Then—*pssssssst!*—the glowstrips in the air lock went out, and the air went out, and the outer hatch opened, and he saw stars up above and total dark below . . .

At the same time, a violent feeling as if he were blowing up like a balloon . . .

Air jetting up his throat and out through his lips, his chest like a pancake . . .

Cold that burned, a volcano of cold all over . . .

He was in space, naked.

Raw, wild panic—

If you panic, said his old, wise voices, you will die. Quickly—do what the old woman told you.

Milo straightened his mind like an arrow and aimed it at the problem.

He pushed with his toes and caught with his fingers at the hatch—it burned! Everything burned all over, like sticking your tongue on a lamppost in a cold snap.

Something awful was happening to his eyes. They were getting foggy, fast!

The other hatch . . . He looked where he'd been told, and there it was. How far away?

(*Swelling all over, like rising bread. Inside, he fizzed like soda pop . . .*)

Gripping the edges of the hatch, he pulled with his arms and pushed with his legs and shot himself through the dark, toward that light.

His eyes blurred. He was almost blind.

No sense of movement. Nothing.

(Except an agony of swelling, volcanic cold, fizzing—————
————————————)

Unbelievably, he woke up.

How could he still be alive? He wasn't too happy about it, frankly.

First he became aware of pain. As if he'd been sunburned inside and out.

He still couldn't see.

Voices came to him, as if from the bottom of a tin can.

"You probably feel sunburned," said a female voice. The woman with the blue eyes.

"You look like shit," said another voice. Thomas.

"You're not sunburned," said the woman. "There's no star nearby, so you don't have to worry about radiation. Now, what is my name?"

"Arabeth," Milo grunted.

"Good, good. You did exactly the right thing," said the woman. "Got yourself moving in the right direction, and your unconscious ass just sailed right into the open air lock. You're not always going to be so lucky. Best work on staying awake."

What? They wanted him to do this again?

His vision came back, a little at a time. Two vague forms squatted over him.

"Hardly anyone passes the test," the woman told him. "Lucky boy. You're going to be an athlete. For a little while, anyhow, until you die."

They didn't have much in the way of entertainment on Unferth, Thomas explained, back at their tiny home. They had fights, of course, and competitions to see who could swallow the most of such and such a chemical. But diving was the only true spectator sport.

It was basically a race. You put three or four naked people in an air lock and opened the door. They scrambled out, and the object was to be the one who went farthest before turning around and coming back. The winner was the one who went the greatest distance and made it back to the air lock alive.

"Almost every time," said Thomas, while shitting into a bucket, "there's at least one that doesn't come back. They pass out and tumble away, or they start bleeding inside, or their eyes go out on them and they get lost and miss the hatch coming back."

"I didn't know you could put a person out in pure space," said Milo, "without a spacesuit. I thought they'd get killed instantly."

"People are tough," said Thomas, wiping himself with a handful of burlap. "They can take just about anything for a little while."

Prisoners, he explained, liked to place bets on the divers, with whatever they had to offer. Cloth. Labor. Food. Muscle. The divers themselves sometimes made money.

"What made you think I could do it?" Milo asked.

"Gob tried to hang you, and you lived. Your body knows how to hold on to oxygen, and your mind knows how to not panic. That woman, the one with the blue eyes? Arabeth? She's the most famous space diver ever. She got rich enough to quit. Now she gets paid to run the games."

"How rich do I have to get," Milo asked, "before I don't have to do it anymore?"

Thomas laughed.

"You're not going to get rich at all," he said, handing Milo a bowl of protein sludge.

"What do you mean? What do you mean I'm not going to get—"

"You belong to Gob and me. If you win, we get a cut. You get to live."

Milo's eyes stung. He flung his bowl across the room.

"I'm not your fucking slave!" he screamed.

Thomas struck like a snake. His fists cracked Milo's head. In an instant, his full weight squatted on Milo's chest.

"Yes, you are," said Thomas. "Of course you are."

Just to make his point, Thomas stayed there for at least twenty minutes. Long enough for Milo to have an asthma attack and pass out.

When he awoke the following morning, Milo's first thought was that Thomas had stayed on top of him all night long, had fallen asleep, and was still there. He opened his eyes and tried to sit up but couldn't.

"Thomas," he wheezed. "You've got to let me up, let me breathe—"

But Thomas was behind him.

"Shut up," he said, and cuffed Milo's ear.

A great Halloween mask of a head, half metal, leaned over and peered down at him.

Gob.

And another face. A fat face, bald, with burn grafts and a metal skull patch, like Gob's.

"This is Seagram," rasped Gob. "He's here to improve our investment."

"Good morning, Milo," said Seagram. "Do you know what this is?"

He held out something like a metal oyster, with a red ball in the middle of it and a tail made of braided copper wire.

Milo didn't answer.

Seagram started to explain something, but Gob interrupted.

"It's a bionic eye," he said. "Give you a few more seconds of vision in space. Give you an edge."

"Now, wait—" Milo gasped.

"We should at least get him drunk," rumbled Thomas.

"Just get it done," said Gob.

Oh, God! No way—

It happened fast. Someone pried his right eyelid wide. Someone dumped home-brewed alcohol all over his face, and everything became a stinging blur.

Something like a fishhook stabbed his eye, yanked, and Milo felt his eyeball pop free.

He screamed, and Thomas pushed his jaw shut.

A knife scraped out his empty socket, way up inside his head.

Milo tried to make himself pass out, but no dice. He felt every slice and stab and insult as they worked wires into his brain. Lights flashed and fires raged and he heard a French horn, far away. Then they screwed the eye itself, the metal oyster, into his socket.

A red blur, a high-pitched whining, and there was Seagram's fat, burned face in front of him. Reddish, but in good focus.

"Zoom in," said Seagram.

The eye seemed to know what to do. Milo simply tried to look closer at the guy, and the image magnified. Blurred, focused.

Blurred again.

"Close your good eye when you do that," said Gob.

"We done?" asked Seagram.

"We done," answered Gob, releasing Milo.

Seagram stood over them, rubbing his jaw.

"He looks like he might win a few," he said. "Instead of straight payment, can we talk shares?"

"No," said Gob. "Straight barter."

Barter?

"After the dive tomorrow," Thomas told Milo, helping him sit up, "you're going home with Seagram for a week. And he better tell me you were nice to him."

Milo blinked. His new eye whizzed, zooming in on the floor.

Dive tomorrow?

He had tried, since his imprisonment, not to think about his other life, before.

He was completely unsuccessful. No matter how hard he tried to shape his intellect, to shut useless thoughts and memories away, they swam at him in dreams and walked his mind like ghosts when he was awake.

Some of it was just daydreams, thoughts of young friends and summer days on the sculpted college yards. Books. Dinner with his parents. This or that girl. Music that drifted in his mental ear as clearly as the real thing.

Mostly he missed his mother, but he found himself crying, unexpectedly, for his father. At the end of things, in the courts, the old dark lord had been unmade, revealed for the first time as a small man like any other, with a heart that could break. More than anything, Milo wanted to know this new father.

At first, Milo fought against such thoughts. They were an impediment to him, in this dark arena. Especially thoughts of Ally, which made him angry and led him into self-pity like a bottomless cave. Self-pity made him weak and small; he could feel it. Remembering Ally was something he could not afford.

He could afford only that which aided his survival. Memories and wishes were deadly illusions.

The old voices agreed that his memories were dangerous. But, they said, memories are not like other illusions. Memories shape our humanity.

Milo eventually came to agree with this. He would not let Unferth reduce him. He would not be an animal, with nothing but animal thoughts.

The night after he received his mechanical eye, everything was so quiet and calm that Milo even ventured to speak to Thomas the way one human speaks to another.

"Thomas? What was your life like before you came here?"

Thomas had been busy repairing some kind of crude tool. He did not stop.

"There is no before," he said.

Milo opened his mouth to press the issue, but Thomas turned his head and looked at him. It was a look of total calm and honesty, and it said that if Milo made another peep, he would kill him.

So Milo was silent and watched a mind movie of an Easter morning some years ago, a soft pink blur in his head.

Arabeth cradled Milo's head in her hands and tilted it back and forth, scrutinizing Seagram's work.

"Looks legal enough," she told Thomas and Gob. "Who's to say it ain't?"

They were meeting in the same room as before, where they'd

thrown Milo into the air lock. Except it was crowded in there this time.

Three other prisoners for the air lock.

An old man, built like a whip, with springs wired into his legs.

A younger man with one arm gone, covered in hair like a troll.

A woman who could have been a man, except that she was naked, so you could tell. She had blue eyes like Arabeth's.

Were the bionics all Seagram's work? What did the blue eyes do, and the springs?

Made them faster, obviously. Made them see better, go farther, last longer.

Milo clenched and unclenched his fists. He wanted this over with, one way or another.

"You better win," said Gob, squeezing his elbow, "or I will eat your face."

"If you don't win," said Thomas, "better just stay out there."

Milo was the only slave among the divers. The only one with owners on hand to threaten him. The others, it seemed, were volunteers. Lucky. Stupid?

Over by the window stood five men with what looked like cameras.

"Sportswriters," said the man-woman, stepping up beside Milo. "Just like back in the world."

"I thought so," said Milo.

"They're the ones who'll flash around pictures of your dead face after I check you on the rocks."

"That's great," said Milo.

Arabeth sprayed the divers down with . . . what? Hot water?

"Glow," said the trollish diver, seeing the puzzled look on Milo's face. "It'll make you visible out there, so people can come see your body floating."

"Good luck," Milo told him.

The troll shook his head, and then they all climbed through the hatch.

No preliminaries, no countdown.

Just *pppppppppssssssssssssssst! Thump!* And the four of them were in space.

Milo knew he had to be aggressive. He had to be faster than—

He wasn't.

Space grabbed at him and vacuumed him in all directions at once.

Hands and feet slammed him back and down. He felt his skin tear down one side of his cheek. Raw tissue started bubbling out of the wound.

They looked like ghosts, leaping through space, flying just above the cratered surface. Glowing nakedness in pure dark.

Milo did the arrow thing, just like before. Off to one side, as he flew into the void, he saw the ready-room window, with the reporters staring out through their lenses.

It didn't take Milo long to realize his mistake.

He had launched himself at the opposite air lock, with its light. But this race was different. He had forgotten. He was supposed to dig in and go back the way he'd come. Could he still do that? Did he have enough consciousness left?

He saw the troll reach down and drag his fingers along the surface, slowing, and bringing his feet to bear against uneven rock. Pushing off like a swimmer, the troll reversed course back to the air lock. Seconds later, Milo could tell he was unconscious. Had he aimed well? Hard to tell.

Milo looked around for some way to stop himself, to start back. But he had aimed too high; rocks and crevasses slipped by just out of reach.

Well, shit.

(*Cold like a million tiny ripsaws . . . fizzing and boiling . . . swelling like dough . . .*)

The last thing he knew before his mind emptied was the old man shoving him aside, off course.

Milo wondered who had won, and then————*Boop.* Zero. Dark.

———

He woke up.

Had they come and gotten him?

No. He was still out there. Floating across the crater. Gravity must have slowed him, finally. He could reach down and stop himself if he wished. So he did. He turned and looked back the way he'd come.

Not too far away, he saw the reporters in the window.

Also not far away, he saw his three competitors, floating at various speeds back toward the open air lock. The first, the man-woman, would reach it within seconds. Then the old man. The troll was off course. He was going to float off and die of exposure, Milo saw.

Hurry, advised his voices.

His hands, pawing at the ground, were like balloons and sausages, and he bubbled inside, like before. But his head was clearing. Why? How?

No time.

Milo pushed, launching himself through space, and almost instantly he was back among the other divers—*too fast!*

He slowed.

What the fuck? You can't slow down in space!

But he did.

What is happening? he asked himself, asked his old-soul self, but the wise ones were just as surprised as he was.

Later, the entire viewing audience of Unferth would be surprised. And impressed. And wild to know more.

Wherever digital screens could be viewed or wherever still pictures could be pasted on stone walls, the story of Milo's first competitive space dive was all over Unferth.

The videos and pictures showed Milo zooming out of nowhere, unexplainably awake and functioning, and then slowing down.

They showed him reaching out with swollen, frozen hands, stopping the old man and the man-woman. Leaving them behind, slowly turning, softly glowing.

The pictures showed Milo sidestepping—still conscious, mind you!—across five yards of airless space and tugging the troll back with him. Pulling himself into the air lock—clinching the win!—and then pulling all of his rivals in behind him. Then the air lock slammed closed, and that was the end of the prison news, which looped right back to the beginning.

"Who and what is Milo Hay?" inmates were asking, all over Unferth.

"Who is he?" asked the groups and crowds and individual cons who started crowding the passages outside Thomas's cliff dwelling. "*Where* is he?"

"He's at the fucking hospital!" yelled Thomas, who didn't like getting his picture taken, and threw rocks at them. "Where would *you* be if you spent a whole minute dicking around in outer space in your birthday suit?"

Milo was not at the hospital.

The other divers went straight there, of course, as always, with varying degrees of damage. They survived, with the exception of the old man, who tried to hold his breath, when he should have known better, and died of a shredded lung.

Milo, to everyone's astonishment, had staggered out of the air lock, blinked a few bloody tears out of his remaining natural eye, and looked around for his owners.

Gob and Thomas stood shaking their heads. They acted as if they wanted to slap Milo's back but thought he might be fragile.

"I don't know what I just saw," said Thomas.

Arabeth said nothing. She herded the sportswriters out of the room and followed them down the hall.

"I think I've earned a share," Milo had the nerve to tell Gob.

"You got a date with Seagram, is all," said Gob.

———

So that's where Milo was.

Seagram's place was a laboratory and a studio and a shop. It was like hanging out in a museum. Over here, racks of sheet-metal plates. Over there, lenses and microscopes and actual computers. Seagram even had a handmade fish that followed him around, hovering over his shoulder. No one else in Unferth had a fish, not that Milo had seen.

Seagram served something like wine in tin cups and cooked something like real food. It looked like chicken and tasted like pork.

"What is this?" Milo asked. "It's like real meat."

"You know what it is," answered Seagram.

Yeah. Milo knew. There was only one kind of animal in Unferth.

He was hungry. Screw it. He ate.

After dinner, Milo was grudgingly pleased to discover that Seagram possessed an actual mattress (in Unferth, just like everywhere else, the money was in resources and technology). He was also relieved when Seagram turned out to be gentle, even kind. That was a first since his arrival.

Still. All that lumpy, burned skin . . .

It's just flesh and bones, said his old soul. Let it go.

"You're a telepath," said Seagram, after.

They lay on Seagram's mattress, side by side, watching shadows on the stone ceiling.

"Telepath?" asked Milo.

"Telekinetic, too, obviously. I suspected it when I wired your eye. Psychic brains are folded differently. Have you always been able to do . . . what you did?"

"When I was little," Milo said, "I could float things. But then I got in some trouble, and—"

"They stuck a mole on you," finished Seagram. "They'd have done the same thing before they sent you here, too, if they'd thought you had the talent. You might have gone into remission with it, but it's back. Big-time. My wild guess is that your brain got desperate and gave your talents a jumpstart. That happens; people get in an accident or bump their heads or have an intense emotional experience, and—*whammo!*—they wake up able to do and see things they couldn't before. Whether you meant to or not, you controlled your circulation to slow your oxygen consumption. Maybe even propelled yourself through space. The video doesn't lie."

Seagram rolled onto his side and stroked Milo's shoulder. Milo recoiled.

Seagram backed off. "You don't have to, if you don't want to," he said.

Milo glared at Seagram, his red eye zooming in and out.

"I *don't* want to!" he shouted. "Why didn't you tell me that before?"

Seagram looked hurt.

"I'm sorry," said Milo. "I'm not . . . I don't like men that way."

Seagram rolled out of bed and wrapped a robe around his fat self.

"It's okay," he said, busying himself at one of his benches. "I didn't, either, before. But you will eventually, probably. Most do."

"Well, not me."

"That's fine, Milo. Go to sleep."

It was the first time in Unferth he'd been called by his name.

The next day, Seagram gave him clothes to wear. Just a simple burlap shirt with no sleeves and short pants with a length of twine for a belt.

"People are looking for you everywhere," he said, after a breakfast of cold leftovers.

"If I talked to them," said Milo, "what would I say?"

"I wouldn't tell them the truth. It'll scare them. Just go back to Thomas and let him figure out how to keep them away from the door."

Milo's brow furrowed. "Go back now? I thought I was staying here for a week," he said. "Is it because I don't—"

"No, no. I'll give Thomas a good report on you; don't worry. I just don't feel well. It happens. I get headaches."

Milo didn't want to go back to Thomas. His rectum tightened at the thought.

"Listen," he said. "Let me try something."

"Try what?" Seagram's eyes narrowed.

"Trust me."

Seagram said, "Boy, if you're thinking of stabbing me, you should know: It's damn hard to kill a fat man—" But then he stopped talking. Some thought or feeling seemed to catch up with him, and he said, "All right. What?"

"Close your eyes."

Seagram closed his eyes, and Milo walked around the table, stepped up behind him, and put both hands on Seagram's great, fat head.

If he could make himself space-proof by accident, maybe he could make Seagram feel better. How? He didn't know. He closed his own eyes.

A "nothing" feeling, for a moment, and then something like holding an ocean between his hands. Something warm and full, with electric tides.

Seagram's *self.*

It was a vast thing, a dreaming strangeness, a *boa* very much like his own, but different. Older. Deep with memories.

Pain.

The longer Milo held Seagram, this other self, in his hands and his mind, the more it became like a weight. Here was a soul that had been wronged and hurt until it was in danger of becoming a mere creature.

Milo heard himself gasp aloud under it. Like his own pain, he sensed, it was something you could get lost in. He remembered that he had done this for a reason, taken hold of Seagram for a reason. He felt himself peeling back shadow and distractions and illusions, until it seemed to him that he found something that was simple and human.

A door. A door in the dark sea bottom, where something of value had been forgotten and locked away.

Milo opened the door and light spilled out. He felt it in his hands, saw it inside his own mind.

Seagram jerked. He said, "Jesus on a stick!"

It was just chemicals, Milo knew. He had moved neurochemicals around in Seagram's head. But neurochemicals, like memories, made the man.

Yes, Milo! cheered his old soul.

He let go of Seagram's head.

Seagram sat with his mouth agape.

"Your headache is gone?" asked Milo.

Seagram leaped up, with impressive energy for a fat man. "What did you *do?*"

"I think I made your brain work better."

Seagram stared around his shop as if it was all new to him.

Something new in his eyes. Something you didn't see in Unferth. Milo couldn't give it a name yet.

"My God," he breathed. "Thank you."

"So, can I stay?" asked Milo. When it came to avoiding Thomas, he was very goal-oriented.

"You can," said Seagram. "But I think you shouldn't. You shouldn't hide or run from something."

"He can hurt me. He can kill me."

Seagram shook his head, nearly crying with happiness.

He said, "Not if you do to him what you just did to me."

Milo couldn't imagine trying that. He spat on the floor. But, whatever. If Seagram wanted him to go, he'd go.

He nodded goodbye and set out through the dark stone labyrinth.

As he went, he felt around in his own brain. Navigated his own black ocean. Groped until he found his own hidden door. Broke it open . . . wider and wider and wider . . .

Seagram lived on Level Two, many corridors and four villages away from the dwelling Milo shared with Thomas. Milo discovered that if he gave his head a little internal tap, he could sniff out the way he'd come. He actually made it back to the edge of his home city before other prisoners glimpsed his face, recognized him from video, and started following him. They grabbed at him, shouting questions.

"What the hell did you *do*?" they asked. "Are you magic?"

"I don't know," he answered. "I passed out, and then I woke up."

"Lying-ass punk! What do you know you ain't telling?"

"Nothing," he answered.

Someone grabbed his arm.

Let go of me, he thought.

And they did, for just a second, as if they'd gotten a shock or felt something slimy. But in a moment their hands were back, gripping, twisting his clothes.

Let *go*! he thought, and bolted for Thomas's house.

He came tripping across the threshold, out of breath, and there was Thomas on the floor with some work he'd brought home with him: pipes and elbows and wrenches and things. Milo went down in a heap against the far wall as the crowd behind him blocked the door, made it dark.

Thomas roared to his feet, a pipe in each hand.

Smack! A broken jaw. A howling intruder.

The crowd dissolved.

Thomas turned to Milo. His eyes burned.

"You're back early," he said, through his teeth. "I told you, you better make him happy, or—"

"He is happy," Milo said, sitting up. "Listen—"

But Thomas wasn't listening. The crowd had pissed him off.

"Seagram give you these?" he snarled, tugging at Milo's clothes. He bunched his fist to tear the shirt off, and Milo grabbed his wrist.

Thomas slapped him.

"You lost your mind, boy?"

Milo didn't let go.

He took one hell of a beating, but he gripped Thomas's arm with everything he had. Something muscular coiled in his mind and extended to his hands. He climbed channels of light and bone, until at last he had Thomas's self—a smaller ocean than Seagram's—in hand.

And he shouldered the pain and shrugged it away until he found the buried door, and the pain came flooding out.

He opened his eyes to see Thomas vomiting in the corner.

Milo fetched him water. Helped him drink. Cleaned up as best he could.

At last, Thomas was quiet. And he sat in the middle of the floor and lifted his shaggy head and looked straight at Milo, and just said, "Yes."

Gob was much more difficult.

Thomas had to tackle him, or try to, anyhow. He distracted him long enough for Milo to daze him with a lead pipe, which distracted him long enough for Thomas to knock him out properly with a *larger* lead pipe. When Gob was asleep, Milo took his head in his hands and opened his door.

It was a small house. Its innermost room didn't contain a lot of light. Gob wasn't going to be anybody's self-renewal poster child.

He also didn't vomit and shit himself when he woke up. He just said, "Better," and started to cry.

Freedom! Kind of.

Milo finally got his own room, or cell. With Thomas, Seagram, and Gob, he showed up in a doorway belonging to a sad, tall man wearing nothing but a burlap turban.

"Would you like to be happy?" Milo asked him. "Would you like to have something to live for?"

"Say yes," Thomas softly advised.

"I'll break his arm," offered Gob, but Milo stopped him with the lightest of gestures.

"Yes," said the man. And Milo grasped the man's head and opened his neurochemical door.

"Go out and walk around and see how good everything is," Thomas advised. "Milo needs your cell."

So the man gladly left and did as Thomas said.

Later, eating dinner out of the turban man's bowls, Milo, Thomas, Gob, and Seagram had a very simple but important talk.

"What is it?" asked Thomas, "this thing you can do?"

"Something natural," said Milo. "Something the brain does, a talent some people have."

"What's next?" asked Seagram.

"I don't know," said Milo.

Seagram cleared his throat and spoke with quiet humility, looking into his bowl.

"I think I might have an idea," he said. And he told them his idea.

Seagram thought they should "cure" the whole prison.

"How wonderful it would be," he said, "if, instead of living like animals, we could have a civilization in here. A real one, where people work together and take care of one another. Where they do things not because they're being beaten and killed but because they enjoy their lives. People have to have something to live for besides just staying alive; that's what animals do. We need to *evolve*."

"So Milo will go out," said Gob, "and evolve everybody?"

"I think it should be their choice," answered Seagram. "When they see how it's made things better for us, they might trust him. But it's going to take more than that. We'll need to start teaching and learning from one another, or the brain-chemical thing, I'll bet, will just wear off. Once they—*we*—have a new vision of what being alive is, we'll behave differently."

They sat silently. Meditating.

"We should get everyone to come to a meeting," said Thomas. "One village at a time, starting here."

"Yes," said Milo, even though his very first thought was: Fuck no, they'll just eat us.

They did not get eaten.

But they weren't convincing, either.

Getting inmates to attend a gathering was pretty easy. Most of them were bored, so anything different was an automatic draw. But that wasn't the same as being open to ideas.

They sat attentively through a brief talk by Thomas and Seagram. They even applauded testimonials from Gob and the naked turban man. But that didn't mean they'd learned anything.

"We live the way we live," said a man with a 100 percent–tattooed body, "because it works for us. The strong eat the weak. It's natural."

Murmuring. The crowd liked that.

"Yeah," said Seagram. "But is that really working for you? Are you happy?"

"Is your mother a whore?" asked the tattooed man.

Laughter.

"Let me show you," said Milo, advancing toward the man. "Maybe if you all saw—"

A small rock bounced off his shoulder.

"Ow!" he yelped. "Seriously?"

The assembled convicts moved in a single wave. They didn't know what they wanted to do, but they felt threatened and wanted to do *something*.

"Let's go," said Milo, turning to his confederates. "Let's go *now*."

They might not have made it, except for Gob. The giant lifted people out of the way, and Thomas followed, throwing punches. Seagram waddled along, concentrating on protecting his own fat head. And Milo came last, every now and then shouting, *"Off!"* and people would back off long enough for them to get past.

They left the city and fled up corridors, working their way toward the surface. Some of the crowd lost interest; others kept following and throwing things.

"They want *me*," Milo huffed. "Let them follow me. You guys take off down this next—here! Go that way! We'll meet at Seagram's tonight!"

"No!" yelled Thomas. "We'll stay together and think—"

"Gob," said Milo.

Gob grabbed Thomas and ran off the way Milo pointed, with Seagram following.

Milo turned left into the space divers' ready room and threw himself bodily at the controls. The hatch opened. He took a minute, hyperventilating, soaking his body with oxygen, until he heard footsteps and shouting in the ready room itself.

Then he stepped into the air lock, shouted his lungs empty, and told the door to open.

Scraaaaaaape . . . pssssssssssssssssssssssssssst!

The remaining pressurized air shot Milo into space, across the rocky surface.

And he swelled somewhat. And became cold and numb. Became fizzy and full and uncomfortable, as if his whole body wanted to sneeze but couldn't.

But he slowed it all down, all his flowing and exchanging and burning. Slowed it down until he felt sleepy but not faint.

Then he got his feet under him in the light surface gravity and walked back to the hatch and the window and gazed calmly in at the mob, crushing and shrieking on the opposite side.

He tried to understand them. He tried to love them.

Good, said his old self.

He closed his eyes and meditated for a few seconds. Then he turned and loped away, out of their sight, across the broad, stony landscape that was almost totally dark, except as it was lit, just faintly, by the slowly turning firestorm of the stars.

He ran for a mile or more before choosing a hatch and imagining that it opened.

It opened.

When he reached Seagram's later that night, his friends were waiting for him. Thomas looked a bit sulky.

And there were others. Milo recognized faces from the mob that had chased him, the mob that had seen him stroll away into space. There were ten of them, maybe. It was a start.

"You obviously know something we don't," said the man with the 100 percent–tattooed body.

Six months passed and found Milo living in a protein garden.

It was like a garden anywhere else in the galaxy, on a planet or in a greenhouse up in orbit. There were growing things, and not just slime. They had found ways to grind stone and waste into soil. They had engineered artificial seeds and built banks of blue-light generators.

Most people were smart, if you gave them time and peace of mind.

If you gave them a world where people weren't terrified all the time, or angry.

The garden didn't have a sky. It had stone. It didn't have fresh smells and breezes. It had mildew and damp, the breath of caves and people. Milo and his first disciples tended the garden.

Everyone had jobs, and this was theirs. Milo planted and harvested. Gob maintained the machinery. Seagram engineered things. Thomas sprayed things and watered things and made soil out of stone and shit and dead inmates.

And there were others, building schools. Others, making drawings and paintings and nice things to put here and there and make the walls look nice, because if it didn't look like a prison, then maybe it wasn't a prison, really.

Yes, said Milo's old voices, which were getting more and more smug by the day.

When they came to him for teaching, they came to the garden and sat in a great circle and touched hands all around. And Milo would start it off, a wave of images and sensory suggestions, and the wave would pass through them all until they opened their eyes and found themselves on warm green grass under a blue sky with white clouds. And flowers and birds all around. For a while.

That was the teaching: this imaginary garden that they could take away with them and remember and dream about.

Sometimes he went out and walked among them. They always gaped when they saw him in the corridors and the cities, as if he were something that belonged in the afterlife, or at least in hydroponics. They didn't mob him as he passed. They just touched his linen suit (they were making better clothes now) and felt blessed if he turned his red robot eye on them, this boy who had made them men and women.

He was always humble, at least on the outside. He took time to stop and talk, to tell jokes and be human. At first, he couldn't stop thinking what a bunch of idiot scum they were and how he wished to God that some beautiful young women would commit crimes and get sent here to be his holy concubines. But he was getting better and kinder all the time, just like the rest of them. And he stopped thinking of them as low and dirty and dumb, especially when he saw the builders and designers and artists they became.

We're going to make it this time, he thought he heard his ancient soul say.

Milo didn't know quite what that meant, except for a deep sense that everything was perfect. That something wonderful was being achieved, just by letting things be the way they were supposed to be.

"Let it be," he told his disciples and all his people.

"Let it be what?" they asked.

"Let it be perfect."

"Oh," they all said. "Okay."

Sometimes he went to the space-diving air lock and let himself out. His favorite thing was to take off his clothes and tie a three-hundred-foot length of rope to a davit inside the air lock, and, instead of propelling himself across the surface, he would leap out into space with the rope fastened around his ankle and drift there for a time, his own self seeming to vanish into the starfield.

Soon, he was going out to the air lock every day. When he wasn't inside cultivating the gardens or out being worshipped, he was floating in space, the most incomprehensibly happy life-form in the universe.

He was out there floating like that the day he saw the approaching cruiser.

He zoomed in with his mechanical eye, watching the ship fire thrusters, slowing down.

It had been a while. He wondered what sort of criminal they were dropping off. Whoever they were, they were in for a nice surprise. He gave his rope a tug, drifted back to the hatch, and made his holy way back to the garden. Soon enough, they'd come to tell him about the newcomer.

The door to the garden opened up, and two uniformed officials stepped in.

He saw them speak with Thomas and saw Thomas point down the rows of radishes, lettuce, and corn. Saw them walk in his direction, so he met them halfway, among the pumpkins.

A man and a woman, wearing court badges from Bridger's Planet.

"Are you Milo Hay?" asked the man.

"I am," he said.

How strange to hear his common name. For months now they'd been calling him *"The* Milo."

The woman beamed at him and said, "We're here to take you home."

They had a hard time explaining to him that Ally Shepard had finally done enough weird and not very nice things to convince her family to send her to the hospital. There, they decided that she was a victim of a rare dissociative disorder that made it nearly impossible for her to distinguish between right and wrong. The thing that had finally gotten her family's attention was that she gathered up a group of children from the park and took them on a "field trip" to a construction site, where one of the children was slightly bulldozed, escaping with bruises.

Under observation, she admitted that Milo Hay had not raped her one bit and that she was so sorry he was in prison now and probably dead, and when could she go home?

None of this could be explained to Milo while he was leaping over garden tables, trying to get away. He might have made it, possibly, but they threw stun whips around his head and dragged his unconscious, holy self back out of the garden.

Stun whips did it for his disciples, too. Even Gob.

Milo woke up, somewhat, out in the corridor and was fully awake by the time they reached the ready room. He screamed, crying and grabbing at things, scraping his hands bloody, before they were finally able to stuff him through the hatch and aboard their ship. With a *thunk!* and a *hiiiiiiiiiiiiiiiisssssssssssss!* and a flare of mighty engines, they carried him across hyperspace, home.

His parents were no big help.

They understood that their son had been the victim of a terrible injustice, but now that he was home, he might as well give it all to the universe and its crazy God and let it go.

"I call it 'Random Value Shift,'" his father explained. "It's how a professor of zoology with five PhDs gets eaten by a tiger in the jungle. Doesn't matter who you are; things will happen to you. It's one of the primary tenets of divine allegory."

Milo didn't give a shit. Nobody cares less about theology than a god.

His parents didn't understand why their brilliant, once-ambitious son was now content to waste away in front of the living-room window, talking to himself. Or why he got up at night to go stand in the backyard, naked.

He barely spoke. He barely breathed. The only time they were 100 percent sure he hadn't died was when they took him to the hospital and he screamed while they removed his holy eye.

His old soul was in shock. All the memories of all his past lives couldn't begin to understand what it must be like to be torn away from Unferth and his disciples and brought back to this small, silly place where he was a kid too young, still, for a driver's license.

Milo, said his ancient soul, his old self: Understand it and accept it. This is small behavior. Overcome it.

Milo ignored the old voices. He tried to shut them up in their own little room, at the bottom of his mental sea, but none of that happy brain magic was working since they'd hit him with the stun whips.

It was like being amputated from himself.

After a year, he made an effort.

He tried until he was thirty years old. For fourteen years, he dragged himself through the trivia and the dullness of normal, everyday life. It was like trying to run a marathon race without legs.

He finished college with a C average.

He found that if he drank, he could be social, in a way. Could stand to sit in a room with people and listen to them babble. So he drank.

He got a job going to people's houses and fixing things. Complicated electrical or nuclear devices. The work occupied him just enough to keep him awake, and it was not necessary that he talk to anyone very much.

At home in the evenings, he watched shows on his fish or on the wall unit until they put him to sleep. Sometimes he would buy marijuana. These things became a respirator for his soul.

Quite often, he found himself remembering a certain night in Unferth when he struggled with his memories of home.

To have nice, useless, distracting memories, or not to have them? He faced the same problem now. He reminded himself to be distracted, and imperfect, and human.

He was supposed to accomplish something, wasn't he? Let alone saving the minds and souls of prisoners. What had happened to Lord Byron, the poet he was going to be? Or at least the professor he might have been?

He sprawled in a dull gray armchair. Here was what Napoleon might have been, if the army hadn't worked out for him.

Milo put his hands on his head and tried to move neurochemicals around, but it was like searching an empty shoe box.

One day when Milo was thirty, Ally Shepard came to see him.

Ally was well. She was an associate professor of dramatic literature. One tiny phase-wave tweak to her cerebrum had put an end to being crazy and doing odd, inappropriate things.

She was happy, except for one thing. It agonized her, what had happened, long ago with Milo.

She knocked at his apartment door. This wouldn't have worked, normally. Milo didn't answer his door or his fish. But he came walking up the stairs just then, carrying a bag of groceries, including a twenty-ounce clamshell package of dope. He stopped on the top step when he saw her there.

"Ally," he said.

(Milo, whispered his sleepy, long-ignored ancient self. Do this right. . . .)

"Milo. You look good."

And damned if he didn't rise to the occasion. Maybe because it wasn't a small, tedious thing. It was a big thing.

He invited her in, and made dinner for them both, and got them both high. And when she lost her cool and dissolved in tears, trying to apologize and make up for all that trauma with mere words, he held her and let her apologize.

"Ally," he said, "you don't need to worry about that. You were sick. And you made it right. And besides, I enjoyed it, to say the least."

Ally went home much improved.

The next day, also much improved, Milo bought a ticket to an orbital resort, where he ate lunch from a vending machine and then managed to find an air lock on a mechanical floor, with no one watching and no one likely to come by soon.

It was no particular trouble for him to get around the codes and make the switches work. He opened the hatch and, wearing gym shoes, slacks, and a light jacket, stepped through into the lock.

No, Milo, protested his very sad soul. It was the voice of a soul that had been on its way to a birthday party with dancing and free beer but was hit by a train before it got there.

Without preamble, he threw the emergency toggle inside the air lock and let the instant decompression blast him into space.

It was painful, since there was sunlight and radiation this time. Drifting away, between space and a twilight ocean, he roasted on one side and froze on the other. Within, he popped and fizzed and went dark.

For his last thought, he tried to think something holy, but a dying brain is a slippery thing.

I wonder, he thought, if the brothers of the Damocles Society still have that goddamn goose.

CHAPTER 15

Lifting Elephants, Juggling Water

Milo woke up on the sand beside a slow clear river.

The sun in the white sky was a small, fierce, fossil sun. The sun of bleach and bones.

His memories of eight thousand years came back, as usual. He welcomed them and his sense of his larger self, as usual.

What was unusual was the feeling of gray melancholy in his stomach and soul. This, he knew, was left over from his suicide. It took a degree of emptiness to end your own life, and that emptiness didn't wear away between worlds.

"Take your time," someone said.

A pale man, thin and angular, with softly blazing eyes, crouched in the sand at Milo's feet. Long black hair wrapped him like a shroud, or maybe like wings.

Death. One of them, anyway. Not Suzie.

"Where am I?" Milo asked.

Death said, "You're right where you're supposed to be," and vanished in a burst of dust and hot wind.

Asshole.

A heavy, oceanic sadness filled Milo.

Suzie. He sat paralyzed for a while, remembering.

Then he shook himself and did his best to come alive. He had forced himself out of bed on half a million Monday mornings and knew how to do this.

Okay. To begin with, once again, where was he?

The afterlife, like time, was infinite, but he had a definite sense of having been dumped beyond the fringes. Like, if he usually woke up in Boston, this time he found himself on the moon.

At least he was dressed for it. He found himself wearing the robes of a desert traveler.

Milo had been a Bedouin nomad in a former life and knew it was foolish to travel in the heat of the day. So he pulled his robes over his head to make a kind of tent and closed his eyes awhile.

He woke up shivering under a star-washed sky and hiked along the river in the night.

Just after dawn, when the heat had begun to rise, he came upon the river's source: a tiny oasis with green weeds and a single date tree. Beyond this splatter of life, the desert stretched like a windblown tortilla.

Would it be best to backtrack, Milo wondered, hoping the water led to bigger water and maybe to people? Maybe he could just stay here and become the official Water-Hole Hermit.

As he stood there, considering, someone called, "Halloooooo!"

He beheld a rider on horseback, leading a camel, atop a nearby ridge.

Milo waved. The rider waved back and nudged his horse downhill.

He was, Milo observed as he approached, a man with a proud beard and an air of cheerful assurance.

"Do we find you in need of assistance?" this person asked Milo.

"A state of indecision," answered Milo, "at least."

"You'll make slow headway on foot," the bearded man predicted. "I offer you my companionship and the loan of a camel."

Milo bowed his head and said, "Thanks." He held out his hand and said, "Milo."

The traveler shook the hand and said, "Akram."

Akram began unloading camping equipment from the camel. Milo assisted by leading the horse to drink.

The tent Akram pitched bore a logo, advertising, in silver letters, AKRAM THE REMARKABLE.

"Remarkable what?" Milo asked. Astronomer? Dogcatcher? Beard grower?

"Juggler," Akram explained. He tossed some tent stakes into the air, whirled them around in a lazy circle, then stomped them into place.

"Remarkable?" asked Milo. "Not 'Great'? Not 'Astonishing'?"

Akram lowered his eyes and said, "Modesty intercedes."

The juggler was kind enough to share his tent, and the two of them slept through the heat of the day. Milo dreamed about Suzie.

Her voice, in the dark. Far away.

"Milo!" she called faintly. Was this a sign? Was she still in the world, in the afterlife? At twilight, Akram shook him awake.

"Milo!"

"Suzie?" he croaked.

"Well, no."

There followed an hour of pulling down tents, loading camels, and brewing fresh coffee over a fire, after which Milo climbed aboard Akram's camel.

The beast tried to bite him. Succeeded a little.

Milo shrugged. How would he feel if a stranger climbed on him? They would get to know each other, and their rapport would improve.

Later, the camel kept wandering off course and wouldn't listen when Milo shouted and flicked the reins. Akram would have to trot after him and tow him back. Minutes later, off course again.

Each time he redirected the animal, Akram murmured, *"As-salāmu alaykum."*

"'*As-salāmu alaykum*' means 'God is good,' right?" Milo asked.

"It does."

"Then why, when this excellent camel needs correcting, over and over—"

"It's better than cursing. Curses darken the soul. I am sorry he's so troublesome."

Milo recalled from his own life as a Bedouin how to be virtuous and grateful.

"Satan is a fine animal," he assured Akram. "Merely headstrong. Is he young?"

"Yes, he is."

"Then I'm sure he will mellow and provide many good years of service."

"If you appreciate him so," said Akram, "he is yours. I gladly make you this gift."

Aw, sonofabitch, no!

But refusing a gift was rude.

"*As-salāmu alaykum,*" said Milo, bowing his head.

Akram's horse tossed its head proudly, almost dancing across the sand.

"That sure is a nice horse," said Milo.

Akram didn't answer.

It was a long, starry night.

Followed by a hot day with hot winds, spent dozing in the tent. Followed by another starry night. Then, an hour after dark on the second night, lights appeared over the horizon. Gradually, soft grass and date palms rose around them, and they found themselves on the outskirts of a grand oasis.

Grand enough to have buildings and streets. The streets were lined with candles and colored lanterns and people. It smelled like food, incense, animals, and burning wood.

Satan did his best to ruin the moment. He drooled a thick, sustained rope of snot, saliva, and vomit, leaving behind something like a snail trail. People made faces as he passed.

Milo stayed focused on the good things.

I might stay here awhile, he thought. Maybe a long while.

It seemed like a happy thought. Underneath it, though, was Milo's awareness that he had no reason to be anywhere else.

They stayed in town that first night, just long enough to eat a couple of chicken dinners and drink some beer. Then they rode back out into the desert a little ways, where other nomads had pitched their own temporary neighborhood, and set up camp in the midst of it.

The next day, Milo became part of Akram's remarkable magic act.

Here's how that happened:

Akram woke him around midday and said, "You may wish to come into town with me. I'm going to get some breakfast and maybe put on a show."

"Sure," said Milo, shrugging.

They left the tent and the animals behind and made their way toward the heart of the oasis.

Milo pointed out that Akram hadn't brought along anything with which to juggle.

To which Akram replied, "How mysterious!" and said nothing else.

There was, Milo noted as they made their way to the bazaar, no shortage of entertainers already hard at work. Anywhere you looked, anywhere there was room, were people doing a whole spectrum of things to get travelers to stop, look, and maybe toss some coins in a hat.

There were jugglers already. Some better than others. There were snake charmers, hucksters, and musicians. People who would draw caricatures of you. Fortune-tellers. Face-painters. Body-painters.

Not all of the entertainment was in the form of talent. Some of it bordered on the mystical, like a man who had tied himself into a complicated knot. For a dollar, you could try to undo him. Milo tried and failed. There was a woman who could talk to animals, and a man, prudently concealed behind a canvas drape, who would shit you a gold necklace for five bucks. It was all very interesting, but it made Milo uneasy, too. These were people who had been hanging around the afterlife for some time and had no plans to be reborn anytime soon. They had found their way to the edge of things, for whatever strange reasons.

Anonymity? Apathy?

"How long has it been," Milo asked Akram, "since you lived an Earthly life?"

"Five years," answered the juggler. "Maybe more."

They stopped for burritos and coffee.

"How long," Milo asked, "before you think you will go back again?"

Akram sighed and chewed.

"There are these two universal women," he said, "named Obong and Glee. They are my counselors. Everyone has them, yes? Well, they blew in on a sandstorm one day and suggested I go back to Earth as a tax accountant. I told them I would think about it. I have been thinking about it for some time. In my last life, I was in a coma for seven years. With apologies, Milo: The world of the living doesn't interest me much."

Milo began to ask another question, but Akram forestalled him.

"They will not allow me to wander forever, I suspect. I know this. Eventually I will throw off the precious balance of things and have to go be a salesgirl or a mule or a coffee bean, and I will be sad. No, no more questions. Peace."

They purchased Milo a tent of his own.

"Not that I mind sharing," said Akram. "I just might wish to entertain a houseguest or two, some evening, if—"

"I get it," said Milo.

So now here he was, walking down the bazaar, balancing a load of canvas and tent poles over one shoulder. This left him blind on one side. He turned to make sure Akram was following.

He wasn't.

"Akram?" Milo called.

The crowd milled around him. No one answered.

Then something caught his eye. Several paces away, amid the crowd, something shiny flew into the air, caught the sun with a flash—it was a brass lamp, the kind you burn oil in—and came back down.

A moment later it rose again, followed by a wooden bowl.

Finally, the lamp ascended a third time, followed by the bowl, a basket, someone's hat, and a plastic spray bottle of some kind. At this point, the crowd spread out to make room for whatever dervish was causing these phenomena, and of course it was Akram.

It didn't take a genius to figure out that Akram had collected a bunch of merchandise from one of the stalls and begun tossing it into the air, quite without permission or explanation. The shopkeeper stood before him, throwing a fit.

"Good people," Akram said to the crowd, "you will now be treated to a demonstration of aerial sorcery! I heartily recommend that, afterward, you visit this fine gentleman's stall—what's your name? Bill? Visit Bill's stall. His goods are not only aerodynamic but of the finest quality, priced to move."

Mollified, Bill the shopkeeper withdrew. Milo returned his merchandise.

"Now," said Akram, cracking his knuckles, "someone throw me something to juggle."

Someone tossed Akram a pair of sandals and a straw hat. He tossed these things in a lazy circle.

"Make it interesting," he challenged the crowd.

Someone called out "Yo!" and tossed him—what? Something long, like a question mark in the air, something that moved—

"Holy shit!" cried Milo and a lot of other people.

A snake!

Akram cried out, too, but he caught the creature, and around and around went the hat, the shoe, and the snake. The snake hissed, twisted, and tried to bite, but Akram winked and boomed laughter.

The crowd showered him with applause. He tossed the shoe and the hat back to their owners, leaving him with the snake, which he let slide down his arm and off through the crowd. This caused some jumping around, but most of his audience remained to see what would happen next.

They were happy they did.

Akram performed for another half hour. They threw him knives, bricks, hot coals, and stools.

Akram seemed perfectly at ease, even when they threw him a whole sack of golf balls all at once. He snatched them from the air, his hands so fast that he and the golf balls became like a cloud. He wasn't perfect. He dropped one or two but easily flipped them back into play with the toe of his sandal and kept smiling.

His only failure, if you could call it that, was when someone threw him a bucket of water. Not the bucket itself, just the water. Akram stood there dripping, looking unsurprised. He bowed to the woman with the empty bucket.

"My congratulations, madam," he said. "You have offered me the one thing that can not be juggled."

The crowd applauded. Akram concluded his act by juggling three pretty girls, collected his earnings, and waved to Milo.

"We're rich!" he said. "For the moment. Tonight we'll buy baked cheese and beer."

He was kind enough to shoulder Milo's tent for a while as they walked back out of town.

"How strong *are* you?" Milo asked, thinking of the three pretty girls.

Akram shrugged. "It's all in the wrist," he said.

Later, after a lot of food and drink, they were struggling to put up Milo's tent, and Milo blurted, "I want to work with you."

Akram hiccupped and said, "I work alone."

They succeeded in getting one part of the tent to stay up, and another part fell down.

"God is great," said Milo, instead of cursing. "Okay, but listen: If you had a partner, you could do stuff like juggle things back and forth.

And we could talk and have patter, you know, instead of just standing there grinning."

"Again," said Akram, "I decline. I am thinking of writing a book or buying a horse farm."

The whole tent collapsed again.

"Forget it," said Milo. "I'll just think of it as a very expensive sleeping bag."

And he walked off to gather the animals and take them to the pond.

The beasts drank, and Milo sat with his feet in the water, trying to juggle three stones. The best he could do was to keep two of them in the air, while the third either thumped to the ground or splashed into the water.

A voice behind him said, "There's a trick to it, you know."

Milo turned to find Akram behind him, juggling beanbags.

"I can teach you how to juggle in less than five minutes," Akram said. "It's easy. Stand up."

Milo stood. Akram handed him two beanbags.

"Hold a bag in each hand," Akram told him. "Toss one bag from your left hand to the right, so you wind up with both bags in one hand."

Milo tossed. Easy.

"Now do it again, except this time, when the first bag is in the air, toss the other bag so that it crosses behind it, in the air, and catch it in your left hand."

It took Milo a couple of tries to get this right, but he got it.

"That's the trick," said Akram, shrugging. "Toss, crisscross, repeat."

It took only a few minutes' practice before Milo could get all three beanbags popping and circling in the air.

"Wow," said Milo. "Thanks!"

"So here's what we'll do," said Akram. "Now that I've shown you the trick, it's up to you to figure out how to juggle more than three. When you can keep seven things in the air, I'll show you how to juggle knives without stabbing yourself in the face."

"Thank you?" said Milo. "That's nice of you? What made you change your mind?"

"The mind is a blessing and a mystery," Akram replied, departing.

Milo had purpose again.

He was a lowly student, studying under a great master. He was the sorcerer's apprentice. It was a role he knew, of course. In his thousands of lives, he had learned kung fu and how to fly airplanes. He had been a poker champ, a pool-hall hustler, and a prima ballerina. He knew by now how to learn a thing and practice it until it looked like magic.

It wasn't easy. That was the first thing about learning anything worthwhile; you had to have patience. You had to know that if you tried to do a thing a thousand times, you could usually succeed in doing it, and if you practiced that thing a million times, you could do it very well. And so on. Mastering a thing was not magic, just hard work.

Chop wood, carry water, as the Buddhists said.

So Milo worked hard. He kept the animals fed and watered. He watched Akram. And he practiced. This became his life.

Of course, you had to have a *reason* to work that hard, to practice like that, and Milo did. He wanted very much to do what Akram could do with a crowd. Not only that, but he wanted the strange, easy peace that seemed to come over the master when he had a bunch of knives or shoes or kittens in the air. As if he weren't there, almost.

Sometimes he found himself dreaming of juggling instead of dreaming about Suzie. Sometimes.

"Who's Suzie?" asked Akram one morning when they were eating donuts in the bazaar.

"Why?"

"You call her name at night."

Milo didn't want to talk about it. Or think about it, or dream. He stuffed his whole entire donut in his mouth and glared into the sun.

"As you wish," said the master. "Obviously this is a mystery of some import. Now chew, please."

———

How to juggle more than three things?

Milo watched Akram. He did exercises. He whirled his arms and flexed his hands. He learned to roll marbles between his fingers. He did push-ups in the sand.

Satan liked to bite him and step on him when he did push-ups. He practiced dodging Satan.

The aha moment, when it came, was not what he'd expected. He had been juggling beanbags all morning, trying new ways of criss-crossing, when it suddenly hit him.

Ask.

So Milo walked to the bazaar, caught a tall, dark-eyed juggler at the end of his show, and said, "I'll give you fifty bucks to show me how to keep more than three things in the air," and the dark-eyed juggler said, "You throw them higher."

"And faster, too, right?"

"Nope. Just higher." And the guy took his money and walked away. Aha!

Milo practiced for a month before he went to Akram and said, "Watch this."

"Now is not a good time," said Akram, who had a bunch of paper and a pen and was busy writing. "I told you I might write a book. Well, I am doing it. The story of my life and also my teachings about juggling."

Milo popped five beanbags into the air. This did not seem to impress Akram much, but he stopped writing to watch.

Milo added a sixth. Then a seventh. The bags whirled higher, now circling a crescent moon.

"I've seen worse," said Akram. "Of course, it's been a *month*—"

Milo added more bags, reaching into his robe for one more, two more, ten more. While one hand was busy fetching new bags, he kept the rest of them going with the other.

Akram's jaw dropped open. He put down his pen.

Milo caught each of the beanbags, one by one, and stowed them away in his robe.

"Well?" he said.

"Well, indeed!" said the master, wide-eyed as a child.

"What were you writing about in your book?" Milo asked. "What's it called?"

"It's called *The Day Milo and Akram the Remarkable Started Working Together as Partners*."

Milo offered a grateful bow.

"God is good," said Akram.

"Fuckin' A," said Milo.

They practiced juggling together, passing things back and forth. And Akram spent some time teaching, finally.

"There's a secret," he told Milo, as they passed seven beanbags back and forth, "to juggling anything the crowd throws at you."

"Like the snake that one day?"

"Precisely."

"What is it?"

"In the air, an object tends to spin on three axes—three separate directions—and you need to get it to hold still and just go up and down."

And this is exactly where Milo's training took a complicated, technical turn. His days became a montage of science and repetition. Throw this, throw that. Learn how objects move in the air. Some of it Milo already knew; in his many lives, he had been a scientist. He had flown the trapeze in the circus. He had pitched baseballs and swung swords.

Time passed. He practiced, survived injuries, and practiced more.

Akram worked on his book. Sometimes he showed Milo an interesting passage or two.

"I juggled an elephant one time," he said, handing Milo the book. "Read."

"It says here," said Milo, "you juggled only one elephant. Is that really juggling?"

"It is when it's an elephant."

"Akram, Jesus! How strong are you?"

"As strong as I need to be. Go do your push-ups."

Milo did a thousand push-ups, and Satan stood over him and drooled something like a dumpling all over his back.

Time passed. Nomads came to the oasis and went away again. Milo dreamed dreams. Heaven and Earth turned. Desert winds blew, wearing things away and burying things, as desert winds do.

The first time they performed together in the bazaar, it was Milo who began the show.

First he grabbed three I'M HOT FOR THE DESERT T-shirts from a young shopkeeper's stall.

"Hey!" cried the shopkeeper, leaping after him.

Within seconds, Milo got the T-shirts spinning up and down in the air, flying like swans.

"Ooh!" said the crowd, circling around.

"Good morning!" Milo called out. "Friends, you will now be treated to a demonstration of highly scientific juggling feats. I heartily recommend that, afterward, you visit this fine gentleman's stall—what's your name? Moudi? Visit Moudi's stall."

Moudi backed off.

It was a routine show, up to a point. Milo asked the crowd to throw him some things, and they threw him their sandals. Threw him a Frisbee. He juggled these things backward and forward. He juggled three turkeys and a dozen eggs.

"Come on, folks," he said. "We can do better than this."

And that's when someone threw him a baby.

It cried as it came whirling toward him over the front row of spectators.

Milo nearly froze. Like everyone in the crowd, he gasped. But he caught the thing, just as one should always catch a baby, neatly across his forearm, supporting its head with his palm.

But then another baby sailed his way, and another.

Milo had no choice. Reflexively, he caught them all, and before he knew it, he was juggling three wailing infants.

The crowd raised helpless hands in the air, surging forward, then surging back, not wanting to get in his way. The crowd grew then, as the noise drew attention, and people farther down the bazaar came running, saw, and stayed, hardly daring to breathe.

It wasn't long before Milo—having been a father and a mother and a baby countless times—realized that something was amiss. Something about the babies was too stiff, their cries too much the same . . .

Dolls.

Some bastard had grabbed a whole display of baby dolls from a stall, and—well, here came the shopkeepers now, gesturing.

One, two, three—Milo tossed them their merchandise.

One, two, three—the crowd caught on.

A moment of disturbed, uncertain silence. And then a blast of re-lieved applause that went on and on and on.

There was Akram, amazed and relieved like the rest of them.

"Bow out, and let's go," Akram said, drawing close.

"But!" Milo protested. "We haven't even done our tandem act, with the swords and—"

"You can't do better than what you just did," Akram said. "Finish at the top of your act, whenever that comes. Now let's go!"

Milo bowed and collected his pile of coins, and they went and got some tacos, and that was Milo's debut as a professional juggler.

That night he had a wonderful, awful dream.

Someone in the crowd threw him a woman. It was Suzie.

"Suzie!" he cried, tossing her up in the air and catching her with expert grace.

"It's no use," she said to him, and before he could answer, she was pulled from him, just like before. Stretching away. Her hand trailed along his face as she left him.

"No!"

Her fingers grew long, soft and warm on his face, as she vanished across dimensions—

Milo awakened. He could still feel softness and warmth on his cheek. Up above him, in the dark, hot breath and wet chewing noises. A long, damp shadow thrust through the tent flap—

"Aw, Jesus on a stick, Satan!" Milo screamed, shoving the camel's head aside, nearly uprooting the tent as he staggered out into the night. Wiping at his face, feeling for the water bucket by starlight, washing away strings of camel drool.

"Milo!" called Akram, emerging from his own tent. "Milo, what's amiss? Are you sick? Are we besieged?"

Milo, sputtering, explained.

Akram laughed.

"It's not funny," said Milo. "He's making my life hell in his nasty little ways."

"What's funny," said Akram, "is that, one: Yes, he's nasty. He's a camel. But, two: You do not see why he pays you all this attention? It is his way of showing that he loves you."

Milo sat down in the sand. He said nothing. Akram went to buy them some cinnamon rolls.

It was true. He felt the truth of it. He even felt his own heart softening a bit. But . . .

"Why?" he finally asked, when Akram returned.

Akram shrugged. He handed Milo a roll, and they ate in silence.

"Because you are kind and good to him, despite his faults? Because you were a female camel in some distant life? Who knows these things?"

Satan emerged from the tent. He found Milo and came near, breathing on him.

Milo reached up and patted the beast on his gross, sweaty neck.

Satan made a horrible noise and bit him tenderly on the arm.

The next day, Milo and Akram managed to perform together. They threw pretty girls back and forth. They threw apples back and forth and ate them as they threw. They juggled knives and fire, china plates and glass figurines. In a sort of slo-mo dance, they juggled bubbles and balloons.

They hauled coins by the sackful back to their tents.

Time passed.

They juggled buckets full of water one day, a feat of strength and timing. That was Milo's idea and design. Another time, he figured out how they could juggle rubber balls and let some of the balls bounce on the ground, as if the two of them were a human popcorn machine.

Quickly enough, it became obvious that the student had surpassed his teacher.

Akram did not seem to be the jealous kind. More and more, his book started to be about Milo.

The time Milo juggled three sleeping girls without waking them up.

The time Milo juggled a pile of sunbaked bricks, so that it went from being a pile over *here* and became a pile over *there*.

The time—the many times—Milo howled, *"Suzie!"* in his sleep, but wouldn't talk about it, and acted like a child if you asked too many questions, and was obviously in denial, and was hiding something . . .

One evening, Akram came out and stood over Milo, who sat staring at the moon and flexing his fingers in the sand. Satan knelt nearby, sleeping, snoring like a steam engine full of puke.

"Friend," said Akram, "you need to get out from time to time. Let's go into town and find some trouble."

"I'm good," answered Milo, his voice barely audible.

Akram heaved a sigh. "You can't just disappear into your work," he insisted.

Milo roused himself a little.

"It's not disappearing," he said. "It's concentration. It's how you become great at something. Others think you're obsessed, and you're the only one who understands what you're looking for."

"Which is what?"

"Perfection."

"Bullshit, respectfully, my friend. You're running from something."

"So are you. So are half the people out here. We're circling the drain as slowly, as far out, as we can get."

"That's true. Fine. Very true. But I've never seen anyone do what you do. You practice. You perform. You sleep. You sit here with your evil camel. That's neither life nor afterlife."

"It's my business."

He stopped flexing his fingers in the sand.

Akram went into town by himself.

The next day, some newcomers came riding into town, making their way through the bazaar on elephants.

"Elephants," said Milo to Akram.

"Elephants, indeed!" said Akram. "Magnificent creatures! Have you ever been an elephant? I have. Once, back when—"

Milo had a certain look in his eye.

"Milo," said Akram. "No."

But Milo was already approaching the first and largest of the new arrivals. A wonderful animal, draped in jeweled cloth, with painted tusks and a howdah full of well-dressed nomads on its back.

He began talking pleasantly to the people up in the howdah, and they seemed to be amused by what he was saying.

"Milo!" barked Akram, stepping up beside him. "No!"

"You did it."

Akram twiddled his thumbs.

"I may have, and I may not have," he said.

"It's in your book."

"Lots of things are in my book. It's just a book."

The nomads climbed down, and Milo stepped under the elephant.

"God is good," said Akram, "and protective of fools."

It didn't work.

Milo trembled, pushing up against the elephant's belly. Every muscle in his body—and these had grown to be considerable—vibrated visibly, but the trouble seemed to be that there was nothing, really, to push against. The elephant grunted. It didn't seem put out; if anything, it seemed to want to help, if it could only discern what this strange, eerily focused two-legs wanted.

But some things are impossible. There are limits and absolutes.

Akram drew a circle in the dust with one sandal. Maybe this was the sort of lesson his friend needed. Maybe afterward they'd ride out of town, go someplace else for a while.

Then the back end of the elephant rose into the air, just a little.

"Ooh!" gasped the crowd.

The elephant made a slight trumpeting noise.

A long second later, the front feet left the ground, as well.

Complete, stunned silence.

It didn't last long, and the elephant didn't go very high. Maybe a couple of inches. But it was an undeniable, visible fact that, for an instant, there was a man holding an elephant in the air.

With an exhausted "whuff!" Milo fell to his knees, the elephant landed daintily, and the crowd shouted and hurled money.

Akram bolted into the street, nudged the elephant aside, and helped Milo to his feet.

Milo wouldn't stay on his feet, though. He got about halfway up and then sank like a ship.

"I think I broke myself," he whispered.

"What did you expect?"

"I expected to lift the elephant. And I did."

Akram lifted Milo over one shoulder, fireman-style, and carried him out of town.

"It's hardly juggling," he said.

"Save it for your book," said Milo, and passed out.

Milo slept.

Akram laid him out in his tent and checked on him now and then, stepping over Satan to do so.

The sleep became a coma. Maybe a half coma, because he woke

now and then to drink water and even eat a little. But then he'd slip away again.

Time passed. Specifically, a week.

Then, in the middle of a cool, breezy night, the flap of Akram's tent lifted, and Milo stood there in the dark.

Akram lit a candle.

Yes, it was Milo. Awake finally, and looking pretty good. A little slimmer, maybe, but overall good. At least that's what Akram thought until he saw his friend's eyes.

The eyes had already developed a strange, inward glow before the elephant. That glow had somehow intensified, as if stoked by a week's worth of constant dreaming.

"I came in to say goodbye," said Milo. "And to tell you I'm grateful."

"Goodbye? Where—God is good, Milo!—where in hell do you think you're going? You're in no condition—"

"I am going off alone somewhere," Milo interrupted, "to learn to juggle water."

Outside, a breeze kicked up. Satan belched.

"Milo," said Akram, "please listen. Water cannot be juggled. No, listen: The elephant was just a question of degree. It was heavy, but at least it had substance, something to hold and move . . ."

Akram fell into a helpless silence.

Milo said, "God is good," and slipped out.

He spent a solid week riding Satan across the desert. Milo let the beast go where he liked. What difference did it make? He flexed his hands as they went. He juggled stones.

After a time, entirely by accident, Milo found himself at the same spring where he had first met Akram. The source of the clear river that led who knew where.

And there he stopped, and pitched his tent, and dipped his hands in the water.

———

Travelers who found him at his oasis called him the Juggling Hermit or the Staring Hermit or the Splashing Hermit or the Hermit with the Unholy Camel, depending.

If they were lucky, nomads discovered him in a relatively expansive mood, juggling nuts or rocks or mudballs. He might even put on a show for them, juggling anything they tossed his way. Other times, they might find him sitting at the very edge of the water, staring down without blinking. Not at his reflection, it seemed, but at something deep and invisible.

Sometimes they found him splashing in the water like a child, although he seemed not the slightest bit embarrassed to be caught out. In any event, he was always gracious and welcoming, if somewhat withdrawn. His camel, unfortunately, was off-putting, but you didn't fault a man for that. Especially a holy man, which this specimen obviously was.

The stars circled, and the moon and sun passed overhead, and the desert rolled and changed.

One day, Milo was staring down into the water, trying not to see Suzie's face, trying to see the secret thing in the water that would give it form, when a large traveler in a bright-green robe appeared from downriver. Masked in a tightly wound headdress. Leaning on a tall walking stick.

"Ah!" said this apparition, drawing near. "There you are!"

Milo looked up and blinked. Sometimes out here he saw things that proved not to be real.

The traveler was real. She unwound her headdress, knelt, and reached for him with big, fat, wonderful arms.

"Mama," he rasped, and let her hold him.

He found food, and fetched her a cup from his tent, and warned his camel not to vomit at her. They sat and ate quietly, until the sun finished going down and she asked him, "Milo, what in the scarlet goddamn hell do you think you're doing?"

He mumbled about juggling water.

"That's the dumbest thing I've ever heard in my life. You can't."

"If I could, though," he argued, "it would be an act of Perfection."

Mama unwound her travel robes and waded into the water.

"Is that what this is about?" she asked, floating amid reflected stars. "Because it doesn't count in the afterlife, you know. You know?"

Milo said he supposed he knew that.

"You know what it's about," he said.

She swam out just far enough to become featureless. Just a shadow. Just a voice.

"Yes," she said. "I know."

Silence.

Milo was good at silence. He let this one go a long, long time.

"If she's been smooshed into the big cosmic soul," he finally said, "then what's the point?"

Mama swam closer. One great warm hand reached up out of the water and grasped his ankle.

"I can't answer that for you," she said. "I know you have to decide whether to sit here pouting like a child or go do something about it. Maybe you won't get what you want. But is this it? You're going to just quit?"

Milo started to say something.

"Look at yourself," Mama said.

Milo did what she said. It took a while, but eventually his eyes adjusted in the starlight, and he saw his own reflection for the first time in a long time.

He was a skeleton, pretty much. Drawn flesh, hollow eyes. His desert garb hung on him like a shroud.

"Go back," said Mama. "Go back and at least try."

"Try what?" he croaked.

"Try *what*?" Now she was pissed. "Are you kidding me? What's wrong with you, you selfish dumbass? Try and be perfect! Try *something*! What's the coolest life you've ever lived? Maybe not cool, maybe that's not the word, but—"

"Captain Gworkon," said Milo.

"Really? Okay. Well, good choice, I guess. Captain Gworkon certainly wouldn't have sat here in the afterlife, rotting away in front of his own reflection. He would have gone back and spent another lifetime—"

"Juggling," said Milo.

Mama's grip tightened on his ankle.

"Dammit, Milo, if—"

"I'm kidding. Fighting evil. He would have gone back and spent everything he had fighting evil."

He stood up and started unwinding his robes. Behind him, Satan stood, too.

Why not? Being born was a way of getting lost, too, wasn't it?

"Go," said Mama. "Fight evil. Do it perfectly. Then come back and we'll see."

Bullshit, thought Milo.

But he forced himself. He was, after all, the veteran of half a million Monday mornings. It's something a wise man or a wise woman knows how to do: shake off your self-pity and your obsession, and put one foot in front of the other and keep moving.

And you wade into the dark desert pool a little way and sort through the lives you see. And just when you're about to make yourself dive in, there's a dumb, sad *honk!* from the riverbank, and you look and there's that animal, that gross, hateful animal that loves you and maybe thinks you're a girl camel in disguise. And it has that look animals get when they don't know if you're coming back or not.

And you've had enough dogs and been enough dogs to know that it doesn't help when you go back and say goodbye, but you do it, anyway. And the animal drools on you and pants and sweats, and its heart breaks, and there are hearts breaking all over the place like popcorn in this big stupid desert. And you're bitter. And you feel sorry for yourself, and that's what's on your mind when you dive in and the water takes you down and makes you forget all, all except the singularity of You, the escape pod of your soul, moving on and starting over for the nine thousand nine hundred ninety-eighth time in a row.

CHAPTER 16

The Green-Apple Game

She faded a little more each day.

She could see the sun through her hand quite clearly now. Like a bright red tattoo.

Shit, thought Suzie.

Sooner than she liked, she would vanish completely.

How did she feel about that? It depended on the moment. It depended, specifically, on her frustration level. Some days she was perfectly happy to get canceled out and not have to deal with anything anymore. Other days she had a gritty kind of hope. Milo would find her, or she would find him. The universe would decide she was right after all . . . that a little imbalance wasn't such a bad thing after all.

She wandered.

She blew from place to place, leaves and wind. Sometimes she let the currents of the afterlife just take her. She materialized on shores and in restaurants. In parks and on boats and in kitchens and recycling centers.

The universe didn't seem to think she was serious about quitting her job; it took her to the bedside of a dying Nigerian king, once.

"I told you," she said. "I quit."

The universe flexed its *boa*. It growled and creaked around her and around the Nigerian king.

"If you and the universe would take your quarrel elsewhere," sighed the king, "I would be most grateful, as I am engaged in a difficult transformation."

Wind and shadows. Suzie hit the road.

Was Milo even here? Or was he down there, on some planet, living one of his final lives?

Her instincts seemed to take her away from busy places, out onto the fringes. The places people went when they were tired, or running from something, or looking for something.

Once, she passed through a place where Milo had been. She could feel him there, like a troubled footprint in the sand. Gone now. Leaving behind a catastrophically unpleasant camel.

Dust and wind and faraway places.

Humans had a thing for these kind of places, she had learned. More than any other creature, they needed sometimes to simply flee. To reduce themselves to zero and make something new out of nothing.

She found herself thinking of someone she had known once. A friend she'd had. A human, besides Milo, who might have understood her a little. A man who had gotten her into the biggest fight of her life.

His name was Francesco. He lived in Italy.

Francesco had a rich family, and gorgeous surroundings, and was handsome and smart and fashionable. He spent his early years having a hell of a good time, drinking and singing and getting laid with his friends. Then one day it became necessary for them all to go off to war. Their families dressed them in armor and bought them horses and sent them off singing and laughing and flying colorful banners, and almost right away they were captured and tossed in a foreign prison.

This was kind of embarrassing, but the young friends tried to make the most of it, singing songs and telling stories, seeing who could kill the most rats or eat the most bugs, and eventually the war ended and they went home, still singing.

Francesco's father exclaimed, *"Bentornato, figlio!"* and kissed him and put him to work in the family business, buying and selling fashionable clothes.

Maybe that's what caused Francesco to get sick.

Something sure did. In fact, they thought he had died and draped a shroud over him. Suzie was about to kiss his forehead and send his soul off to the afterlife, when he suddenly sat up and said, *"Gesù, non so cosa darei per una ciotola di zuppa,"* which means, "Jesus, what I wouldn't give for a bowl of soup."

This happened sometimes. Ordinarily, Suzie would have flown away home, but something about the young man intrigued her. There was a light about him, some madness or goodness set free by the illness.

Indeed, as he recovered, it seemed Francesco had gone crazy. He kept skipping work, spending his days out in the meadows and woods, chasing birds and skinny-dipping in streams and trying to pet the deer. His friends and neighbors laughed and laughed, but Francesco only laughed back, took off all his clothes, and walked stark naked out of town. He went to live in the ruins of a stone chapel out in the wilderness, eating berries and nuts and doing as he pleased.

"Questo è folle!" gasped the townspeople. "You can't just go around being happy and doing whatever you like!" Some of them even went out to the wilderness to tell him so.

Francesco didn't answer them with words. He just kept right on being happy, right in front of their faces. This made some of his visitors angry, and they went home and kicked things around the house. A few of them, however, decided to stay. By and by, a little community formed: a group of the nicest people you ever met, wearing rags and living on berries, fixing up the old chapel stone by stone. Animals even started coming around. Birds and deer and squirrels and frogs and toads and such.

Suzie couldn't believe it. Humans usually had some weird addiction to suffering and toil. These freaks, insisting on simplicity and happiness, reminded her a bit of Milo (currently off living a life as a Japanese bunny rabbit). If they weren't careful, one of two things was bound to happen. One: They would spread their happiness to others and make the world a better place. Or two: They would make people uncomfortable and get burned at the stake.

Suzie even put on a human form and warned Francesco about this. "Happiness scares the crap out of people," she told him.

He only smiled and went on doing what he was doing.

Something happened then, while they were talking.

They saw each other. Really *saw* each other.

Francesco saw who she was. He looked surprised to discover Death hanging around his little chapel. But he wasn't upset. Death was part of nature. Death was a door. She was also, apparently, not bad-looking.

And Suzie saw waaaaay into Francesco. She saw that he would become a famous example of peace and goodness and make the world a better place. It was terribly important that he continue what he was doing, so that these things could come to pass.

Suzie saw something else, too. Something bad.

Francesco was still sick and didn't know it. The sickness was sleeping inside him, and very soon it would wake up and kill him. She saw it the way you sometimes see a shadow down in the water.

She decided to not let it happen.

She found some rags to wear and pitched in helping to fix the chapel.

Her feet and hands grew rough. She tried to pet the animals, but they recognized her and kept their distance.

Francesco walked to Rome (with no shoes on) and had a talk with the pope, and the pope liked him and blessed him, and after that more people started coming to the chapel. Not to laugh or be uncomfortable but to see and learn.

Not long after that, the sickness inside Francesco bloomed and grew, and Suzie felt the urge to kiss him on the forehead and make him be dead. But she didn't.

She didn't make the same mistake she'd made with the whale, though. Didn't let his soul escape and then try to stuff it back inside. She focused on the shadow instead. Stuffed it back under whatever interior anatomical rock it had been hiding and told it to stay put.

Francesco was down with the sniffles for a day, but that was the worst of it. By evening he was well enough to take some of his disciples out to look for lepers to feed.

There would, Suzie sensed, be hell to pay.

Sure enough, about a week later, she was out in the meadow looking for a good keystone to anchor the chapel door when she saw a tall, pale figure riding down out of the woods.

One of the other Deaths. He called himself Zaazeemozogmelaffello-Ba-Tremuloso-Ba-Jalophonso-Umbertoaawiigsheetossalavagredorro-Ba.

"Well?" said this universal slice, approaching Suzie. "Where is he?"

Suzie had just found an especially likely looking pile of rocks. She picked up a good one and held it in a way that, she hoped, looked mildly threatening.

"Where is who?" (She tried to look innocent, as well.)

The other Death just looked disgusted and turned to ride on toward the chapel.

"You can't have him," Suzie called out. She gripped the stone harder. She'd throw it if she had to.

He stopped.

"Suzie," he said. "What's going on? You know this isn't how it works."

She nodded.

"Still," she said.

He looked uncertain and climbed down off his horse.

"What do you propose?" he asked. "And would you put the stone down, please? We both know you're not going to throw it at me."

She dropped the stone.

"He's important," she said.

"I'm sure he is. I'm sorry. This is how it balances out."

"Sometimes the balance is wrong."

"That's not for you to say."

Suzie's eyes flared.

"I've decided that it *is* for me to say," she told him. "How do you like *them* apples?"

"Apples?"

She had an idea. "You can have him," she said, "if you beat me at a game."

"Like what?" (Death was a sucker for a challenge. They all were.)

She reached into her pockets and drew out two little green apples.

"We throw these apples," she said. "Whoever's apple goes farther gets to have their way."

He looked puzzled and wary.

"That's not really a game," he said. "As such."

She tossed him one of the apples and said, "One."

"As you wish," he said.

"Two," said Suzie, and "Three!" and they both threw as hard as they could, and a crow came swooping down out of the air and grabbed Suzie's apple and carried it off over the trees, out of sight.

The other apple landed in an old posthole, at a respectable distance.

"That doesn't count," Zaazeem-etc.-Ba complained.

But he got back on his horse and rode away, embarrassed by the way he'd been tricked.

Suzie didn't tell Francesco what had happened, just as she hadn't told him the whole truth about his bout with the sniffles.

She also stayed up all night watching the door, in case Zaazeem-Ba tried to sneak in and take Francesco in the dark. But he didn't.

The years passed. Summer and winter gave way to each other, in turn. People came to the chapel to watch and help. Some of them started their own communities in other places. Suzie finally got the animals to let her pet them. Some of them died, but they seemed, overall, to sense that this was okay.

Every now and then, one of Suzie's colleagues would come riding across the meadow (or whirling on the wind or falling with the rain or creeping with the twilight), and she would challenge them. And she managed to send them away, by hook or by crook.

Until, finally, the dark thing inside Francesco came out from under its rock and wouldn't go back, no matter what she did. He caught the sniffles, and his eyes grew hollow. Suzie pushed at him and pulled and fed him certain things and even yelled a little, but nothing was working.

When parts of him began to turn black, Francesco looked up at her and said, "Suzie, enough."

He was right.

She kissed him on the head and sat there holding his hand while he dimmed and went out and rose up and became one with the cosmic hoo-ha.

Suzie closed his dead eyes and gave the cosmic hoo-ha a taste of the old middle finger.

Now, centuries later, Suzie thought about Francesco often. A lot of people did.

She thought about him whenever she felt particularly lost out there on the edge of things. Wandering the moors, the empty roads. Sometimes looking for Milo, sometimes not. Too tired and angry to be happy.

Sometimes fellow drifters would look at her with the long, long stare they all shared and ask where she was headed.

"I'm just trying to avoid the universe," she would answer.

CHAPTER 17

A Real Thing, with Substance and Power

Captain Gworkon.

Milo had fought against evil in many lives, but Captain G was the most conspicuous.

It happened in what most people would think of as the future. He won a galaxy-wide lottery and spent the whole bundle on bionic surgeries. He had himself built into a flying atomic cyborg, descended on the fortresses of powerful space pirates, and towed them to justice in chains.

Crime in the fourth galactic arm dropped off by 50 percent.

This was not, to his surprise, entirely appreciated.

"You saved us from the bad guys," a grad student once said to him. "Who's going to save us from you?"

He didn't let her question bother him. People like that usually thought differently when their own lives were threatened.

Two nights later, he saved the same grad student from a pack of wild synthetic pig-dogs.

"I'm sorry about what I said," she said, kissing his metal cheek. "It was a failure of imagination."

"Most failures are," he answered. "No prob."

———

Evil.

Sometimes it was something that stood up and announced itself clearly. Like the times when he was born a Muslim, and the Christians were evil, and the times he was born Christian, and the Muslims were evil. He thanked God, in those lives, for making it so obvious.

Other times, it was still obvious but harder to fight. Like the time he was a laborer and signed up to help build a tunnel under the Crook-shank River. And sometimes the air locks failed and the tunnel flooded and men drowned. But if you complained about safety, thugs would come into camp at night, looking for you, and say how a man who fit your description had broken into some houses, and they'd have wit-nesses. And away you'd go, and the message was to keep quiet and take your chances and suck it up.

Milo spoke up and wouldn't stop, even when they came for him. He had an accident in jail and died spitting blood.

Sometimes, the fight took place in the most commonplace of ways.

In the twenty-first century, they made it illegal to buy cheap pre-scription drugs online. The pharmaceutical companies paid lawmakers to keep it that way, and medical expenses were bankrupting people, killing people. Milo ignored these bullies, and bought whatever he wanted from whoever he wanted, and fought evil that way.

Sometimes superheroes are regular people, and there are millions of them, typing away at their keyboards.

Many centuries ago, Milo led a thousand peasants in a protest. They marched up to the lord's castle and demanded lower taxes. They didn't have enough to eat.

The lord got up from his turkey dinner and ordered twenty soldiers to go up on the walls and fire some arrows at the peasants.

Ten peasants fell down amid the wheat and the wildflowers and died.

The nine hundred ninety remaining peasants turned around and ran like hell.

"What's wrong with you people?" Milo screamed after them. He tossed rocks at their retreating backs. "There are so many of you and about forty of them!"

It was like watching a horse get bossed around by a horsefly.

Milo was a saxophone player called Mookie Underwood, and he walked across a bridge into Selma, Alabama, with hundreds of other men and women. On the other side of the bridge, policemen waited with clubs.

"Turn back," called the policemen.

The marchers didn't turn back.

The cops clubbed them down and beat them.

The marchers ran and were chased and horribly beaten.

Cameras flashed. Cameras rolled. All around the world, people saw.

"Let them watch," Mookie choked through his own blood. "Let them see. It's their ass, too."

Fighting evil was often a secret undertaking.

As a shoemaker named Milosevic Kocevar, he had defied the Waffen-SS by hiding books beneath his floorboards. Some in the resistance shot at soldiers, some destroyed railroads, others hid books and paintings and kept them out of Nazi hands.

Milosevic, for his part, preserved a rare library of Polish pornography. When the war came to an end, he returned it to the museum, which hid it away with secret pleasure. To this day, you have to ask to see it.

When he got to the afterlife, after that particular Polish life, Milo found that Suzie had a perfect copy of the entire pornography collection.

"You risked your life for this?" she asked.

The expressions on her face were dramatic and varied widely. Some of the drawings and photographs were quite surprising. Some of them involved ponies.

"When people try to destroy art or thought," Milo explained, "it makes all forms of art and thought valuable. It's a slippery slope once we start saying what people should or shouldn't see. It's a real evil, a thing with substance and power. I was helping to preserve people's chance to see and to choose."

"I see," she whispered. "I understand."

For a solid month, every time he turned around she had one of those books open.

"I'm fighting evil," she'd say.

"*Rozumiem,*" he'd answer, in Polish. "I understand."

CHAPTER 18

Slaughterhouse

COVINGTON, OHIO, 1948–1972

When a soul has been born almost ten thousand times, birth comes easier.

Milo recovered in good form from all the squeezing and the sudden brightness. Of course, he didn't understand right away who or what he was, any more than any other infant did. But time passed, and he learned.

He learned emotions. Sometimes he was filled with huge, sunny goodness. Sometimes he was apprehensive or calm. Sometimes he raged. When he raged, he was fed. He noticed this.

Aside from a certain smartness and confidence, Milo was mostly like other babies all over the world. But something in his brain—that wonderful brain—was different. Something like an OFF switch. The switch, like the rest of his brain, wasn't finished forming yet.

What was it an OFF switch for?

Unknown.

Milo lived with another person, called "Mommy." They lived in a trailer on a farm. Mommy (whose name was Joyce) worked for the Smoker family, who owned the farm. She helped with the cows. There were a hundred cows, and Joyce was always busy.

One morning when he was three, Milo was left to wander in the barn during milking time, within sight of his mother. He heard something scratching in the corner, behind a rusted manure spreader, and discovered a giant, nasty-looking silverfish.

The insect stared up at him through glossy, awful eyes. In its last life, it had been a pimp.

Milo picked a rusty nail out of the dust. With a look of mild concentration, he stuck the nail through the silverfish and pinned it to the boards beneath.

The insect spasmed, like a dry leaf throwing a fit.

All kids do things like that. Then they feel bad. Milo's OFF switch kicked in, preventing the bad feelings. (It did *not* prevent a hard-to-breathe feeling he often got when he was frightened or excited. His mother called it "asthma.")

Five minutes later, the milking was done, and Mom was ready to move the cows out for the day. "Milo!" she called.

"Coming, Joyce!" he answered, and ran to meet her, to take her hand.

He left behind a systematically dismembered silverfish: Wingless, wings arranged in a row. Legless, legs arranged in a row. Headless, the head in his pocket.

In fifth grade, a girl named Jodi Putterbaugh moved to Covington. Her parents, like Joyce, worked on a farm. She got on the bus the first day, walked straight to Milo's seat, and said, "You look like you might be in fifth grade."

Milo nodded. He was busy reading a science-fiction book.

"Do you mind if I sit here, so I'll know when to get off the bus? My mom says this bus stops at three different schools, and I'd hate to accidentally get off at the high school. My name's Jodi Putterbaugh."

"Milo Wood."

She sat down next to him and left him alone with his book.

Milo couldn't focus on his book, after that. He thought about Jodi Putterbaugh sitting next to him, with her long brown hair and cow eyes. New switches started opening all over his brain. The hard-to-breathe feeling raised its head, just a little.

The OFF switch stayed quiet, studying the situation.

On the playground later, after a long September rain, Milo was stomping on worms when he heard a sharp "Oh!" behind him.

Jodi Putterbaugh, looking stricken.

"What are you doing?" she asked.

"Nothing."

"You're killing worms. Why?"

Milo didn't have an answer. He didn't like the way Jodi was looking at him.

"Maybe I won't do it anymore," he said.

She nodded but kept walking away. Milo started having a tiny little heartbreak feeling, but the OFF switch shut it right down.

Jodi's family started an organic farm on the north side of Covington, raising food that was chemical-free. They raised pigs for pork but were very nice to the pigs while they were alive. Jodi invited Milo and some other fifth-graders to her birthday party in June.

"That's Henry," Jodi's dad told Milo, when a loose pig nuzzled his leg and began chewing on his jean cuffs. They were all sitting at a picnic table, eating yellow cake.

"You name your animals?" Milo asked. "But—"

"We're going to kill them, yes. But that doesn't mean you can't show respect. Lookee here." And he got down on his knees and took Henry's head in his hands.

"Look in his eyes," said Jodi's dad. "There's somebody in there. Henry's alive in his head, just like you and me. He appreciates kindness." (Mr. Putterbaugh was right. Just a year ago, Henry's soul had been a retired painter in Buenos Aires. His kindness to his neighbors had been legendary. His short, happy pig life at the Putterbaugh farm was a reward, not a punishment.)

"I'm going to change the way the world treats animals," Jodi told Milo.

It's funny, the things that cause people to fall in love. In Milo's case, it was Jodi reaching over and squeezing his hand. Later, under an apple tree, at that perfect moment of dusk when the lightning bugs are coming out, they said, "One, two, three," and kissed each other on the lips.

Milo heard a whispering deep inside his head just then, as if, say, there were ten thousand old souls trying to be heard and offer advice. The voices seemed to approve of the kissing.

It's going to be all right, said the old souls.

The old souls were wrong. The dead switch knew how to wait.

Years passed. Fred Smoker, the owner of the farm, took Milo hunting with his own sons. For Milo's first kill, Smoker marked his forehead with blood. When the blood touched his skin, Milo moaned a little. He couldn't help it. And he didn't tell Jodi.

The Putterbaugh family moved away, pushed out of business by a gigantic new Dinner Bell meatpacking factory over by Casstown. Milo's heart split wide open, but the OFF switch came out of hiding to squelch the pain.

Something was wrong, his old soul sensed, in a sleepy, overconfident way, but didn't know what.

Milo learned farm chores from his mom, and these developed into paid work as he grew and filled out. He lost his virginity to one of his mom's friends, Debbie Fair, out in the woods one night.

Then, suddenly, he had a high school diploma and an apartment of his own—a room over the Lucky Mart Gas and Sundries, right on the edge of Covington. He was a *person*. He planned to save money and go to college before long. The plans made him feel good and made his soul feel good. His soul reminded him that you had to make money in order to save money, so he needed some kind of job.

Fair enough, agreed Milo. He got drunk with a meat-packer named Tom Littlejohn one night at Walt's, and Tom got Milo a job at the Dinner Bell plant, killing cows. (Ah, shit, said his ancient soul.)

He carried a stunner, a kind of air hammer, and a hundred times a day he held the muzzle between a cow's eyes and—

SssssPOP!

—a steel slug punched through the cow's skull and stunned its brain. Sometimes this killed the cow outright. Other times the cow might just tremble and roll its eyes at you. Milo's dead switch engaged automatically during work hours; he could kill an animal no matter how it looked at him.

One time they had a three-hundred-fifty-pound Duroc hog named Orlando, to be specially butchered for a charity dinner at the Cincinnati Oktoberfest. Don Sweeney, the senior hand on the killing floor, tried to knock Orlando out with the air hammer, but Orlando bounced back up, squealing with rage. Sweeney came vaulting out of the pen, laughing, "That's enough for me, boys!"

Milo grabbed the hammer from Sweeney and hoisted himself over the wall. Before Milo could even get balanced right, Orlando came grunting at him, pig feet flying, jaws agape (he had been a pig for six lives in a row and was really good at it).

Milo was focused, fearless.

SssssPOP!

Pig and pig-slayer went down together.

Milo got up first and gave Orlando another slug (SssssPOP!), right in the eye.

Gore jetted all over his smock.

Still the mighty pig whined and kicked and looked as if he might make it back to his feet. Milo leaped up as high as he could and came down on the pig's ribs with both feet, driving his heels down.

Snap! Crack!

Orlando screamed and thrashed.

In one final, fluid motion, Milo reached behind him, picked up a nine-pound sledgehammer, and smashed the pig's jaw.

Again, the hammer whirled and smashed. When Milo backed away, chest heaving, eyes dead, there was nothing left of the pig's head. It looked like rags and Jell-O.

"Jesus, Milo," said Sweeney, in a tiny little voice.

At home in his apartment later, Milo shook as if he'd been in an accident.

You should feel something, whispered his old soul.

Milo tried to cry. His breath shuddered. He sat there for an hour, shaking, trying to be normal.

He would go to college for engineering, he decided. After a month's research, he found a program that would cost four thousand dollars a year. Five years at the slaughterhouse might give him what he needed to start, without having to bury himself in debt.

That's good, said the wise voice. More!

Milo put his plans in writing, complete with a timetable. He contacted the college about financial aid, about meeting with an admissions officer. He felt more like a person than ever.

To celebrate, he spent his college savings on an air rifle.

He began going for walks in the woods at night, sitting for hours in the trees along Route 41.

It seemed as if the only time he could ever get his mind to spin down and be still was when he crouched among the insect noises of the night woods with his rifle to his shoulder, lazily tracking cars as they passed.

Breathe in. Breathe out. The rest was silence.

For his birthday, he bought himself a telescopic scope and an insulated set of winter camos.

In midsummer, he did something that surprised him.

Hidden fifty yards from the road, he fired a shot that cracked the windshield of a passing Toyota 4Runner. The truck swerved, then sped up and vanished toward Springfield.

Aw, shit! That was dumb. That was serious. It was the kind of thing that drew attention.

Milo checked the papers the next day. Nothing.

Was he disappointed? Relieved? He didn't know.

That same day, Milo went down to Zwiebel's Market for baloney and horseradish sauce and ran into Jodi Putterbaugh.

He stared at her over a pyramid of Miller beer twelve-packs. He knew she was familiar, but couldn't quite . . .

"Do I know you?" asked Jodi.

She was cute, in an off sort of way. Dressed in sweats.

"Not sure. I'm Milo Wood."

"Oh, my God, Milo! Milo, I'm Jodi Putterbaugh. From fifth grade!"

Sometimes our memories make us do strange things, especially if we are strange people. Milo said, "Hey, Jodi," marched around the beer pyramid, grasped her by the arms, and planted a huge kiss on her lips. Not just a friendly kiss, either.

Obviously that long-ago dusk, with the kiss and the fireflies, had been lurking around in his head.

Woo-hoo! crowed the ancient souls.

"Okay," said Jodi. And they put their arms around each other and stood there by the beer for a time.

Where had she gone?

Iowa. Then she was in the hospital for years, having hallucinations and, finally, brain surgery. She was dumber now; did it show?

Her parents?

Dead.

"Shit, Jodi. I'm sorry."

He *was* sorry. It got past the switch.

Jodi said, "Thanks. I'm going to be driving a school bus, when school starts up in the fall."

Meeting Jodi Putterbaugh at the store and then having grilled cheese and Cokes with her at K's made Milo have to get his thoughts in order. For that, he needed quiet.

Night found him in the shadows by the highway. Thinking. Breathing.

Waiting. Pulling the trigger and—*crack!*—starring the driver's-side window on a little blue Mercury Lynx. The driver kept his nerve, didn't swerve, but sped up.

That shooting made the paper. The cops also mentioned a previous report, a Toyota. Someone called him "the Route 41 BB Sniper."

Why'd they have to go and put "BB" in there? Made him sound like a little kid.

He went and got a real rifle and real rifle bullets. He threw all the bullets but one out the car window. That one bullet, he kept in his pocket.

They had dinner at the Brewery, looking out over the Miami River.

Man, she looked nice. Not just cute, like that first day at Zwiebel's. Now she'd had time to grow in his mind, and he'd made room for her there. She made it hard for him to breathe, that's how beautiful she looked, wearing a blue dress and an enormous mum in her hair. The mum looked like a second head.

He had gone out and bought a tie.

"Do you miss living on a farm?" he asked her, over salads.

Jodi nodded. "Yeah," she said, "except for the work. I miss the animals, but you have to work really hard to live on a farm. Does that make me lazy?"

"Nah," Milo answered. "There's different kinds of work, is all. Different kinds of energy."

She gave him a nice kind of look then. He'd said the right thing. For a minute, spearing the last of his lettuce off his plate, he felt the rightness of his life like a boat sailing on clear water. But it made him nervous, too, because he had to tell her sooner or later where he worked.

They talked about college. They were both saving up.

"Maybe we could take a class together over at Edison," Jodi suggested. "To try it out. A class about poems. I know you probably don't want to take a class about poems, especially, but it can be interesting sometimes if you look at the way we put words together in regular life. Like last week I made a grocery list. It said—you want to hear what it said?"

"Yes."

"'Red lettuce and shoestrings.'"

"So that's like a poem?" asked Milo.

"No. It's just some things that wouldn't come together anywhere else but on a list."

Milo shrugged. "Who says that's not a poem?" he said. "Just because it came together at random?"

Jodi's face brightened. She leaned forward.

"You actually get it," she said, reaching out, touching his forearm. "I thought you might get it, and you do."

"I work at the Dinner Bell plant," he told her.

Their entrées came.

"Jeez, Milo."

"Gotta put food on the table," he murmured. It was just like when she caught him squishing the worms.

"You know what they do with baby pigs they can't use?" she asked. "I read about this slaughterhouse in Pittsburgh. They just pick them up by their hind legs and bash their heads on the floor. They have contests to see who can get the brains to splatter the farthest."

A single table candle burned between them. It was too tall, and unless he peered around the side, it left a bright halo in the middle of her head, and all he could see was the mum sticking out.

It bothered him, the tone in her voice. The dead switch armed itself. So, she wanted to tell horror stories?

"They had a contest once," he said, leaning forward into the candle-light, "at Dinner Bell, with the steers. The air hammer went on the blink, and the night shift had to process two hundred beeves before they clocked out. So they went ahead and hooked the steers onto the overhead trolley without using the stunner. Which basically means they're hanging upside down, totally alive and scared to death, instead of brain-dead like they're supposed to be. And they had a contest to see how far they could process a beef before it died. They had one steer come down the line that had been skinned and had its, you know, its organs gutted and had gone through one steam-spray, and when it got to the guy who was supposed to cut off the flank steaks, it twisted and went, 'Moooo!' right in his face. I mean, it wasn't even a cow anymore, it was just a meat thing, and it goes 'moo' like that. The guy quit."

He peeked around the candle to see if Jodi was shocked. She was staring into her lap.

The dead switch snapped off. Better judgment flooded in. Aw, man . . .

"Listen," he said, "it wasn't really a contest. The floor works like an assembly line—"

Jodi winced at the sound of his voice. He shut up.

They ate their dinner.

Milo found himself making lists in his head.

Things to talk about: Craziest things you ever did. Shoot cars on the highway.

No! cried his old souls. He kept silence.

Dinner forks. A picture on the wall. Picture that might be an eye or some water going down a drain. Hard to tell.

Milo drove out to his tree on Route 41.

Why had he told Jodi that awful story?

People sabotaged themselves all the time, Milo thought. For exam-ple, why was he driving out to the same tree, the same spot where he'd already shot at two cars? Wouldn't they start watching this area? If the

Route 41 BB Sniper were smart, he wouldn't snipe on Route 41 anymore.

He hiked back to his car.

He drove to the edge of Troy, out past the old covered bridge and past Experiment Farm Road, until he found a hill overlooking I-75 itself.

He left his truck parked on a gravel turnout, a mile or so from the interstate. Carrying both guns—the air rifle and the rifle rifle—he picked his way over a barbed-wire fence and sat down beside a tree, four hundred yards away. Out of headlight range.

The highway roared and whined. The headlights approached like starships, transforming into streaks, then taillights. It would be a challenge to try to hit them just as they passed. He'd have to lead them by . . . twenty feet? Part of it would depend on whether he used the air rifle or the real thing.

He went with the air rifle, although it grated at him. BB Sniper, my ass. The rifle bullet in his pocket seemed to announce itself, to clear its throat, to grow hot against his leg. He ignored it and screwed the scope on. Took his time calibrating, firing four shots into a pop can down in the ditch.

Patience, the dead switch whispered at him.

He *was* patient. Couldn't have said what form of Perfection he was waiting for. Didn't the headlights all look the same? And the longer he sat there, the more chance some cop would get curious about his truck, parked for no reason back there, with the empty gun rack in the rear window.

He wound up choosing a truck. A Peterbilt tanker that got his attention by pulling its Jake brake a mile upstream.

Milo let the Peterbilt fill his scope. Let the reticle hover off-center. He wasn't trying to hit the driver. Moved his shoulders and arms and hands together, swiveling just slightly, letting the reticle pull out ahead of the truck, like a sprinter making his move.

Timing his breath, exhaling.

His lungs emptied. The oxygen in his blood hit maximum, leaving his eyes at their sharpest. He squeezed the trigger between breaths, when his body and mind were at their most still.

His ears, hyperalert, heard the *crack* of the shot and the distant *crack* of the pellet on the windshield. An adrenaline bomb went off inside him. He had a moment of Perfection that even his ancient soul enjoyed.

Then a universe of noise and confusion as the truck locked up its brakes and skidded to a stop—*incredible!*—less than a hundred yards down the shoulder. The stink of scorched rubber filled the night. Cars swerved and scrambled to give the truck room. A horn blared.

Milo's body tightened up, and he almost bolted. Then the dead switch kicked in.

He exhaled. He sat like a stone.

The driver appeared, walking fast. Not your usual trucker type but a skinny guy in nice pants, with his shirt tucked in.

Flashlight.

The beam played up and down the ditch. Then up the hill, way to Milo's right.

Milo reasoned with himself. He felt as if he stood out like a bonfire in the night, but that was just mind panic. He imagined what it looked like to the trucker, down there on the shoulder. He made a list of things the trucker saw.

Shapes. Shadows. One big rock and some fast-food trash.

Needle. Haystack.

The beam jabbed in his direction. Milo covered his scope with his hand, so the lens wouldn't reflect.

The light passed over him without pausing.

In the dark that followed, he raised the rifle to his shoulder and focused in on the driver. The guy started walking again, back toward his cab. Milo zeroed the reticle on the back of his head. Followed.

Breathe, whispered the dead switch. Squeeze.

He didn't. The adrenaline bomb in his chest fizzed and subsided.

The driver had hopped back up in his cab, but the truck didn't go anywhere. He's radioing the highway patrol, Milo thought. He won't leave until they come.

He backed away through the weeds, uphill, crouching. Down the fenceline the way he'd come.

Dead grass. Duck under branches. Racing heart. Grunt. Gasp. Dodge a gopher hole.

Sirens. Fuck! If they had any brains, they'd send somebody down Experiment Farm Road, too. Goddammit. Even if he got to his truck and got on the road, a cop might pull him over, if he passed one.

Shit. He unslung the air rifle, wiped it down with his sleeve as he ran. When he judged it was print-free, he cast it aside, to the left, into a strip of woods.

Jogged through the tall roadside grass until he drew even with his truck, and thirty seconds later was on the road, fiddling with the radio. Rifle in its place, up on the gun rack.

He drove casually into Troy and out of danger, and the main thing on his mind was that he still wished he hadn't told Jodi that slaughter-house story.

Let a little time pass, he thought. Be patient, just like with firing the rifle. Make it perfect, and she'd let him in again.

Radio. Washer-and-dryer sale. Slow song. Static.

One day when school had been going about three weeks, Jodi stopped the school bus at the Kosmal driveway, out on Tick Ridge Road, to pick up little Rachel and Skye, and there was Milo Wood, in a brand-new Cincinnati Reds ball cap. There was his truck, parked just down the road.

"Milo!" gasped Jodi as he climbed aboard the bus.

"Hey," he said, smiling a warm smile. "Can I sit up here in front?"

A week ago, he had sent her flowers. Five yellow roses, two red roses. A low-pressure bouquet.

Three days ago, a note on stationery paper, saying he was sorry. Saying he had a surprise for her.

At home, he built a little Jodi shrine. A plastic toy pig. A grocery-store receipt. A candle. A picture of some mums. A picture of a school bus.

Now here he was, half on, half off the actual bus.

Ten little kids and two young teens sat perfectly still, observing.

"I'm not supposed to have riders," said Jodi, keeping it quiet. "Extra grown-ups, like friends or whatever you are."

"Not supposed to" didn't mean "no." Milo started climbing the rest of the way onto the bus, but Jodi reached for the lever, slowly closing the door.

"You can follow me back to the garage," she said. "Now, get down; you're going to get me in trouble."

All right. He stepped down. The door closed in his face.

He followed the bus to fourteen more driveways and three schools, with kids piling up in the backseats, staring. One of them made a face at him. He made a face back. The kids laughed. He could see them turn around to tell Jodi.

Schoolkids, he thought. Thumbs-up.

"I quit the slaughterhouse," he told Jodi after she parked the bus at the district garage.

"So much for putting food on the table."

"It's okay. I know somebody who knows somebody over at SynthaGro. They might put me on."

SynthaGro was a company in Troy that would come and spray little pellets on your lawn and keep bugs and weeds from doing what they did. If he got hired, Milo would be wearing a green uniform with his name on it and pushing a little green spreader—kind of like a lawnmower—around people's yards. It didn't pay as well as Dinner Bell, but hey.

"Dinner Bell is like *The Texas Chainsaw Massacre*," said Jodi. "Anything but that."

And she kissed him on the cheek.

For some reason, this made the dead switch perk up. In the space of his own head, Milo whipped around with a savage grin, teeth exposed, and made the switch disappear.

I'm going to have this, he thought, lashing out. I'm going to have this one good thing. And then another good thing after that. And another.

His old souls peed themselves, spiritually, in amazement.

He kissed her back.

Roses. Letter. School bus.

"What are you thinking?" Jodi asked.

"I'm doing poems in my head," he answered.

She wouldn't sleep with him unless they were living together.

"So move in," he said, shrugging. "Your apartment's the same as mine. What difference does it make?"

She squinched up her eyes.

"*That's* romantic," she said.

"It's practical," he said, but then he wheeled around and grabbed her and kissed her and took her hand. She shook his hand off and put her arm around him. They walked out of K's with their arms around each other.

"The kids are asking when you're going to follow the bus around again."

"I thought you were going to get in trouble?"

"I *did*. Someone called the school. I'm lucky I didn't get written up."

It might be fun to be a teacher, he sometimes thought. Once he got to college, anything could happen, really.

She moved in that same evening.

Jodi paused in total silence when she saw the Jodi shrine he'd built. He didn't explain. Just stood worrying, making silent finger-snapping motions.

She didn't say anything. Just moved on, kept moving in. The second all her things were inside and she'd cleaned the bathroom, she pulled him into the bedroom and said, "You may take off your clothes."

He saw that she had arranged some things beside the Jodi shrine. A simple Milo shrine: the word "Milo" on a piece of paper, and a candle.

Bright skin. The lamp. Twisted sheets. Breeze. Open window.

And then the list stopped. The poem stopped, if that's what it was, and there was just her and him, one thing, breathing perfectly.

After, she lay half on top of him, stroking his chest. She said, "I love you. You know that, right?"

"I do," he said. He loved her, too. He wanted to, anyhow. Wasn't it the same thing?

So he said "I love you" back to her, and the dead switch screamed as if he'd poured acid on it.

It was a lazy afternoon and evening. They unpacked some things and arranged some things. Argued in good humor over whether to use his couch or hers (hers), which TV to use (hers), which plates to use (hers). Three times, they stopped to make love.

The dead switch calmed down and took a softer tack.

What are you doing? it whispered. This could be good or bad. You had to have *something* bright and human and *normal* going on, right? Otherwise the *beautiful* things you did might come to light.

After the second time, they didn't bother getting dressed again. They sat on the living-room floor, sorting records, naked. Jodi had a tattoo of a dolphin on her shoulder.

"See my dolphin?" she asked, leaning forward, almost into his lap.

"It's nice," he said. It was blue.

"I like your armband," she said.

Milo's forearm said "Jodi" around it, in a ring.

"It's not a real tat," he said. "I drew it on with a marker."

"Wow."

"We should both get real ones. Real armband tats with our names." She shook her head.

"What?" he said. She wasn't excited about the idea. He had thought she'd be excited. Why wasn't she?

"Don't make a big deal out of it," she said.

Yeah, said his thousand voices. Don't.

They were right. Milo nodded, looking away. He sat quietly, tracing her dolphin tattoo with his finger, pulling her close.

Okay, he thought. Breathe out. Be still. It'll all be so good if you'll just be still and let it.

After she fell asleep, he went for a drive.

Parked his truck off-road and hiked to a bluff overlooking Tick Ridge. Part of Jodi's bus route.

He needed someplace totally new, after all, if he was going to shoot again. No doubt they had their eye on I-75 now.

Full moon.

Breathe in . . . let it go . . .

Crack! The sound of a real rifle, the kick of a real rifle against his shoulder.

The *punch!* of a real car window disintegrating.

Squealing tires. Headlights going all sideways. The car slid backward into the ditch on the far side of the road.

Warmth bloomed in Milo's gut and spread through his chest. His groin tingled.

Had he . . . ?

He waited.

Faint car radio.

Scraping noise.

The driver's-side door opened, and a woman got out. Walked to the middle of the road and stood there with her head down. One hand on her hip, the other rubbing the back of her neck.

Okay.

That was good, right? She wasn't hurt. Right?

The old voices and the dead switch locked grips and wrestled.

When he got home, Milo was momentarily startled to find Jodi sitting on *her* couch in *his* living room, wrapped in one of *his* blankets, watching *her* TV.

When people move all their things in together, it takes a while for their minds to follow.

"Where were you?" she asked.

He leaned over and kissed her.

"I drive around when I can't sleep," he said.

"Well, watch out," she said. "There's those asshole kids that shoot BBs at people."

Two days later, he had his first day wearing the SynthaGro uniform.

There wasn't even any training.

"It's just like a lawnmower," the foreman told him. "When you're done, put up three or four of these tags." He handed Milo a bundle of wire stakes with little yellow flags on them, warning people that the lawn had been treated and to stay off the grass for a couple of days.

"Good to go?" he asked.

"Very good," said Milo. And he climbed into his SynthaGro truck, which smelled like poison. It burned a little, just the smell going through his nostrils.

But it was the smell of having a job, too. It was the smell of having a real life and of someone at home, someone he liked being with. It was the smell of love.

He sprayed three lawns and then stopped at the pay phone outside the Stop-N-Go in Troy.

Jodi answered the phone.

"Hey, precious," she said. "Whatcha doing?"

Want to meet for lunch?"

"Maybe."

"Pizza Hut."

"Healthy choice. Okay. Now?"

"I'll wait for you. I'll get a table; I'm like a mile away."

Jodi made a kissy noise as he hung up.

———

Four minutes later, Milo died on his way to Pizza Hut.

He was going down Main Street thinking how Velma from *Scooby-Doo* was actually hotter than Daphne, although you were obviously meant to think the other way around. Now, why *is* that? his brain had just begun thinking, when the thing that happened happened.

It was fast and bad.

A Camaro came screaming down Main Street, decided Milo was going too slow in his SynthaGro truck, and screeched by in the oncoming lane. (Jackass.)

The Camaro went slightly airborne over the railroad tracks by the Sunoco station.

On the other side, a church bus full of kids, on a road trip from the Liberty Baptist Church in Columbus, swerved to avoid the Camaro. Swerved into Milo's lane, just as Milo came over the tracks. Milo had about a tenth of a second to quit thinking about Velma from *Scooby-Doo* and process whether to hit the bus or take his chances in the ditch.

Fast fast fast: Milo yanked the wheel and rolled the truck into the ditch. Fell through the driver's door when it flapped open. The door scissored back on him, chopping him in two and trapping both halves under the truck, with lawn chemicals pouring all over. His dead switch didn't have time to arm.

It took him three seconds to die, but it was a long, terrible, slo-mo three seconds.

Jodi passed the wreck on her way to Pizza Hut, and by then there was a collection of vehicles on-site: the bus, the Camaro, five cop cars with lights flashing, an ambulance, and two fire trucks.

She stopped. She knew. She started shaking.

The same instant, the chemical smell washed over her.

"That might be my boyfriend," she told one of the cops, gagging as she spoke, covering her face with her hand.

The cop nodded. He looked sympathetic but raised his hands, saying, "You need to back up, ma'am. Please. There's some nasty stuff spilled here."

Jodi backed off.

She stared into the ditch.

Truck. Chemicals. Crashed and smashed. Part of Milo. Red lights blue lights.

She thought of all the different things that could have happened or not happened, and how different things were going to be now from the way they would have been.

Looking down, Jodi noticed that she had forgotten to put on shoes.

Barefoot. Asphalt. A faded Pepsi can. They wouldn't have let me in Pizza Hut, anyway, she thought.

CHAPTER 19

The Most Amazing Girl
You Knew in High School

Milo woke up half in, half out of the water. As if he'd washed up there like a dead animal.

For a moment, it was very nice. The smell of earth and grass and wildflowers, the cool of the water on his skin. Then, as always, memory came. First a whisper, then a roar, and Milo gagged on it. The memory of the rolling truck and the chopping in two and the crushing and drowning in chemicals was still immediate, still tangible.

This memory backed off, leaving him wild-eyed. Leaving him with other memories, things he had done, like shooting at people. Things he was probably going to do, if the accident hadn't—

He rolled over on his side, convulsing, and puked all over some dandelions.

His whole body shook.

Milo wasn't surprised by his condition. He had led enough questionable lives to know that bad things worked their way into your soul. When you had done wicked things, you arrived in the afterlife with a berserker of a hangover.

Footsteps approached, crashing through soft grass. Milo winced.

He didn't look up. He spat, cleared his throat, and said, "Hey."

"Indeed," said someone. "Hey."

Someone who was not Suzie.

A cat trotted up and rubbed noses with him, then trotted off again.

Towering above, wearing something like a ruffled funeral dress, Nan frowned at him.

"And how," she said, crossing her arms, "would you say *that* went?"

Milo took a few seconds to get his thoughts in order.

"I almost killed people," he said, shuddering. "I think I would have."

Nan pursed her lips. But when she spoke, Milo was surprised at how gentle she sounded.

"You *were* making progress," she said. "There's something to be said for that. Let's get you home."

She reached down and, with a surprisingly strong grip, helped him to his feet. He stood quivering for a minute, and they made their way along the river.

"I couldn't help but notice," said Milo, pausing to throw up again, "that I have not become part of the Oversoul."

"Noticed that, did you?"

They crossed a bridge and walked through town. Past fancy neighborhoods. Past suburbs.

"I suppose," said Milo, "I have to come back as a tapeworm now."

"Stop whining."

"Well, I didn't *accomplish* anything."

Nan stopped. She gave his elbow a yank and turned him to face her.

"Sometimes," she said, "the value of a life is in what it *doesn't* do. Imagine if Hitler had resisted the voice inside him and spent his life keeping bees? What a great life."

Milo considered this.

"Driving into the ditch instead of hitting the bus," said Nan, "is why you don't have to come back as a tapeworm. Be satisfied with that. You didn't reach Perfection and you didn't win any prizes. Now, hush. Here we are."

They had arrived in the middle of a trailer park, in front of a rusty old Airstream with broken windows. Off to one side towered what had to be a thirty-year pile of beer cans.

"Home sweet home," said Nan.

"Mmmm," said Milo, entranced by the beer cans.

They were all his mind had room for, just yet.

The inside of the trailer matched the outside. Stained chair, peeling walls, and some kind of smell, a combination of feet and banana peels.

Milo didn't care. He aimed for the bedroom at the rear, collapsed on the damp mattress, and zonked out.

Time passed.

He didn't sleep well. Kept waking up if anything happened, like if a bird flew by or a leaf landed on the beer cans.

He hid his head under a moldy pillow, but it didn't help.

It didn't help because it wasn't the light and the noises and things that were keeping him awake. It was Suzie.

Don't think about that! warned part of his brain.

Last time, in the desert, he had listened to this part of himself. Now he gave it a violent shove.

For eight thousand years, he had awakened by a river, and Suzie had been there, and everything was fine. Now everything was bullshit.

He could feel the shape of her, where she would be if she were lying there with him. He would have zipped out to buy some dry sheets, of course, and would spray some afterlife version of Lysol. They would have made love and talked.

Milo screamed into the pillow and got a mouthful of mildew.

They had fallen in love at a time like this. The day he died for the hundred-and-first time.

For his first hundred lives, they had been friends. They had long talks; they watched TV together. They traded books and argued about desserts.

"I'll have some of yours," she would say, not ordering her own dessert.

And Milo would say, "No, you won't," and he was serious. He was territorial about his food. He loved food and wanted everything on his plate. And he would make her order her own. Friends do things like that to each other.

Then everything changed.

One day, he was down on Earth leading one of his less admirable lives: a Scottish rascal named Andrew Milo McCleod, who made a living stealing other men's sheep. The sheriff had caught him and tied his hands behind him and was getting ready to cut off his head.

Milo was looking around at the high hills and the mist, thinking about things. Maybe he could get his arms free and make a run. He thought about his chances of getting into Heaven and wished he'd bedded more women. He thought about Lord Donnel, who owned these hills and the sheep he'd stolen, and wished on him a pox that would make Swiss cheese of his private bits. That's what he was thinking when a pale woman in a black dress appeared in front of him, saying, "Mind what you wish for, Milo."

And he'd tossed his head, winked his eye, and said, "Well, then, lass, I wish you'd give us a kiss."

She seemed amused. And she did kiss him. Kissed him good. It made him dizzy and made him wish to keep his head. He was going to suggest that she help him to his feet so he could make a run, at least. Get to the woods and—

But she stepped aside to make room for the sheriff, who had sharpened his broadsword. He kept a string of human ears along his belt; that's how nasty this sheriff was.

"I love you," said the woman.

He loved her, too, Andy Milo McCleod did. Very much! Just as he loved the morning air and the low clouds and the sun that was hiding behind them and the sheep dotting the far hill and the sea and the rocks it crashed on, and how he'd love to kiss this girl again, whoever she was—

The sword whistled.

A sharp, electric jerk.

The world rolled, then stopped, and he lay facedown in the grass, trying to blink the clover out of his eyes. Then the sleep shades came down.

He found himself beside the pale girl, looking down at his disconnected head.

His soul memory floated together until he knew who the girl was.

"I am so, so, so, so sorry," she said.

"That was a good kiss," he answered. He wanted to kiss her again. It was all he cared about.

"Did that hurt?" she asked. "It looked like it hurt."

"It hurt more than you'd think," he admitted, rubbing his neck. "I think it has something to do with, you know, cutting through the spine. It's hard to describe."

She reached up and put her arms around his neck and pressed herself against him.

Had she said "I love you" before his head came off?

"Yes," she said. "Oh, fuck it. I've wanted to tell you for a long time. In the afterlife, we have to be so careful, and I wanted everything to be just right."

Milo looked around at the head and the blood and the sheriff over there having a pee.

"It's perfect," he said. He put his arms around her.

And there was a repeat of the kiss, and they both knew they'd have to get going.

"I know how to describe it," he said. "When your head's chopped off. It's like hitting your funny bone super-hard, except it hurts like that all over your body for a second. Especially, you know, your neck."

"Thank you, love."

They kissed tenderly while the sheriff walked over and picked up the severed head by its long red locks and dumped it in an old barley sack.

———

After that morning in the Highlands, a lot of things had changed.

They had begun sneaking around, for one thing. They weren't sure it was necessary, but they didn't want to be split up, so hey.

That night, in the afterlife, Nan and Mama and Suzie had brought him to his house (a crappy old shack by the water-treatment plant), then gone off and left him. Then, beginning a long tradition, Suzie had come back in through the kitchen window, all dry leaves and cool wind. They held hands and walked to his rickety, crooked old bed and didn't speak at all for the longest time.

It was, and was not, what he'd expected.

It was warm and perfect. They had always felt "at home" with each other. They felt even more at home now. Familiar, as if they'd been making love for centuries.

It was not wildly supernatural. Milo had expected that making love to Death would involve weird fires and shadows and whisperings in the dark—perhaps even pain—but there was very little of that. Only the soft red glow in her eyes. The occasional drawing of blood. The sudden flutter and leathery warmth of being wrapped in wings, once or twice. And once her eyes had widened until they seemed to drink him in, and he felt himself falling and his whole self being drowned out by something larger, like a single note in a symphony, and he screamed and screamed—

Other than that, it was all surprisingly normal.

Afterward, they went out to dinner, and he let her share his dessert. A giant slice of peanut butter pie. Not because he *wanted* to but because being in love is different from being friends.

Which was why, centuries later, Milo got up off his moldy bed and left his damp, trashy trailer without getting a wink of real sleep and went to find her, whether the cosmic God-soul liked it or not.

What if she's been sucked into the universal yin-yang? wondered a part of him. What if she no longer exists here, really?

He told that part of himself to stick a pickle in it and kept putting one foot in front of the other.

He stopped at a sundries store for canned food and a can opener and some bottled water. He made a knapsack out of a pillowcase, slung it over his shoulder, and headed for—what?

A red moon lurked in the trees.

Milo walked until he came to a railroad crossing. There, he put down his knapsack and waited.

A crow came and sat on the railroad sign for a while, then flew away again.

A train howled from far off, then rumbled closer the way trains do, throbbing and groaning and slicing along the rails. It blasted its horn as it went past, and Milo reached up to keep his cap from flying off.

He threw his knapsack into an open boxcar and jumped after it. Tumbled through dust and straw and rolled to a stop in the dark.

He scooched back to the door and rode there awhile, in the wind, watching the moon until he fell asleep.

He woke up because something at the dark end of the boxcar made a noise.

Animal?

"Someone there?" he called.

"Hell yes," someone said. "A coupla someones."

"Well, hello."

"Hello yourself."

Milo peered into the dark until his eyes made out three forms seated against the back wall.

Milo had ridden the rails before, down on Earth. If this were Earth, he'd take out his knife now and whittle a piece of wood. To look casual and cool, and to show he had a knife. But he didn't have a knife, and this wasn't Earth.

Milo said, "I'm looking for somebody."

"Well, you *found* somebody."

"Somebody in particular," said Milo. "Death.

"She's my girlfriend," he added.

Clickety-clack.

"You're talking about Suzie," said one of the shapes, one of the voices. "You're Milo. I heard o' you."

"Ten thousand lives," said another voice. "You're like Superman."

"Well," said Milo, "I don't know about all that."

"I heard from a guy who heard from a guy that you threw an elephant up in the air and it never came back down."

Milo raised his eyebrows.

"Superman or not," said the first, "y'ain't supposed to date *them*. That's like the man who married the ocean. Ever heard of that?"

"I've been warned."

Clickety-clack.

"What's it like?" asked one.

Milo considered the question and found it fair.

"Think about the most amazing girl you knew in high school," he said. "Not your girlfriend or some other girl you hooked up with. I mean the one you *never did* hook up with. The one who haunted you and still haunts you. Know what I mean?"

They knew. Every man knew.

"Marsha Funderburg," said one, in a quiet voice.

"Wu Ping," said another.

"Vicki Tuscedero," said a third.

"Well," said Milo, "it's like that."

Outside the boxcar door, a few lights passing. Someone's farm, probably.

"Well," said the first voice after a while, "ain't seen her. Sorry."

The train slowed. Milo gathered up his knapsack and steadied himself against the door. When it slowed a bit more, he thought, he'd jump.

"Is it true," one of the shadowmen asked, "there's a place where you step off a sidewalk and turn into nothing?"

"It's true," answered Milo.

Click. Clack. Slower.

Lights ahead. Town.

He jumped.

He walked into the town and found the police station.

Not exactly a police station, per se. But most towns and cities had a place where you could go if you needed help, and this town had a nice one. A brick building right downtown, with a cement eagle over the door.

Milo found a tired-looking sergeant sitting behind a tall desk.

"Hi," said the sergeant, in a friendly-enough tone for the middle of the night.

Milo said, "Hi. I'm looking for someone."

"The someone got a name?"

Milo told him the name.

The sergeant appeared to freeze for a second. Then he leaned forward and surveyed Milo like a schoolmaster.

"That would make you Milo, I gather?"

Shit. "That's right," he said.

"Well, it shouldn't really surprise you that I have instructions not to tell you anything. In fact, the instructions I have say that if you show up asking about Ms. Suzie, I'm to recommend you find some other way to focus your energies. There's something of a tone to the message, if you don't mind my saying so."

"I'll bet."

"I'm also supposed to ask you to wait here," said the sergeant, "if it's not inconvenient, until—"

Milo was already gone.

He didn't go far. Just a few blocks down, close to the railroad, where he stretched out on a park bench for a while and tried to sleep.

Woke up at some hour in the night with that feeling we all get of having just missed someone calling our name. He sat up and listened.

A breeze circled his bench. Shadows teased his eye.

Nothing. Across the park, a cat or a possum darted through the pool of a streetlamp.

Unable to get back to sleep, he shouldered his sack and walked back to the railroad tracks.

———————

"Haunted? What do you mean, 'haunted'?"

Milo sat in the middle of a crowded boxcar on a fast train, rocking and clacking. Sometimes when a train was well populated, it could become almost like a party. This one had become a great conversation, illuminated by flashlights and old-time lanterns, fueled by a whiskey jug making its rounds and an enormous knapsack full of Cajun hot fries.

Someone, an old man in gumboots, had said there were parts of the road that were haunted.

"How can anything here be haunted?" asked a woman with a henna tattoo across her forehead. "It's the afterlife."

"You can die in the afterlife," said the old man, who was curious in his own right, just for *being* an old man. Everyone up here was young-ish. Weren't they?

Yeah, sure. Just like everyone was happy, and eager to get born again, and couldn't wait to join the Oversoul.

"If you die in the afterlife," asked a number of people, "where do you go?"

The old man explained that you go Nowhere.

"But you might take a while going," he said.

Milo shuddered.

He slipped off the train at moonrise, with the jug tucked under his jacket, and drank his way down the road. Some road in the middle of nowhere. A stray dog joined him for a while.

His days and nights became a blur of towns and conversations.

"Death? *The* Death? She came for me, is all I know."

"I'm not allowed to tell you anything, friend. There's a message here—"

Sometimes he stuck out his thumb, and sometimes he'd catch a ride.

Sometimes he'd get a lecture or a cautionary tale.

The guy who tried to date the Northern Lights. The gal who loved the Jet Stream.

Everywhere, he kept thinking he'd walk into a bus station and find her selling magazines. Maybe she'd be on the bus itself, so he rode the bus sometimes, searching faces.

Sometimes he was recognized. He was, after all, famously old and wise, and famously in deep shit.

"Is it true," they asked, "about the place that goes Nowhere? Is it like a tunnel? Is it a stormy place or, like, a big hand that reaches down and grabs you?"

"It's just a sidewalk," he told them.

He wandered through nights and days, and in and out of weeks, and almost over a year.

He got skinny, like a stick. He learned not to be hungry except when he had to be.

He began to smell musky, like an animal.

He went from living "up there," as some would say, and learned to live "down here."

He worked at a grain elevator for a time, earning some food and a warm bed. Then the air began to feel as if it might snow in a week or two. Maybe he should head south.

He went south until he smelled the salt and the sea islands, but he still felt cold. Felt sort of thin, and it occurred to him maybe it wasn't the weather or the season.

He was riding atop a long, rusty train under a full moon when it occurred to him. He had made himself a fire—just a little hobo fire, a stick or two—and was trying to warm himself against the slipstream when he noticed something that startled him.

He could see the fire through his hand.

He jerked and said, "Fuck me!" and jammed his hand into his coat pocket.

Later, when he'd got up the nerve, he raised his hand against the moon, and . . .

"Fuck me," he whispered.

The road *was* haunted. By him.

As if a switch had been flipped, he saw them all along the old train, like riders on a mythical snake. The moonlight shone through them, but it ran over them like water, too, and made them visible.

Some of them sat; others stood. All stared ahead but with a hollow disinterest in where the train was actually going. Many of them had allowed themselves to age, leaning like old barns. Many of them had fires, like him. None of them looked warm.

A cross-breeze caught Milo. A stream of milder cold, bearing dry leaves.

"If you can see them," said the cross-breeze, "maybe you can see me, too."

The breeze took his hand, and he turned his eyes toward the moonlight.

She was like steam over softly boiling water. Barely there.

"Suzie," he said, and they sat there by the fire for a while, holding hands, touching foreheads, leaning against each other as much as this was possible. Parts of them were like mist. These parts flowed through each other.

It was the saddest joy Milo had ever known.

"I'm not being dragged into the Big Whole," she told him. "I'm getting the sidewalk treatment."

Goddamn them, Milo thought. Or it, or whatever.

"It's just reality, love," she said. "Death isn't a person. She's Death. If she's not Death, she's nothing. Two plus two. You quit moping around out here in the Empty, and go back and live. Go do your Perfection thing."

A tunnel loomed. All along the spine of the train, the ghosts lay down side by side and held their breath against the smoke and steam of the engine.

After the tunnel, the night itself seemed more clear. The train rolled and whistled down a long timbered trestle over a lake. It might have been Lake Michigan. It was endless.

"I don't know what to do," croaked Milo. "If I go back."

The engine whistled and moaned, miles ahead.

Suzie waved one ethereal hand, indicating the ghostly riders up and down the hundred boxcars.

"No one knows what to do," she said. "It's a crapshoot. Haven't you figured that out? Please let's not have this conversation; we're short on time."

WAAaaaaaAAAaaaaWOOooOoooOOOoo! moaned the train. "You *do* know what to do," she said, "actually."

"Oh, yeah?"

"Yeah. It's like when you were trying and trying to figure out how to juggle more than three beanbags. You got tired of getting nowhere, and you went and asked somebody. Don't act surprised; I've been digging around in your mind."

"A teacher," said Milo.

"A teacher."

"Like, the greatest teacher ever."

"Something like that."

Dawn touched the great lake. Up and down the train, the ghosts became hints of themselves. Milo held on to Suzie's hand while the sun burned through the morning fog. Then he stood and performed a fairly credible swan dive off the train.

It was a long way down, and it hurt. Jolted him unconscious when he hit the lake. But he wrestled himself awake and drifted down through the cold, searching images and shadows, searching possible lives, sinking through more than two thousand years.

Kind of a shame you had to go that far back to find a really, really, really, really, really, really, really, really, really, really, really, *really* fine teacher.

CHAPTER 20

The Discredited Economist
Who Fell from the Sky

Milo had tremendous respect for learning.

Learning was the most important thing a soul could do. There was an infinity of things to learn and to teach. There was an infinity of ways to get the learning and teaching done.

You could learn from mistakes, to begin with. That was pretty common. Milo's first mistake, as a baby in India, had been to reach out and grab a Ghaasa spider. The Ghaasa spider bit him on the thumb, and part of his thumb turned black and fell off. And he screamed, and wisely let it go, and didn't do that again.

You could learn to do things no one had ever done before, if you could imagine them being done. As a Moroccan inventor named Abass Ibn Firnass, Milo decided that it was time for his own species to conquer the air. Constructing himself a framework of wood and heavy paper, he flung himself from the highest roof in Andalusia, and damned if it didn't work.

For nearly ten minutes, to the wonder of crowds far below, he swooped and glided among the towers and minarets, until at last his momentum slowed and it came time to effect a landing. At this point, he realized that, in so thoroughly studying the elements of flight, he had neglected to develop a protocol for landing. Birds flew with their wings, so he had built himself wings. They land on their tails, however, and Abass had failed to provide himself with one. He survived a hard landing with considerable injury but no regrets.

"You are an angel!" gushed a local poet.

"You are kind," answered Abass, "but I am a scientist and a friend to man, something a hundred times greater."

He was an old copper miner whose job was to teach rookies how to drill holes and stuff them with dynamite and then get away before the dynamite was detonated.

He took this teaching very seriously.

So did his students.

Teaching is more likely to be a fine art when a passing grade means you don't get your ass blown off.

One of the most mysterious of Milo's lives was lived as Rabbi Aben ben Aben, a revered Jewish mystic. All his life, he sat bent over scrolls and texts. One day he staggered to his feet, a wild look in his eye as if he had unlocked something unlockable, learned something unlearnable.

"What is it, *rabboni?*" whispered his fellow scholars.

"It's a trap!" he cried, and fell down dead as a stone.

This was probably an important teaching, except no one, including Milo, understood what it meant.

Milo learned about money and became a famous economist.

He invented the field of "cryptoeconomics."

It was like the field of "cryptozoology," which concerned itself with animals that weren't real, like Bigfoot and the Loch Ness Monster.

Some economists, Milo noted, went around saying that if you helped rich people get richer and didn't make them pay taxes, eventually that would help out the poor people, too.

"That's the economic version of Bigfoot," Milo said on TV.

And he went around talking about cryptoeconomics and making a lot of rich people mad, until one day two strange things happened. One: A lot of economists (in the employ of big companies run by rich people) got together and said that Milo was full of shit. And then two: Milo was on a private-jet flight when the emergency door by his elbow blew out and popped him out of the plane. A farmer who saw him fall out of a clear blue sky did not see the jet, just this guy in an awesome suit who came down in his wheat field.

The big companies became the resource cartels that almost cannibalized the human race.

There are things out there that certain people don't *want* you to learn.

Milo had one of those lives where he just couldn't get ahead. He worked at Subway, and made car payments, and paid rent, and had to buy food and pay the electric bill.

You have to learn a trick or two to live like that. You almost get some money to put aside for school, and the car breaks down. You finally save enough to pay the electric bill, and you get pulled over for having a taillight out.

Milo learned how to use thrift stores and learned how *not* to have any kids until he got his degree and—

Pow! He had a kid. Happened just like that.

Sometimes the things we learn, Milo noted, don't help us very much.

———

Sometimes Milo learned simple things that were sort of like poetry.

He was ten years old, and his gramma taught him how to take care of plants.

"You get a rock," she told him, shuffling around her greenhouse, "and you put it in the dirt beside where the plant sprouts up. And when you go to water the plant, you pour the water over the rock instead of straight into the soil. That way the water sprinkles gently all around inside the pot and doesn't kick up the soil and disturb the roots."

"You water the rock," said Milo.

"You water the rock," said Gramma.

CHAPTER 21

The Buddha in Winter

INDIA, 500 B.C.

Long ago, there was a tiny Indian village called Moosa.

Moosa was not an exciting or remarkable place in any way. In fact, the village and its people had a reputation for lacking any particular shining qualities. They were honest enough, and good enough, but generally not too bright, ambitious, charismatic, or lucky.

It was Milo's fortune, good or bad, to be born in this place. He did not, predictably, stay there, and the thing that propelled him out into the world was a man named Horsa Chatturjee.

Horsa Chatturjee, true to the spirit of Moosa, was not a scholar or an athlete or a great warrior. He was not an inspiring man in any way. He was a man who fell into a hole and broke his leg.

This was a big, important event for the village.

The local elders had gathered around, and were discussing how the hole had gotten there and why Horsa hadn't been looking where he was going, when someone suggested they actually lift Horsa out of the hole and carry him someplace where he could be helped. And that

voice came from little Milo Raj Ram, who had a habit of offering un-
welcome advice to his elders (Milo already suspected that Moosa was
not the seat of a future empire. As he stood by and watched the older
men treating Horsa Chatturjee's leg, this suspicion deepened).

"Pull on his leg," said the eldest, a shirtless old fart with a gray top-
knot, "until the bone slips back under the skin. Pull until it pops into
place. Then pack goat shit around the torn flesh until the bleeding
stops."

Milo was pretty sure that putting goat shit on an open wound was a
terrible idea. He tried to say so but was boxed on the ear for his trouble.

He went up a tree to sulk, as boys will do.

While he was up in the tree, three things happened.

One, some voices in his head told him not to mind the old men,
who were foolish and stubborn. Milo had been hearing these voices for
some time and understood that they were the voices of lives he had
lived. He had great respect for them.

Two, he began to feel short of breath. This wasn't uncommon; he'd
been having these little attacks all his life. They usually abated once he
quit running around, climbing, or feeling upset.

This time, however, he kept feeling worse and worse, until the
world began to swim around and Milo fell out of the tree.

That's when the third thing happened.

A traveling healer walked into the village.

The healer, a holy man, wore a beard so long it had to be braided
into ropes and tied off in six places to his belt.

When Milo fell out of the tree and landed at his feet, the healer
frowned and probed at him with a long, beaded stick. Milo stared up at
him, blinking and catching his breath. At this same moment, a terrible
cry arose from the eldest elder's hut.

"Aaaaaaaaaaaaaaaaaaaagaaaaah!"

"What's that?" asked the healer.

"That's Horsa Chatturjee," Milo told him. "The elders put goat shit
on his broken leg."

"Ah," said the healer. "This must be Moosa."

By now others had noticed the healer and gathered around.

"I will examine your friend," offered the healer, "if you like. In exchange for supper."

"Aiiiiiiiiiiiiiiiiiiiiiiiiiiiiiiiiiiiiiiiiii!" screamed Horsa Chatturjee.

The healer was fed and made welcome.

Milo watched the procedure from outside the hut, peering over the windowsill.

The healer washed away the goat shit, revealing a very red, angry, evil-smelling leg. He burned the wound with a torch, nearly sending Horsa into orbit. Then he knelt at Horsa's feet and prayed, waving a torch. Milo hunched at the window, enraptured, thinking, This is the way they do things in the big city!

He was still there when the healer shuffled out of the house and said, "Alas, a demon has been at work here. Someone fetch an ax. The leg will have to go."

They fetched him an ax, and he performed the surgery himself.

After, the healer would accept no payment, taking only the goat that had produced the offending goat shit, saying, "I'm doing you good country people a favor."

"With a teacher like this," Milo mused, enraptured, "a diligent student could launch a golden age!" And he swore that when he came of age, he would seek out such a master, if it meant he had to search the whole wide world.

The day after his coming-of-age ritual, still wearing his yellow prayer cord, Milo showed up at his parents' breakfast table and said, "Goodbye. I'm going off into the world to seek knowledge. God knows I won't find it here."

"Smart move, kiddo," said his father, and sent him on his way with some bread and a new pair of sandals.

Milo hiked for weeks, through villages and across bridges and rivers. He talked with fellow travelers and slept by the fires of kind strangers. Just as he'd anticipated, things got bigger and less pointless the farther he went. Along the way, he heard of armies lurking beyond the mountains. He heard of a strange mystagogue called the Buddha, whose disciples were so holy they didn't need to eat or drink. He heard of great floods and seas and ships and women so beautiful and skilled that the men who bedded them died from pleasure. The more he traveled, the more he heard and saw and the bigger his world became, which was just as he had hoped.

One evening, Milo was enjoying the hospitality of a rich beet farmer and his field hands, and the farmer asked him if his wanderings had a particular purpose.

"I am seeking a teacher," Milo answered.

"A teacher of what?"

Milo shrugged. "I'm not sure it matters. Something new. Something wonderful or terrible."

A murmuring around the farmer's table.

"We can teach you about beets," someone said. "That's about it."

The tallest of the field hands—a thoughtful-looking fellow—spoke up.

"I understand what you're saying," he said. "It's something I want, also. Maybe the teacher you're looking for isn't a regular sort of teacher at all. Maybe he is, in fact, someone more like a farmer or a blacksmith."

Milo knew wisdom when he heard it.

"I would like to come with you," the field hand continued. "But I have promised my employer here to work through harvest time. Perhaps you could work with us until the beets are ready to pull, and then we can travel together and see what we find."

Milo accepted, and became a beet farmer for a while, and was thankful.

———————

He learned.

He learned about getting up early and carrying water. He learned about beets. Beets, beets, beets. He learned to fix things. He grew stronger.

After the beets were in, he and the field hand—whose name was Ompati—set out to find a teacher, and it was one of the most pleasant times in Milo's life. They hiked long roads, and met other travelers, and traded stories and songs. Once, they spent a night in a brothel, where Ompati was robbed of his wallet. Twice, bandits tried to rob them at knifepoint, but Milo and Ompati had done farmwork and had knives of their own. They swam in rivers. They slept under the stars. They saw strange and wonderful things: a leper with no legs, who had determined to crawl to Calcutta. They saw a magician who could separate himself from his shadow. Staying overnight with a holy man in a village called Moon Smoke, they drank the blood of a snake.

Milo came to understand that a great many holy men and others who seemed wise were, in fact, just out to get your money.

Don't let that discourage you, said the old voices in his head. There are real teachers out there. Keep looking.

"All right," said Milo softly. "I will."

Once, Milo and Ompati marched alongside a mighty army for several days, trading jests with the soldiers and marveling at the great war elephants. On the fifth day, they began encountering men with shaved heads, in orange sashes, who laughed and waved at the soldiers as they passed.

"Pilgrims," Ompati explained.

As the sun continued to rise, they saw more and more of these holy madmen.

"Disciples of the Buddha are teaching nearby," came the rumors and whispers, down through the ranks.

That evening, the army came to an unexpected stop.

News rushed like a weather front: not just *disciples* of the Buddha, but the Buddha *himself*! He and his entourage had met the army at a crossroads up ahead, and the army had stopped to let him pass.

"I don't understand all the excitement," said Milo.

"Maybe his teachings haven't traveled as far as Moosa," said Ompati, "but in places of consequence, they say he is the greatest soul that ever lived. They say he defeated the demon lord Mara in single combat, without even standing up. They say he just touched the earth with his hand and beat Mara back with pure *wholeness*."

"Which means what?"

"I don't know. No one does."

Milo and Ompati got a nasty surprise the next morning when messengers came riding down the lines, shouting to the sergeants and marshals. They looked excited.

The sergeants and marshals, in turn, screamed at their units.

"Quick-march, forward!" shouted the marshals.

Before them and behind them, soldiers, elephants, chariots, and armored horsemen all moved with purpose, looking tough.

"I propose," said Ompati, "that we will only be in the way here."

So they left the army behind and waded away between trees.

Arrows started falling around them. One stuck in the ground, nudging Milo's ankle.

"We seem to have wandered *toward* the fighting," observed Ompati.

Milo struggled to breathe. Red-hot terror had a grip on him. He was pretty sure he'd peed himself. Up ahead, and all around, he heard battle cries and shrieks and brave little speeches.

Soldiers rose out of the underbrush. Mean-looking guys in leather armor.

Milo wheezed and blacked out facedown in some kind of Asian raspberry bush.

Warm rain.

Milo came awake painfully, feeling sticky. Nearby, someone shuffled in the grass.

Lifting his head and looking around, he discovered an elephant standing over him.

Milo wasn't startled or afraid. It was clear from the very first instant that the elephant wasn't going to hurt him. In fact, it seemed sad and confused and stared down at Milo with a peculiar lost look in its eyes.

"Oh, God," Milo whispered. The elephant's trunk was half severed. The warm rain that had awakened him was blood misting in the air as the beast exhaled.

A single tear welled in one great eye and rolled down its cheek.

The surrounding forest looked as if it had been stepped on. Everywhere, broken trees, smashed people. Milo wondered what had happened to Ompati.

Focus, said the old voices in his head.

Milo pried a saber from a dead soldier's hand and took a step toward the elephant.

The elephant met him halfway. With a heavy grunt, it knelt in front of him.

Milo patted its head. Then he cut the elephant's throat.

A sheet of blood covered him. The elephant gurgled, rolled its eyes, and died.

Birds called out. Wounded soldiers moaned.

Milo sensed eyes on him and slowly turned.

A figure stood nearby. Slightly uphill, a silhouette against the morning sun.

"That was compassionate," said the silhouette.

Milo nodded. He would have said something, but he hadn't quite recovered his breath yet.

A cloud passed over the sun, and Milo saw that the figure was an old man. He was bent like a gwaggi vine, with a beard like a whip. Like other old men, his skin hung loosely, but under the hanging skin, muscles stretched like old harp strings. His simple wrap, a worn robe, hung on him like a second skin.

That was all Milo saw at first—a poor old man—until the eyes captured him.

X-ray eyes, whispered his many voices.

Milo didn't know what an X-ray was (not in *this* life), but he got the idea. The old man looked at him as if he could see his naked bones and the atoms they were made of.

"*Namaste,*" said Milo, bowing.

The old man bowed in return.

A sudden chorus of shouting from the hilltop.

"*Bodhi!*" someone cried, followed by a chorus of voices. "*Bodhi! Here he is!*"

Milo looked uphill to see several young bald men in simple robes hurrying toward them through the trees, hopping over the dead and wounded.

"Mmmmm," murmured the old man. "Here we go again."

The young men arrived in a breathless little herd.

"It's okay," the old man told them. "I'm having a good day."

"It doesn't matter," said the tallest, "if you're having a good day or a bad day. You're not supposed to wander off without telling Ananda."

"Shhh," said the old man, kneeling to help a bleeding soldier. "Be useful."

He unwound his simple robe until he stood in their midst wearing a homespun loincloth, and he began to tear the robe into strips. His students—as Milo deduced them to be—did exactly as he did, without question or hesitation.

"Buddha," Milo whispered to himself.

The old man heard him. Gave him an X-ray wink.

Milo tore his uniform into bandages and went about the forest, binding wounds.

————————

Milo found himself working with Balbeer, the oldest of the students. They rigged a series of tents at the top of the hill—the beginnings of a field hospital.

Milo asked, "What does it mean when you said Buddha has good days and bad days?"

"We don't call him 'Buddha.' That's a generic term for someone who's enlightened. Buddha is something everyone has inside them, if they can get to it. So we just call him 'Bodhi.' Wise one. Teacher."

"And the good-days-and-bad-days thing?"

Balbeer handed him some firewood. "Be useful," he said.

Milo went off to heat some water.

So, Milo thought, this is what it's really like to be a healer.

He put pressure on wounds that were bleeding. He tied splints around crooked arms. Once, he cut off a ruined leg. He gathered firewood. He cleaned things that needed cleaning.

One day, Milo saw the Master making his way out of the hospital with a pail full of shit, going to dump it in a latrine that he himself had dug.

"That's the teacher I've been looking for," Milo said to himself, "if he'll have me."

"Could you at least take the arrow out of my throat," coughed a soldier at his feet, "before you leave the third dimension?"

Milo's eyebrows shot up.

"Ompati!" he cried. "I'm so pleased you're not dead!"

Ompati started to say something but gagged instead.

Milo made him be silent.

He made himself useful.

The next few days passed in a blur. Milo worked in the makeshift hospital and did what the Buddha people around him were doing. He slept wherever there was space. Ate whatever came his way, which wasn't much. Surprising, thought Milo, when it came right down to it, how little a person needed.

The students seemed happy in a way Milo had trouble understanding. They weren't like other people. Most people had a kind of unhappiness they carried around with them. You saw it in their eyes or heard it in the way they talked. They were always a little bit mad about something, or worried, or sorry. This nagging unhappiness was a way of living that most people had gotten used to.

The Buddha people didn't have this unhappiness. They seemed to have a way of doing rather than fretting. Doing what was in front of them at that moment, whether it was talking to you or stitching a wound or drinking a cupful of water.

As he was noticing this, thinking about it, he realized that Balbeer was standing beside him. Balbeer put a friendly arm around his shoulder and said, "You're already enlightened, Milo."

Milo blinked.

"I don't see how that could be," he said. "I haven't—"

"You haven't had an explosion of light inside your head, or seen the future, or had fire shoot out of your nose?"

"No, I haven't."

"That's not what enlightenment is. It's not some mystical explosion. It's noticing what's going on around you, here and now, and you do that."

"Not always."

"Well, you're not always enlightened."

"So then basically everyone's enlightened, probably, at least some of the time. Like this guy whose leg I had to cut off. He screamed so hard he was drooling, and his eyes rolled back in his head."

Balbeer squinted, thinking. "I don't know," he said.

Milo was surprised. He had never heard a teacher or a serious student say "I don't know." It sounded frightfully intelligent.

"Why does a rhino have horns on its face instead of up on top of its head?" Milo asked.

"I don't know," said Balbeer.

"That's wonderful. How come wood burns? Why do our armpits stink? What does it mean if I dream about being naked in the marketplace?"

"I don't know. I thought I was the only one who had the 'naked' dream."

"I think everyone has it."

They went and got something to eat.

Not long after, there came a morning when all the Buddha people got up and started walking away, down the road. Milo and Ompati got up and went with them. Milo discovered suddenly that he had nothing in the world to his name. A primitive kind of robe, one set of underclothes, and a pair of leather sandals he'd borrowed from a dead mahout.

Ompati picked up a stick from the side of the road.

"It feels good to have *something*," he said, "even if it's just a stick."

They walked in silence for a time.

"I haven't seen the Master for a week," Ompati said. "Is he even with us? Maybe he has gone on ahead."

"He's old," Milo answered. "They say he has good days and bad days."

"Doesn't *everybody* have good and bad days? What does that mean?"

Milo shrugged. He didn't know.

That night, they found out.

They were sitting around a fire at twilight, cooking some beans they'd begged from a passing caravan, when Milo was struck with energy.

"I'm going to go ask him," he said.

"Ask who what?" asked Ompati and a couple of pilgrims who had joined them.

"About the dream I have, where I'm in the marketplace and I suddenly realize I'm naked."

"Everybody has that dream."

"Yeah, but I wonder what it means."

And he was up and gone among the many fires, looking for the Buddha.

The Buddha didn't have a huge, fancy tent or anything. He wasn't easy to find, camped among his followers, because he slept on the ground just like the rest of them. But Milo reasoned that wherever the Master sat down and made his fire, a lot of his people would try to sit down near him. So he went where the fires and talking and laughter were thickest, and there, indeed, was the Master.

Milo expected to find some of the elder disciples sitting in a circle, with the Master sitting in the middle, staring into the fire. But what he found was confusion. There were several disciples, older men Milo recognized from the Master's inner circle, whispering loudly at one another. In the middle of them stood the Master, crying and looking pissed off.

Other pilgrims, at fires nearby, busily pretended not to see.

Milo advanced, anxious to see what was wrong. If someone had hurt the Master . . .

"Why would you say something like that?" the Master was sobbing. "That's cruel, is all. What's wrong with you all?"

Two disciples—one fat, the other short but thin, like a dormouse— were having a spat of some kind, off to the side.

"Why did you argue with him?" asked the fat disciple. "You know you're not supposed to contradict him when he's like this! He doesn't understand. It just upsets him."

"I know!" whispered the dormouse, looking pained. "But he was fine, that's the thing. One second he was breezing along, saying mountains are like rivers, only slower, and he was having a great day. Then he said, natural as you please, 'I must remember to ask Yi if he still has that bit of volcanic glass,' and before I could catch myself, I said, 'Master, Yi has been dead now for seven years. Remember the tiger?' and he came unglued."

The fat disciple seemed to calm himself.

"We have to be careful," he said. "I know you would never upset Bodhi on purpose."

Strong hands grabbed Milo by the shoulders and spun him around.

Fuck! The Buddha had goons! Who knew?

Balbeer.

"Milo," said Balbeer, his eyes sad, "just go and eat. You can't help here."

"But what's wrong?" he sputtered.

Balbeer steered Milo out of the woods. Behind them, the Master's voice rose angrily.

"He's old," said Balbeer. "Old people get confused sometimes."

"But he's—"

"He's not a god."

Milo found his way back to his own fire and sat down.

"Did he have an answer?" asked Ompati. "About the dream?"

Milo sat with his shoulders hunched.

"I couldn't find him," he said.

He tried to sleep, and couldn't.

Every time he closed his eyes, he saw the Buddha in tears, frightened of his own friends.

He closed his eyes and tried to meditate. Maybe that would help.

Meditation was something the Buddha people did. It seemed to help them be cool about things. He had been trying but without much luck.

"See and listen to what's happening in your mind," Balbeer had told him.

"My mind is noisy," Milo had answered. "I can't see or hear."

Balbeer had shrugged and closed his eyes and appeared to ignore him.

Milo tried again now.

Breathe in. Don't think of anything. Breathe out. Notice that you are breathing.

What's wrong with the Master? his mind asked.

Milo noticed the question.

Do people live on the moon, wondered his mind. No matter how hard he tried, random shit just kept floating up.

My ankle hurts. I haven't had an asthma attack in a long time; maybe I'm cured? Do Buddhists have sex? What was that noise?

Shut up, he thought. Shut up, shut up. Breathe! Stillness . . . breathe . . .

I can feel my hair growing.

"Fuck!" he roared.

"Shhh," admonished some nearby pilgrims. "We're meditating."

The next afternoon, the travelers reached a place called Sravasti.

Sravasti was a town. The Master had been there many times. A long time ago, they had built a whole complex of monasteries there. It was one of the main places people went if they wanted to learn the Master's teachings. Some of his best students and disciples taught there, and the town was sort of an ongoing Buddha-fest. You could hardly go downtown to buy bread without stumbling over meditating pilgrims.

When the Master himself came to town, it was like Jesus entering Jerusalem, except Jesus hadn't been invented yet.

The traveling throng became a parade, showered with blossoms and song. They were all bowed to and knelt to and touched with reverence. Part of this was because the Sravasti crowd was primed to honor anything remotely associated with the Buddha, but it was also because they didn't know which of the travelers *was* the Buddha.

Like most people, these spirit tourists expected to know the Master on sight. He should be ten feet tall, with flames shooting from his eyes. This, they said, was the man who had made a rice bowl float upstream just by asking it to. This was the man who had slain a horrid jungle monster by permitting it to eat him and then burning his way out with Perfection rays. This was the man whose soul was one with all time and the universe.

Yet he passed before them, a hunched old man like any other old man. He had the X-ray eye thing, true, but that was hard to see if he wasn't looking straight at you.

"They don't recognize him," muttered Ompati, picking magnolia petals from his hair.

Milo nodded.

"It's just as well," whispered one of the travelers, walking nearby. "He's been asking about the wedding preparations all day, especially the belly dancers."

Milo frowned. "Whose wedding?"

"His own."

"He's getting married?"

"He *got* married. It didn't work out."

"Oh," said Milo. "Sorry."

"Also," added the disciple, "it was sixty years ago."

That night, amid the soft lawns and simple walls of the monastery complex, torches were lit. The thousands came and sat, waiting to hear the Buddha, buzzing excitedly.

It's like an outdoor rock concert, said a voice in Milo's head (the voice was from a future life).

The elder disciples emerged from the central monastery, plopped a big, fancy pillow on the grass, and sat around it in a semicircle, looking nervous.

Out came the Master. One step at a time, assisted by Balbeer.

The crowd hushed. Insects chirped. Bats zipped between torches.

The Master sat on the pillow, forming the *mudra* with his fingers.

Some time passed.

The moon rose.

The Buddha looked up. His eyes were bright but distant, like faraway fires. Milo recognized the lost look.

Oh, no!

The Master started talking about the wedding.

"I'm getting married," he announced softly, with a slippery kind of grin. "It will be at my father's palace, to my love and my destiny, my cousin Yasodhara. There will be belly dancers."

Looking around, Milo saw the crowd nodding to itself, to one another. They listened and tried to follow.

"You have to admire a good belly dancer," the Master continued. "They don't dance so much as they flow. They're like truth, or a river. Like a wave. Think about that. We're going to ask them to wear emeralds in their belly buttons."

The crowd ate it up. Truth! A river! Unity! Impermanence! No idea that the Buddha was wandering the undiscovered country of his own memory.

His closest disciples watched him with genuine love and awe. But their glances shared a question they dared not voice.

How much longer, they were thinking, can we get away with this?

That night, the first of the monsoon rains arrived.

The Buddha's thousands rolled up their mats and crowded into the huts and monasteries. In the morning, several young pilgrims woke everyone with a great shouting: "Come quick! Something wonderful! Something strange! The Master has to see!"

So the Buddha and his thousands followed the young men down to the shore of a nearby river. The Master wasn't hobbling, Milo noticed. He looked sharp and quick.

The river had swelled, like a boa constrictor swallowing a horse. It plunged and thrashed, gripping whole trees and great branches.

"Look!" cried the young pilgrims, pointing, jumping up and down.

They all looked.

"A monster!" they cried.

Some distance from shore, a single jujube tree stood against the flood, its branches beaten and stripped, and in its highest reaches something awful crouched. Something wet and bad. Something toothy and glaring but also, clearly, something frightened.

"A devil," murmured some.

"A demon!" said others.

"Nonsense," said the Buddha. "It's a tiger."

So it was.

Soaked and muddy, baring its teeth at the flood, it looked ready to fight, if only something attackable would present itself. As Milo watched, it took a big green terrified shit.

Everybody looked at the Master, expecting something.

"Someone bring me a rope," he said. "The longest rope you can find. Long enough to reach the top of the tree."

A hundred pilgrims pelted back to the monastery and into downtown Sravasti, without hesitation or a single question.

Milo leaned closer to Balbeer and asked, "What . . . ?"

Balbeer shook his head, frowning.

Noise and shouting—they were back with the rope! A hundred ropes! The Master selected one and tied it into a wide, lazy lasso.

"No way!" said Ompati. His sentiments were echoed up and down the shore.

Even the tiger took an interest. He watched the Buddha without blinking, licking his chops.

The Master whirled the lasso over his head . . . slowly at first . . . and cast it like an arrow over the water. It settled neatly over a broken branch just behind the tiger.

He tugged the lasso tight and pulled.

He meant, it became obvious, to pull the jujube tree down to the shore, allowing the tiger to leap to safety. But he was, after all, an eighty-year-old man, and . . .

The tree started to bend.

The thousands muttered and gasped.

The tiger knew something was up, but he wasn't sure if he liked it or not. He shifted, glaring.

The Master's hands began to quiver.

"Please be useful," he said to those around him.

Disciples and pilgrims piled onto the rope. Balbeer began a chant, which got them all pulling together. *"Ahn!"* they chanted, and pulled.

"*Bastei!*" they chanted, and pulled, and the tree bent closer, until at last the roots tore free and its top branches hovered just ten feet from the bank.

At this point, a couple of things happened very quickly.

The tiger leaped through the air.

Everyone saw the tiger flying toward the shore and let go of the rope and ran.

Everyone but the Master, who had secured the rope around his wrist.

The tiger flashed its teeth and fangs and went crashing away through the trees without eating anyone.

The jujube tree came loose and went rolling downstream with the flood, yanking the Master off his feet, into the raging river, and out of sight.

As fast as this happened, Milo was faster. He was in the water before he even knew he was going to go, reaching for the Buddha's old bare feet, the last part of the Master to vanish.

The water swirled around him. Branches and gravel and floating dreck scraped at him, but his groping hands found what they were looking for, and down the river they went, the tree and the Master and Milo.

Milo pulled himself up the Master's body, almost climbing him like a tree, until he reached the old man's wrist. Once he had the wrist in his grip, he did what the Master could not, which was to use both hands to unwind the rope.

The tree rolled away toward the ends of the Earth.

Milo and the Buddha bobbed up into the air, gasping. They fought together for the shore, grabbing for weeds or branches, clawing at the mud.

A tall figure splashed toward them. Big, strong beet-farming hands grasped Milo—Ompati!—pulling him, pulling the Master free of the current, until all three of them beached themselves and lay there with their legs in the water, gulping air.

Pilgrims and disciples came running, surrounding them, shouting with joy.

Milo realized then that the flood had yanked their clothing away. He and the Master lay there naked before the growing crowd.

"I've had dreams like this," said Milo.

"Everyone has that dream," said the Buddha.

The Great Tiger Rescue had predictable results.

The story of the Buddha's supernatural strength and compassion flashed across the jungles and villages. Within hours more pilgrims started thronging into Sravasti. A new fable! A new miracle!

The story of how the Buddha had been dragged into the river and had to be fished out did not flash anywhere. It was hushed up, on a solemn and voluntary basis.

You can't blame them, said one of Milo's past-life voices. Imagine if Jesus had been eaten by ferrets. It wouldn't work well, fable-wise.

The disciples and pilgrims didn't even want to talk about it that day. As they sat around in the thousands with their rice bowls, eating the midday meal in a light, cool rain, Ompati said, "Man, I thought it was all over. You guys were underwater for a long time—"

And everyone around them got up and left.

"They don't want to hear it," said Milo.

"You saved his life," insisted Ompati.

"*We* saved his life, I suppose. That doesn't change the fact that he isn't like a normal person. He's more like a story that lives and breathes. Sometimes the story has to be edited."

"You're starting to sound like a wise man," Ompati remarked.

Balbeer approached and knelt beside Milo.

"He wants you to come and see him," he said. "Both of you."

Oh. Cool.

Balbeer led them through the crowd to the Master's central hut. It was a modest home with a brick foundation and a roof of fresh green pwaava leaves, as if the Master lived beneath a huge salad.

Inside, the Master sat cross-legged, eyes closed. When Milo and Ompati sat across from him, his eyes opened.

"Thank you," said the Buddha, patting Milo on the knee, nodding at Ompati.

"You're welcome," they whispered.

"Of course," said the Master, "a life is like a wave in the river. It rises and then disappears back into the river. It rises again somewhere else. The rising and falling doesn't make a lot of difference."

"You mean it doesn't matter," said Ompati, "if Milo saved your life."

"It doesn't matter," said the Master, fixing his eyes on Ompati, "to the river."

Ompati looked at the ground, corrected.

"Now," said the Master, "meditate with me."

Eyes closed again.

Milo closed his own eyes and tried.

Tried not to think about chickens, and why rocks were hard, and a bare-breasted woman he had glimpsed once, and string, and his belly button, and snow . . .

The Buddha and his traveling disciples left Sravasti in the middle of the night.

"We're going," whispered Balbeer, awakening Milo. "Before he has another bad day."

"I don't think they'll talk about it," yawned Milo, "even if he does. They don't want to see it, so they don't."

"They'll see it," said Balbeer, "if it happens enough."

They were on the road for days and days, begging food along the way. Every night, Milo and Ompati joined the Master in quiet talk and meditation. The rest of the Buddha world might want to forget the almost-drowning, but the Master himself obviously considered the young men to be good and worthy friends.

"I suck at meditating," Milo blurted one evening. He wanted to meditate so badly, the failure was giving him stomach cramps.

The Master raised a quieting hand.

"Meditating is mostly breathing," he said. "Breathing is our most

intimate contact with the world outside ourselves. We bring it in"—
the Master inhaled—"and we push it out"—and exhaled. "When we do
that, the world outside becomes part of us."

They breathed together, the three of them. In, out. In, out.

"So," said Milo, "it doesn't matter that I can't help thinking about
monkeys or my big toe?"

"The mind can't help being noisy. Last night, trying to meditate, all
I could think of was cats."

"Oh," said Milo, surprised. "What about them?"

"Nothing. Just cats, cats, cats, cats, cats, cats."

"Cats, cats, cats, cats, cats, cats, cats," repeated Milo. Ompati
joined in.

"We're meditating, aren't we?" asked Milo.

"We were," said the Master.

"I don't get it," said Ompati. "You're supposed to clear your mind,
but it's okay to think about cats. You're meditating if you think about
cats, but not if you think about meditating."

The Master closed his eyes and appeared to weigh this.

They waited awhile for him to continue, until he began to snore
softly.

Sitting with Ompati at their own fire, later, Milo was silent for a long
time.

Not meditating silent, just silent. Thinking.

"They say the Master has achieved Perfection," said Milo eventually.

"It's kind of obvious," Ompati replied. "You know it when you see
it."

"Yeah, but it's not what you'd expect. I mean, sure he's all spiritual
and everything, but he also has the practicality thing going on. He has
trouble meditating, like me. But he makes a success of it. His mind is
falling apart, but he makes a success of that, too. And then things like
the tiger. That was amazing!"

The fire popped. Sparks rose, whirled, and died.

"Is there a point?" asked Ompati.

"There is. It's this: I want Perfection."

"Doesn't everyone?"

"No, I don't think so. I think most people want a little bit of it but not the whole package, where they leave the cycle of life. I think—no, I know—that I have lived thousands of lives. I may be the worst meditator ever, but I'm beginning to know things. Almost like my other lives are slipping me notes. Don't look at me like that. Anyhow, they have been telling me—I think—that until now I never wanted real Perfection, because I never saw it in the flesh. Not like this. It's something I've been rebelling against for a long time."

"Rebelling? Against Perfection?"

"Yes. But not anymore. It's necessary somehow. I can feel it. I've been fighting against becoming part of the Oversoul. But now I want that more than anything."

Milo could hear the voices in his head dancing around and singing.

"Let me get this straight," said Ompati. "You've been rebelling against Perfection, but now you've changed your mind because the Master is perfect but in practical, groovy ways you can understand?"

"Yeah. That's what a teacher does, right? Gets you to understand? Well, I understand."

The voices in his head presented him with some cool dancing lights and sitar music.

Milo hadn't known they could do that.

"Wow," he said. "Beautiful."

He reached down and touched the Earth. For a moment, he could feel it turning beneath him.

"What in hell are you doing?" asked Ompati.

"I'm not sure. Something wonderful. It's making me have to go to the bathroom."

And this felt quite Buddha-like to him, and quite perfect, and maybe it was.

———

After that, a string of bad days.

If you weren't part of the Master's inner circle, you might not even know. If you were one of his old disciples or one of his new friends, though, it meant more work.

Balbeer dropped back through the ranks of marching pilgrims and took both Milo and Ompati by the arm. "Can you do something for the Master? He's not at his best today."

"Anything," said Ompati.

"We'll reach a village soon. Take his food bowl, and when you beg for food, fill his bowl, as well."

They bowed. "Happily," they said.

At the edge of the village, the disciples stood in a tight circle around the Buddha and smiled at the pilgrims as they passed with their food bowls.

"All is well," said those smiles.

"We're going to be late for the elephant races," called the Master, from inside the circle.

The villagers were generous. They were always generous. Especially when Milo raised the Master's bowl and said, "One more, if you please, for the Buddha himself."

Afterward, he and Ompati sat among the disciples around the litter. The Master crawled out on his hands and knees to join them. They passed him his food bowl, and he ate without relish, as if eating were an afterthought. His eyes, Milo noticed, seemed far away but not empty or lost. He was working on something in that brain of his.

After a while, the Master turned to Balbeer.

"I wonder," he said, "if you would do something for me?"

"Of course," said Balbeer.

"When we have finished eating, will you go upstairs and tell my mother I wish to see her?"

Milo's heart sank and took his appetite with it.

"Of course, Master," said Balbeer, looking as if he might cry.

———

They rested all day at the village. Milo found a dignified old bo tree to sit under and meditated his ass off for three hours.

Cats. Rain. Trees. Love. Dogs. His penis. Night.

His mind was noisy. Nothing he could do about it. But the breathing part, that he could manage.

In. Out. Be aware of the air and the world coming in, going out.

There was something familiar about the exercise. Not because he'd been breathing all his life but because he had breathed this way before. Expertly. Consciously. He had a mental flash of his naked body floating in space. . . .

Perfection. In some other life. But he had lost it. He didn't recall how.

Groovy. And tragic. This time he wouldn't lose it.

He opened his eyes. There was a noise but not a jungle noise. Voices in distress, from the outskirts of the village. Milo jogged out of the woods, to find the Master's disciples fluttering around like panicked storks.

"What is it?" he called. "What's wrong?"

"He's missing," answered Ompati, appearing at his elbow.

"Maybe Heaven has taken him!" one of his elderly disciples was saying, nearby. "Look, his robes are here. All his things are here. I tell you, he has been taken up."

"Let's go," said Milo, tugging Ompati's sleeve, and they joined a number of pilgrims to spread out through the village, searching.

It didn't take long to find him, and, again, noise was their clue. Raised voices from down the road, from the village center. Milo and Ompati ran and discovered a small crowd gathering in the marketplace.

Peace, thought Milo. He feels better and has come to the village to teach.

The crowd parted. Milo excused his way through and found the Master standing at a market stall. He held a pomegranate in one hand, inspecting it closely.

He was stark naked.

The crowd, now that Milo glanced around, didn't look awed or spiritual or even curious. They wore the faces of a schoolyard crowd, the faces of children who have found an injured bird to torture.

"Perhaps it is wash day," someone suggested.

Laughter.

"It's awfully hot," said someone else, and someone said, "He is in the market for a tattoo!" and then someone threw a stone at him. It bounced off his shoulder.

Milo didn't see who had thrown the stone, but Ompati did. He grabbed the young man's arm and threw him to the ground.

Several other young men stepped forward.

Milo, who had raised his hands, lowered them.

"Peace, friend Ompati," he said. "This isn't what we've learned. It isn't what we teach."

He breathed in. He breathed out. The air and the crowd and the town were part of him.

He turned to the Buddha and took him by the arm, saying, "Our friends are waiting, Father." He didn't call him "Master." Maybe the crowd didn't know. They didn't need to know. This wasn't a story the future needed.

"I want this pomegranate," griped the Master.

"I don't have any money," Milo whispered in the Buddha's ear. "Neither do you. I'll bring you one later."

The Master subsided. "This one," he said, putting the pomegranate back. "I want that one."

"Fine. But for now we have to go."

Ompati took the Master's other elbow, and they steered through the crowd. The young men noticed the look in Milo's eyes, which was a look of peaceful power he had gained, like an ocean wave, and they parted before him. Some even bowed and looked ashamed. They noticed the look in Ompati's eyes, as if he wanted an excuse to kick someone in the balls, and they made way for that, too.

———

After they dropped the Master off with his old friends, Milo went back into the trees, alone. He found the bo tree again and sat down to think.

You wouldn't call it meditating. Meditating didn't look like this, with the furrowed brow and the dark eyes. It was the look of a man who is trying to find courage.

The Master needed help.

The kind of help he needed was so, so difficult. He needed an act of Perfection.

Milo meditated on that for a while.

Part of meditating was knowing when to put meditation aside and get up and go do something.

So he got up. He left the trees, carrying his food bowl. He asked Balbeer for the Master's food bowl and walked into the village.

"Wait up," called Ompati, running behind him.

They begged enough food for themselves and the Master. Milo made a pitch for some coins, too, and their last stop was the marketplace, where they bought the Buddha his pomegranate.

Sitting around the litter an hour later, Milo noticed a brighter look in the Master's eye.

"How do you feel, Master?" he asked.

The Master didn't answer right away. He looked at Milo for a long time, without blinking. Then he looked at the sky.

"I feel good, Milo," he said. "Thank you. It is an excellent evening."

They all felt good. The evening was warm and filled with birdsong. Flying clouds laced the sky like shredded cotton, turning gold at the edges as the sun slipped away.

"I won't preach tonight," said the Buddha. "Let's have music instead."

So they had music. Villagers came with *rudra veena* and lyre.

The sunset colors spun from gold into pink and purple and dark. The stars brightened and began to turn, and the Master ate his pomegranate. Half of it, anyway. The other half he handed off to Ompati.

Green eyes surrounded them, glowing in the brush. They moved and came closer. Shadows like tiny people.

"Monkeys," whispered Ompati. As soon as he said this, an old grandmother baboon walked out of the dark and sat gazing at him in the firelight. She reached out with a thin dark paw and let her fingers rest on his knee.

The stars turned. The *rudra veena* sang.

"It's okay, friend Ompati," said the Master. "You've taken no vow of celibacy that I recall."

The disciples' laughter drowned the music for a time.

In the morning, the Master felt unwell.

"I think we will stay here another day," Balbeer announced.

At noon, the Master felt worse.

"Say prayers," asked Balbeer. To Milo, he said, "Take the Master's bowl and see if you can bring back some kale, some aloe, and some didi juice. Something bad has got into him. We need to get it out."

Balbeer's voice was calm and even, but Milo saw real fear in his eyes.

He did as he was asked, and when Milo returned, Balbeer and the disciples were sitting in a loose circle around the sleeping Master, looking grave.

"Set it down," said Balbeer. "He won't take anything."

They all pretended to meditate.

The sun crept down the sky.

Ompati mixed leftover fruits and greens into a salad and split it with Milo for a snack.

The Master stirred after a while. He sat up and then, despite Balbeer's remonstrances, stood. Hunched at first, and looking a little green, but then he straightened up and peered around at them all with his cosmic eyes.

"I am going to die," he announced.

Voices clamored, but the Master raised a hand and silenced them all.

"Why should this bother you?" he chided. "I'm eighty years old. My soul is going out into the Everything. Be happy for me."

His stomach made a horrible noise.

"If you would," he said, "please ask in the village if they would bring some blankets and pillows and make for me a bed in that grove, just there." He pointed to some sal trees, not far away. Then he excused himself and made for the woods at an awkward trot.

By late afternoon, they all knew. Every last pilgrim and student and hanger-on had gathered in the sal-tree grove, in concentric circles, with downcast eyes. The Master had arranged himself on a mound of simple blankets, resting his head on a nice tasseled pillow. His face was greener than before, but he appeared composed.

"Listen," he said. "I just want to clear something up, so there's no confusion when I'm gone. I haven't chosen anyone to take my place. I don't want you guys to keep hiking around India; we look like a circus. Split up. Go home. Spread what you've learned."

"What does Perfection feel like?" cried a desperate voice, somewhere in the grove.

"How do you feel right now?" asked the Buddha.

"Sad," answered the voice. "Scared."

"That's what Perfection feels like," said the Master. "Don't worry. In a while, it will feel different."

Soft voices, confusion.

"Listen," said the Master, coughing. "Don't search the ends of the Earth looking for your happiness. Perfection is being happy with what you are right now."

"What if you're an asshole?" someone called.

The Master offered a weak smile. "I doubt very much," he said, "that many happy people are assholes."

Then he died.

Ompati stared off into space. His eyes glazed with shock.

"His last word was 'assholes,'" he observed.

"I don't think he would have minded," said Milo. Then he said, "Look!" and pointed. Lots of people were pointing.

Flowers were dropping from the sal-tree branches. Light red blossoms fluttered like moths on their way to the ground, drifting over the dead Master, over the grass, and over the pilgrims.

"That's better," said Ompati.

Milo found his bo tree once again and had a seat.

He would meditate. What else could he do?

He could go back to Moosa. Why not? No one needed to hear the teachings of the Master more than the idiots of Moosa.

Ducks, he thought, closing his eyes. Cats. The moon. Death. The wind.

He could hear the villagers at a distance, gathering over in the sal-tree grove. They would let the Master lie there for some time that way, so that he could be seen. In three days, like it or not, they'd have to cremate him.

Maybe they'll let me have some of the ashes, he thought.

Did he deserve that? He still didn't know.

He hoped his older voices and past lives would offer some kind of remark, but the voices had gone eerily silent. He was left with a feeling that they had been super-happy with him and that he had screwed this up.

"Open your eyes," said Ompati's voice. "You know you can't meditate for shit, so just open your damn eyes."

Milo opened his eyes.

Ompati stood before him.

"You did it, didn't you?"

Milo squinted. He looked up at the sky.

"I don't know . . ." Milo began.

"Don't dishonor yourself!" Ompati shouted.

"All right," said Milo. "Yes. I did it. I found a mushroom in the woods before I went to beg for his dinner. A certain kind of mushroom. I mashed some of it into the pomegranate I brought him. There you are. That's your answer."

Ompati trembled visibly. "Why?" he asked.

"You know why. His story is more important than his life. He knew it. We all know it. I did something that was necessary. I am, perhaps, his greatest friend."

Was this true? He felt doubtful. He could hear his soul voices, darkly muttering.

He would meditate on it, he decided, all the way back to Moosa.

"I'm sorry," said Ompati.

"Sorry for what?" asked Milo.

"I'm afraid I mixed the uneaten half of the Master's pomegranate into a salad."

Milo's stomach gave a seasick lurch.

"Yes?" he asked.

"The salad we split for a snack, earlier."

A bird called. Milo watched the moon among tree branches.

"Ah," he said. "Well, the wave returns to the river."

"Indeed," said Ompati, sitting down beside him.

Together, they waited, meditating about beets and monsoons and gods and brothels and other fine things they had known.

They breathed in. They breathed out.

"Cats," said Milo.

"Shhh," said his friend.

CHAPTER 22

Escape to Chinese Heaven

Milo didn't wake up beside the river this time.

He didn't even wake up in the desert.

He was sitting at the bottom of a deep well. Sort of like a jail cell but without a sink or a toilet.

"Great," he muttered.

It didn't take a wise man to guess that this was where you went if you murdered the Buddha.

"Hello?" he called.

No one answered. Would they just leave him here and forget about him? Were they that mean?

Dammit, he had one more life to live! Somebody was going to listen to him, by God. He began looking around for a stick, for some rocks, anything he could throw. He would throw one hell of a fit, if they thought they could just stick him down here—

Something interrupted the light and came tumbling down the well.

A rope ladder. It snapped to an end just in front of his face and swung back and forth.

"Climb up here," snarled Nan's voice. "Want you to see something."

Milo growled in frustration. He had really been looking forward to throwing his fit.

He climbed the ladder.

At the top, there was Nan, with a cat or two, standing in what looked like someone's backyard.

Most of the yard was packed with people—standing, sitting on blankets, sitting on lawn chairs. They were all facing the same direction, paying not the least bit of attention to Milo.

Even Nan ignored him. She, too, was turned away, watching something.

The house and the backyard were built on a hillside, and the hillside overlooked a river. Most of the landscape was hidden beneath a crowd like Milo had never seen, spilling down the hill and stretching for miles.

It was a festive crowd, to say the least. They wore bright colors. There were flags and hand-painted signs. There were shirtless drunks with painted chests and eighteen thousand different kinds of music playing. It was Woodstock Meets the Super Bowl.

Milo stepped up beside Nan.

"What—" he began.

"Shut up and watch," Nan barked. "You might learn something in the hour or two you have left."

What?

His heart pounded. They meant to space him. Or "Nothing" him, or whatever you wanted to call it. God . . . what did that mean for Suzie? She had been nearly gone, that night on the train. What about now? Was she still out there? Or had she gone ahead of him, into Nowhere?

The crowd grew louder. They sang out in raw joy and gladness.

The source of the joy and gladness appeared, not far away, downhill.

It was the Buddha, arriving in the afterlife. He made his way pleasantly, humbly, through the crowd. He was young again, Prince Siddhartha, with shining black hair falling over one shoulder.

Would the Master recognize him? (Help him?)

Milo waved both arms and shouted, "Hey! Up here!"

Nan elbowed him in the gut, sneering, "Keep still, you. That's the greatest soul that ever lived, down there. You're just the bastard who killed him."

Milo wheeled on her, turning red. "I should have known you wouldn't understand!" he bellowed. "I did the most difficult thing imaginable, for the good of the Master and everyone in the world—"

Nan elbowed him again.

"You get everything wrong," she muttered. "You always go too far."

Down below, the Master had drawn near the river, and the air above the water began to shake and glow.

A golden light spun itself out of thin air and cast a perfect cosmic dawn over the multitude. It made everything beautiful and simple. Made everything clear, like the air and the light after a rain.

Surely, thought Milo, the Buddha himself understood what he had done.

Maybe he would say something at the last minute. Any second now he'd stop and say, "Hey, we're forgetting someone! Why, without Milo, the Master would just be a story about some old coot who forgot his own name and sat around meditating in his own drool. C'mon down, Milo!"

But the Buddha did not say these things.

He waded out into the river, wearing a breezy expression.

"Please," said Milo. He didn't have the energy for anything more. Time and space had clamped onto him with a corkscrew and twisted everything right out of him.

He was done.

How could a person be so wise and so good, generally, and wind up with the whole universe against him?

The Master became a mere shadow in the wild flood of light. Then the Sun Door overwhelmed him and absorbed him, and he was a part of it.

The great light closed and faded.

"That's pretty much the opposite of where you're going," said Nan. But Milo barely heard, because his own ancient voices had begun to speak up, taking rather a pissy tone.

You were on your next-to-last chance to get life right, said his soul, and you murdered Buddha. Oops.

Oh, come on! Milo thought. You were *there*!

You. Murdered. Buddha.

I tried to do something complicated and beneficial, Milo explained. Tried to, anyway. Inside, he suddenly felt a feathery kind of flutter. A violence that was soft, angelic.

Milo's own soul was trying, in its metaphysical way, to beat him up.

The light was just evening light now, over the river and the town and the bridge and the multitude. But the excitement wasn't quite over, the great day not quite done.

Blinking, the crowd turned and buzzed and seemed to be seeking something. Slowly, following pointing fingers, they all found what they were looking for and raised their eyes to the hill, to the backyard where Milo stood, to Milo himself.

As one, they pointed.

"Him," they said.

"Oh, fucking hell," said Milo. *"Really?"*

Pop! Mama materialized beside him.

"Sorry I'm late," she said. "I didn't want to miss the receiving line down there."

"Ma!" cried Milo. Hope!

"Thank God!" he said. "I was about to—"

"Hush," said Mama, turning away. "Please, just hush."

Milo felt himself collapsing inside. Indeed, he would have fallen, but they caught him. Not Mama and Nan but the backyard people, the crowd people. And they raised him up and carried him the way crowds have sometimes carried saints to the stake or queens to the chopping block. Downhill, along the river.

Milo closed his eyes and let it happen.

Over the bridge, toward the neighborhoods and their sidewalks.

He heard the names they called him. They weren't very creative.

"Buddha killer." "Buddha poisoner." "Buddha's Judas."

Now and then someone would give him a poke or throw something at him. Something wet splashed over his shoulder. Something hit his knee.

Milo remained silent. He didn't want them saying, later, that he raged and panicked like a madman or a killer, but just then someone let him have it with a stick, right in the funny bone.

"God fucking *dammit!*" he howled.

All around him, eyes bugged.

"See?" they said, pointing. *"See?* I'll bet he was always like this! All ten thousand lives, like a time bomb, waiting."

That's it, Milo thought. If they can be mean, I can be mean. I have more experience than these losers, anyhow. And he began fighting to turn himself over, opening his jaws as wide as they would go. He would begin by biting some fingers off. And then some faces. What did he have to lose?

And then he was flying.

It happened in an instant. A storm of leaves and dust, snatching him up and out of their grasp. Up and away into Nowhere, into Nothingness. Nothing but wind and something that wrapped around him and felt like legs, looked like bottomless eyes, felt like a tongue.

"Lover," said the dark and the wind and the nothing.

When the whirling and the dark settled down, they were someplace far away.

Twilight. A soft breeze and wind chimes. Colored lanterns here and there. A harbor, with old boats that rose and fell as if breathing.

They materialized aboard one of these boats. A long, spacious sampan, like a big canoe with a roof.

Chinese Heaven, thought Milo. Cool.

He looked around.

"Suzie?"

Something like a gasp and a whisper from the shadows at the sampan's far end.

He didn't see her until the moon broke out from behind clouds. Then he saw her, draped like a rag over the gunwale, dripping like heavy mist.

"Aw, shit," he said, rushing to her. Trying to hold her. Trying to find something solid enough to touch.

"You have to hold me," she breathed. "I'm all used up. You have to let me take from you."

He held her. He shuddered with rage and fear. How long before she faded into nothing? How in hell had she managed the strength to scoop him up and fly off with him?

"I know," she sighed. "Shut up."

Even her voice wasn't all there.

God, he thought, when you loved someone, every day was Opposite Day. Being with them made you feel weak and also strong. They made you want to laugh and cry. Get dressed up and get undressed. You wanted to keep them forever and eat them like a bucket of cheese fries.

"I killed Buddha," he told her.

"He understood," said Suzie. "He knew it was the smart thing, what you did."

Milo stomped both feet in frustration. "I knew it!" he yelled. "I knew it! Goddammit, Suze, how come he didn't *say* anything? All he had to do was look at those universal slice bastards and say, 'Don't be too hard on Milo, you soulless bipolar butt-suckers; he was only trying to ensure a future of peace and goodwill,' but noooooooooo—"

"He was busy," she said calmly, "being transformed into pure eternal light. I missed you, by the way."

Well, yeah.

"I missed you, too," he said. "We didn't get to see each other much last time."

"We might not get to see each other much this time, either. Depending on how badly they want to chase you down. Depending on . . ."

She waved one hand in front of a lantern, and the hand became invisible.

But he was able to read her eyes, and they were love eyes.

See, now, Milo thought. *This* is Perfection.

"Maybe if we go into the pure eternal light together," Milo said, "we'll dissolve together or something, and sort of be together still."

She nodded.

"Maybe my expectations have diminished," she said. "But that would be okay with me, too."

Milo sat, leaning back against the gunwale. Suzie lay down with her head in his lap. She matched his breathing.

"Buddha made me see something about Perfection that I hadn't seen before," he said.

"It's better than oblivion?"

"It's about evolution. That guy kept evolving. When he started losing his mind, you'd think he would have slipped into death. But he didn't. He kept getting up in the morning, and doing things, and learning. And when death *did* come, he was okay with it. He kept evolving. Taking the next step. And that's how it should be. And the next step, if I can earn it, is the Sun Door."

Suzie made a questioning noise of some kind.

"We'll figure out what to do about you," he said. "We just need to keep ahead of them long enough to figure it out."

True night had fallen, afire with stars. Paper lanterns, fueled with candles, rose like butterflies over the city and the bay.

"I wish we'd done this long ago," said Suzie.

The stars and the lanterns cast reflections in the water.

It was as if they'd run away to outer space.

Time passed. They lived on the sampan, sometimes staying in the same harbor, sometimes moving down the coast. Over days and nights, and in and out of weeks.

Once or twice, Milo thought he sensed unfriendly eyes turned their way. Sensed plans and bad intent moving around them. Sensed balance seeking to assert itself. When that happened, they waved. They sailed. They anchored up rivers, under vast, overarching flowering trees.

They were the most beautiful fugitives in all eternity.

Even as fugitives, they knew that life was for *doing* stuff.

They read books together. They ate and drank at festivals. Once, they made a paper dragon big enough for the two of them to hide inside and wove through the crowds, ringing bells and roaring. Delighted children followed them.

They made love so slowly—how else can mist make love?—that they fell half-asleep, the way you do lying in warm grass. She was like a shadow, or warm water, moving against him. Somehow, making love was still making love, whether both were completely there or not. Making love was powerful shit.

One morning, Milo was sitting in the stern, washing socks in a bucket and watching game shows on a tiny battery-operated TV, when he saw a phalanx of universals walking down the pier. Walking toward them with a purposeful stride, bearing quarterstaves.

"We should go," Milo called down into the galley, where Suzie was taking her turn at cooking.

He didn't have to say anything more.

She gave an exhausted sigh but did what needed doing.

Whir! Rustle! Whoosh! They left.

They lived up on a mountainside for a while.

Not a long while. Milo had a feeling that their time and their luck were both running short.

The souls who lived on the mountain harvested tea every day, and Milo and Suzie joined them. The tea grew in narrow hedgerows on steep terraces cascading down the mountain. Sometimes mist rolled in from the sea and left them isolated on the mountain, above the clouds, like a cartoon vision of Heaven.

They herded goats, which ate weeds but left the tea alone and nourished the tea shrubs with their poo. They lived in a round wooden house with three hundred other people. The house was like a whirlpool made of walls and windows and laundry hanging down. They all ate together and launched paper lanterns together at night and heard everybody through the walls and open windows when they talked or sang or loved. The house was six thousand years old, and everyone who had ever lived there had scratched his or her name on a wall, on a stair, on the roof, somewhere. The house was like a library of names. Milo and Suzie wrote their names on the little wooden platform around the well. Milo wrote "Milo." Suzie wrote her true name, which all universals and natural forces have; it was a puzzle of seven interlocking infinity symbols made of streams of numbers representing letters. If you touched it, it burned and moved under your hand. Underneath, she wrote "aka: Suzie."

One day, a universal slice in a poor burlap robe walked up the mountain—at first Milo thought it might be Mama, and he tensed.

It wasn't.

The universal helped them pick tea without saying a word to anyone.

Milo and Suzie disguised themselves in sunglasses, just to be safe.

The universal launched paper lanterns with them and ate supper with them. He introduced himself as Mohenjodaro Bo-Ti Harrahj Nandaro, the Fifth Way of the Fifth Light of the Fifth Sign of the First Night, He Who Is Both Near and Far, an Incarnation of Work.

He wrote his name on their big wooden salad bowl. It took him fifteen minutes.

Mohenjodaro never said a suspicious word. He did all the dishes, spent the night in the tool barn, and was gone before breakfast.

"What's on your mind?" Milo asked Suzie after breakfast. They had chosen to stay home in bed that morning, because Suzie was feeling especially transparent and worried.

"I don't like running scared," she answered. "I'm sick of running, and of running out like a slow hourglass. I want to feel at home. I want my candle shop back. I want us to . . . to—"

"Live our lives," said Milo, standing at the window, looking out on the green mountain rising from the sea of mist.

"Yes," said Suzie, her voice quivering. "But they're not going to let us do that. The *boa* isn't going to let us. It'll catch up, sooner or later, like a wave spreading out."

Silence.

This is what giving up feels like, Milo thought.

Far below, the mist thinned and parted for a moment, affording a glimpse of the shore below and the river winding away.

Milo's breath caught. His eyes took on a soft and peculiar blaze.

"I know what to do," he whispered.

She gave him a doubtful look but said, "Let's hear it."

"Follow me," he said, and they left the whirlpool house, holding hands.

Down through the tea shrubs in the fog, to the river's edge.

Suzie understood.

"You're going back to live your last life," said Suzie. Her eyes saddened, but Milo saw her steel herself and straighten. "That's as it should be," she said. "Go, while you can, and—"

"You're coming *with* me," he said.

Her head tilted. Curious and confused.

"We'll get it right, together," said Milo.

"No," said Suzie. "You mean, like, I would live a life . . . I'd be human?"

"One life. Get it right or get it wrong, and we'll either win or lose together. Everything, or . . . nothing. The sidewalk."

"Baby, I can't do that," she said gently.

"Suzie," said Milo. "Sweetheart? Lover of eight thousand years? I love you so much, but don't be a stubborn ass. What have you got to lose? Either of us?"

Suzie's eyes flared, wild and desperate.

"I'm the wisest human soul in the universe," he reminded her. "Give me the benefit of the doubt, this once."

She said nothing, but they began walking again, crossing the narrow, rocky beach.

There, in the gray water before them, were thousands of possible lives.

Suzie lifted her hand. "Look," she said. "That one."

Milo looked.

"You've got to be shitting me," he said at first. But the more he looked, the more her choice made sense.

"Peace," he said. The Master would approve.

"Peace," Suzie repeated.

She waded out into the water.

"I wonder what it's going to be like," she wondered aloud.

"Like being a god," said Milo, "except without any of the god stuff."

"You sound like you hate it."

"I hate being *born*. It's gross."

Waist deep in the waves, she hopped up and kissed him on the lips.

"All or nothing!" she said, and turned and dove.

Milo was right behind her, sliding into life one last time.

CHAPTER 23

Julie DeNofrio's Impossibly Elaborate (and Strangely Hypnotic!) Tattoo

Milo's lives flashed before his eyes. That happens sometimes when you die and also when you're about to be born.

Not all of his lives flashed. Just certain ones. Lives that went with what he'd learned from the Buddha. Lives where he'd done something Peaceful with a capital "P."

Once, he had been a tree for five hundred years and thought of the world outside himself as something big that changed and moved and had fire in it. When the wind blew, he bent. When fall came, he shed his leaves. When they came and chopped him down and made a house out of him, he was a damn fine house. He had grown so old and thought and felt so slowly that he was able to understand these things and to know that they all had their place.

His every moment and every thought were Stillness and Peace.

———

On Gorm 7, an experimental planet where they were trying out different ways of living, Milo lived in a neighborhood where the comptrollers doubled the rent one year.

The people in the neighborhood did not storm the comptrollers'
offices. Instead, they took off all their clothes and went to live in the
woods.

"Back to nature," they all said.

"Hey!" cried the comptrollers. "You can't do that! That's not a
choice! You *need* our houses!"

The naked people didn't answer. They disappeared among the trees.

Milo happened to be walking behind his (former) neighbor Julie
DeNofrio. She had an impossibly elaborate—and strangely hypnotic!—
tattoo on her back.

He never would have seen that if not for this peaceful—and highly
effective!—consumer protest. You never know what little surprises will
come along when you choose to evolve.

There had been peaceful changes up in the afterlife, too. Not long
after he and Suzie became lovers, she had decided to open a greenhouse.

"You're going to grow and sell plants?" Milo asked. "I heard you
right?"

"Yeah," she said. They were eating burritos. She stopped eating
hers. "Why?"

She could read his mind, so he tried not to think about how Death
didn't seem like someone who would have a green thumb.

"Nothing," he said. "I'll help you if you want."

She started eating her burrito again.

The greenhouse was a success. As it turned out, death was a huge
part of growing plants. Things died and went in the soil. Leaves died
and fell off, or you trimmed them. Plants died and made way for new
plants.

She was especially good at carnivorous plants. She grew a Venus
flytrap one time that ate one of Nan's cats.

"Maybe she won't notice," said Milo.

And she didn't.

Way in the future, the people on different planets didn't bother one another much, except to trade. But in 3025, the people of Kurgan 4 attacked the people of Pondwater 3.

"You're going to work for us now!" roared the Kurgans.

But the people of Pondwater 3 (Milo was one of these) said, "No."

The Kurgans shot some of them. But the Pondwater people still said, "No."

The Kurgans tried to beat them and twist their arms and get them to work and help out and go where they wanted them to go, but the Pondwater people either just stood there and ignored them or said, "No," or went limp and lay down on the ground.

Sometimes they quoted the Parable of Jonathan Yah Yah, a famous teaching about how you can't force someone to do something if they're not afraid of you.

Eventually, embarrassed and puzzled, the Kurgans said, "Aw, fuck you guys, anyway," and knocked over some potted plants, got back on their ships, and went home.

Milo was one of the unfortunate few who got shot. As Milo lay dying, a man in a ball cap came and looked down at him and said, "It's not really an end, you know. You're like a wave that rises up and then returns to the river. The wave will rise again."

"I know," said Milo. "But the wave would still like, maybe, a little slice of pizza before it goes."

So the man in the ball cap went and got him a slice of pizza.

That was a nice thing to do.

The small things, Milo thought as he died, were really the big things.

Suzie, too, had given Peace a nudge now and then.

Of course, because she was Death, Suzie's nudges could be confusing and might not look like Peace at first.

She had gone to the horseraces once. To the Epsom Derby, in 1913.

It was nice. It was festive. Lots of dandy British people in fancy hats.

The women's hats were *enormous*. Suzie couldn't get enough of the women's hats. She wanted one.

That was one of the things she hated about her job. You got to go to these wonderful places sometimes and have a great time for a while . . . until it was time to be Death and throw a wet blanket over everyone's day.

She was there because of a woman named Emily Davison.

Emily Davison was a suffragette. She had been jailed a bunch of times for fighting for women to have equal rights—voting, mostly, but other things, too. A couple of times she had gone on hunger strikes, and prison matrons had to force-feed her liquids through her nose.

Suzie was standing by the rail, watching the horses line up for the next race, when Emily Davison stepped up beside her and said, "Well, hello."

"Oh," said Suzie, surprised. "Hello."

Emily was a wise old soul, and discerning. Some people could recognize Death whether she had decided to make herself visible or not, and the suffragette was one of these.

The bell rang, and the horses took off down the track, out of sight. Suzie admired Emily's hat.

She almost wanted to ask if she'd mind taking it off, before, so it wouldn't be ruined, but didn't. She wasn't tactless.

"You're not going to try and talk me out of it," said Emily, "are you?"

Suzie shook her head. "I think it's a brave thing," she said. "And necessary, unfortunately. Good things will happen for a lot of people after this."

Emily nodded. She stood very, very still, watching the track with wide eyes.

Hooves thundered as the horses began coming 'round.

"I'm frightened," Emily said.

Suzie laid a gloved hand on her arm and opened her mouth to say something reassuring. But what exactly?

"It's all right," said Emily, managing a weak, breathless smile. "You can have my hat, after, if you like."

With that, she ducked under the rail and onto the track and flung herself in front of Anmer, a racehorse belonging to King George.

The crowd convulsed and gave a single, sickening gasp. Followed by screams.

Suzie stepped out onto the track, amid running race officials and confused horses and men with box cameras and a doctor. She found the hat, and Emily herself, quite ruined.

The country had been ignoring the suffragettes up to that point. After fifty thousand people attended Emily's funeral and clogged up the London streets, they couldn't ignore the suffragettes anymore.

"How brave," Suzie kept saying to herself, watching the funeral go by.

Emily Davison came back as a suffragette in her next life, too, and then as an electric eel, and then a suffragette again.

As long as some people were *that* determined, Suzie often thought, how bad could things really get?

"How bad could things really get?" she said aloud once, but she felt an awful dread in her belly when she said it.

"Pretty friggin' bad," she imagined the universe saying, shaking its fat, pretentious head.

CHAPTER 24

The Family Stone

Milo was born inside a machine.

He lived there with his family and ten thousand other people.

The machine's job was to crawl all over Ganymede, Jupiter's biggest moon, and make it like planet Earth used to be. It pumped things into the atmosphere and did things to the soil, and the people inside drove its engines and cooked its chemicals and lived sweaty, grunting lives.

Officially, Milo's name was JN010100101101110. As far as the resource cartels were concerned, this was all the identity he needed. Only his family called him "Milo."

His boyhood friends called him "Mildew," because that's how boyhood friends are.

His friends were Frog and Bubbles. Their ball fields were the corridors between turbines in the engine rooms. Their hiding places were tangles of hoses and storage pods. The haunted places they dared one another to go were too many to count: Where someone had been drowned in the algae pumps or died fixing the mighty lobster claws. Places where people had been crushed, steamed, frozen, or recycled.

There were occasional wonders, like the crawler's scattered windows—portholes where you could look out over Ganymede's craters and see Jupiter filling the sky like a magical whale. Sometimes they glimpsed cartel drones hopping across the sky . . . watching, listening.

They were on the residential deck one day, poking at some kind of engine jizz oozing down the wall, when screams exploded from a nearby family pod.

"God, no! You can't do this! We'll pay you! It was an accident!"

"We will find a qualified family, off-planet," answered a hard, amplified voice. "Now let *go!*"

Two Monitors emerged, bulging with police gear. One of them cradled a baby.

"Our neighbors had an extra last year," whispered Frog, his voice low. "They tried to hide it, but how do you hide a baby?"

"If they're taking it off-planet," Milo wondered aloud, "how come they're headed for the kitchens?"

Years passed. Milo began working with his dad in the crawler's great central ventilator.

The day everything changed, Dad found him standing way on top of the lung, riding it up as it breathed.

"Goddammit, Milo!" bellowed Dad, "you're going to get us fired."

Milo didn't argue, because getting fired was always a possibility. And if you didn't have a job, you couldn't live in cartel housing. And because the crawler couldn't support homeless people, you'd be sent downplanet. No one ever came back from downplanet.

"How's Mom?" Milo asked, sliding down. Mom had been ill lately.

Dad ducked down a steam tube, grabbing a wrench from his belt.

"Keep working," he said. "They're watching."

Milo followed.

"That's why I came looking for you," said Dad. "I've been thinking about what you said. Your buddy Frog."

Frog brewed and sold affordable black-market meds these days.

"You oughta think twice about that," Milo warned. "Speaking of getting fired. Or shot."

Dad stopped. He whistled, and his fish dove into his hand, displaying schematics. Dad read the schematics and surveyed the gas lines overhead.

"Our cartel insurance can't cover any more of the cartel medicine," he said.

"So she's worse."

"Well, you'd know that if you came home nights, instead of blowing your pay at that . . . place."

Shit! Milo thought. Dad *knows* about that?

"That" was Dreamscapes, a discount brothel on the rec level. Women could earn additional income as licensed prostitutes while they got a refreshing, narc-induced night's sleep.

"I'm going to go fix something," said Milo, heading back the way they'd come.

"You do that," said Dad.

Home was a circular pod, with sleeping cells in the walls. Mom stayed in her sleeping cell during the dinner hour that night. Milo heard her coughing.

Dad wasn't feeling too social, so Milo talked to the twins.

The twins, Milo's four-year-old brother and sister, had come along on his twelfth birthday. Good thing their family had a top-drawer skill assignment and was permitted three kids. Carlo and Serene were their own universe of two, sometimes communicating in a language of their own invention. Laughing at things no one else heard or understood.

"Zee too," said Serene.

"Mak lo," answered Carlo, with his mouth full.

"Muk luk," said Milo, and they just looked at him.

After dinner, Milo took Dad down to Frog's.

By the time they got there, a couple of other people were waiting in the hall. One by one they buzzed in and buzzed out and scurried away. By the time Milo buzzed in, seven people had shown up all at once, fidgety and coughing.

"Something's going around," Milo said to Frog.

"I'm shutting down for the night," answered Frog, sweating over his pill cutter. "They're going to get me pinched. 'Zup?"

"My mom. This same cough everyone's getting."

Frog handed over a zip bag with five lozenges.

Out in the corridor, it was getting noisy. More people. More coughing.

"That's a schedule-one antibiotic," said Frog. "Gimme sixteen. That's friend prices. Then out you go."

Dad handed over the chits.

When Milo opened the door, the latch sprang in his hand, and he fell back under the sudden weight of three big coughing pipe fitters.

"I got nothing!" he heard Frog shouting, panicking. "I'm just a dishwasher, swear to God!"

In the corridor, heavy boots. Monitors!

Dad grasped Milo's elbow. Together, they got to their feet and hunkered down, pushing for the door.

They broke free and stumbled into the corridor.

But the corridor was worse. Full of coughing people, too many to count, and Monitors among them, smashing skulls. Milo heard the howl of an anaconda around the corner.

Everywhere, fists and elbows.

The zip bag got loose.

"Retards!" Milo gasped, clawing after the bag.

"No time," grunted Dad, pulling at him.

A Monitor grabbed him by the collar, pulling the other way.

"Your SPLAT has been scanned!" roared the amplified voice. "Now, up against the wall!"

The anaconda appeared—a massive vacuum hose, wrangled by Monitors in exo-frames, sucking up screaming rioters. They flew away down its cavelike throat (to *where*?).

The thing turned toward Milo. The slipstream pulled at him.

Dad, gritting his teeth, grabbed for something, anything.

Suddenly there was this girl.

She interposed, all flying black hair and waving arms and crazy eyes.

"No!" she screamed at the wranglers. "They're with me! Undercover 6065650!"

She waved some kind of plastic badge in the air.

The vacuum pulled the girl off her feet. The anaconda swallowed Milo and Dad, too—

—almost. The wranglers shut it down. Louvers slammed across the great mouth. Dad fell, and the wranglers kicked him to his feet.

"Follow me!" barked the girl, darting around, then running down the hall.

They followed, bewildered, as fast as they could.

The girl led them straight up to the commercial ring just as the shift whistle blew. The whole concourse trembled as the twilight shift came off, passing the grave shift going on. Boots thumped, voices growled. Toolbelts clanged.

The girl shook long dark hair over her face and gave Milo a look he couldn't interpret.

"What you told them," said Milo, "about the undercover—"

"They scanned us," whispered Dad urgently. "They have our SPLAT codes."

"Listen," said the girl, flashing the plastic badge. "It's not mine. It's from an enforcement volunteer in our hall who died in one of the abandoned seed cages. I'm not a snitch. I help make food."

"The kitchens." Milo couldn't help a tone of disgust.

"Not the kitchens," said the girl, rolling her eyes. "I said 'food.'

Medicine isn't the only thing you can buy under the table, you know. You guys have never been pinched before, have you?"

They gave her identical dumb looks.

"By now they've scanned a thousand codes. Way more than they can process. If they didn't get you with the anaconda, you're clear."

In the corridors behind them, noise and shouting. The Monitors in Frog's corridor had obviously failed to contain the chaos.

"It's turning into a real thing," said Dad.

Milo grasped the girl's elbow and asked, "Why did you help us?"

There was that unreadable look again. It was the only answer she gave.

Rioters spilled into the concourse.

"You dropped this!" said the girl, pressing something into Milo's hand.

Mom's pills.

Then she was gone, slipping away downstream.

Dad kept them close the next day. Even the twins had to follow him around in the tubes and tunnels.

"Rioters'll break into the pods on the skilled level," he explained. "For food."

Dad gave the twins his fish and let them read important numbers to him.

From the corridors below, the smell of smoke.

"They're burning the unrefined fuel," said Mom.

"Idiots," sneered Dad. "They'll use up the air. Don't they *realize?*"

That's when the Monitors showed up. Five of them.

"Ventilation one one zero one zero zero one zero one?" the commander barked, his speaker cranked way up.

"That's me," answered Dad.

"Shut down the lung," said the commander.

Dad's whole body jerked, as if he'd gotten a mild shock.

Mom started to say something, but a sudden cough silenced her.

"That'll kill the oxygen," said Dad.

The commander leveled his burp gun.

The twins watched in silence. They understood that something important was happening.

Mom closed her eyes, trembling.

"No," said Dad.

And he looked straight into their masks as they shot him.

His whole chest came apart. He fell, gagging, and died.

Milo's jaw dropped. Before he could move or say anything, a handful of rioters spilled onto the gantry.

The Monitors' burp guns sprayed green gas.

Milo felt his body go numb. He dropped to the floor for what seemed like a year.

He woke up underwater.

His eyes opened, and he saw sunlight and waves overhead. Felt himself immersed and sinking. He kicked and swam and broke onto the surface, gasping, treading water that stretched everywhere, as far as he could see.

Above, a flying machine whined and rumbled, then shrieked away.

He'd been dumped in the water—the ocean? Was this an ocean?

Shouting and panic, all around. Fifteen people, he guessed, struggled in the water.

Jupiter split the sky like a crescent knife. Other crescents—other moons—hung in space to either side. (It was a lot to take in for a kid who'd never been outside, never been anyplace bigger than the lung. If it hadn't been for sims, he might have panicked and definitely would have drowned.)

(Are we downplanet? Is this Europa?)

"*Mom!*" he cried out.

Fwoom! A giant orange fish exploded from the sea and fell toward them, fell on top of them—

A raft! It inflated, grew rigid, and sat turning in the water like a floating fort.

There was Mom. There were the twins, already clambering over the side.

Giggling. Pushing each other.

Milo crawled over to his mother, and her eyes brightened. She grasped the back of his head and brought their foreheads together. They sat like that without a word.

The twins, meanwhile, gamboled in the middle of the raft.

"Whootoi!" yelped Carlo.

"Nok beta," answered Serene.

Then they turned to Milo, turned to Mom, and together said, "Dad."

There was nothing to do but shake their heads. Milo felt his mother trembling.

The twins fell silent, holding hands.

"Land," someone said.

What? Milo wasn't sure what to look for. Except in movies and sims, he'd never seen a horizon before.

Something like a dark wall, way ahead. Cliffsides rising above the waves.

The island seemed to race toward them.

"Tidal currents," coughed Mom. "We might get carried right past."

Milo gave her a curious look. She and Dad had lived in other places, off-crawler. They had something called "education."

"Europa practically sits in Jupiter's lap," Mom explained, "in an elliptical orbit. So it's got huge tides that squeeze it like a rubber ball."

The island loomed close. At the top, jungle trees and vines bristled and hung. At the waterline, the ocean hissed and swirled, exploding on sharp rock.

"Ho!" someone yelled.

People and boats surrounded them, darting between waves. Dark, naked people. Long, skinny boats, like things made from scraps, with ragged curving sails. The dark people threw cables over the raft. Passengers grabbed for these lifelines.

"Hold tight!" bellowed the dark people. Some of them, Milo noticed, had breasts.

He grabbed a cable—like nothing he'd ever touched before, rough and unfamiliar—and gripped tight. The raft slowed.

The water did things he couldn't understand. It seemed to be rising, swallowing the island whole. The water climbed and climbed. Was the island sinking?

"Tides," repeated Mom. "Hundreds of feet high."

The twins clung to her arms and to each other.

They rode the rising tide like that, with their mysterious saviors grinning all around them and the sea racing by.

The sea reached the top of the cliff, and there it stopped.

It crashed against a long white beach.

It lifted the boats and the raft and let them scrape gently onto land, where the dark people leaped out and helped the newcomers onto dry sand and grass.

Beyond the grass, houses of the same materials that formed the boats and the cables.

Wood, Milo realized, remembering his classes and sims. Vines and trees. Wonderful!

Beyond the little houses, a great crowd of green and wood and vines—a forest!—which rose up the flanks of steep hills.

More islanders came running from the village. All dark, like their rescuers, and all naked.

"Thank you," said Mom, her voice raw.

The strangers nodded.

"You're the third package in two days," said one of the strangers, a man with long gray hair and a missing eye. "What in the star-spangled hell is going *on* up there?"

The man's name was Boone, and he didn't waste a lot of time on chitchat. He introduced himself, shook some hands, and then called out, "Where's Jale?"

"Here, Boone," answered one of the rescuers, sitting in the grass.

One of the rescuers with breasts, Milo noticed. His own age, maybe a little younger.

"We need you to go back out again."

"Aw, dammit, Boone, we just—"

"We're out of redfish. O-U-T out."

They glared at each other, the girl and the one-eyed man. Then the girl stood and waved her arms up and down.

"Fish Committee!" she shouted. "Pony, make sure freshwater bags are aboard, and Chili Pepper, baby, check the nets, will ya?"

The dark, naked people who had rescued them—nearly all kids and teens, Milo now realized—popped up and ran in various directions, grabbing this and that. Most of them converged on the skinny wooden boats they'd just arrived in, yelling back and forth. Singing, some of them.

Jale—the leader of this wild young navy—took three long steps across the sand and stood looking down at Milo.

"Come fishing," she said.

"I . . . we just got here," he stammered.

"You've seen about all there is to see," said Jale, shrugging. "It ain't complicated."

"He'll go," said another voice, behind him. Another girl.

Squinting against the sun, Milo looked back over his shoulder, and there was the girl from the crawler, from the night the riots began. And she was naked.

Milo produced a croaking noise.

"Go!" called his mother, not far away, one twin in each arm, surrounded by islanders.

Then they had him by the arms, the two girls and a variety of children, and he was aboard a wooden outrigger. Twenty or so island kids splashed alongside, pushing the boat into the surf. The girl from the crawler ran with them, laughing. Then they all vaulted into the waist with him, balancing expertly.

Jale clambered up to the prow and crouched there, tugging ropes, freeing a sail, which snapped open like a wing.

The ocean and the wind whipped them away from the island.

The girl from the crawler sat facing him. Looking at him. She seemed amused.

She's beautiful, Milo thought. He struggled to focus on her eyes, because she was so, so naked.

"I'm Suzie," she said.

Two other outriggers sailed alongside them, and the three boats were out for three days.

Three clock-days, in crawler time. Earth days. In Jupiter orbit, that was one day. Eighty-odd hours from one dim sunrise to the next.

Milo had time, finally, to think about his father. If he stared into the sun long enough, he could project Dad's face onto the cloud bands of Jupiter. He was wary of tears, though. The people around him had losses of their own. He would handle his loss alone, for now.

I shouldn't have left the twins so soon, he thought. Or Mom.

The islanders leaped around and over Milo and Suzie, pulling ropes, loosing nets. The nets came back with fish in them, and the islanders would sing out and pack them away in a hole up front, covered in palm fronds. Or they would make evil faces and empty the nets back into the sea. Milo glimpsed one fish with a mouth in its belly. Another had tumors for eyes, writhing with tiny pink tentacles.

Suzie, Milo learned, had been a victim of the anaconda, sucked up and jailed less than an hour after rescuing Milo. Like him, she had no memory of being transported downplanet. She had been here for four days. This was her second fishing trip.

"It's beautiful here," she said, "but it's toxic. The terraformers' big learning experience. They need fish—like, lots of fish, especially redfish—for the antioxidants."

"What's an antioxidant?"

"I don't know. We have a lot to learn. Like how to sail and how to walk around on this stupid boat without falling in the water, and how come you still have your clothes on? It's warm. It's always warm."

Because I have an erection, Milo thought.

When in Rome, said a voice inside him.

Seized by a sudden and particular courage, Milo half-stood, worked his way out of his clothes, and cast them overboard.

Suzie eyed his erection.

"Is that because of me?" she asked.

Milo nodded.

"Wow," she said. Then she stood and climbed up to the prow with Jale and asked if someone could please teach her how to work the nets.

They learned the nets, and the sails, and how to read the weather.

They learned the islanders' names. Among the younger kids were Zardoz, High Voltage, and Demon Rum. The teens were Gilgamesh, Talk Pretty, Frodo, Pony, and Chili Pepper, Jale's boyfriend. Jale was the captain; they deferred to her on all three boats.

The sky went through changes. Jupiter changed shape. The distant sun crept between horizons. Smaller moons passed. Dark clouds boiled up sometimes, and they sailed around these when they could.

"You watch the water, too," Jale told them. "Not just the sky."

"For fish?" asked Suzie.

"Fish and tsunami," answered Jale, eyes on the sea. "The tides here make everything bigger."

When they slept, they left a few kids to mind the sails and watch the sea. The crews curled up in the bottom, jumbled together in knots, while Jupiter eclipsed the sun and haunted the sky like a hole with a glowing rim, and the stars came out, and the other moons shined brighter than ever.

Milo and Suzie didn't sleep. Not then.

They slumped together with the outrigger's wooden hull on one side and a pile of sleeping kids on the other. Their bare arms and shoulders touching sent shivers all over Milo.

"You talk to yourself," Suzie whispered.

"Hmmm?"

"You heard me. What's going on when you do that?"

What was he going to say?

"Sometimes my head talks to me," he said.

"Mine, too," she said, and they went back to being silent and not sleeping.

"Redfish!" Chili Pepper called out in the middle of the second day.

The crews boiled into action, tying sails down.

"What about the nets?" asked Suzie.

"Don't use nets for redfish," said Zardoz. "You gots to dive for 'em."

Milo searched the water. All he saw was a school of tiny, iridescent guppies darting around. Leaping and splashing on the surface.

"Dive for what?" he asked. "There's nothing here big enough to eat. Just these—"

"Rainbow minnies," said Suzie. "The redfish come up from under and feed on them. Where you see minnies, there's redfish."

"Get your air!" yelled Jale.

All the older kids, the teens, started hyperventilating.

"They have to fill their tissues with oxygen," Suzie explained.

"Jesus," said Milo. "How deep are the redfish?"

"Deep," answered Demon Rum.

Milo looked thoughtful for a second. Then he started inhaling and exhaling as fast as he could.

"No, Milo," said Suzie.

"Working in the lung," Milo said, speaking on the exhale, "with my dad . . . we'd get gas bleed-off . . . from the waste membranes . . . the cartel gas masks didn't work for shit . . . so we'd have to hold our breath . . . couple minutes at a time . . . I can swim . . . no reason I can't . . . dive and fish . . ."

Demon Rum handed out short wooden spears to the older kids.

"Milo," said Suzie, "listen, you don't—"

"I'm going," he said, feeling light-headed.

"Jale!" shouted Suzie.

"Let him," said Jale.

Demon Rum came skipping back and handed Milo a spear. He tried, without success, to mask a smile.

What weren't they telling him? What didn't he know?

"Go on *one!*" yelled Jale. "Three . . . two . . . one!"

The teens all swallowed one final, great breath and dove over the gunwale. Milo was the first one in the water.

Surrounded by cool, surrounded by blue, he kicked with his legs, pushed with his arms, and aimed straight down, where the water was a deeper, dusky blue. Like a sky in reverse.

Islander kids knifed past him. In a second, they were twenty feet below. Thirty.

What the hell? What were they doing?

They were using their legs and feet, their bodies undulating, the way a dolphin swims.

Milo did the same. He went down faster, deeper, and it got darker all around.

The others were out of sight, below. His lungs began to burn, but he didn't want to turn back yet. The fish couldn't be far.

Something in his head warned him: What goes down must come up and needs time to come up.

Shit.

Milo turned and pulled his way back toward the surface.

You have a lot to learn, he told himself. Take time to learn it.

Goddamn, the daylight and the mottled sun up above were *awfully* far away.

But he made it.

He broke the surface in a universe of shooting pain. Pain like explosions in his lungs. He opened his throat and screamed in reverse, sucking up air like an anaconda; he got water, too, but didn't care. Coughed it up.

Suzie grabbed him and dragged him into the boat.

He was bleeding. He could feel it. His eyes and ears.

"You are one simple fucker, you know that?" Suzie bellowed at him. Was she hitting him? Hard to tell. Parts of him felt sharp and broken;

other parts felt dead. "If that's all the smarter you can be, like a two-year-old, I don't care if it breaks my heart, you asshole, I'll—"

"Leave him alone," said a young voice. Very young. Demon Rum. "Let him come around. He was brave."

"He was stupid," spat Suzie.

"He was learning. Still, Jale's gonna be pissed." By the time Milo was able to move, able to sit up, the rest of the divers were breaching, breaking the waves like fish, gulping air. Some of them, including Jale, had thrashing fish on their spears. Redfish the size of small children, with long red whiskers and narrow fins.

The young kids cheered and helped them aboard.

Celebration! There were extra food and water rations when false night came around and Jupiter eclipsed the sun. And they sang some songs.

Milo sat down beside Jale, who was snuggling with Chili Pepper, and said, "I'll be able to do it right next time."

He didn't know how he would do this, exactly, but he felt that it was true.

But Jale said, "No."

"Listen," he said, "back on the crawler—"

"Forget the crawler," she said. "You wait 'til Chili has had time to teach you right. You and Suzie can both learn, and then next time—"

But Milo was already standing, already heading back toward his place by the mast.

Dammit, he thought. I was just being courteous, anyway. Whose permission—

"Milo," said Chili Pepper, calling after him. "Jale's captain. Her own father does what she says, when we're on the water."

Milo tuned him out by playing some music inside his head.

A day later, when Frodo sighted minnies, Milo grabbed a spear and went over the side right after the others, before anyone could stop him.

"Shit, Milo!" both Suzie and Demon Rum cried.

But Milo had been conferencing with the voices in his head, and they had given him some helpful memories from other lives (so the voices said).

You could imagine your brain was a house, with a toolroom inside. You could open that toolroom and find ways to make your brain work better. He recalled floating in space, at peace, stark naked.

He recalled meditating with the Buddha (yeah, right!). In, out. Breathing was much more than taking in air. Breathing was where your rhythms interfaced with the rhythms of the world.

Even when you were holding your breath.

He passed Jale, who gave him a brief, surprised look. The water darkened around him.

Pressure and movement. Balance.

Glowing dots wriggled through the dark . . . Milo struck with his spear (that was breathing, too, the death struggle and the spear trying to wrestle free).

The fast ascent, into light again, flying up through rolling waves, into warm sun and light.

And climbing aboard by himself, because, oddly, no one held out a hand, no one helped him over the side or complimented him on his fish.

No one even looked at him.

"Oh, I see," he said, but he said it almost silently, because he finally got it.

They had their ways and their captains and rules because those things kept them alive. He had made a successful dive, but he was an asshole for disobeying Jale.

He didn't make eye contact with any of them as they went about the business of storing fish and steering for home.

Suzie sat down beside him.

"*That* time was fucking awesome," she said. "Way better than before. Smarter, you know? You're not as simple as I thought. But Jale's going to rain on you, I think."

"Suzie—" warned Chili Pepper.

"Let it go, Chili," she said sharply. "You turn your back on him, you turn your back on me."

Milo's brow furrowed. He loved her.

A day later, when the island came in sight, they still weren't speaking to him.

Fine. He and Suzie and Mom and the twins would make their own village on the other side of the island. He knew about catching redfish, and they could grow some crops, maybe.

"Hey," said Suzie, waking him up, nudging him with a big toe.

It was the supernatural time of day, eclipse time. The great planet was a hole in the sky, surrounded by misty light and stars.

"Hey," said Suzie, lying down beside him, facing him. "Do you remember me, from before?"

"Sure," he whispered. "From the day the riot started."

"Not that," she said. "Before then. Before . . ."

"I never met you before then. I'm sure we must've passed on the concourse or on the rec level or something, but we must've gone to different classes and sims—"

She pressed her whole hand against his mouth.

"Listen: You know when we talked about the voices?"

"The voices got me in trouble," he muttered.

"I think those are, like, memories from when we've lived . . . before."

Milo considered what had happened when he dove. The things he knew about the breathing, which were things he had never been taught.

"I think," she said, "there's a reason you feel familiar to me," and Milo realized that she had his penis in her hand.

An hour later, there was a general stirring in the boat, and sounds of alarm.

"Shit," said Jale, up in the prow.

Milo followed her eyes and saw that they were home. There sat the island, green and jagged, with its hills and grass and the village behind the long white beach.

And up on top of it all, over the tallest hill, hovered a cartel tanker ship.

It looked like a coffee kettle welded to a toilet, bigger than an ancient football stadium, steaming and hissing.

"What . . ." began Milo.

"Trouble," said Jale, helping to pull the outrigger ashore, forgetting to ignore him.

She assigned High Voltage and Demon Rum to unload the fish from all three boats, then ran into the trees without another word.

They all followed. Everyone seemed to have an idea what was going on. Everyone but Milo and Suzie.

They weren't in shape the way the islanders were, and the island kids left them behind without hesitation. Suzie kept her eye on what little trail there was to follow, and they hopped over fallen trees and around tangled vines, eventually stumbling out of the forest.

There was a factory on top of the hill. Looked like one, anyway. Looked as if giants had stood an old-fashioned submarine on its end and driven it into the ground. A towering, rusty, patched-up engine, clanking and steaming, full of hoses and oil stains. Over that, the tanker loomed.

"What in the name of . . ." Suzie began.

"It's a well," said Milo, who had been shadowing his dad around machinery for at least a decade. "A gigantic well, with a huge, piece-of-shit water pump."

Not far away, Jale and Boone and a whole lot of islanders were arguing with two armored Monitors. One commander, with a red helmet, and a deputy with a burp gun.

Milo and Suzie jogged over to listen.

"This machinery is your responsibility," crackled the deputy, through his speaker. "Either you keep it running your way or we will assist you."

"Is that what you call it?" sneered Boone. "Sending a fifty-year-old grandmother down to fix a valve with a nine-pound wrench?"

"She is your chief mechanic," said the commander.

"Was," said Boone.

Jale slapped angry tears from her face and turned away.

"You may have five minutes to select another volunteer," said the commander. "Or we will choose for you."

"*There is no one!*" roared Boone. "Why won't you understand? The mechanics can't dive that far! Even if a diver *could* get down there, they wouldn't know what to look for—"

The commander lifted Boone by the throat and held him in the air.

"Four minutes," he crackled, letting Boone slump to the ground.

The islanders stood there without breathing or speaking.

"I'll go," said Milo.

Suzie smacked him—hard—across the back. "You don't even know what it *is!*" she hissed.

"They need someone to dive down and fix something," said Milo. "I can do both of those things."

Jale shook her head.

"You're on punishment," she said.

Everyone stared at her in disbelief.

"Jale?" said Boone, picking himself up, rubbing at his throat. "You wanna bring me up to speed?"

Four minutes later, Boone and a team of mechanics led Milo into the rusty submarine—the water pump—and showed him what to do.

The pump was a cave of pipes and hoses and greasy turning things, stinking of scorched oil and exhaust.

"This is what we do," the mechanics explained. "Everyone on the island—everyone on *all* the islands—runs these goddamn pumps for the water cartel. It's a lot of digging and a lot of fixing and a lot of broken bones and skulls."

At the submarine's core, something like an anaconda snaked down into a pool of groundwater. The pool was the well itself.

"It goes down a thousand feet," the mechanics told him. "You have to go down that far to get below the toxins in the water table."

"Holy shit," said Milo.

"He can't dive that far," said Suzie quietly. "No one can."

The lead mechanic (*new* lead mechanic), Big Bird, shook her head.

"The stuck valve is four hundred feet down."

"Christ on a stick," said Milo, "they don't have scuba gear for shit like that?"

"The well is too narrow for gear," said Big Bird, "with the drill head in place."

"Can't you raise the drill head?" asked Milo.

"Not with the valve stuck. It's a safety feature."

Big Bird handed him a crescent wrench so heavy he had to hold it with both hands.

"The valve chuck is a bright-orange nut," she said, "but you won't be able to see it in the dark. It sticks out a ways; you'll probably just hit it as you go down. It's the only thing down there that fits this wrench."

They stood silently looking at each other.

"Righty-tighty, lefty-loosey," she said.

"I know," said Milo.

"Let him get ready," said Suzie.

The mechanics backed away. So did Suzie.

He stood there for a time.

From some distance away, he probably looked to Suzie and the mechanics as if he was meditating.

I have a big mouth, he was thinking.

In fact, the sight of the hole and the dark water and the greasy machinery scared the crap out of him. A lot of *bad* had happened lately. It seemed a matter of destiny that it would come to an end here, with his drowning or getting smashed, just when all he wanted was to go off someplace and have sex with Suzie.

"Milo?" said Suzie, tapping him on the shoulder.

Shit! She could read his—

"You don't have to. You know that, right?"

"Just another minute," he said. "I'm oxygenating."

As Suzie re-joined the mechanics, he felt more focused.

After a minute or so, he jumped in.

Splash!

Sick! The water was what you might expect from swimming inside a machine. Oozy and thick. Too late, he thought to close his eyes, but they already stung.

Gripping the big wrench, he sank like a firebrick, scraping against the anaconda hose, then bouncing against the earthen wall of the well itself.

The water squeezed him. Pressure mounting.

He tried to feel the balance and harmony he'd felt in the open sea, but it just wasn't there.

He tried to open the toolroom in his brain and get the light to shine out, but he couldn't find it.

He tried to meditate, but his mind kept thinking about having sex with Suzie and—

He slammed into something hard and round. It jabbed into his leg and stopped him hard enough (almost) to make him yell out or take a breath. The wrench bobbled loose, but he caught it with his elbow.

Fuck! Idiot. The valve nut. He'd forgotten.

His lungs had begun to burn, but he had time to do what he'd promised, he thought.

He worked the wrench into place. It fit neatly.

Lefty-loosey . . . he gave it a yank.

It didn't budge.

Of course not, he thought.

The pain in his lungs cranked up a notch (I don't have enough air to get back up, he realized, and tried to ignore the thought).

He gave the wrench another pull. Nothing.

At this point, someone put a hand over his face.

He almost screamed. He *did* urinate, which warmed the water and felt nice. And he realized almost instantly what was going on. It was the dead chief mechanic, bobbing around.

It was all Milo could do to convince his body not to panic, but he calmed himself. Even felt the beginnings—way too late—of peace and balance.

He was also left with at least a gallon of adrenaline pounding through his veins. He was aware of this in the same way he was aware of his respiration.

Milo put his whole body into one massive tug, and the nut came loose and turned.

And turned. And Milo heard something *clank* into place.

Up! Now! He launched himself toward the surface even as he felt his consciousness beginning to slip. Any second, his body would gulp for air, whether he wanted it to or not—

A dead hand touched him again. This time it grabbed his wrist.

Wild horror! He shit himself a little—

But it wasn't the dead mechanic. The hand was a living hand, and it pulled him and kicked along with him and took him up . . .

(What? Who?)

Light, at the end of a verrrrrrrrrrrrrrrrrry long tunnel . . .

Splashing through!

Oily, gassy air!

He sucked it up—delicious!—grasping the edge of the well.

He was so damn weak. He was going to pass out and sink.

An arm around his neck. Legs twining around his legs, holding him up.

"Suzie?"

"Just shut up and pass out," she said, and he did.

The well sucked water up out of the bedrock and pumped it into the cartel tanker. The Monitors climbed back aboard the tanker, and the tanker rode its skyhook up into space.

Milo and Suzie lay in the hospital hut, sleeping.

Sometimes people brought them something to drink or a bit of fish to eat.

One time, Milo woke up and his mom was sitting there, naked, trying to feed him some soup (awkwaaaaaaaaaard . . .).

The twins were there, briefly. They gave him a bored look, said,
"Fong!" and scrambled away somewhere.

"They're letting me teach in the school," Mom told him. That was
all he remembered from Mom's visit.

The next time he woke up, it was Suzie who fed him soup.

"That other mechanic finally came to the surface," she told him.
"There's a funeral for her tonight. They have these toxic trees that
burn like crazy, so whenever they have a funeral, it usually means a
bonfire. Except you're not supposed to get too close or breathe the
smoke, or get the ashes on you, or go near the fire pit after until there's
a good rain. Other than that, though, they say it's really cool and burns
different colors."

"What the flying hell were you doing down in the well?" he asked.

"What did you expect me to do? You think you're the only one who
can do that voice-in-the-head thing? You don't listen. It's the past-lives
thing I told you about. We knew each other, and I think I used to be a
queen or something."

"Of that," said Milo, setting the soup bowl aside, "I have no doubt."

"Ooh," she said. She liked that. She let him kiss her.

She let him do all kinds of things.

They left the hospital tent in time for the funeral, which was a simple
affair.

Boone and five other islanders lowered the body into a sandy grave.

"Midnight Rider," said Boone, piling sand over her with a hand-
carved shovel.

That was the name the woman had chosen for herself, because it
told people something about who she was.

"Midnight Rider," everyone repeated, and they lit the bonfire, and
stepped back and stayed out of the smoke, and applauded the wonderful colors.

Then they went about their business and, as far as Milo could tell, never mentioned the woman again.

Afterward, Mom took Milo by the elbow and called the twins with a whistle, and the four of them went to the shore together and stood—cautiously—knee-deep in the sea.

And they talked about Dad. Just talked about him. And cried.

And Mom didn't say they shouldn't talk about him anymore after that. Dad hadn't been an islander. But, as far as Milo ever knew, they didn't. He was part of another world, or a face from a fading dream.

There was another funeral, the next night.

Sometime during the high tide, with hundreds of people around, three sisters had walked right into the ocean, holding hands, and let the monstrous undertow take them.

"No one tried to stop them?" Milo asked Chili Pepper.

Chili Pepper shook his head. "Some people choose not to live like this," he said. "It's like defiance, you know?"

A light rain came down on the funeral that night, so the colors were dimmed somewhat.

There were no bodies to bury, so Boone sprinkled some sand on the wind.

"Betty," he intoned. "Lunch Lady. The Priestess of Mu."

"What does it mean when you sprinkle the sand?" Milo asked Boone later.

Boone didn't know. "Just seems right," he said.

They became islanders.

One of the first things they learned was that the islanders called themselves the "Rock 'N' Roll Hall of Fame." (Booty Dog had a twentieth-century pop-culture book called *I Want My MTV.* They got a lot of their names from this book.)

Other islands named themselves after their own mood and style.

Big, glad names were popular, like the Sexy Geniuses and the Hookah Panthers to the north. There were serious names, like Hope Island, the Isle of Life, and Gateway Atoll.

"Things change," Boone told Milo, "so names change. Last year we were the Twilight Zone."

They traded with other islands sometimes. Here on the Hall of Fame, they grew a kind of grass that was great for twisting into rope. On the Isle of Life, they grew apples that could feed four people for a week. So they traded grass for apples.

"Last year," Boone told Milo, "we traded a girl named Red Rita to a boat builder named Spock."

"Traded?" Milo's eyes darkened.

"Married," Boone clarified. "Relax."

Hall of Famers helped them build houses—one for Mom and the twins, one for Milo and Suzie. Milo and Suzie's hut was made from giant leaves, mostly, and some metal plates salvaged from a cartel trash drop.

One whole wall of Mom's hut was an aluminum strip with part of a faded advertisement on it, advising everyone to watch a TV farce called *Time Lobster.*

Mom made a better islander than Milo would have guessed. She taught in a little bamboo schoolhouse they had and took a seat on the New-Things Committee, a think tank for brainstorming up better ways to live. If you'd had an engineering job or a real education, you got pressed into this group. A man named Raymond Carver, a former cartel lab chief, had been in charge of this board for as long as anyone could remember.

There were other committees, with constantly shifting member-ship.

The Food-Safety Committee, which identified and gathered fruits and vegetables that wouldn't poison you if you ate them. (Suzie took this group by storm, showing them how to dry and preserve certain fruits, and their stores began to increase.)

The School Board. The Fairness Committee.

The Tsunami Committee, whose members learned to read the sea and kept watch on a high bluff with a giant warning drum. This committee had a subcommittee: the Rebuilding Committee.

Milo and Suzie both became members of the Fish Committee. You had to be young and fairly healthy to be on that one, which they were.

For the time being.

Health wasn't something you took for granted here.

Milo noticed a lot of missing arms and eyes. There were people with weird swellings that came and went quickly, leaving misshapen bone. Almost no one on the island was unmarked. Some of the youngest bore strange puckerings and scars on their skin. Demon Rum had a hole in his foot that went straight through (he wore a ring of braided grass through it). A girl named Bug had what looked like extra veins in her throat, and her voice was rough, as if she breathed sand. Many, many people had a bad eye, or a wandering eye, or an eye with a blue caul over it. Several people were blind. There were never any babies. This wasn't talked about.

Milo and Suzie were also assigned to the Water-Pump Committee.

Everyone worked on the giant pump. But the board members were responsible for knowing how the thing actually worked and for keeping it going. They would be the first to suffer if the cartel came for water and didn't get what they wanted.

"You're spending the time and work needed for collecting food," Milo observed, after a week, "on running this dinosaur for those fuckers."

"No shit," said Jale.

"We'd all be a lot healthier if we could send out two, three times as many fishing crews."

"No shit," Jale repeated.

"You're stuck here eating fruit from the island, and most of it's toxic."

"It's poisoning you, too, Diver Man." She pointed out a swelling near his elbow.

His first cancer. Lovely.

They burned it off with a piece of hot steel from the trash.

———

In the first weeks that they lived on the island, Milo and his family attended five funerals. They thought that was a lot. Then the storm came.

It was the kids who noticed it first. Some of the younger fishermen.

They had found a dead fish on the beach and were poking it with sticks when the very youngest, a three-year-old girl named Moo, straightened up, pointed her stick at the horizon, and said, "Storm."

The other kids turned instantly and froze. When someone said, "Storm," it was a slightly less urgent form of the tsunami drum.

They all pointed together, screaming *"Storm!"* over and over, a piercing alarm.

Most of the islanders rushed to the beach.

Suzie and Milo had seen storms on Ganymede, on screens and through windows. But they were fitful, staticky things. Some wind and dust; the milk cries of an infant atmosphere. They had seen video of Earth storms, and of course there was stormy Jupiter with its cyclonic eye. But the thing that came oozing over the horizon that afternoon wasn't just windy and dark. It looked bad and unnatural and out of place.

"It looks like a stomach," said Milo.

It came writhing across the sea, balloon-smooth, pink, and horrible, quivering like jelly. Here and there, parts of it puckered or spilled like guts. The pink gave way to patches of decomposing greens and blues.

A stinking wind flattened the surf and took them by surprise. A wind like burning plastic and rotting feet. A score of islanders doubled over and retched on the sand.

Then they ran for the jungle in one flying mass. The young hit the trees first, followed by the unencumbered grown-ups, followed by those who carried children or belongings, followed by the elderly and the sick.

What exactly was going to happen? Milo wondered.

They ran under a huge rocky overhang—a shelf like a giant hand trying to karate-chop its way out of the Earth—near the base of the volcano.

It started out fairly roomy, but as the older, slower islanders kept arriving, they shuffled farther back, closing in tighter until they were packed like synthetic olives in a jar. Milo snugged up behind Suzie, wrapping his arms around her.

Thunder rumbled, and the putrid wind found them. Milo breathed through his mouth.

Then there were hands on his arms, but not Suzie's hands. Smaller ones, seeking his fingers and holding on.

The twins. Serene was on his left, smiling up at him. Carlo, on the other side, had captured Suzie's hand. They both smiled, but their eyes were troubled and questioning.

"What is it?" asked Serene.

"A storm," answered Milo. "A bad storm."

"We'll be all right," said Suzie, hoisting Carlo onto her hip.

Milo glanced around. "Where's Mom?" he asked.

"I thought she was in here," said Suzie. "Isn't she here?"

Milo turned a full circle.

"Mom!" he called, but the wind had kicked up; other voices were calling out, too.

"Just stay with us," he told the twins. "We'll find Mom after."

Quite suddenly, the air went green.

Flash! Lightning.

Crack! Immediate thunder.

And then the world came apart.

Was this what a hurricane was like? Milo wondered. The wind was like a steam press, pushing them and whipping at them with loose leaves and branches. It shot water sideways at them through the strange green air.

Milo didn't like the feel of the water on his skin. Was it crawling on him, feeling for a way in? That's what it felt like. Beside him, Serene fidgeted, wiping the mist from her face and flinging it from her fingers.

"It's slippery," she complained.

"I know," said Milo.

Serene slid between Milo and Suzie and took hold of Carlo's ankle. "Bood buh ja," she said to him, and Carlo answered, "Parka."

Milo and Suzie shared an amused look.

"Parka," said Milo.

"Fuckin' A," said Suzie.

The rain raised blisters. Everywhere you looked in that crowd under the overhang, there were tiny bubbles on people.

The storm lasted for hours, like something that had decided to hover over them and digest them. They passed the time whispering stories and conversations. They took turns napping and holding one another up. For a while they sang an ancient spiritual called "Margaritaville."

The green air turned pink.

Milo noticed the trees outside, away from the overhang. Their trunks and leaves had developed veins (veins, or rivers of scarring where the rain had touched them?).

Leaves fell. Coconuts fell. Whole trees crashed. He could hear them near and far away.

Flash.

Crack!

The lightning began a barrage that went on and on, and the funny thing was, it lulled them. Milo and Suzie found their way to the ground and lay there with the twins between them and fell into strange dreams and wakeful fits.

When it was over, the older ones hesitated to step outside.

The storm had rolled on. They could hear it growing distant, still rumbling. It left behind a dullness and a stillness and a stink like a bowel movement.

"Let it dry first," said Babs Babylon, a forty-year-old widow, the Hall of Fame's finest toolmaker.

"Screw it," coughed Boone, who had stood the whole time. And he walked out into the wet, through a big puddle that shined ugly rainbow colors, the way gasoline does.

And most of them followed.

"Take the twins," Milo told Suzie. "Will you?"

She nodded. He didn't have to tell her he was going to look for Mom.

First he caught up with Boone, who had stopped among some ferns to puke and catch his breath.

"Where else would people go?" Milo asked. "Did the Storm Committee find another—"

Boone shook his head.

"That's the only one," he said. "She mighta stayed in the huts, probably."

Then he gagged and said, "Let me be, Milo. Go on now."

Milo had no plan.

If Mom was at the beach, Suzie and the twins would find her there. But Milo had an old, sure, unexplainable feeling that they wouldn't.

When he first stumbled—literally stumbled—over a teenager named Miss Nude Mars, he thought she was a pig sleeping in the underbrush. How weird, he thought. Pigs weren't among the animals they'd seeded on Europa. But this animal was pink and round and was snuffling in the dirt.

"Jesus," whimpered Milo, when he saw and understood.

Miss Nude Mars had one enormous tumor swelling along her left side, from heel to skull. It throbbed. He could see it tugging at her, under the skin, with blue blood vessels like tentacles.

She looked up at him with one rolling, horror-filled eye, her right eye. The left was collapsing and leaking yellow water.

"*Fulghussss,*" she gurgled. She raised her right arm as if reaching for him.

Milo ran.

————

Five minutes later, he found his mother.

She looked okay, at first. Just a woman resting against a tree.

"Mom?" he called. And he hurried, tripping over fallen branches and discolored leaves.

Heard her say, "No! Milo, no—"

She could speak. She would be okay; whatever had gotten to Miss Nude Mars hadn't gotten Mom so bad. But what in hell had kept her? How come—and then he saw.

She was pregnant. Except not really. Something low in her belly was growing big and round, burgeoning as he watched. Stretching her. As he stood there, with a low moan starting down deep in his chest, he saw a portion of her skin part like a zipper alongside her belly button, which now popped out, reversing itself.

She raised a hand to shield her face, to not see him, to be invisible.

Through grinding teeth, she uttered a kind of stifled howl. Something old and sure inside Milo made him back away, made him run again.

This time, he ran to the village.

He barely spared a glance at the sodden, sagging huts that still stood, or the few misshapen islanders who lay on the sand, dead or dying. One, he saw, had burst like a fallen, overripe fruit. He grabbed a handmade machete from among the village tools and stole away uphill again, into the jungle.

Milo had to go very far away, inside himself, to do what he did.

By the time he got to her, she was gagging rather than breathing. Her scream was strangled by rising tumors along her throat, but she looked at him when he arrived, panting and crying.

As quickly as possible, with all his strength, he beheaded his mother with the machete. He was insanely practical about this, stepping nimbly away so that the hundred bad fluids that sprayed from her didn't catch him.

Why? What had happened? Had his mother not gotten moving in time? Hadn't known to head for shelter? Hadn't known where the shelter was?

He would never know. He would try not to think about it. Already his mind was putting ice on the whole afternoon, packing it away someplace numb.

He backtracked and found Miss Nude Mars again, but she had split down the back and rolled wide open, and toadstools were growing from the torn flesh. The toadstools had tiny little finger things around their caps. They waved at him.

For a week, maybe more, the Rock 'N' Roll Hall of Fame sat around and didn't say much. Sat looking out at the sea and the sky. One man—a relatively young man, a former free-enterprise flier named Dracula—walked off into the surf and was dragged away. Forty people were there when he did it. They let him do it.

Milo went to Suzie and the twins, meaning to have them scrape the rain blisters off and clean themselves with ocean water (Was that clean? Was anything clean?), but Suzie was way ahead of him. Everyone was doing it.

Over and over, they went to the sea, up to their ankles, and scrubbed at themselves with sand and seawater. A few of them scrubbed themselves until they bled, and others watched them do this and let them do it. Until Jale came hobbling up to Cracklin' Rosie, who kept scrubbing and bleeding and had torn three fingernails loose, and said, "No, Rose. Stop it. Stop," and held on to her until she stopped, and kept holding on to her. And that seemed to shake a lot of them out of it. That seemed to be the thing that got the Rebuilding Committee moving and doing, and got Uncle Sam to hike uphill to check on the tsunami drum, and got them all gathering and speaking and touching one another, even if they flinched at first.

—————

"I buried her" was all Milo told Suzie and the twins, who cried and got
sad and mad, the way people do.

It wasn't quite true. Burial hadn't been necessary. The storm dead
took care of themselves, was how Milo thought of it.

Serene and Carlo came to live with Milo and Suzie, who hardly ever
saw them. The twins came and went as they would, like a windstorm,
nontoxic and indecipherable.

There were funerals, when a week had gone by and they had a good
idea who was gone.

William Hofstettler, Marny deJeun, Pat the Bunny, and Junebug.
Cordero, Napoleon, Wait for Me Zane, Callisto the Stripper, and Wavy
Gravy. Wavy Gravy, some argued, wasn't really dead; he had vanished
into a tumor cocoon, and when he came out, he was someone else.
They voted to go ahead and have a funeral for him, and he attended as
Wavy Gravy 2.

Dr. Hook, Velma Peters, Jalapeño, Kellogg, Double Dip, Jodi Petu-
nia, Boone, Ivan Rue, the Last of the Mohicans, Milk Money, and Joelle
Texas Radio.

"Joelle Texas Radio" was Mom. Milo had almost forgotten.

Time passed.

A month later—two?—the entire population lay out on the beach,
watching Io and a score of tiny inner moons transit Jupiter.

Something sparkled between the moons on the giant planet's upper
limb. Like fireflies or glowing embers.

"That's pretty," said Milo.

"Yes and no," said Chili Pepper, several yards away. "It's cartel ships
on the way."

In the morning, sure enough, a whole cartel fleet came burning down
through the atmosphere.

One of the smaller sleds roared overhead, thrusters blowing, and settled on the beach. The Hall of Famers dropped what they were doing and formed a double line just uphill, like a bunch of naked soldiers.

Milo was on his way up to the pump, almost to the woods. Raymond Carver, who seemed to have replaced Boone, shouted at him.

"Milo! Get down here and get in line!"

Milo opened his mouth to say something rude.

"Just do it!" bellowed Carver, jogging toward the Hall of Famers himself. "'Splain later!"

Milo lined up. So did everyone who wasn't already on duty up at the pump.

Milo took a spot next to Carver as the sled opened and three Monitors marched out.

"It's what they want," Carver whispered. "You don't line up, you could get shot or kneecapped or blinded or—"

"Quiet," the commander boomed.

"We need fruit," said one of his deputies. "Those of you not on shift, go get whatever you have stored, and gather half a ton more."

The Hall of Famers broke ranks and headed for the trees.

"A half *ton?*" said Milo.

Carver walked off, pretending not to hear.

"Is that a problem?" crackled the deputy, leveling his burp gun.

Milo didn't answer. He just walked away. Lazily. Insultingly, he hoped.

When he got to the trees, though, he gathered fruit alongside the others.

"Has anyone thought," he asked, "what *we're* going to eat, the next month or so?"

No one answered him.

Piling fruit on the beach later, Milo saw that the cartel fleet had been busy, too.

They weren't just there to eat fruit. Something big was happening.

Enormous ships had descended on skyhooks and sat over the waves many miles out, forming a distant semicircle.

"They're testing again," said Carver.

"Testing what?" asked Suzie.

"A weapon. I heard scuttlebutt about it before they took away my lab."

"Atomics?" asked Milo.

"Worse," said Carver. "It pulls space through itself, like a needle going through its own eye. They call it the inside-out bomb."

The Monitors over by the sled took notice of the conversation.

"Work!" they all boomed simultaneously. One of them started walking over.

The Hall of Famers bent low, arranging the gathered fruit.

"So," said Suzie, "whatever's in the affected area just disappears?"

"That would be great for mining," said Milo, "if you could control it."

"No," whispered Carver as the Monitor approached. "It's for getting rid of lots of people without a trace. Without evidence."

"There's an awful lot of nothing going on here," crackled the Monitor, pushing his way between Milo and Carver.

They gave him their best dumb looks and dispersed.

They tested the bomb early the next afternoon.

Milo was clambering around on the pump when it happened. Something up on the submarine was leaking oil. They were going to have a fire sooner or later if it wasn't stopped. So he happened to be looking at hose fixtures, and not out to sea, when the bomb went off.

Still, he was momentarily blinded.

The flash penetrated everything, as if they'd been cast into the sun. Milo cursed, throwing his arm across his face. The rest of the day shift did the same.

Except for one, a kid named Christmas Break, who had been looking due south when the thing exploded. He screamed horribly and wouldn't stop.

Milo found the boy by sound, stumbling around in a universe of kaleidoscope-like spots. He grabbed the boy and held him close, restraining him. Christmas Break wanted to poke and claw at his eyes, but Milo held him until he calmed down, his screaming reduced to a steady moan.

In the meantime, Milo's own eyes cleared, and he looked seaward. He couldn't look away.

Out beyond the cartel ships, a crater had formed in the ocean. A perfect half dome, as if a bowling ball the size of a small world had been sitting there and had vanished. Above this impossible emptiness, a dome of clouds formed and whirled to fill empty space.

Wind rushed in from behind Milo, from everywhere, pulling waves and sand and clouds and birds toward the ball of . . . nothing . . . out there.

Water and wind smashed in from all points, booming and roaring.

Milo's jaw hung loose. The spectacle was something on the scale of gods or giants, something human eyes and minds weren't ready for.

The storm settled, leaving something like a wobbly star hanging in the air, a scar left by the bomb's quantum arm-twisting.

Christmas Break whimpered.

"You'll be all right," Milo told him (lying?). "Your eyes should get back to normal before the day is out. Let's get you to your family. Why'd you pick the name 'Christmas,' by the way?"

"Because my parents named me Melissa," said the boy. "They wanted a girl."

Milo kept him talking and not rubbing his eyes until they all got downhill.

The star hung pulsing over the ocean until the next morning. When it finally burned out, the cartel ships headed for the island.

The fleet, Milo sensed, was in the mood to party. And his stomach went dark and sour.

"Will they leave us alone?" he asked Carver, when they lined up on the beach.

Carver didn't say.

The first of the big ships hovered overhead, eclipsing Jupiter and the sun. Other ships, big and small, followed it like a pack of wolves.

Sleds and cargo heavies landed. Soldiers spilled out. Not just armored Monitors, but soldiers in jumpsuits. The soldiers seemed amused by the naked islanders lined up on the sand.

"Go about your business!" hollered some kind of command figure, dismissing them. "We need you, we'll call."

The Hall of Famers broke away and headed for their huts, for the woods, anywhere but that beach.

Milo and Suzie watched from the edge of the woods as the soldiers set up tents and generators. More sleds arrived, spilling cartel people ashore. People in all sorts of uniforms. Military, engineering, corporate types in suits.

Voices grew rowdy. Glass shattered. Music wailed.

Now and then, soldiers marched into the village and forced islanders to go pick fruit or narcotic froojii leaves or "some of that colorful firewood shit."

A knot of Monitors broke away from the party and found Jale at her tent.

"Where's your redfish?" asked the tallest of them. "Show us what you've got, and bring sacks to carry it."

Milo and Suzie, two huts down, listened without breathing.

"We haven't gone out lately," Jale replied. "We've been fixing leaks up at your pump. There's no fresh."

"Dried, then," said the Monitor. "We know you've got dried."

"We need the dried," Jale said. "You've got our month's fruit. The trees are picked over."

A hard sound, as if someone was getting hit.

Milo and Suzie got up and walked over, without discussion.

Jale lay on the sand in front of her hut, cupping a bloody lip with her hand. Chili Pepper crouched over her.

"Can we help?" asked Milo.

The Monitors said, "Fish."

"We'll go look," said Milo, buying time. "But we may have already given the fish out, put it out there with the fruit—"

The Monitor smashed him in the head with the butt of his burp gun, and Milo fell down and went dark.

When he awoke sometime later, things were even busier. Airships and watercraft growled in the air and growled in the surf. Music pounded.

The Hall of Famers kept to their huts, still.

Suzie dabbed Milo's cheek with something wet. Jale and Chili Pepper sat nearby.

"Jale took them to the fish pantry," Suzie told him. "Otherwise they were going to shoot you."

"What the fuck," Milo asked, "are we supposed to eat this month?"

"We get through tonight," said Chili Pepper, "we'll worry about that."

Suddenly, shouting from among the huts out near the trees.

"No!" bellowed a woman's voice. One of the Hall of Fame women went running by, wild-eyed.

Looking after her, Milo saw the source of her distress. Two men in suits had a preteen girl by the leg and were dragging her toward the trees. The girl thrashed and screamed. The woman reached the suits and pulled at them, shouting.

The suits appeared to be interested in whatever the woman was saying.

They dropped the girl, and the woman walked into the trees with them.

Milo stood, fists clenched. "I think I'd rather be dead than—"

"No," said Jale and Chili Pepper together.

"You'll make it worse," said Chili Pepper. "It can get a lot worse."

They heard the woman cry out from the woods. They stayed where they were. Milo's eyes stung. Suzie gripped his wrist hard enough to hurt. He let it hurt.

Thunder rolled. Far off, it seemed. From around the side of the island.

He searched the sky, which seemed clear.

The thunder became a steady pulse.

"That's not thunder," said Chili Pepper, standing. "It's the tsunami drum."

Chili Pepper grabbed both Milo and Suzie roughly, shoving, shouting, *"Go!"*

Down on the beach, Milo found the Fish Committee dashing to get the outriggers in the water. The drunks on the beach seemed confused by the sudden rush of bodies and boats; they milled around and laughed, staggering out of the way. Someone turned the music up.

"Something spooked the moon niggers," Milo heard as he dodged between suits and splashed into the surf.

Dark figures came flying out of the trees: the night shift from the pump, descending on hidden zip lines. They hit the sand and sprinted for the boats.

The fishing outriggers were full, Milo could see, and steering into the surf. Downbeach, Hall of Famers dragged other boats out of the trees. Huge, simple boats, great logs tied into catamarans, with rough masts and sails. There were three of these, and it took hundreds of hands to get them into the water.

"That way!" Milo urged Suzie. "Look for the twins!"

One of the cartel spacecraft flashed lights as the island boats left shore.

Whoop-whoop! Sirens and alarms drowned the music and the shouting.

Finally, soldiers went running for the sleds and heavies, eating bananas as they ran or straining to finish drinks.

———

On the catamarans, hundreds of hands raised the masts. Sails stretched, finding the wind. Milo leaped aboard the second catamaran, gripping wet wood with his toes. Hands steadied him, steadied Suzie as she followed.

"How many islanders can you fit on a boat?" someone called out.

"One more!" they all shouted. "Always one more!"

They found an open place on the woven netting and sat scrunched together, taking up as little space as possible.

Overhead, cartel ships blazed and screamed. The smaller craft rode their rockets into space. The giants waited for their skyhooks to tighten and pull, nosing them upward like rising whales. A few heavies smoked and steamed on the beach still, engines flexing impatiently, awaiting stragglers.

Suzie poked Milo in the arm and pointed seaward.

The horizon had darkened.

"It doesn't look like a wave," she said.

"It won't be a real wave," said someone sitting nearby, "until it gets to the shallower water. Then it'll stack up."

The voice was familiar . . .

"Carver!" cried Milo. "Have you seen my brother and sister?"

Carver shook his head but said, "They got aboard somewhere, I guarantee it. Sharp cookies, your bunch."

Milo had to be happy with that for now.

"Anyhow," continued Carver, "there's a steep drop-off farther out. We're trying to sail past that before the wave gets there."

"We're not going fast enough," growled a woman with a tumor swelling behind her left ear.

Three men adjusted a mighty rope. The catamaran leaned sideways, causing its passengers to dig into the netting with their fingers. The boat gained speed.

Then the ocean dropped out from under them.

The catamaran seemed to nosedive, and Milo understood that the tsunami's trough had reached them.

A mile away, the hump he had seen speeding along the horizon had begun building into a mountain.

"Holy God," said Milo.

Before another breath passed, it was on them. Suzie squeezed his arm as the sea ballooned under them, tilting them up and lifting them into the sky.

Several islanders lost their grip and tumbled into the crazy water. They did not reappear.

Looking back toward the island, Milo saw that the cartel heavies were all clear, their engines torching hard, zooming straight up out of the atmosphere. All except one, which just now seemed to be wallowing in the sand.

The wave intervened as they passed over the crest. For a second, the catamaran might as well have been flying; below them lay the edge of the world and far-flung islands. Out to sea, the ocean was like a dark army—ranks and ranks of swells racing across the blue.

They slid down, gaining speed, their stomachs in their throats, and were thrown back up again as a larger wave took them, lifting. From its peak, they watched the first wave slam across their island.

The last cartel heavy, lifting off, trying desperately to gain speed, was swallowed up without a trace. In an instant, the trees and hills vanished underwater. Only the highest hill and the massive pump machinery remained untouched, surrounded by raging foam and whirlpools like jaws.

"Madness," whispered Milo. "This planet is mad!"

Suzie shut him up with a long, wild kiss. The kind you feel in your throat.

A day later, in the evening, they sailed back ashore.

Not their familiar shore. Who knew where that was? The village was out in the sea somewhere or splintered among the trees in the forest. The tsunami had chewed the island a new shoreline.

They found a wide beach, and two of the great catamarans sailed ashore. They muscled the boats into the shelter of the trees first, before collapsing in the sand. Members of the Rebuilding Committee built a fire and began gathering shore debris for shelters.

"The twins," Suzie said.

Carlo came plowing through the crowd, towing Serene. The two of them looked at Milo. Only looked.

"Good," they said, simply, simultaneously. And they looked at Suzie, too, and said, "Good."

They all roamed the edge of the forest together, gathering whatever looked useful.

The third catamaran didn't come back.

"The outriggers?" Milo asked Carver.

"They're fine. They're faster, so they go farther out, take longer to return. They'll find food while they're out."

Incredibly, they found the tsunami drum, wedged between boulders, its skins and ribs intact. They rolled it to the nearest bluff and assigned a watch—a woman named Jane Eyre, whose husband was missing—and left her there.

The Rebuilding Committee took an inventory of tools they had and tools they needed to make. Milo and Suzie volunteered to dig the new latrine. Cracklin' Rosie, Red Wine, and Matthew left to scout for freshwater.

High tide and low tide came again, and went.

At sunset, they remembered the dead.

"Polly Wolly," read Carver. "Jim Shunk. Justinian the Third. Bead Woman. White Chick. Mr. Henry. Caspar. Big Brad. Old Brad. Shakespeare. Sarah the Librarian. Siamese Cat. Conan the Avenger. Leave Me Alone."

Out of the weird golden twilight, the outriggers rode in and slid ashore. The sailors walked up the beach and came among them without a word, except to join in the litany.

"Boo-Cherry. LoopsyDoll. Captain My Captain. Vaughn Gillespie. Indigo. Demon Rum. Word Salad. The Last Scientologist. Doris Fubar. Danny Bo-Banny. Good Grades, McDonalds, and Pookie of Nazareth . . ." and it went on, seventy names, spoken and repeated and not spoken again.

———————

Things got back to normal.

Things changed.

Like their name. The Rock 'N' Roll Hall of Fame became Sly and the Family Stone, after a famous ancient band.

Seven days after the tsunami, a cartel sled came burning down from space. The Family Stone barely had time to gather on the beach before the Monitors emerged.

"Line up!" barked the commander. "Everyone!"

Uuuuuuuuuuurrrrrrrrrp! He fired his burp gun into the air. Empty cartridges rained on the sand.

They came running from everywhere.

This isn't about fruit, thought Milo.

"We lost a ship," the commander said. "Where is it?"

Sounds of confusion up and down the line.

The Monitors were not playing. All four of them aimed their guns at a little girl named Mango.

"I saw it go down with the wave," said Milo. "It waited for stragglers, and it got in the air too late."

"Where is it now?" asked one of the deputies.

Milo shook his head. "I don't know," he said.

"Chances are it was swept into open water," said Big Bird, right behind him. "At least three waves washed over this island."

"Shut up!" yelled the commander, stepping through the front line and pressing his muzzle against Big Bird's forehead.

"Why didn't you warn us?" he asked. Then, screaming: *"Why didn't you fucking moon niggers warn us?"*

An angry buzz rose up and down the line.

"You heard the drum, same as everyone else," someone said. "You know damn well what it means."

Aw, shit, thought Milo.

Uuurrp! Big Bird's head came apart in a red cloud. His body hit the sand.

Because, Milo wanted to say, the cartel suits and their nerds and goons had been too busy yelling and drinking and trying to drag kids into the woods.

The commander stepped back.

"Because you chose not to warn us," he said, "a disciplinary action will be levied, beginning at sundown."

Fearful muttering in the line.

The Monitors climbed back into their sled, rocketed into the air, and burned out to sea.

Carver and Jale stepped over Big Bird's body, through the front line, and turned to face the Family Stone.

"Listen," said Carver, "those of you who know what's going to happen and know what to do, go do it. If you're new or not sure, listen up."

About half of the population left and walked back to the huts.

"Here's what's going on," Jale told the rest. "It's not going to be easy. The cartel goons are going to be here in an hour, and they are going to come into our homes and force us to hurt each other."

"What do you mean?" someone asked.

"It's something tyrant governments used to do back on Earth," said Carver, "before the comet. So people used to switch houses. They'd send their children to the neighbors or to less-immediate relatives. That way, if the soldiers came and made them do things, at least they didn't have to cut their own child or whip their own mother."

Milo's eyes stung.

We could run, he wanted to say. We could hide. But he knew what Jale would say.

They'd make it worse.

What do you do, he wondered, when you scratch around for courage and it won't come?

You fake it, said the voices in his head.

So he said, "All right."

And Suzie said, "All right."

The whole Family Stone said, "All right," and the line melted back into the village.

"Suzie," said Jale, "you're going to come with me. Chili is going to Rose's hut. My father is going with Milo."

She ticked off other arrangements, but Milo barely heard.

The twins. Dammit, how come they were always out of sight when things got crazy? Then he remembered what Carver had said. *They were smart. They'd figure it out.* And there was nothing he could do for them, anyway. But—dammit! His mind went in circles this way.

He and Suzie kissed. Around them, other families kissed and parted.

He walked to the hut where Jale's dad, Old Deuteronomy, was already waiting.

The sun passed behind Jupiter, and the stars came out, and some of the stars moved and circled, and came in low, and landed on the beach.

In the dark, Old Deuteronomy groped for Milo's arm and gave it a squeeze.

They heard voices among the huts closer to the beach.

There was the sound of the sea on the shore and insects in the jungle.

Waiting. Maybe they had gone?

Voices exploded, shouting. One brief scream, followed by the unmistakable *smack* of fists on human flesh.

Milo and Old Deuteronomy both leaned forward, almost rising, almost yelling out.

Be wise, said Milo's head. He subsided. So did the older man.

Through the door, Milo watched a tableau of shadows and silhouettes. Mostly still . . . the shapes of the village huts, the trees near the beach, with stars beyond and Jupiter's ghostly crescent. But other shadows, too. A helmet, the blunt shape of a burp gun.

Another hut—closer this time—erupted in curses and something shattering.

And another hut, farther down the beach. And another.

Sometimes it sounded as if every single one of the islanders had been pounced on at once, as if the night itself had gone bloodthirsty. Other times there might be just one or two huts getting attention, and you could hear every *thump* of a club, every scream or whimper. Some of the soldiers must have brought whips or belts.

Now and then, gunfire.

Once—for ten minutes straight, it seemed—a small child screamed a singular high-pitched wail of agony, and Milo heard muttering then, all around.

That's how they'll get us, he thought, despairing. Someone will resist, and others will join, and they'll shoot us all.

After that, there was a long silence. Milo began listening for the sled engines, hoping, and he was still listening when three shadows crowded the door.

"Stand up!" roared the soldiers. Before Milo could move, a rifle butt cracked the side of his head.

They jabbed a rifle up under his jaw and forced him to his feet and pressed something into his hand. A whip of some kind, like a squid, with a hook at the end of each tentacle. A gun muzzle dug into his neck.

Fully amplified, the Monitors screeched, *"Up! Get up! Get up, you fucker! You wanna die? You wanna die? Is that what you want, you piece of shit? Get up do it do it do it! Hit him! Hit that old moon nigger! Hit him—"* And Milo saw Old Deuteronomy looking up at him with hard eyes, shouting, "Do what they tell you!"

Discipline.

Incredibly, Milo raised his arm and brought the whip down across the old man's shoulder. Felt it catch. Felt the hooks dig in and the whip jerk to a stop and his arm jerk to a stop. Old Deuteronomy shrieked.

Milo gave the whip a flick, freeing the hooks. Blood spattered. Bits of skin stuck all over the hut.

"Do it again do it again do it again!"

Something hot stabbed him in the leg. One of the soldiers laughed.

Up and down went Milo's arm—*slash—jerk—(flick)—spatter.*

They made him do it nine times.

Milo listened to Old Deuteronomy's breathing, which was weak. The flare had begun to die, and in the fading light he watched the old man rock back and forth, just slightly.

He would hit the old man, Milo knew, as many times as he had to. He would, if necessary, kill him.

The soldiers took the whip from him and left.

"I'm sorry," whispered Milo.

"Yes," said the old man. "Quiet."

Milo didn't know when the cartel ships lifted off. When the sun slipped out from behind Jupiter, they were gone, and the Family Stone went through a blank, staring time.

About half of them had scars now, on top of their tumor welts and bent limbs.

He looked for Suzie.

Here she was! Looking dazed and blood-caked, part of her left ear sawed off.

"It's okay," she kept saying. She let Milo steady her.

Milo felt his undamaged body like a new kind of nakedness.

"They made Carver shoot Chili," Suzie whispered. "Wrapped his hand around the gun and squeezed *his* hand with *their* hands."

Chili, thought Milo. But it was an empty thought just yet. Just a name. Some kind of feeling would come and fill it in later. Wouldn't it?

He walked off alone, looking for the twins.

He found Serene in minutes. The sea had dropped away to low tide, and she sat near the precipice with Cracklin' Rosie, who wore a poultice over one eye.

"Hey!" Milo yelled, rushing forward.

Serene glanced his way, then went back to staring at the horizon.

Where was Carlo? Milo realized he had never seen one twin without the other.

When he drew closer, Milo realized Serene was shaking so hard, so fast, that it looked like stillness.

"Did they . . . ?"

"They didn't touch her," whispered Cracklin' Rosie, stroking the girl's hair.

Relief.

"I don't know how they knew," said Rose. "We put them in two separate huts, but they went and found Carlo and brought him and made them . . ."

Her voice trailed off.

"Made them beat each other?" asked Milo.

Rose put a hand to her mouth and closed her eyes.

"No," she said, so quietly that Milo had to read her lips.

Minutes later, Carlo came down from the village with Number One, Rose's brother. Slowly, self-consciously, the boys sat in the sand next to Serene.

None of them spoke. There was a terrible awkwardness between them now.

Milo sprang up and walked away before they could see him cry.

In the days that followed, the Family Stone was quiet and hollow-eyed. They did their work without speaking.

Milo took tsunami watch for a month. Suzie left the village with paper and charcoal, saying she was going to map the island.

Some people walked into the sea.

The cartel dumped off newcomers, who walked into the sea or stayed and became islanders and took new names. Christopher Noonguesser. Rome. Posh. Sir St. John Fotheringay. There was a whole family of crawler saboteurs: Mr. Jones, Mrs. Jones, Yoko, and Fyodor, all of whom became pump engineers.

Milo watched the water and tended the drum. He let the stone and the sand and the wind have him.

"Gotta show you something," said Suzie, hiking up to the tsunami drum one morning. "It might be important."

She kissed him on top of the head. He turned and gave her a squeeze.

Suzie had brought Christopher Noonguesser to mind the drum, and she led Milo to a distant cliff.

Pointing straight down, she said, "There."

An iridescent patch on the water, right where the surf broke.

That's how they found the missing cartel ship.

They climbed down and dove to the wreck. The pilot still sat in his chair, strapped in tight, bones stripped by fishes. His passengers drifted behind him, bones in party clothes, swaying in the current.

Later, back ashore, Suzie said, "We won't tell the cartel."

Milo nodded. He acknowledged her with burning eyes.

They told no one.

Ten more people walked into the sea.

They had a big, fat funeral.

Jale said the names this time.

"Hobbit," she said, followed by, "Doris, LoJack, Gavin McLeod, Peter McPeter, and Orm. Jilly, Nathanial the Digger, Mustang Sally, Nellie and Nellie's Husband and Nellie's Other Husband. Michael Ben-Jonah, and Carter, and Shane."

Instead of a bonfire, everyone made a little wooden boat and set it on fire and sent it burning out to sea. Milo thought the surf would eat the boats, but the night was eerily calm, and they burned for some time and spread out and out, like stars.

———

Milo resumed his vigil at the tsunami drum, but he didn't sit there draining away, like before. He meditated about things he remembered. It was like watching his mind play movies.

Movies of his dad. Movies of playing with Bubbles and Frog and favorite times with Suzie. Things he was proud of, like when he dove down deep that first time, without training, and the time he had saved the Buddha from drowning.

His inner voices were much clearer suddenly. He remembered being in Vienna and having a fiftieth anniversary party and falling to his death and surfing and being a father and living in Ohio and almost being murdered in Florence, Italy.

He sat there for five weeks, remembering, and talking with his voices.

He remembered quite a bit about Suzie. She came up to bring him some redfish and hikipikiiaki berries, and he made love to her on the spot.

"You remembered," she said afterward. "Just a guess."

"Yeah. I remembered."

"Took you long enough."

And eventually the idea came. It wasn't brilliant or complicated or new. It was just perfect for that particular place and time.

It was an idea that began with a story.

After a while, High Voltage came up to ask if he wanted a break, and Milo said, "Hell yes," and took his story down to the village.

They were having another funeral. Kind of a mix this time—some were suicides; some were not. It had been a bad cancer week.

Milo stood quietly, a safe distance from the fire. The story would wait.

They watched the fire afterward, and when a little time had passed, Milo cleared his throat and said: "Listen."

The Family Stone turned and looked at him, and eyebrows were raised. Milo had smeared some kind of black shit all over his body. On top of that, he had smeared some kind of white shit, in the shape of bones. He looked like a child's drawing of a skeleton. They gave him their complete attention.

"I'm going to tell you a story," he announced. "Afterward I'll tell you why I think the story is important, but for now just listen. Okay?"

Silence.

"A long time ago," he began, "on an island somewhat like this one, there lived a man named Jonathan Yah Yah. And Jonathan Yah Yah was one of those people who are afraid of everything. When a bully beat him up in school, he was afraid to fight back, for fear of making things worse. All his life he was in love with Marie Toussaint but never once brought her flowers, because what if she didn't like him? As long as he kept his love secret, it was possible that she might love him back. If he brought her flowers and she laughed at him, then this illusion would slip away and things would be worse. Later, when he was poor and had a dull job at a toilet junkyard, he was afraid to look for a better job. What if he didn't find a better job, and his boss found out and fired him? Things would be worse than before. Things could always be worse.

"And then he died.

"They carried him up to the boneyard and buried him. And Jonathan Yah Yah lay there in his coffin, feeling all sad because of the crappy life he had settled for. Because of all the things he hadn't done, because he was afraid. How silly it was, being afraid like that. Either way he'd be in his grave now. The only difference was, he might have had a fine life to look back on and be proud of. As it was, here he lay with his memories of the toilet junkyard.

"As it happened, Baron Samedi, a powerful voodoo *loa,* was sitting atop a nearby crypt at that moment, having a cigarette, and he called out, 'Jonathan Yah Yah! Come up here and talk to me!'

"And Jonathan Yah Yah climbed out of his grave and dusted himself off and waited to hear what the *loa* had to say.

"Baron Samedi said, 'Jonathan, you have my sympathy, because you have missed your chance for a happy life. But you also have my contempt,' and he crushed out his cigarette on Jonathan's forehead, 'because you have let fear make your decisions for you. So I am going to do you a favor. And I am also going to do something cruel.'

"Jonathan Yah Yah asked, 'What is the favor?'

"And Baron Samedi answered, 'I will allow you one day more to walk on the Earth with the living, to do whatever you wish.'

"Jonathan Yah Yah bowed and was grateful.

"'And what,' he asked, 'is the something cruel?'

"And Baron Samedi answered, 'I will allow you one day more to walk on the Earth with the living, to do whatever you wish.'

"And the *loa* vanished in a great cloud of ash.

"In the morning, the sun came up, and Jonathan Yah Yah walked out through the cemetery gates. He meant to make the most of the day, more than any day before.

"The first thing he did was find the man who had bullied him as a child. He was going to punch the man in the face, but then fear spoke up.

"What if you are jailed? said the fear.

"But Jonathan thought about this and said, 'Let them jail me. At the end of the day, I will be in my grave!'

"And he punched the man and broke his nose. This felt good, and the man looked afraid to hit Jonathan back and afraid to call for the police.

"'I should have done that years ago,' said Jonathan to himself.

"Next, Jonathan went to the house where Marie Toussaint lived with her husband, and he brought her flowers and gave her a lingering kiss on the lips. He saw a light in Marie Toussaint's eyes that he liked very much, and he thought, I really should have done that long ago! Then her husband punched Jonathan in the face, but Jonathan didn't care. 'I am for the grave, anyhow!' he said, and bowed his way out.

"Last, Jonathan Yah Yah went to see a cattleman he knew and said, 'If you would hire me to tend your cattle, I would be attentive and thorough and take pride in doing good work.'

"And the cattleman said, 'Very well. Come back tomorrow, and I will give you a horse and a rope, and you can work six days a week.'

"On his way back to the boneyard, Jonathan politely quit his job at the toilet junkyard, something he had wanted to do for years.

"As he climbed the hill to the boneyard, Jonathan began to feel a terrible sadness. Why, he thought to himself, there was so little to be afraid of! Pain? Sadness? Death? All these things came to me, anyway, and I have nothing to show for them. How easily I might have had dignity. A family. I might even have been a cowboy.

"It was much harder now, lying in his grave, knowing that he might have lived happily with far less grief than it took to live afraid. That was the cruel thing Baron Samedi had meant for him. And he passed into death that way, full of regret."

Milo paused.

No one said anything for a bit.

"So," said Sir St. John Fotheringay, "the thing with the black paint all over you, and the skeleton, that's meant to illustrate, basically, death, right?"

Milo nodded.

"You're saying you're dead," said Yoko Jones, "and so are we. All of us."

Milo nodded and smiled.

"It's about the cartel," said Jale, speaking from beyond the firelight.

Milo nodded and held up a skeletal hand.

"We are living as slaves," he said, "and pretending that it's okay because there's nothing we can do about it."

"There's not," muttered Fotheringay and a lot of other people.

"We have absolutely no power—" said Old Deuteronomy.

"We have *all* the power!" interrupted Milo, with unusual force. "Because the cartels and their goons depend completely on us for work. The cartels could not exist if people didn't choose to work for them."

"We don't choose," said Fotheringay. "They force us!"

"Force?" said Milo. "That's not possible. What are they going to do, come down here and move our arms and legs for us? They need us to do it ourselves, and we only do it because we are afraid. That's not force. That's *fear*, and it's a *choice*."

The Family Stone chewed on that awhile.

"If we stop working," said Fotheringay, "they'll kill us."

"They can't kill us all," answered Milo. "Like I said: They need us."

"They only have to kill a few of us, is the idea," said Yoko Jones, "and then the rest of us will chicken out and go back to work. Right?"

"Wrong," said Milo. "Because we won't be afraid."

"The thing is," said Fotheringay, "I rather think we *will* be afraid."

Milo pointed at the fire with one hand and at the sea with the other.

"We take our own lives by the score!" he shouted. "We're already poisoned, already sick, already half dead! How many of you are thinking about walking into the ocean right now? Raise your hands."

No one.

Then one hand.

Then a hundred, and then everyone. Even the children.

Milo let them sit there like that with their hands raised. No one spoke.

He raised his hand, too.

"We are already dead," he said. "Let's make it count. Let's create a world, a solar system, in which the following is true: If you put out your hand and try to bully people into serving you, those people will always choose not to serve. Very soon, no one will try that anymore. It would be like trying to juggle water."

Silence again. The hands went down.

One hand went back up. Gilgamesh.

"I don't get it," said Gilgamesh. "In the story, are we the zombie guy or the Baron guy?"

More hands followed.

"Are we supposed to be ready to die for real or, like, metaphorically?"

"Is the woman in the story supposed to represent freedom? Or is it a sex thing?"

"Does that paint itch? It looks like it itches."

Milo closed his eyes. He backed away, out of the firelight.

———

The next morning, he walked down to the beach and helped push the fishing outriggers into the surf. He wore a fresh coat of black and a fresh coat of bones.

"Good weather!" he wished them, "And tons of fish!"

"Thanks!" yelled Jale as they slipped away, raising sail.

Jale had drawn a bone on one arm, he saw. Good.

He sat down on the beach and meditated.

He thought about spiders, for some reason. He couldn't help it.

The twins joined him, wearing complete skeleton paint. Carlo had six hundred arm bones and an extra eye.

The next day, he climbed up to the pump.

He wore a special greasy variety of the skeleton paint, because someone was needed to dive down into the well and jar the drill head loose again.

Two of the engineers had painted their faces like skulls.

The dive he made that day was deeper than any he'd ever attempted. By the time he resurfaced, he was blue. You could see it through the paint.

The next day, he walked the forest with members of the Food-Safety Committee to taste-test a new kind of banana the soil had begun sprouting.

Two of them, Sage and Nosferatu, wore skeleton paint. The three of them walked together, searched the trees together, and, when the committee found what they were looking for, it was the three of them who volunteered to taste a little bit.

Just a little bit.

Before he even got his banana peeled, Milo's fingers blistered.

Nosferatu had no reaction, but he dropped his banana the second he saw Milo's fingers.

Sage lost an eye. A tumor swelled up in her eye socket and just— *pop!*—burst her eye.

But she joined them in meditating on the beach afterward.

"I can't do it," she complained. "I keep thinking about my eye."

"Me, too," said Milo.

The next day, the whole Food-Safety Committee wore skeleton paint. So did a lot of others. Maybe fifty. Some accessorized with dry leaves and sticks. Milo saw green skeletons, yellow skeletons, blue skeletons. No red. It was hard to make red.

Milo was thinking about making another speech, when something awful happened.

He and sixty other people were sitting on the beach pretending to meditate when something bristly and silver came tearing out of the sky. It raced for the island, guns flashing, and then thundered straight back into space.

The cartel was still mad about their lost ship.

Most of the islanders ran uphill along the coast, to see if the tsunami drum was all right.

It was not. It was blasted in two and burning.

So was the watcher, a little boy named Marcus.

The next day, the entire Family Stone came out in skeleton makeup.

They were waiting outside Milo's tent when he woke up. All of them, in a big semicircle, weaving in and out among the huts, all the way down to the beach.

They waited in total silence. The only sound was the wind in the lovely, deadly trees and the constant sigh of the ocean.

Finally, it was Sir St. John Fotheringay—in blue skeleton paint—who cleared his throat.

"Was there something in particular," he said, "that you wanted us to *do*?"

"Yes," said Milo. "Go fishing."

———

They went fishing. All of them. Instead of doing their cartel work.

It took them two weeks to build enough outriggers to carry them all. But every day they went to the forest and cut trees. Afterward, they practiced breathing. They meditated. Even if they couldn't quiet their minds all the way, they learned to control their breath and their rhythms.

They swam out to sea and practiced diving. Deeper and deeper every day.

Some of them drowned.

"Jennadots," Jale intoned, by the fire at night. "Holly Timm, Mrs. Jones, Axelrod, and Fantasia."

Finally, they put out to sea. The whole Family Stone. And they stayed there for an entire week and rode the sea and ate like kings.

Milo was pretty sure they'd find the cartel waiting for them when they got back. But they didn't.

The cartel had *been* there, all right. They had burned the village to atoms.

The Family Stone didn't even talk about it. They sailed around the island and found a better beach. The Rebuilding Committee gathered wood and leaves for huts. The Tsunami Committee commissioned a new drum and new catamarans.

Everyone kept busy, either preserving fish or cooking fish or building something or searching for vegetables, or teaching or learning or watching for giant waves. And they were happy doing it, more or less.

"The blue skeleton paint itches," Suzie complained to Milo. She had made her own blue paint out of raspberry juice, mud, and something like a lemon.

"Don't use it anymore," Milo advised. He kept waiting for the stupid paint to start raising tumors and killing people. But that was his only needling concern. Other than that, things were as they should be.

That was the status of the Family Stone when the cartel came scorching down with two heavies full of Monitors, bellowing over their loudspeakers.

Milo tried to stay busy doing his work, winding leafy fibers into thread for fishing nets, but he had a hell of a time not watching the goons out of the corner of his eye.

They gathered in a cluster, like they always did, burp guns at their chests, obviously expecting the Family Stone to line up. They looked silly, standing in their little knot, being ignored.

Eventually they approached the first islander in sight: Mr. Jones.

Mr. Jones was filleting redfish and hanging the fillets to dry on a crude wooden rack. He was decked out in blue skeleton paint and scratching himself when the Monitors walked up.

Milo couldn't hear what was said, but he could imagine.

"Why the hell aren't you moon niggers lined up?" the Monitors would ask.

"We are busy doing our work," Mr. Jones would say, continuing to work.

"Your work," the Monitors would continue, "is to operate the wells and be prepared to provide water for our tankers."

Mr. Jones would ignore this nonsense, because it was no longer true.

The Monitors would probably get mad and—yep, there they went, beating the living shit out of Mr. Jones. Mr. Jones, as rehearsed, wrapped his arms around his head and tried to endure. He even tried to return to his work, but they clubbed him back to the ground and left him there, bloody and motionless.

"Dammit," Milo whispered.

Briefly, the Monitors split up and tried to drag a few people down to the shore. But the people they grabbed went limp and became a real pain to move.

"How come you're all wearing this skeleton shit?" Milo heard a Monitor ask Christopher Noonguesser, trying to pull him away from his work.

"We're dead," answered Noonguesser. "There's nothing you can do to us."

The Monitor gave Noonguesser a smart kick in the teeth and left him there.

"Dammit," said Milo. He kept letting his thread get loose, which meant starting over. What he needed was a drop spindle. Rootabeth, the resident expert, had told him that at least three times, but he'd been too lazy to carve himself one. He would do it tonight, he decided, if they didn't all get shot today.

The Monitors were having a conference by their spacecraft now.

Crackle, crackle, crackle.

They would get on the loudspeaker and make some kind of threat, Milo knew.

But they didn't.

They got back in the heavies and swooped away over the outgoing tide, up and gone.

The Hospital Committee rushed to help Jones and Noonguesser.

"What now?" asked Suzie.

"Now I'm going to go find some wood for a spindle," he said. "You?"

"I'm going to go scrape off this fucking blue paint," she said.

At least eighty other islanders went with her into the woods, scratching and cursing, all silently proud and feeling brave to the point of tears.

The silent treatment could work both ways, Milo discovered.

The next day, the goons were back. Several sleds and heavies landed. One large ship hovered over the beach, not quite landing.

The cartel stooges who got out and walked around were engineer types, with a few Monitors. They crackled to one another by speaker and radio and said nothing at all to the Family Stone.

The big ship opened its bay doors, and something like a giant coconut fell out.

It did not strike the ground. It bobbed in the air as if it had reached the end of an invisible tether, and there it stayed. It had an odd look to it, as if it might or might not be glowing softly. It blurred around its edges, as if it might not quite be there.

The ship nosed up and rode its skyhook back into space.

The smaller craft followed, except one. A single heavy, steaming at the edge of the cliff.

A loudspeaker spoke to the islanders as they built and cooked and fixed things.

"We will return in one week," said the loudspeaker. "At that time, we will expect the pump and well to be functioning and at least forty thousand kiloliters of detoxified water available for loading."

Then the heavy rumbled off the sand and shot into orbit.

Christopher Noonguesser came walking up. Noonguesser wore a bandage around his jaw and had lost about half of his teeth.

He pointed up at the coconut thing, hovering and blurring overhead.

"That's one of those things they've been testing," he said. "It's an inside-out bomb."

"It's an inside-out bomb," Milo announced to the whole Family Stone, at around noon. It seemed only right to share what he knew.

"Great," said Christmas Break, still mostly blind from the first test they'd witnessed.

A lot of islanders—maybe a hundred—got up and headed into the woods. Headed, specifically, in the direction of the pumps.

"Aw, fuck," said Milo. And he opened his mouth to shout, to get them to hang on and hang together, but Suzie put her arms around him and said, "Shhhhh, baby. Don't police them. It works or it doesn't. The dead don't force things; they just go about their business."

She was right.

Still, it made him so mad. How could people give up like that? He sat down to try meditating again (couldn't stop thinking about whether his butt was getting bigger as he got older. Did that happen to everyone? Why?) and almost managed to get some kind of peace back.

Suzie sat beside him, doing the same thing.

He got up around twilight, at the very beginning of the eclipse, and was getting ready to go find wood for his damn drop spindle when Suzie pointed at the trees and said, "Milo, look."

He looked.

A hundred islanders emerged from the forest in a line like a triumphant hunting party, all carrying some kind of machinery, or sheet metal, or small motors or transformers or pipework.

Parts from the cartel's precious pump.

They piled them in the middle of the village, and the Rebuilding Committee got busy sorting through the parts, discussing what could be useful and how.

Many of the islanders, Milo noticed, now wore traces of red bones on their skin.

"How'd they manage to get red paint?" he wondered aloud.

"Easy," Suzie answered. "It's blood."

The day before the cartel had promised to return, Milo quietly put out the word for the Family Stone to gather on the beach.

Skeleton by skeleton, committee by committee, they all came.

Milo arrived with a package of some kind tucked under his arm—a roll of sailcloth, it looked like.

"I brought something to show you," he announced. And he unrolled the sailcloth to reveal ten communications fish. Black, sleek, and military-looking.

A gasp went up. Islanders could get their faces shot off just for *mentioning* fish, let alone having ten of them actually in their possession.

Milo picked up one of the fish and held it high.

"A couple of months ago," he told them, "Suzie and I found the missing cartel ship, and we dove down to the wreck. Suzie salvaged these from inside the cockpit, and we haven't told you about it. I'm sorry about that. We should have told you. At the time, it seemed like we might have to keep secrets from one another."

The Family Stone made forgiving noises.

"You have a plan," shouted Carver, way in the back, "don't you, Milo?"

Milo put the fish down and clapped his hands two times.

"Let me tell you about my plan," he said.

Milo's plan called for the cartel ships to come down and look around to see if their slaves had wised up.

Which they did.

Fa-zoooooooooooom! At midmorning, about fifty ships came slamming down out of space and circled all over the place. A lot of them circled more than forty miles out. Big ships, like the first time they'd tested their bomb. A few heavies landed on the beach.

The Monitors on the beach looked around, and Milo could see them getting madder and madder as they saw tons of pump machinery helping to support huts, forming launch docks for the catamarans, forming . . . was that a playground?

The soldiers boomed and crackled and waved their burp guns.

Milo almost wished they *would* shoot. Noonguesser had gotten every one of the fish activated, and five of them were in the woods now, filming.

But the goons all got back aboard their spacecraft and left the island and circled far away.

Overhead, the inside-out bomb made some eerie noises.

Okay, thought Milo. This was being filmed, too. Not just here but far out at sea.

Ten miles out—that was his plan—the Fish Committee was supposed to have left their outriggers spread out and sea-anchored. They were supposed to be treading water, and five of them were supposed to be filming. Filming the fleet, filming the island, filming anything big and awful that might happen.

But here was where Milo's plan differed from what everyone else wanted to do.

The Fish Committee, since his big speech, since the Parable of Jonathan Yah Yah, included nearly everyone. Milo's plan was for nearly everyone to leave the island aboard the outriggers, film whatever happened to the island, and broadcast it in one military-priority burst, reaching everywhere from Venus to the Neptune ammonia mines. Then they were to *survive*. To dive and swim if they had to, avoiding the fleet, and going on to live their lives.

That morning, however, the Fish Committee had told him no.

"No," said Jale, whose hair had gone white since Chili's murder. "Are we dead or aren't we?"

"We are," they all said, the whole Family Stone.

In the end, it was mostly the children who took the outriggers out. They could work the fish as well as grown-ups and hit s e n d when the time came. They could sail and dive and swim and had a lot of years to look forward to, if things changed.

If people under the cartel thumb, from Venus to the Neptune ammonia mines, heard the Parable of Jonathan Yah Yah and learned about being dead.

"Because they're the Family Stone, too," Carver said as they formed a circle. "We refused to accept the cartel rules; it's why we're here. But we're not the only ones. There're others like us everywhere, and they'll know what to do when they see what happens on this island. When they see this thing of beauty the cartel has built for them."

Christopher Noonguesser was with the children, out there hiding among the waves. So was Old Deuteronomy. If they survived, they would help explain what had gone on here.

Most of them, though, stood right here under the bomb.

They pretended not to be watching it.

Most of them pretended not to be afraid.

"Milo?" said Fotheringay. "I'm afraid."

"I was trying to meditate," said a man named Wild Bill. "But I keep thinking about that fucking bomb."

"Me, too," said a lot of people.

Milo noticed the bomb getting bright around the edges.

"I've always sucked at meditating," Milo said. "Sometimes I can't think of anything but cats."

"I always have to go to the bathroom," said Calypso.

"I think about not thinking about things," said Yoko Jones. "I can't help it."

"I think about getting old," said Suzie.

"Food," said someone else.

"The alphabet."

"Making love."

"My missing eye."

"My kids back on Ganymede."

"Music."

After that, they didn't talk anymore. The moment was simply too busy, too heavy.

Now? *Now?*

Would it hurt? Would they burn like stars or just end suddenly?

Now?

If you were Sir St. John Fotheringay, you began doing a little dance at this point. If you were Yoko Jones, you tried to hum in perfect sync with the Everything.

If you were Milo, at that point, you decided that these last moments were the perfect time to finally meditate for real, and you looked straight into Suzie's eyes and your eyes locked and you meditated together.

And it worked, in a way.

There never was such a moment, after all. If you were supposed to be in the moment, this was the one, all right. There was this one idea going out to all the people on all the planets that maybe you couldn't get people to stop being predators, but you could get them to stop being prey. That from now on there would be this great big peaceful future, and either it was going to be or not be, depending on what people did with this one moment, the whole future waiting on this one breathless moment, like an elephant on the head of a pin. Maybe things will change after this, and we can all stop living the same idiotic greedy mistakes over and over, lifetime after lifetime, and finally evolve into the kind of people who insist on living well—

"No, no!" you growl, because even though these are worthy thoughts, they are *not* meditating, and just this one damn time—

But it can't be helped, because it's not just your head, is it? It's the head and soul of all the voices of all your ten thousand lives and eight thousand years and all their pasts and futures, all the cavemen and race-car drivers and milkmaids with pale cheeks, all the spacemen, crickets, economists, and witches. The voices are full of the things people are full of, the things they will carry with them into whatever future takes shape, things like waffles and hard work and things you hope no one finds out. Things you fear, and things that defeat you, like spiders and children and forgetting to set the clock. Gothic shadows like the Hook Man, escaped and haunting the woods. Things like barbarians and taxes and red and blue lights in the rearview mirror and the feeling that's always there, like a haunting, the most human thing of all: the feeling you forgot something, forgot something, left something undone. The voices in your head, your thousands of years and lives, talk about Perfections you have known, like the time you were catapulted over the walls at Vienna, the time you left the first footprint on the moon, the time you dove in and saved Stacey Crabtree's little girl from drowning, the time you played a violin note that broke the stained glass in St. Patrick's Cathedral in Troy, Michigan. The voices talk about the masks you wear, like the wife mask and the husband mask and the mask where you pretend you know what you're doing and the festival mask and the masks of ennui and joy. They talk about the thing behind the mask, the greatest and most mysterious thing of all, the source and object of all fears and hates and lives, the last thing we see and know before we die, which ties it all up in a nice glowing bow of Knowing, and Silence, and Peace.

Except it hardly ever works that way, including Now, and you look at Suzie and she looks at you in those moments before the *great big thing* happens and the end comes, and you kind of fall together, laughing at each other for trying to be so serious, laughing for the same reason you do most things, which is a reason you still don't know, and neither do wise men, moo cows, or Death.

CHAPTER 25

The Sun Door

They did not wake up beside the river.

As Milo's soul memory came flooding back, he realized that this was unusual and a bad sign. He remembered waking up in the well last time.

No flowers, and no sunshine.

Just dark.

"Are you kidding me?" said Milo. "What, are they still mad about the whole fugitive thing?"

Hello? Where was Suzie?

"Hello?"

"I'm here," came Suzie's voice. She sounded frightened, uncertain, which wasn't surprising. She had never died before.

There she was, on his left, grasping her head, looking sort of wild.

He took one of her hands and held it, waiting.

"We died!" she gasped. "I died! Wow. *Wow.* I used to *be* Death. I'm like a goddess. Omigod omigod omigod."

It was a tall order. Most people got to the afterlife and remembered that they'd once been truck drivers or ostriches.

"We're supposed to wake up by the river," she said. "That's where I always met you. Why aren't we by the river?"

"They're still mad about the whole fugitive thing. Maybe. Just a guess."

As their surroundings came into focus, Milo saw that they stood in the middle of a library of some kind. Paneled in dark wood. A fireplace with a sculpted fox over the keystone. Leather chairs. A low table in the shape of a sea chest.

"Maybe it'll be okay," Milo ventured. He gave her hand a squeeze.

Suzie shrugged. "Maybe for you. It was like a betrayal, going off and doing what I did. Universals aren't supposed to *live*. We're supposed to *watch* people live and give them shit about it."

Something was going on outside the little library. There was light of a sort, filtered through shuttered, deep-set windows. And voices . . . a dim murmur. Not unlike the sound of a crowd gathered on the other side of heavy walls. Not unlike the mob that had tried to carry him to the chopping block last time.

"I don't suppose you have any of your cosmic powers left?" he said. "You could just whoosh us out of here, or . . ."

Suzie flexed her fingers. Blinked her eyes.

"No," she said. "Nothing."

Milo's eyes widened then. Suzie was—

"Solid!" he yelled, grabbing her up and squeezing her. "You're solid! You're not fading!"

"I noticed that," she said. "Neither are you. I don't know what it means."

Neither did Milo, now that he considered it. But if it meant that she wasn't going to fade into oblivion, that was good. Is that what it meant?

A door at the end of a hall flew open, and Mama came charging in, between the leather chairs. Her great arms and mighty hands reached out.

Mama wrapped Milo up like a boa constrictor. He couldn't breathe.

Suzie squirmed and fought beside him; Mama had captured them both.

They sank into her as if she were a warm, oozy version of the Europan Sea.

"I was wrong," he heard Mama say. "I should have understood what you did with the Buddha. And then you went down and taught one of the most powerful lessons in history. Well done."

Suzie's grip tightened on Milo's hand.

Had they done it? Had they been successful?

"Yes," said Mama. She sprayed tears. *Sprayed.*

"You mean . . ."

"Perfection."

Suzie gasped. Relief flooded through Milo, and he had to clench up to keep from peeing.

Nan's voice came down the hall from another room.

"Congratulations," she croaked. A couple of her cats wandered into the library.

"Took you long enough," she added.

"Everyone's waiting," said Mama, spreading her arms again and ushering them toward a set of mighty oaken doors. "And I do mean everyone. You might even have a bigger crowd than the Buddha, believe it or not. You're the oldest human soul ever, Milo. And, Suzie—if I can get used to calling you that—you're a real original. In fact, no one's really sure what's going to happen with you. I mean, you came from the universal mind but not as a human, and now here you are going back, after being human—"

"I'll risk it," said Suzie. "It beats the alternative."

Milo found himself slightly faint and wobbly. It was too much to understand. In a way, it was like a graduation, except not. It was like . . . he didn't know what it was like.

Nan's voice, behind him.

"I promise you," she said, her voice low and warm, the voice of a mother or grandmother, "there is nothing on the other side of the Sun Door but joy and wholeness. You'll see."

She gave Milo a hug from behind. It was like being hugged by a well-meaning twig.

He believed her.

"About that," said Suzie. "About the Sun Door."

On the other side, the crowd hummed and roared.

Mama and Nan both said, "Mmm-hmm?"

"We're going through together."

Mama and Nan looked at each other. Conferred silently. Shrugged.

"You can try it," said Nan. "It's not how it's done. In the Oversoul, *everyone's* together, see—"

"We're not asking," said Milo.

Nan and Mama looked a little nervous, but they nodded.

Milo took Suzie's hand, and they faced the double doors together.

The doors swung wide. Light flooded in, blinding them. Shouting and screaming deafened them.

There was nothing they could do but shuffle along as Mama, like a pillowy tugboat, herded them out into pandemonium.

Fingers touched them as they walked. Mama pushed. The multitude squeezed them along like peas in a tube of toothpaste.

Like the Buddha's well-wishers, they were everywhere. The hill and the floodplain, the bridge—all seethed and crawled with waving, with singing, with colors and banners. In the town beyond, they stood on rooftops. Zeppelins and balloons floated and whirred.

They were in the river, too. Where it was shallow enough, they waded and stood, applauding, cheering. They were joyful, purely joyful, and it was like a tangible thing. They were joyful because they looked at the wonderful thing happening to Milo, to Suzie, and knew it would be their day someday.

The air above the river warped and shivered, as if an invisible someone had struck a great invisible gong. Shock waves of light and joy radiated, forming something like a tunnel.

They reached the riverbank and splashed through the shallows.

Suzie grasped Milo's shoulder, and their eyes locked. They slipped arms around each other, trusting in the crowd to move them in the right direction.

Suzie, wild-eyed, didn't speak. Milo leaned in to kiss her, saw her eyes close and her lips part—

The door enfolded them, drew them in.

They were two swimmers in a flood. Milo felt their souls spreading out like peanut butter. It was perfect. Even sort of sexual, in a way. They flowed through each other, leaning in for a long, hard, wet kiss, and swam through the Oversoul together.

Together.

For about three seconds.

CHAPTER 26

The Oversoul

Imagine if you were an earthworm.

Imagine that you have an earthworm girlfriend, and the two of you have been together as long as your worm brains can remember. You love each other in a crazy, primitive, soulmate kind of way. You can't even think what it would be like without her. You can barely think at all.

Then one day you wake up and you have turned into a human.

You are huge, like a human, and understand all the things humans understand. You have a beer belly and a New York Rangers cap. Holy shit! Yesterday all you knew about was crawling in the dirt. Today you have a bachelor's degree in sports marketing. Today you understand about taxes and the solar system. You read and write Spanish and English. You have a best friend, an ex-wife, and a kid you see on weekends. You have been to Brazil and Europe, which, to an earthworm, would be like visiting distant galaxies, except that the very idea of "galaxies" would melt an earthworm's mind.

Do you think you'd be all heartbroken about losing your earthworm girlfriend? Your earthworm self?

You wouldn't.

Actually, here's the thing: You and your worm girlfriend are actually both in there, smooshed together in your vast new brain. You and a trillion other worms.

You do not think about being trillions of separate earthworms. Why would you? You move ahead with being your new, awesome, ancient self.

Everything makes sense to you now.

Time. Gravity. Which fork to use. Zippers. Infinite dimensions. Tacos.

It's all part of a dream you are having.

A billion years pass.

Or they would, if time weren't just part of the dream.

So you dream a billion years. What's the difference?

The billion years pass like a great sleeping ocean.

And then one day you dream that you are an old soul named Milo, standing knee-deep in a river, holding hands with an old soul named Suzie.

Everything comes back around. *Everything.*

You forget that it *is* a dream.

And you pick up where you left off, with a long, deep kiss.

(You remember understanding gravity and Chinese, but it's fading.)

After a while, you walk out into the river, and let it take you, and give way to the weirdness of being born.

You hold hands. Nothing tries to pull you apart.

You hang together in the water, between lives and worlds. The river carries you, time enfolds you, and catfish swim through you.

CHAPTER 27

Blue Creek, Michigan, and Other Lives

They came back separately, somewhat back in time, and didn't meet until they were practically adults.

Age sixteen found Suzie working as a cleaning lady at St. Thomas's Cathedral, in Sauvignon. One night she heard strange noises from inside the crypt of poor old Archbishop Guilliaume. Swallowing her fear, she pried the lid loose and found a handsome—if somewhat dusty—young man crouched inside.

"Well!" sighed the young man. "I can breathe again!"

They fell in love at once. Otherwise he may not have confessed to her that he had jarred the lid shut while attempting to rob old Guilliaume's grave, and she might not have suggested that he go ahead and rob the eighteen other honored crypts in the cathedral and that they run off together before dawn and make a life for themselves in the South of France.

"Done!" said the young man, and he gave her a splendid, stirring kiss.

It was an oddly full kiss, in its way. Full of strange knowings and mysteries.

"Mon Dieu!" gasped Milo.

"Mon Dieu!" gasped Suzie. "That was one hell of a kiss!"

BLUE CREEK, MICHIGAN, 1882

Milo Falkner and Suzanne Cobb met on a sleigh ride, at Milo's birthday party, the year they both turned ten. They didn't hold hands right away, but they smiled at each other a time or two and blushed.

Milo's father (a notorious rakehell) was running on strong home-made beer that night, making free with the whip, and turning left over the dangerous end of Sand Lake, where the ice was often thin.

Snap! Once or twice, the lake protested. *Bang!* Like a gunshot.

Which was, finally, the cue for young Milo and Suzie to clasp their mittens together.

The sleigh reached shore. They still held hands, blooming inside like candles.

Suzie, upon reporting the sleigh ride to her parents, was forbidden to have anything more to do with Milo and "that whole family of misbegotten reprobates," all born, it was said around the county, with snakes for umbilical cords.

He wrote her a letter; it was intercepted. *She* wrote *him* a letter, which was also intercepted, and which earned her a week of copying Bible lessons.

Then, horror: Suzie fell ill, the way children in those days were prone to do. She paled and evaporated until, at last, when she said, "Milo," ever so softly and cried a single tear, her father had him sent for.

And Milo was brought up to sit with her and to talk to her about things. Swimming. Frogs. How he liked books and would teach her to hunt ducks.

"Not ducks," she breathed. "I love ducks."

"Geese, then," he said.

And she lived.

Her father, fearing the worst, had already bought her a grave plot over at Grassby's and, being a practical sort, had gone ahead and kept it. In the years that followed Suzie's recovery, she and Milo sometimes took picnics there.

On a future planet, a millennium away, Milo and Suzie came back as responsible parents and taught their children the most famous story in all the interstellar colonies: the Parable of Jonathan Yah Yah and the Martyrs of Europa.

They told how the martyrs had died to broadcast awful truths about the ancient, greedy cartels. They told how miners and engineers all over the solar system followed their example and refused to work, even though some of them became martyrs, too, before the cartels fell apart.

All good parents taught their kids this same lesson: If everyone agreed to suffer pain or death rather than be treated unjustly, greedy people could never again gain power.

"We've had fifty generations of justice now," they told the children. "Don't be the generation that blows it."

"We won't," said Shaggy and Little Red Corvette.

BLUE CREEK, MICHIGAN, 1892

The year he was to have begun law school, Milo became the first person to drive a motor vehicle across Petoskey County. The vehicle itself was a great, noisy thing, mostly a clumsy steel boiler with a smokestack on it. Newspapermen followed (or outpaced him) on horseback, telegraphing dispatches as fate permitted. Sometimes Milo drove for miles without incident or delay. Other times, he spent hours making repairs.

After a journey of fifteen days, Milo pulled up just after eight o'clock in the evening at Toastley Hall, a dormitory at Casper Teaching College, marched up to the chaperone's desk, and asked that his sweet-heart, Miss Suzanne Cobb, be sent down, in order that he might kiss her for the photographers.

"No," said the chaperone, a sour and suspicious person who, in a former life, had been a cornstalk. "Curfew is strictly seven-fifty, and no gentlemen after six."

Milo said, "Please."

He was refused again, and the exchange escalated, until the news-papermen observed Milo—with an unholy look in his eye—carrying the chaperone out of the dormitory, across a manicured yard, and down a gentle hill, to dump her with a noisy *splash* into a convenient willow-shrouded golf pond.

This proved controversial. Milo was fined by local authorities and excused from his law school for the space of one year. He took work as a grave digger at the Blue Creek Cemetery.

Suzie, visiting her beloved in the graveyard one summer lunchtime, only remarked, "I'd have thrown that old pea-wit in the pond myself back in September, if I wasn't afraid of hurting the ducks."

Then she gave him a kiss, there between two open graves. A good kiss, too. The kind it's nice to give—deliciously, thrillingly so!—but not at all polite to talk about.

They came back as a couple who met in Paris between wars. Milo had a movie camera, and she had a brace of performing birds.

They made movies together. Little short films. Jerky black-and-white movies like tiny whirring storms. A girl with a flower cart, sped up until she seemed to dance on frenzied strings. A man getting beaten up by street children. A fat woman disrobing. They filmed her husband and his wife. Almost always, it was something a bit grotesque.

Her birds performing.

People reacting to a fake spider.

Opium addicts sleeping, with rats crawling and sniffing among them.

Two midgets sharing a wheelchair.

One time they filmed an entire rainstorm, beginning to end, with puddles and people hurrying and lightning reflected in shop windows.

They filmed themselves walking away, down the street, past a cat, past a man with a guitar, farther away, receding until someone—a fleet and criminal shadow—stole away with the camera.

BLUE CREEK, MICHIGAN, 1897

Suzie and Milo married. For a few years, they lived the life of a young, free couple with bright prospects. They hunted pheasant, quail, and wild turkeys, raising Irish setters to run and fetch. Suzie became the better shot, almost as if, when her finger found the trigger, something quiet and ancient moved in her.

The first two children—Charles and James—came as planned, with one year between, and then Edith, a surprise.

The same week Edith was born, Gerald Wedge, the Petoskey County prosecutor, handed Milo a capital case.

"Got to cut your milk teeth sometime," Wedge told him.

A local businessman—Graydon Ornish—had found an intruder—Heinrick Mueller, a repeat offender—in his house and thrown him out. But he didn't leave it at that. Ornish discovered where Mueller lived and burned his house down. Mueller and his wife both died.

The community—one part of it, anyway—wanted Ornish acquitted. They cried out that Ornish was a good man, defending himself against a recidivist who was no good to anybody.

"He would only have gone on robbing people," insisted Ornish, "and maybe hurt someone."

The community agreed, noisily. In Petoskey County, in those days, as in many other places, the local courts often bowed to public opinion.

Milo, however, knew his own mind and conscience.

"The law has to prevail here," he declared to a belligerent courtroom, to an uncertain jury, "not the way we feel about it. We aren't here to discuss what Mr. Mueller *is* but what Mr. Ornish has *done*."

Young as he was, Milo stood there like an old tree, with thick glasses and hawkish nose, and in later years more than one of the spectators would say it was as if a grown-up had appeared out of thin air in a room full of foolish children.

Ornish went to the gallows.

Milo attended the hanging, which unfolded in its own dreamlike pocket of time, from the creak of the lever to the twitching and the dribbling of urine on the floor. It wounded him the way lightning will sometimes wound someone, on the inside.

Five years later, when Gerald Wedge died, the party men came to Milo and said that naturally he'd want to step in as acting prosecutor, and he surprised himself by saying, "No, fellows, thanks."

He stopped being a prosecutor and became a defender.

"What happened?" Suzie wanted to know.

What had happened was that Milo had had a powerful dream. He had a lot of powerful dreams. They both did.

"I dreamed," Milo explained, "that I lived in South Africa, in a village, and that I committed a terrible crime. I hurt someone and took his money. But I wasn't punished."

"You weren't caught?" Suzie guessed.

"I was caught right away. But in this particular village, when someone did something destructive, they gathered around him or her in a circle and told stories of all the good things he had done in his life. Hardly anyone ever committed a second crime. We need something like that here. Something besides punishments that only make people worse."

Suzie would always remember that evening, always remember him sitting sideways at his rolltop desk, one elbow at rest among papers, glasses perched on his forehead, hawkish nose dividing his face into light and shadow.

They were quiet together for a while.

"This may be a bad time to mention," she said, kissing his forehead, "that I want to open a gun shop."

Milo and Suzie were born again and again, and sometimes their life together didn't go as they might have hoped. In one lifetime, they had planned to get married when they graduated from high school, but Suzie had a seizure while swimming in a pond and drowned before she turned seventeen.

Her headstone was one of the new kind: engraved polished marble. It would last. It would pass through time like an arrow.

For years after, Milo was like a piece of wood, splintering apart from inside. But he slowly got moving again and worked and grew gardens and owned cars and let the years pass. He kept her picture on his wall until it had been there for fifty years.

Suzie's headstone lived up to the hype; fifty years later, it might as well have been new.

In the last summer of his own life, Milo planted a garden that grew to surround the house, nearly seventy yards of radishes, carrots, and beans, with marigolds to keep the rabbits out. Sad stories grew up around him like weeds.

BLUE CREEK, MICHIGAN, 1932

Thirty years went by.

Suzie and Milo built a new house above the country-club golf course and raised the children in it. Unbelievably soon, the house wasn't new anymore. Empty spaces opened up: when Charles went off to Dartmouth, and when James went to U of M, and Edith went to Miami, down in Ohio.

And Milo stepped back from his project, his three-decade project, which was a diversion program for kids who broke the law, sending them to classes instead of vomiting them into the jails. He took stock of it all and, like a good wise man, knew when to step aside.

Suzie, by contrast, had bought the whole building above and around her gun shop. Hunters all over the world were proud to own Falkner rifles. She brought in way more money than Milo ever had.

The grandkids came. Nancy, Kimberly, Wanda, Norman, Andrew,

Catherine, Curtis. Charles bought the law firm. Edith was in a horseback-riding accident.

One day, around the time the grandkids started becoming teenagers, Milo found himself looking out at the great steel cars over in the country-club parking lot and at airliners thundering overhead. The radio squawked in the living room, behind him. Some new music called jazz.

He thought about the sleigh-ride days, when everything had been horses, horses, horses, horses.

"What the hell planet are we living on, anymore?" he asked aloud.

"The Pepsodent Theatre of the Air," said the radio, "brought to you by Pepsodent and NBC."

Centuries later, when people perfected the OZ drive and started going out among the stars, some of them wanted to take pets along.

Cats turned out to be perfect for space dwellers. They were excellent at floating. Didn't seem to mind that there wasn't really an up or down. They tended to stay out of the way.

Milo and Suzie, born to separate litters on a space station in Pluto orbit, were among the first space cats to cross the interstellar voids. They were like two furry rockets, shooting through hatches, flying across pods. They were impeccably neat, which helped and kept cat food from getting into the ventilation.

They grew long and thin, became like aliens.

They napped for years at a time.

BLUE CREEK, MICHIGAN, 1942

Norman went off to fight in the war. His parents, Charles and Lydia, got a star, like a receipt, to hang up in their front window.

Milo made an unofficial star out of linen and hung it in the front window at the big house, on the side away from the golf course.

He and Suzie went hunting. It became their way of keeping watch over their grandson, in whatever far field he camped in or marched on. Norman marched across northern Africa; his grandparents marched the fields and woods around Sand Lake.

When Norman was killed at Anzio, they looked at each other and leaned against each other, the only alternative to sinking down on the floor. Then they geared up and went hunting, anyhow, stomping the winter-brittle weeds and wheat, skirting the frozen lake, taking note when the dogs quit the trail at their feet and sniffed the air instead.

A bear rose out of the winter wheat just yards away. An old bear, with a fading coat and scars.

"Dogs!" barked Milo, a simple command and a simple gesture, and the dogs sat down, as they'd been taught.

Suzie aimed quickly but with care.

Crack! Crack crack! said Suzie's rifle. The bear lay dying, fast and painlessly, shot straight through the eye and then double-tapped through the heart.

"Jesus, Suze," said Milo. "I thought it would be like a poem, where we look at him and he looks at us, and then we just let each other turn away and go. Later on we'd tell how he was close enough that we could see the specks in his eyes and the wind in his fur."

"This isn't a poem," she snapped.

When they got home, Milo went out and bought some crayons and made them an unofficial gold star to hang in the window. He took down his original star and laid it on the coffee table, unable to bring himself to throw it away.

Suzie came along later and put it in the trash.

They came back, in more than one life, to live in the wine country (who wouldn't?). They came back and lived in villages, in forests, and in huts by the sea.

They learned kung fu and knitting. They learned more ways to make love than any other lovers had ever known. Sometimes they remembered the things they had learned from other lives. When they were seven years old on Rapa Nui, in 1700, they remembered that they had flown on starships. They saw the starships in their dreams, and carved surfboards in their image, and learned to fly on the water.

They came back as two Navajo women. They came back as lungfish and banana farmers.

Sometimes they died together, or a few minutes apart, and sometimes one or the other faced long years alone.

BLUE CREEK, MICHIGAN, 1947

Two years after the war had come to a stop, Milo and Suzie sat on their front porch swing, on the evening of their fiftieth wedding anniversary. Their thin, veiny old hands lay tangled together in her lap. Their children and grandchildren bustled inside the house, preparing supper. The homemade gold star hung in the window still, for Norman.

The dogs curled up together nearby, faking sleep.

Milo leaned close and said, "I'm proud of you, Suzie."

Cooking smells drifted out through the screen door, as if the house were breathing pumpkin pie and onions.

Suzie said, "Mmm?" because she didn't hear well, so he repeated, "I'm proud of you."

And she squeezed his hand and rested her head on his shoulder and laughed, and said, "That's all right, love. I'm tired of you, too."

ACKNOWLEDGMENTS

Every book has friends.

Some of these friends are people who actually help the book get written. Maybe they read and offer advice. Maybe they're agents or editors or people who spark ideas. Others are people who are friends of the book because they are friends of the writer in some way. And of course there are readers, the best friends any book has.

Man, this book sure has a lot of friends.

The list begins with my wife and friend, writer and poet Janine Harrison. Janine has been excited about *Reincarnation Blues* since I first mentioned it and has been a tireless cheerleader and adviser. She is also much more, of course.

My agent, Michelle Brower, dropped into my life by telephone one day some time ago, saying, "I like your style. Would you like to try and publish books together?" She changed my life, and I thank her with all my heart. It should not go without saying that this book was actually sort of dumb as a first draft, and Michelle guided me toward the light. Everything that's good about *Reincarnation Blues* has her mental fingerprints on it. Her assistant, Annie Hwang, can also share in whatever credit is due.

Tricia Narwani, my editor at Del Rey, was wild about the book and is also fun to drink beer with. She, too, guided me through some changes. In the nicest way. You know how some writers will tell you that working with their editors and publishers was pure, raw hell and that the book they wound up with was hardly their book anymore? I have never experienced that. Tricia and Del Rey have been good and gentle friends.

A humble thank-you to Alice Walker for her pamphlet *Sent by Earth: A Message from the Grandmother Spirit After the Bombing of the World Trade Center and the Pentagon* (Seven Stories Press, 2001). The story of the wise, loving people in chapters 9 and 27 is inspired and informed by Walker's account of the Babemba tribe, appearing in this essay.

I have had valuable input and encouragement from many of the usual suspects. Josh Perz. Ted Kosmatka. Rachel Mork. Mary-Tina Vrehas. My dad, Don Poore, basically told me how he thought I should rewrite the first chapter, and he was right.

As always, Mom and Bill have been a source of encouragement and support. Plus it's nice to go hang out at their house, which has a pond and a cool indoor-outdoor porch kind of thing, which is a perfect place to write and watch the ducks.

Sometimes a book's friends are *groups* of people.

I'd like to thank Janine's group of writerly students from Purdue, the First Friday Wordsmiths, especially Kevin Shelton and Kayla Greenwell. I started this book during a FFW retreat on a farm in southern Michigan, at a farmhouse table full of young people drinking coffee and tapping away on laptops. In the evening, there was a bonfire and stars and lightning bugs. What a fine setting for starting a book.

There's a group of people in Muncie, Indiana, who have been so good to me I don't even know where to start. Writer and professor Cathy Day and I exchanged books and became friends some time ago, and she got poet Sean Lovelace to invite me down to Ball State for a reading. That evening remains one of my favorite nights ever. Cathy, Sean, Silas Hanson, and several of the young writers I met that week— Brittany Means, Sarah Hollowell, Jackson Thors Elfin, Jeff Owens, and Jeremy Flick—have been with me in my head and heart ever since.

As always, the writers of the Highland Writers' Group have been a trusty source of criticism and support.

And the Mean Group, the meanest and most snack-eating crit group ever. We're back together and meaner and snack-eatinger than ever.

And thanks to those who have read and continue to read. I offer you a courtly bow.

ABOUT THE AUTHOR

MICHAEL POORE's short fiction has appeared in *Glimmer Train, Southern Review, Agni, Fiction,* and *Asimov's.* His story "The Street of the House of the Sun" was selected for *The Year's Best Nonrequired Reading 2012.* His first novel, *Up Jumps the Devil,* was hailed by *The New York Review of Books* as "an elegiac masterpiece."

Poore lives in Highland, Indiana, with his wife, poet and activist Janine Harrison, and their daughter, Jianna.

michaelpoore.live
Facebook.com/michaelpooreauthor
Twitter: @michaelpoore007
Instagram: @michael_poore227